Life Before

by

K.L. Romo

Published by K. L. Romo

Copyright © K. L. Romo, 2015

This book is dedicated to all the empty-nesters
out there.
Don't worry—the adventure is just beginning!

Chapter 1

Elaine Grace Dearborn

2011

Dallas, Texas

If someone were to tell me I had a propensity for prostitution, I would have laughed hysterically and said they were a lunatic.

Whenever anyone asked if I believed in paranormal happenings or mysticism, I always said *no*. Ghosts from the past just appeared in movies. I didn't waste my time even thinking about it. There were more important things in the world to consider than whether mystical things were possible. I didn't have the inclination to consider the highly improbable possibilities.

I was a mom and a housewife. The person who picked up dirty clothes from the floor, day in and day out. The person who washed the laundry, wiped the dust from the furniture, and vacuumed dog hair from the carpets. Now my job as mom is basically done, my kids basically grown. My days of changing diapers, wiping bottoms, and kissing boo-boo's have long since passed. The sticky fingerprints which covered every smooth surface have long since faded into the memories of my kids' childhoods.

I am ending one phase of my life and beginning another.

Of all the terms used to define who I am now - *middle-aged, mature woman, empty-nester* - I believe I despise the word *empty-nester* the most. *Empty* describes one who is devoid, vacant, hollow, depleted. A person whom I've never considered myself to be.

Since my children have now gone off into the world to make a way for themselves, the word *empty* seems to have branded me, regardless of how hard I try to believe it doesn't apply, and to pretend all of the women I know don't place that label on me. When so many people think of you in such a way, after a time it no longer matters if you're different. Your mind eventually begins to believe them.

Elaine Grace Dearborn. The stay-at-home wife and mother. But I'm now a stay-at-home mom with no one to care for. My life has somehow dwindled into monotony, devoid of purpose.

But I am also Elaine Grace Dearborn, the English major. The wanna-be novelist who'd decided her career could wait a little while longer while she raised her kids.

Well, now it's time.

My laptop looks sleek and impressive, though I've done absolutely nothing with it but play solitaire and send emails. Nothing. Now it seems to dare me every time I walk by. *What are you afraid of?* it whispers mockingly, just loud enough for me to hear. It throws down its challenge as if we were destined for a death duel.

Just sit down and start, I keep telling myself.

But self-doubt seeps in like a poisonous gas.

What if I can't do it anymore? What if I've lost my talent with words? The *what-if's* are doing battle with the *go-girls*, and so far they're winning.

I'm scared to death. This is the part of me I've been saving for later, holding in reserve until the kids were grown. The part that's not the wife and mother.

This is who I *am*. A writer.

But what if I truly can't do it? The *who-I-am* would first dry up into the *who-I-dreamed-I-could-be,* and then shrivel into nothing. I'd lose myself. Not the *Mom Me,* or the *Wife Me,* but the *Other Me.*

I have no back-up dream.

Once again I sit at my beautiful desk my husband made me for Mother's Day, in front of my shiny laptop, and decide it's do-or-die.

The house is totally quiet, except for the muffled ticking of the mantel clock, insisting that time is moving on, with or without my fingers even hitting the keyboard.

I have no idea what to write about. Who cares about what happens in a boring-stay-at-home-mom-life on any given day? I place my work-worn hands over the computer keys, noticing the multitude of wrinkles I already have at age forty-four. What will they look like at fifty-four? At seventy-four? Can I get them to do what I need them to do? The charms on the bracelet my kids gave me for my birthday seven or eight years ago dangle from my wrist. Beautiful reminders of how much my family loves me, all hanging there, just waiting.

Just get the fingers moving. A trick from school. Just start writing something. Anything. The words will start like a small stream, running downhill faster and faster until it turns into a swiftly-moving river that you couldn't dam up if you wanted to.

Just write.

Without thinking about it another second, I start typing, my charms making a soft tinkling sound as they hit each other over the keyboard.

W H A T   I F   I   W E R E   S O M E O N E   E L S E ?

The words appear on the screen, and I stare at them blankly. It's as if someone else's fingers had typed them. *Why did I write that?* I don't know. But I'd learned in school to trust my instincts. Sometimes our brains take us to strange destinations, with no rhyme or reason, and we should let it. Sometimes we just need to let the emotion pour itself out, like spilled milk spreading across the breakfast table.

Strangely, the letters seem to magnify themselves. They begin to blink, first one at a time, and then in an unsynchronized rhythm. Twinkling Christmas lights strung across my field of vision.

Oh shit! Not another migraine! The sight is the first thing affected; the beginning of the aura. Written words are no longer decipherable. Letters disappear in no particular pattern, like my brain takes a pencil and erases the ones it doesn't like.

The silence in the room is deafening. *Ha!* I've always thought that was a silly oxymoron, but now I understand it totally. Through the years with kids, I'd yearned for quiet. Now lately there's been too much. But this silence is different; I don't even hear the clock ticking. No traffic sounds from the busy street behind our house, no birds chirping in the trees. Just the tinkling of my charms as I move my hands. But how can these four small charms make such an entrancing, distinct sound? As if I were in a beautiful garden, and a warm summer breeze suddenly blew through a thousand tiny crystals hanging in a tree. The sound of mystery and magic.

The mesmerizing notes get louder as the letters on the screen continue to blink. I'm enchanted by them, as if I'm in a trance. The room seems to shimmer around me, like dizziness and blurred vision combined.

Then I'm in darkness, the only light coming from my screen, a pinpoint that gets bigger with each passing second. As if I'm traveling through a tunnel. I've never seen anything so realistic on a computer before, not even with 3-D glasses. I could swear the tunnel is swallowing me, getting bigger with each passing second.

Voices come from my computer speaker, at first so faint I can't make out what's being said. Women's voices, getting louder.

"Eliza, how many more hours will you need to finish the Harrison gown?"

The light at the end of the blackness expands, and there is movement. The chimes are louder and the tunnel seems to be devouring me. For some reason I'm not afraid. I have no worries. Just a peacefulness I want to keep forever.

The scene at the end of the tunnel is moving closer. I can see a woman, sitting in a chair sewing, with needle and thread poised in her hand. Shiny pearls cover her lap, sparkling with the light that surrounds them.

Glimmering pearls and shimmering music.

My body begins to tingle, tiny exhilarating pinpricks cover my skin from scalp to toes. And then I am weightless, no longer twenty pounds overweight. No longer any weight at all.

My God! It's like I'm in the Twilight Zone! What is happening??

I stare at my lap, at the pearl-covered bodice of a cream-colored gown. And then pain, as the needle pricks my left index finger. *Ouch!* I wince, as a pinprick of red quickly blossoms.

The last words I remember thinking are *What the hell?*

Chapter 2

Eliza Genevieve Darling

June 2, 1907

Dallas, Texas

The Virginia K. Johnson Home & Training Center For Women

"Eliza, how many more hours will you need to finish the Harrison gown?" Ms. Dixie asked me as she passed through the sewing room. "Mrs. Harrison is chomping at the bit to get that dress."

I stared at my lap, at the pearl-covered bodice of a cream-colored gown. And then pain, as the needle pricked my left index finger. *Ouch!* I winced, as a pinprick of red quickly blossomed, causing more panic than it should have been worth. Lord, if I stained Ms. Eudora's gown with blood, I'd most likely have to shred it up and start over.

"I'm working as fast as my fingers will go. My lands! Who has ever heard of wanting two thousand beads on one dress! You'd think *she* might be considering the life of a sporting woman!" I answered, shaking my head as, one by one, I sewed the pearl beads onto the bodice of the gown ordered by Ms. Eudora Harrison. A fine lady needing fine clothes.

The only precious thing I'd ever owned was the locket my father had given to me the day I turned thirteen, not long before I would become fatherless. My fingers instinctively stroked the letters etched into the gold - EGD. Eliza Genevieve Darling. Rubbing my fingers over the fancy letters was like fingering a worry stone; it was my usual habit when I was vexed or worried. My father had handed me the small black box and told me it was a special gift to celebrate the day I was no longer a child. My mother, of course, had been upset that he'd spent so much of his hard-earned money on such a trivial luxury. But my father had just winked at me as she complained about his extravagance. It was his way of letting me know how special I was, and no one, not even mama, was going to stand in the way of his showing me. My mother had been right to label it expensive, but quite wrong to call it trivial. That locket had gotten me through many a hard night. It was my constant reminder that I'd been special to *someone;* that I was a person worth loving.

The only time I ever knew anyone who'd worn a gown as fancy as Ms. Eudora's was at Madame Dixie's Orpheum. My home away from home, I'd always called it. The place I'd spent the last five years of my life. That is, before I came here. This is my home now, and will be for as long as I can see into the future. The Virginia K. Johnson Home and Training Center for Women, across the river from where The Orpheum had called home. In Oak Cliff.

Ms. Dixie raised her brows in her usual amusement at my temporary vexations. "Well now, Eliza, you know as well as I do that money talks. I imagine if they can pay for it, they can have it. Never mind how ridiculous or gaudy," replied Ms. Dixie in her practical way. As a former madam, catering to the fantasies of the men who could afford her upscale parlor-house had been her only business plan. She was smart and level-headed. Her place, *The Orpheum*, had been the best of the parlor houses in Dallas. Her thriving club had been a testament to her skills as a shrewd businesswoman.

"Well, I know Ms. Dixie. But I certainly don't understand what the dad-gum hurry is. It's only June. I don't understand when Ms. Eudora imagines herself to be wearing a gown as heavy as this before the dead of winter. She'll melt down to nothing. And you know it only gets to be bitter cold in Dallas no more than one out of every four winters," I said, shaking my head at the absurdity of it. I had my reservations about making a dress for Eudora Harrison anyway, considering she was one of those leading the charge against the *unfortunate* women still earning their living as working girls. It was almost as if I were a part of the wealthy elite of the North Dallas League as well, and it made my blood hot under my collar. Ms. Dixie knew this, and yet here I was, sewing my heart out on this dang gown.

"Eliza, you're a seamstress now. You work with needle and thread, and now you're even lucky enough to be operating a sewing machine. You don't get the chance to decide who your customers will be. You just do the sewing. And be glad you're able to earn your living this way, instead of selling your body to the highest bidder," Ms. Dixie replied with her usual frankness.

"I suppose so, Ms. Dixie," I said. What else could I do but agree?

I set my lips in a thin line of frustration as I thought about those *reformers,* trying to rid Dallas of *depraved* call-girls, sinners of the flesh. Why, I bet half those polished hypocrites didn't love their husbands, and had sold themselves for a family life. I know I'd seen several of their husbands at Ms. Dixie's more than a few times. I pushed the needle through a particularly thick part of the bodice with my thimble, continuing my slow progress with the pearls on Ms. Eudora's dress. Lord knows I didn't want to work so fast that I pricked myself again and stained her dang dress. But maybe that could be my unique signature. *Marked by the blood of Eliza Darling.* Ha! That would certainly cause Ms. Eudora to suffer a dizzy spell.

I pushed the needle up through the underside of Ms. Eudora's bodice, through the pearl bead, and back down again. A repetitive task that allowed a girl to sit and think about things while she got her work accomplished. But in this case, my musings got in my way; I was late in realizing that I was almost out of beads.

"Damn it!" I cursed under my breath, occasionally returning to some of my former habits when I was truly vexed and wasn't thinking as a *lady* ought to think.

I was sure Ms. Eudora would be by any time to check on her gown; I was sure she was most anxious to model for herself in the looking glass.

Now I'd have to go buy more. It was another one of those Texas days that threw us a slight surprise, June 2 and already a sweltering ninety-eight degrees outside, the air sticky with moisture. None of us were expecting it to be this hot so soon. I didn't relish the thought of making my way downtown, just for the purchase of something I should have had enough of to begin with, had it not been for Ms. Eudora's pride in wanting a gown with more pearls than a bay full of oysters. Wearing a long skirt and high-collared blouse, it didn't take long for a girl to become overheated and in search of an electric fan, though they were hard to come by.

I left the sewing room, and walked downstairs, finding Ms. Dixie in one of the schooling rooms. She could usually be found there, tirelessly helping some of the younger girls with their numbers and sums. It was such a dang shame that most of the girls at The Johnson Home didn't know how to read any better than a newly born puppy, or even know how much change they should be getting back from the store clerk at the pharmacy. The youngest girl living with us at present is only fifteen years old, and expecting a child no less. Her mama and daddy didn't know how to read or do simple arithmetic, so she'd gone out into the world knowing how to do only one thing. Well, fortunately for her, Ms. Dixie was going to make sure that changed.

"Ms. Dixie, Ms. Eudora's monstrosity gobbled up all my pearl beads. I'm afraid I have to go downtown and buy more."

Ms. Dixie looked up from the sums she was writing on Delilah's chalk board with a pensive look on her face. "You'd better go to the mill for more thread too. I don't think the delivery came yesterday as it was supposed to. Two spools should be enough."

Ms. Dixie rose and walked with me to the office where Ms. Virginia kept the cash box. It was a smart idea on her part to keep some money readily available should we need it. And invariably we did. "Pick up a half pound of jelly beans, while you're there," she told me with a mischievous twinkle in her mint-green eyes. "You know my sweet tooth gets the better of me more times than I'd care to admit. I'd like to shake the hand of the genius mind who invented those little chewies. So much easier to eat than that sticky Turkish Delight." She handed me a nickel, which was more than enough to replenish her jelly-bean stock for a month.

Ms. Dixie was right. I'd never seen a woman so drawn to sweets. She'd been sporting a sweet tooth for most of her life. It struck me as ironic that the former madam of the most popular bordello in town had only the vice of being addicted to sweets. If only we could all be so lucky.

"Of course I will," I told her. I put the money in my pocketbook, and walked toward the stairwell. That was another advantage of living in a three-story building. We all got a great deal of exercise, traveling up and down the wide mahogany staircases all day.

Both the cotton mill and Sanger Brothers' Dry Goods were located Downtown, so I'd have to ride the trolley. But even with the heat, I guess it was nice to get outdoors for a bit. I held my skirts as I made my way to the sidewalk; I'd just cross over one street to Bishop Avenue to catch the North Loop Streetcar. As long as I was on Bishop, I could flag it down anywhere. No need to have a designated stop; it moved so slowly we just waved to the trolley-man as he came down the street and he stopped for us. Couldn't be much easier than that.

It took only three minutes for the streetcar to stop in front of me. And with electricity being its method of movement, one no longer had to worry that soot or smoke would wash over a girl's dress like a coat of black watercolor. It was distressing to think of the dark film of dirt and grease that had routinely settled over our skirts like a veil of heartache, even though I couldn't usually see it on *my* clothes. All of my garments were black or gray, the color of guilt. I'd long ago stopped wearing any color that might mistakenly portray innocence, because I knew I had none. The girls at The Orpheum had found my clothes so peculiar they'd given me the name Somber, an initiation into their ranks. A new name for a new life.

A smidgen of dust was all that blew upon me now. I pulled myself up and easily took a seat on one of the wooden benches. At least the movement of the train, albeit slow, caused a whisper of breeze to blow through the car and chase away the perspiration. It wasn't long before we were making our way over the Trinity River, the dividing line between Oak Cliff and downtown Dallas. The Trinity had never been a very pleasant river to look at, being brown and murky. And it wasn't even very wide, only truly looking like a real river after it rained for at least a few days. It wasn't much good for anything, not even fishing, but even so, I saw a handful of men and boys down along the banks, with their rolled-up pant legs and fishing poles. It was scary to think of eating something pulled out of that river; I believe I'd have to be on the verge of starvation to even consider it. But then, maybe they *were.*

After twenty minutes, my ride was over, and the streetcar dropped me downtown at the corner of Main and Lamar, right in front of the Dallas Cotton Mill - the only place that sold the over-sized spools of thread we couldn't buy anywhere else.

I looked up at the huge, ugly building that took up an entire city block. The mill was a three-story brown-brick and concrete building. Tall windows lined every floor, like straight teeth in a huge sneer. And all of those windows were closed. Lord, how could anyone work in this stifling heat without a breeze from the outside? It seemed more like torture than a way to make a living!

I could hear the deep rumble of the machinery before I even went inside, like a constant angry thunder. My lands, what must the noise be like in the innards of this monster?

I opened the door to a small greeting room – I imagine they didn't get many customers walking right in off the street. Horse and buggy, or if they were lucky enough, a gas-powered delivery truck would be used to deliver thread and cloth to most of their customers.

The wrinkled man behind the counter looked up as I opened the door. "Mornin'," he almost shouted. "What can I do for you today ma'am?" he asked in a loud voice, with somewhat of a perplexed look on his face. I was most certainly not a delivery man.

I found I had to shout back, just to answer him. "My goodness, that noise is loud. How in the almighty stars do you tolerate that?" I asked, shaking my head, more rhetorically than anything else. How thankful I was that I didn't have to listen to that deafening rumble all day, every day.

"You get used to it, ma'am. What can I do for you today?" he asked again.

I felt the sweat bead on my forehead, and fanned myself even harder. My little oriental fan was apt to just fall to pieces and blow away, I'd already used it so much in the last few weeks. Summer had just begun its six-month visit, and already it had almost worn out its welcome. At least as far as I was concerned, and I imagined most of the women I knew. Dresses buttoned to the neck and sleeves to the elbow didn't allow for much breeze to cool a girl down. And not putting my hair up served to increase my discomfort ten-fold. I couldn't bear to have my scar on display for everyone to see: cutting my hair fairly short and leaving it down around my face covered it somewhat.

I'd been relatively cooled by the breeze while riding the streetcar, but now I was standing in an oven. I didn't understand how they managed in that heat. "Well, sir, I need two spools of cotton thread please. I'm a seamstress and close to being out of thread, queer as that may sound. So now I'm in a bit of a tight situation - I have to finish a dress before my customer throws a tantrum; her patience has gone by the wayside. Well, if she ever had any to begin with."

"Oh, one of those, huh? Well, we better just fix you right up. I'll just go to the back and get them. It might take me a few minutes," he said.

My brow was melting. "Thank you so much," I answered. My lands, I couldn't suffer the stifling heat one more second. "You know, I think I'll just wait for you out front."

"Yes ma'am," he answered as he disappeared into the bowels of the factory, the sound swallowing him up as if it had a hungry body of its own.

As I opened the door, hot air flew into my face, as if it were being sucked into a breathless vacuum. At least it was air that was moving, never mind it being hot. Just getting out of that sweltering building was a blessing. The air so still in there it was more like standing in a closed-up crypt that in a greeting room. I continued fanning my neck and face, hoping to keep my hair from becoming soaked through.

I looked down the street and noticed a young girl coming out the side door of the mill. She sat down on a wooden bench that stood by the door, and leaned her head back against the brick wall as she stretched her legs out in front of her. I thought I'd prefer to wait while carrying on a nice conversation rather than standing by myself, so I made my way over to her.

There was no shade to cover her, the sun beating down on her tiny form that was already covered in a sheen of perspiration. Small pieces of cotton lint covered her entire body like a fine fur, clinging to her damp skin, her auburn braids, her worn dress and apron, and her bare feet. I couldn't believe this girl wasn't even wearing any boots! Under her veil of dust and lint, I could see she was a pretty little thing; as pretty as I'd ever seen, even at Ms. Dixie's.

"Well, hello," I said as I made my way to the bench where she sat. But she didn't stir. Her eyes remained closed, her head still leaning back against the wall. As if I were a specter that she couldn't hear approaching. *How curious.*

I was now standing right beside the little thing. "Hello," I said again, leaning forward as if this gesture improved my chances of carrying on a conversation. This time her eyes flew open, as if I'd suddenly startled her. She was squinting up at me in the bright light, as she cocked her head to see who I was. When she saw I was wearing more clothes that the working women of the mill, she stood up in greeting.

"Oh, hello ma'am," she answered, with a slight curtsy, as if I were royalty instead of a common seamstress living at Ms. Virginia's.

"The sun'll do us both in today if we're not careful. Not much shade for you out here; actually, none at all," I said. "Don't they give you any cover from the sun?" I asked.

"Well, there's a covered porch around back, but this door is closer to the spinning room, and I don't have much time. I just wanted a little fresh air and some breeze, before the machines start running again. The sun will just have to shine where it shines." She didn't seem much concerned about the heat, as if it were just another fact of life she'd learned to deal with. And I suppose it was.

"My name's Eliza. Eliza Darling," I said as I held my hand out to her. "Nice to meet you."

She held her small hand out to me as well. "I'm Mamie Carroll. Nice to meet you, Miss." But the girl looked at her dust-covered hand as if trying to decide whether she should have offered it in its present condition

"My lands, Mamie. Where in the world are your boots?" I asked.

Mamie looked down at her small, dirty feet, with considerable consternation. They were quite fuzzy with stray cotton fibers. "I usually go without in the summertime. I can keep my balance on the spinners easier if I don't have boots on. I fall more when I'm wearing my boots."

I didn't quite understand what she was saying to me. "Why do you have to stand on the spinners?" I asked.

Mamie seemed to remember that some people weren't familiar with the inner workings of a mill, and acted as if it were quite an odd thing to be talking to someone who didn't work inside, as if it surprised her that someone from the outside would even care. The mill was her world, and I imagined she didn't speak with many other folks who didn't live in that world with her. "Oh, for a number of different reasons. I have to piece-up the threads when they break, and also clean under the roller. I must admit, I'm small for my age, and I can't reach the very top of my machines. So I have to climb up. I can get a better grip on them if I hold on with my toes."

This poor girl had to get her job done one way or another.

"My goodness, Mamie. I just went inside for a brief minute to buy a spool of thread, and about wilted from the heat. How in the world do you work in there all day?"

"Well, I must admit it's hard to do, ma'am. There isn't any breeze 'cause they have to keep the windows closed tight.

And the water pipes are always raining sprinkles all over everything. So with the two, it's sticky as molasses in there," Mamie said.

I looked up at the massive three stories in front of me, and stared at the large, closed windows, trapping that stifling air behind their glass, close to smothering those unfortunate people who worked inside. I'd never heard of anything so daft. "But why in the world would they keep the windows closed on hot days like today?" I asked in disbelief.

" 'Cause the water droplets and hot air make it steamy and kinda wet inside. The cards of cotton – that's the strands – they stay nice and moist, and aren't as apt to break apart," Mamie explained. "When they break apart, we have to hurry and piece them up, that is, tie them up, so that the spinning machine can keep running. It's so hard to piece the strands quick enough, I think I'd rather just have the heat and stickiness than have a whole bunch of broken cotton strands one after another. Too many to piece-up so fast, and my fingers start hurting something fierce."

The poor girl suffered one way or the other, it seemed.

Mamie then stood to go, the tinkling of metal sounding from her large apron pocket as she took a stretch, and one last breath of fresh, dry air. Air without cotton fibers floating through it, like summer snowflakes. "I'd best be getting back. The spools ought to be changed by now. Nice meeting you, Miss Eliza," she said to me, once again holding out a hand that had seen enough work to belong to a sixty-year-old lady, instead of to a beautiful young girl. Mamie's thin smile looked as if it would tear apart any minute, a fragile disguise to her weariness.

"Well, nice to meet you too, Mamie. You take care of yourself," I said as I shook her hand, taking in the loveliness of the girl hidden behind her circumstances. I lingered in saying goodbye, as I thought about the shame of her being more a slave to this roaring concrete monstrosity than an employee.

Had I listened to mama, that would have been me, I thought as I walked back toward the greeting room to pick up my thread. I'd left young Mamie, but the image of her sweat-soaked body, covered in tiny fluffs of cotton lint like a baby chick, was etched into my brain.

Yes, that would have been me.

Chapter 3

The Diary of Eliza Genevieve Darling

Dallas, Texas

1907

Of all the words used to define who I was before - *sinful, unvirtuous, wayward, fallen* - I believe I despised the word *fallen* the most. Fallen from what? Grace, I would imagine. That word describes one who has given up, lapsed, degenerated. A person whom I've never considered myself to be.

Although I left the life of prostitution behind almost four years ago, the word *fallen* seems to have branded me for life, a permanent mark regardless of how hard I try to believe it no longer applies, pretending the upright citizens of Dallas don't still place that label on me. When so many people think of you in such a way, after a time it no longer matters if you're different, if you've changed. Your mind eventually begins to believe them.

For me and most others I've known, being a prostitute was just a means to an end, a way to gain my independence from my mother. No more, no less. I learned early on that my body could be used as a tool to get what I wanted, and to make money. More money than I'd made as a shop girl. More money than any other position would pay. And wasn't that what employment was all about?

My daddy died a week after my thirteenth birthday. He'd been killed on the street one night, by persons unknown, most likely when he was leaving the local pub he was known to frequent. We didn't even know the reason, but I'd heard Mama cursing him under her breath for being sodden with the whiskey. But the one thing we did know was that he was gone, leaving a wife and five children to fend for themselves.   Mama didn't know how we were going to survive, so she sent me out to search for a job. I was the oldest, after all. Mama sent me straight-away to the cotton mill to inquire. She was certain that working at the mill in the spinning room was the only respectable job a thirteen-year-old girl would be able to hold. But as was the usual case, I had other ideas. I thought there would be nothing worse than being a spinner, standing on my feet all day, just watching hundreds of strands of thread wind themselves around their bobbins. So instead, I ventured out to look for something else. I'd always excelled in my schooling. Reading and writing were easy for me - I'd devoured as many books as I could get my hands on, and loved writing stories about people I knew. I would dream up a different life for them, letting my imagination run in whatever direction the paths in my brain decided to take. Ms. Hallfield, our teacher, had told me I might just be the next Harriet Beecher Stowe or Louisa May Alcott. I was good with numbers and sums as well. Needless to say, doing mindless, monotonous work as a mill-girl did not appeal to me in the slightest.

Setting my sights quite high, I'd gone into Sanger Brothers' Dry Goods, the largest store in Dallas, hoping and praying that someone would give me a chance. That someone had been Mr. Gramercy. He hired me, and put me to work on the very afternoon I'd come inquiring.

I was a feisty young thing at thirteen. At Sanger Brothers, the boys would always come around to flirt with me, which I took as a compliment *and* an opportunity. Mama was from the *Old Country*, Poland, and didn't believe much in pampering or paying too much attention to any one of her five children, especially me, since I was the eldest. So when those boys hovered around me like bees around a blooming honeysuckle vine, I felt like a princess who was quite in control of her subjects. I would even daydream it were so, and almost imagined I could point my royal scepter at them and command them to do my bidding. I could feel the power of my youth and beauty, almost creating a spell over those boys, as if I were a fairy or a witch. I loved wielding my magic, my own personal weapon; better even than a knife or gun used to force their victims to obey one's commands. Those boys hovered close of their own free will. I had them vexed as if they'd been given a magic potion that made them slaves to my affection. I actually had power over someone else, and I won't lie – I loved it. Mr. Gramercy had warned me to be careful around those young men, as he referred to them, but I just couldn't make myself stop. I think I was just as drawn to them as they were to me.

But those boys would prove to be my downfall, especially Samuel. And my downward slide would continue swiftly until I was at the very bottom of the hole I'd managed to shovel for myself. My life would forever be that of a different person. My, oh my, how those seemingly quick and innocent decisions can change a person's life forever.

I worked behind that counter with Mr. Gramercy for four happy months, until my life took a terrible and unexpected turn. It seemed within the mere twitch of an eye, I went from selling cloth and dry beans to selling myself. It had never been my intention to travel down that path; what thirteen-year-old girl in her right mind would even consider it? Mr. Gramercy had done his Lord-almighty best to defend me, trying valiantly to prevent my downward spiral into disgrace. But he failed.

I admit I'd let my vanity get the better of me. Just like most young girls my age, I'd grown more concerned with my appearance, and my attractiveness to the opposite sex. I'd put back a penny a week until I'd saved enough of my salary to buy *Beautall's Pearline Tooth Powder*. For some reason, I'd developed a fixation on pearly white teeth; I wanted them to be beautiful, shiny and very, very white. Like pearls from an oyster. When I first saw that tooth powder sitting on the shelf at Sanger's, it was like my brain had been seized by an idea that just wouldn't loosen its grip. I had to try it. Once I'd finally saved enough, I bought a bottle and hid it under my mattress, the only place I thought I would stand a chance of keeping something that was mine, and only mine, away from mama's prying eyes, and the sticky, curious fingers of the hands of four younger siblings. But I was wrong. Mama had felt it necessary to turn my mattress only three days after, and had found it there. I'd tried to explain it to her, but she didn't understand. She *never* understood any of the modern-day products.

"You waste our money on this potion? You would allow your brothers and sisters to starve just to feed your sexual perversions? You disgrace my home?!" Mama screamed at me when I'd gotten home from work, holding my tooth powder as if it were a gift from the devil himself. Her accusations shot across the room like arrows, piercing my soul just as easily as if they'd been made of flint. How could something so innocent as tooth powder bring about disgrace and evil? How could it make *me* disgraceful and evil?

"Mama, the powder is for cleaning my teeth!" I cried back, in self-defense of both my honor and morality.

"Don't lie to me!" mama screamed as she slapped my cheek, the impression of her hand seared into both my flesh and memory. Mama had never slapped my face before, and I think the emotional pain of it was much greater than the physical. She threw the bottle of tooth powder into the fireplace, where it landed between two burning cedar logs, sending sparks flying, as if my hopes and dreams were being chased right up the chimney. Through my tears of anger and hurt, I watched the flames consume the product of my vanity, the label on the glass bottle shriveling into blackness, which quickly turned to ash. The life of a teenage girl in the modern world had no place in our house. She'd made her point.

That day, and the next, I wore my anger like a funeral shroud, hoping it would take me to the next stage of my life. I didn't much care where, as long as it was away from mama, and her icy-cold heart.

Samuel Strayhorn came into Sanger Brothers almost every day, buzzing around my counter with his confident manner and sweet words. He was from Highland Park, the new neighborhood where all the well-to-do folk lived. Samuel never seemed to be wanting for much. He always had at least a nickel in his pocket for an elixir or some candy sticks. He came by every day after his lessons were finished and walked around and around the store, pretending he was looking at the merchandise, when in fact the only thing in that store he was really interested in was me. As was his ritual, he'd finally end his wanderings right in front of my counter, trying to make what small talk he could, and ending his conversation with an exclamation point of a peppermint stick. He would smile and hold that candy stick in front of me until I reached out and took it from him, as if that small gesture made it clear that I felt the same way about him.

Then each and every night, Mama asked me where I'd managed to get a candy stick. And each and every night, after answering her with a silent, secretive smile, she'd accuse me of spending my hard-earned wages on something so trivial and selfish. As if I didn't know she needed the money I brought home to put food on our table, to feed my brothers and sisters. How could she believe I thought anything otherwise? That was the entire reason I was working at Sanger's every day instead of going to school. That was the *only* reason. Why else would a thirteen-year-old girl be spending time working when what she'd rather be doing was anything else? Especially learning? When Mama told me I had to quit school to go to work, I cried until my nose was so plugged-up I had to breathe through my mouth. How I'd yearned to stay in school like most other girls my age. I had convinced myself I was destined to be a spinner of stories that would capture one's imagination. I was a writer. All I wanted to do was write, and learn even more. I loved my schooling.

"I didn't spend money on it, Mama," I always told her. "It was a gift."

"From who?" she would ask, looking upon me with her usual icy glare of suspicion.

I never answered with a name. Until that last day.

"From a boy, Mama. Samuel is his name," I finally told her, with a dreaminess in my eyes that angered her more than the candy stick.

Mama grabbed that candy from my hand as if it were made of poison, and promptly threw it into the waste can. In fact, she did consider me poisoned, but not by the candy.

"First you bring the powder into my house, and now gifts from a boy. Girl, the evil of the flesh has taken over. You bring disgrace upon our home!"

"I am *not* evil!" I protested, unsuccessfully trying to convince her.

Then one Friday afternoon not long after, Sam Strayhorn once again hovered in front of my counter, waving that candy stick at me. He asked again if I might want to make a plan for the evening. I'd always told him *no* before. But not that day. I no longer cared what mama would say. I knew she was going to believe the worst about me, whether or not I tried to be well-mannered and proper. I decided then and there that since mama already considered me a depraved girl, I might as well not disappoint her expectations. And I was more than anxious to get away from her for a time.

"Well, I would love to go to dinner with you, Sam," accepting his invitation playfully.

My descent into waywardness had begun.

Our harmless dinner on that Friday night turned into a tryst that lasted the entire weekend; his parents had been away, visiting family in Tyler. It was so much more satisfying to be the object of an almost-grown-man's undivided affections, instead of just a girl receiving scornful stares from her own mother. Why put myself through the suffering I felt from her revulsion? I was happier being the object of Sam's desires, and being free to do exactly as I pleased. Totally free.

But on Sunday night when I was walking home, after Sam had dropped me three blocks down the street, my skin began to prickle as my front door came into view, as if my body were somehow trying to warn me of the danger I was walking into. And sure enough, when I was close enough for mama to see me through the window, the front door opened and a policeman came out. He met me on the front walk, and told me my mama had reported me as a runaway child who was now selling herself for money. He asked me if I knew that prostitution was a crime. I told him I was in no way practicing prostitution; I'd just been spending time with a young man who'd caught my fancy.

"So you're saying you gave yourself to him for free then?" that policeman asked, not really expecting or wanting an answer.

Before I even opened my mouth, he took my arm and turned me around, marching me away from my house.

I turned my head and looked back, as if my glance would somehow cause mama to regret calling the authorities, but I immediately realized my hope was totally misplaced. The last thing I saw was mama's face, watching me continue my fall from respectability. She had neither worry for me, nor saving grace. Only anger framed her features, her brow creased under its weighted presence. It was clear she intended to have me suffer through the punishment she plainly felt I was due. My front door closed, and with it that almost-innocent chapter of my young life.

"What did I do wrong?" I asked the policeman as he pulled me down the street, wrenching my arm with the same determination that I put forth trying to free it. "What did I do!?" I screamed.

"Young lady, you are being arrested for the practice of prostitution," he told me with the grim face of a hangman.

"But I didn't sell myself! I'm not a prostitute! Ask Samuel! Samuel Strayhorn. He's the boy I've been staying with. He'll tell you!" I tried to plead my innocence to him but my words were falling on ears that just wouldn't hear. He said not another word to me until we reached the jail-house.

"Here is where you'll stay until the judge decides your punishment," the policeman said as he shut the door to my cell, and turned the key. The click of the lock was the sound of my life being changed forever.

How could mama have done this to me?

Chapter 4

The Diary of Eliza Genevieve Darling

My Descent

Descent.

Walking down a staircase. An acorn falling from a tree. A girl whose craving for attention causes her to spiral downward on a course she never would have predicted.

My fall from respectability.

My fall into another world.

The next day I was taken before the judge. Mama was there, but so was Mr. Gramercy. He held his bowler in his hand with the worried look of a lost puppy. I thought he might just break down and cry right there. I wanted to cry too, but I wasn't about to give mama that satisfaction, so I decided to just hold my head up as high as it would go. As far as I could determine, the only thing I'd done wrong was not letting mama know where I was all weekend. I certainly didn't consider staying with Samuel a crime, and I wasn't about to act like I'd committed one.

Mama proceeded to tell the judge how I had sullied her good name with my lewd acts of perversity. How I had ruined my innocence by staying with a young man for two whole days.

"She has prostituted herself for sheer pleasure and monetary gain, dishonoring her family," my mother said, as she glared at me, as if I were a foul and objectionable creature, not even meant to keep company with reputable people. "She cannot return to my decent home. She is wayward, and must be punished!" my mama barked, more of a demand than a request. "My daughter should remain in jail, for her own good, and the good of our home. Maybe after being treated as a criminal, she will acknowledge her sinfulness, and return to her senses."

I'd gotten pleasure, yes, I thought, *but not money!*

I listened to my mother talk about me as if I weren't her daughter. As if I were some shameful villain whose main purpose was to ruin all decent existence. She stood stoically in that courtroom, stating her case without shedding a tear. Instead of worry, she was consumed by a passionate wrath. She wasn't concerned about my fate. It was her own reputation at stake, not mine.

Did mama not remember me sitting on her knee when I was small, listening to stories about her childhood? Had she conveniently forgotten the times I'd been a good and obedient daughter, cooking dinner in her stead, or cleaning the house, or caring for my brothers and sisters? And what about quitting school at her request, disposing of my dream to be a writer so our family would have enough to eat? We were now like two strangers; it seemed that neither of us had met the other. The thought that maybe my mother was demented entered my mind. Had she lost her sanity after my father died, and I just hadn't paid sufficient attention to notice?

Mr. Gramercy, on the other hand, testified that as far as he'd seen, I was an honorable girl. I came to the store on time every day, and worked diligently at my job. Although he admitted that boys did hover around my counter, he argued that this was only a natural occurrence, especially considering that I was such a pretty young lady.

"How could attention from the opposite sex not be inevitable?" he asked the judge. "It's like putting a spoonful of honey on the windowsill and not expecting the bees to start buzzing around it. It's just nature," he argued.

"My daughter must be taught a lesson," my mother countered. "Her younger brothers and sisters must see that there are stiff consequences to such behavior. She sets a bad example for her siblings."

"But she's a good girl!" Mr. Gramercy blurted, shaking his head as he squeezed the brim of his hat. "Your honor, surely there is some other punishment more befitting a thirteen-year-old girl than being confined to a jail cell! Please!" he cried out.

The icy hand that squeezed my heart after hearing my mother's words loosened its grip as I listened to Mr. Gramercy's plea. He sounded more like my parent than my own mother, and I would be forever grateful that he stood up for me and was so distressed by my predicament.

The Judge looked from my mother to Mr. Gramercy, and then to me, considering his options. Then he banged his gavel forcefully on the dais. "Guilty as charged. Thirty days in the city jail!" he boomed, with the authority of his position.

My mother looked at me with an air of righteousness and walked from the room, leaving me to suffer the consequences that she herself had mandated.

Mother, please don't leave me here! I'm sorry I caused you worry! I'm sorry!!

The little-girl part of me wanted to run to her, and hold on for dear life. The terror coursing through me demanded that I cry and beg for another chance. Anything to escape being kept in a cell.

But the other part of me - the stubborn and rebellious part - wouldn't let me do it. I would *not* embarrass myself; I wouldn't let one tear fall, nor give mama the satisfaction of begging for mercy. Although I felt the dam might break any second, I didn't say a word. Just tried to pretend I was watching the goings-on of someone else's fate, not my own.

How could this have happened? I felt as if I were in a play being performed for an audience of strangers. *I* felt like a stranger. Who were the actors in this ghastly drama?

"It will be fine, Eliza," Mr. Gramercy told me quietly, trying to give me what comfort he could. "You'll see. The time will pass quickly, and your job will be waiting for you," he stated, his expression of concern and apprehension belying his hopeful words of encouragement.

A cold and roughened hand then wrapped itself around my upper arm, its owner seemingly apathetic to my fate, and I was straightaway marched back to the jail and placed in my cell. The click of the lock was like a punctuation to the judge's gavel, finalizing my sentence with its cold, metallic exclamation.

I was given a rough frock made of sackcloth to wear, and made to change right there in that cell, with nothing to hide behind but my shame. It was chilly that March, and I remember being cold the entire time I was in that place. I was disgraced, and I knew that was the point. Did mama think that once my dishonor was fully paid for, my degradation would convert me to a *proper* daughter? If so, her plot was foolish. My situation did nothing but strengthen my determination to be my own person.

In that jail cell, I learned first-hand of the hypocrisy of the law; I learned that the rules of my confinement were whatever the jailers wanted them to be, regardless of what was considered a crime as was written in the ordinances. As I sat alone each day and considered my situation, I observed the policemen who were on duty each shift. I quietly listened to their conversations with other men in uniform who came in and out during the day, and I soon came to the conclusion that they were men just like any other, and they would put their own needs before those of the town and the common good. Their satisfaction would always have a greater priority than that of the people they were sworn to protect. I was sure I could use their human needs to my good advantage.

I came to know who among my jailers was the weakest link in the chain, and I put that knowledge to good use during his next shift. On the sixth day of my predicament, I put my plan into action.

"Excuse me, officer," I said rather demurely, trying to make myself appear as dainty and innocent as possible. "Would it be at all possible for me to sit out there with you, so that I can just look out the window for a bit? I haven't seen the sun in almost a week, and am prone to becoming quite sad without it. My mood seems to need sunshine. I promise to just sit quietly and gaze at the sky."

He considered my request, and assumed it would cause no harm. After all, how could a thirteen-year-old girl, who was slight of figure, overcome such a large and powerful man of authority such as he?

"I guess I could let you sit by the window, just for a while," he answered without concern.

The burly officer unlocked my cell and let me sit beside him, I feigning to take in the sunshine while he completed paperwork at his desk. After a small while, I placed my hand on his knee, hoping against hope that he would be *just a man.* Like I'd surmised, he didn't disappoint me. He looked me in the eye for a brief moment, as if he were going to chastise me, but then just as quickly looked back down at the paperwork on his desk. He made no mention of my hand on his knee, nor did he make any attempt to remove it. I was one step closer to my freedom.

After sitting in that fashion for a while longer, I ventured to suggest a compromise. "If you would possibly consider giving me my freedom, I might consider giving you some special comforts and attention. A man such as yourself must surely need relief from the stress of such a demanding job."

Our eyes then met in that way when two people seem to read each other's mind. It was lucky for me that the fine officers of the Dallas police department apparently didn't hold themselves to any higher standard than would a normal man about to induce a young woman to commit an offense. I was being fully introduced to the hypocrisy of men taking *favors* from women but bearing no blame themselves.

My jailer rose and ushered me into a small closet in the back of the building, filled with mops and pails and cleaning rags. The small room was musty and dusty, but he certainly didn't seem to mind our surroundings. He had only one thing on his mind. He turned over a pail on which he motioned me to sit, and proceeded to unbutton his dark blue trousers. I was now certain his trousers were put on one leg at a time, just like any other man's. And unbuttoned, just like any other's. I proceeded to service him, with no more thought than how long it would take me to gain my freedom. It most certainly wasn't any act of love or lust, at least on my part, but just a task required in trade for something else. Just like working. It was no more personal to me than selling a man a pair of socks at Sanger Brothers. Socks in return for money. A *favor* in return for freedom. The principle was the same.

It took longer than I would have liked to satisfy the officer, but once he was done, he buttoned his pants, and told me to follow him back to the desk while he did the paperwork. "I'll prepare a release form for you that states your fine has been paid. If asked, just say you don't know who paid it." Of course we both knew who'd just tendered it, and he smiled as he recalled the form of payment I'd just given. "You're free to go, Miss Darling. I'll get your clothes."

I walked out of that jail with my head held high, as if I'd just been visiting a relative. It crossed my mind that I should have been bothered by what I'd just done. But in fact, I really wasn't. Or at least I didn't think I was. I told myself it was just the law of supply and demand. Bartering. If I had what someone else wanted, there was always the possibility of negotiation. Then it occurred to me that if I could get what I wanted by providing sexual favors, I had a skill that would get me what I wanted in life. Not only the necessities, but the luxuries as well. I had no thoughts of going back to mama and the children. It was no longer my home. As far as I was concerned, mama had given me up to the world, and I was bound and determined not to return to someone who would have me locked up, with no more thought that having the dog catcher take away a stray. I would miss my brothers and sisters, but would never give mama the satisfaction of returning to beg for forgiveness. I wanted no mercy from her. I just wanted my freedom.

The sun on which I'd based my ruse had vanished, swallowed up by the dark and ominous Texas rain clouds that could form out of nowhere, then empty their fullness in the flash of a lightning bolt. Like the Lord emptying buckets of tears for the meek and meager. Water drenched me as I marched myself away from the precinct house, vowing to myself that I would never return.

The rain notwithstanding, being wet and chilly and bedraggled didn't stop me from doing what I had to do. I walked straight-away to Emma Street and chose the fanciest house on it as my new home. I would start my new life with what I had to offer. Myself. I was certain it would be an easier way to make a living than being a store clerk, or Lord forbid, working at a mill. And there would be no mama constantly wearing her disappointment in me like a death shroud, always reminding me that I was not the kind of daughter she was willing to raise.

I would just have to take care of myself from here on out.

Chapter 5

Elaine

June 2, 2011

Dallas, Texas

I'm almost in a state of shock as I stare at my laptop screen. I am breathing hard, my body almost not able to contain the fright that has smothered me like a down pillow pressed over my face.

Oh my God! I whisper as I shake my head, and try to will the tears not to spill.

What just happened here? One minute I'm trying to decide what to write about, and the next thing I know, I'm having a hallucination about the early twentieth-century. It seemed so real, like I was actively participating in some strange four-D movie or something. My body trembles as my brain tries to process what has happened, trying to decipher the facts through the weirdness of it all.

I am terrified that my latest life-change has caused me to once again lose my state of balance, to lose myself to mental fragility. But instead of nightmares while I sleep, I'm having a hallucination, fully awake.

My laptop screen is still illuminated, the screen-saver not even on. I can now hear the usual daytime noises floating in from the other rooms of the house - the clunk of ice falling from the ice-maker into the bin, the soft hum of the refrigerator, the ticking of the clock. I can hear each second moving to the next, the total, inexplicable silence from before replaced by the familiar sounds of a normal day. But something is definitely off. *Way* off.

WHAT IF I WERE SOMEONE ELSE?

Those words still stare back at me, from the top of the page. But halfway down the screen, there is also something else.

ELIZA GENEVIEVE DARLING

Who in the hell is that? And how did that name get there?

I don't remember typing that. But there it is, right in front of my face.

I am totally unnerved by my fear that the depression and anxiety I suffered so many years ago have navigated their way back, reminding me that yes, oh yes, I am still vulnerable to their erratic surprise attacks. I consider the very real possibility that my feelings of uselessness have caused my mind to once again travel down the dreaded path that eventually merges with the road to insanity. I come very close to slamming my laptop closed, and retreating to the safety of my bed, like a little girl hiding under her covers. The fear of anti-depressants and therapists grips me as I remember my dark days. I don't want to go back.

But then I look again at the screen in front of me.

There are nine words, and I'm positive I didn't type the last three.

Who is Eliza Genevieve Darling?

I look up at the clock on the wall above my desk, and am totally freaked-out, teetering on the edge of hysteria. Its hands point to ten minutes past nine. I feel as though that clock is just another prop in this weird *Twilight Zone* episode I've been starring in. *How in the hell could that be?* I didn't even sit down to write until a few minutes after nine. I look again to make sure the second hand is ticking, and it is. I try to convince myself that time appears to have stood still because the batteries in the clock must need replacing.

I turn off the desk lamp, shaking my head in a moment of defeat and pain. My creative juices have just been swallowed by a whirlpool of fear. Or insanity. I'm giving up before I really even start. I try to clear my head as I make my way to the kitchen.

The digital clock on the stove reads nine-eleven. I almost race to the bedroom. Nine-eleven. The ticks from the clocks almost sync with the thumps I feel inside my chest. I'm frightened. I'm really scared. *What if I am losing my mind?* The thought was like a huge lump stuck deep inside my throat.

I walk back to the den in an almost trance-like state, and stare at my laptop as of it is a living, breathing thing. I need to hide its taunting face, and put it into the quilted sleeve my sister made me for my birthday. Pink and purple paisley material, with my initials   *E G D* embroidered in a large and fancy font, squarely in the middle. It occurs to me that the name *Eliza Genevieve Darling* begins with the same initials. More cause for worry?

Has my mind gotten craftier in its deceit?

I spend most of the day halfheartedly paying bills and doing laundry. Cleaning a kitchen that was already spotless to begin with. Running a dust cloth over our antique furniture, even though any dust that might be present is too little for the naked eye to see - I'd just dusted a few days ago. I am an automaton just going through the motions, trying to take my mind away from the anxiety that has attacked me like an enemy. Trying to temper my bizarre episode with a sense of normalcy that comes from the mundane. But I'm certainly not focused on the tasks at hand. Ever since I turned my laptop off, I've been filled with such a strange sensation, like my body and my spirit aren't meshing as well as they did yesterday. I almost feel uncomfortable in my own skin.

By three o'clock, I feel as though I've been run over by a freight train. I don't understand why I'm so tired, having done almost nothing all day long. But go figure; stranger things have happened.

Stranger things.

I lay my head on the pillow for a nap, and wonder if I will dream of turn-of-the-century prostitutes and cotton-mill spinners. I'm so afraid, like a little girl scared of the boogie-man in the dark. There is still that vicious little voice whispering in my inner ear, taunting, and once again announcing that I might just be losing my mind.

Chapter 6

Elaine Grace Dearborn

History

Damaged goods.

A package crushed by UPS. A glass with a crack running through it. A car stuck in a hail storm. A sixteen-year-old girl who has an abortion.

Me.

For me, being a good wife and mother has always been the ultimate goal. Don't think I believe I'm a perfect mom, because I don't, and I'm not. Far from it. I'm not a perfect wife either. I've made mistakes, some so devastating that I still feel like crying when I think about them. But I decided long ago that I have no choice but to own them, and try to make up for them and move on.

My son Andrew was a year old. He was healthy and happy and everything a one-year-old should be. But his mother wasn't. I was supposed to be happy. I *should have* been happy. I *knew* this. But knowing something and *feeling* it are sometimes two different things. Mind versus heart. Intelligence versus that deep-seated belief that I was a failure as a mother. As a person.

I made a mistake. I knew it right after I'd taken the action that can never be undone. I was so young, and trusted my parents to guide me in the right direction. They believed they were doing just that. But it hadn't worked out that way.

I got pregnant when I was sixteen. I had hoped and prayed that my period was just late, although it never had been before. I finally broke down and bought a home pregnancy test. It felt like a time bomb in my hand. The magic wand which would tell me of my fate, whether my life was to explode before it even had a chance to really begin. The test was simple - pee on the stick and see if a blue line developed. If not, I was the luckiest girl in the world. But if it appeared, my life as I'd known it was over.

That was the longest five minutes of my life. Sitting on the edge of the bathtub, behind a locked door, hoping no one would knock before I knew whether my world was to crumble around me. I looked at that stick lying on the bathroom counter by the sink, next to the Tinkerbell soap dispenser that I'd not yet been able to make myself replace. A remnant from my childhood. Seeing those two items in such close proximity was outrageous. I wanted to cry.

I wanted to be the little girl again who'd begged her mother for that soap dispenser.

The blue line seemed to scream at me as I held that stick in my hand, trying to convince myself that maybe blue was the color of an overactive imagination. I just stared at that stick in a state of suspended animation, my thoughts moving in a hundred different directions, along with my confidence. That blue line was a revelation, mocking me. Telling me I had no business trying to act like an adult. My one act of being a woman had slapped me in the face. I'd just wanted to know what it felt like, if it was the epitome of womanhood my friends constantly talked about. God knows, I'd listened to them long enough. I'd been an outsider, just looking in, but I wanted to be an insider.

I didn't love the boy, really didn't even know him at all. He was just a vehicle for my journey into womanhood. How did this happen after only one time? I knew it could - we'd had the sex-ed lessons in school, and my mother had explained it to me more than once. But I never believed it could happen to me! What were the chances?

Apparently much higher than I'd thought.

Two words a parent hopes they will never hear spoken by their teenage daughter.

"I'm pregnant."

I told them right away - the fear of my situation outweighed the fear of my revelation. At first, they were just in shock. Then my mother cried, and my dad left for the gym to work off his anger. But they quickly came to terms with the situation, much faster than I'd expected. They weren't really angry, they said. They were scared. My parents told me it was just a mistake. It shouldn't have happened to me but it did.

"We can fix it," my mother said, as if she were talking about a broken toy, or a dress than needed hemming.

How can it be fixed? I wondered. Pregnancy is like being dead - you either *are* or you *aren't*.

"We'll go to the Planned Parenthood clinic tomorrow," Mom said. "You'll just have to take the day off from school. One day shouldn't hurt."

I just looked at my mother in a state of confusion. She saw that I didn't understand.

"Elaine, there's really no choice but to have an abortion. It's safe now," she told me simply.

I said nothing.

"You've got plans to go to college. Of course, having a baby while you're trying to get your degree is out of the question," mom said, matter-of-factly, as if it didn't require any more thought. "Not to mention the fact that you've still got two years of high school to get through."

My parents had made their decision, made *my* decision for me. They never asked me what I wanted to do, and I really didn't even know. I was so scared; I just wanted it to go away.

The next morning my mother took me to the clinic. It was in a strip mall not far from our house, squeezed between an ice cream parlor and a dry cleaner. It didn't look like a clinic at all, just another store. I listened to my mother discuss my *situation* with the receptionist. It was surreal, as if I were listening to her talk about someone else, a neighbor or the daughter of a friend. Not me. I knew I was the reason we were there, and I knew what was to happen. But my body just went through the motions, as if it belonged to someone I didn't know.

The nurse had me take another urine test, just to be sure.

"Yes honey, it's positive," she told me. I had held out no hope that it would be negative.

I was taken into an exam room, and told to put on a hospital gown.

"Now, this procedure shouldn't hurt," the nurse told me, "but you will feel some pressure, and some discomfort." She then put fuzzy socks on my feet - it was freezing in that room. "The doctor will insert a tube through your vagina and into your uterus, then suction out the tissue."

Tissue.

The baby, I thought. Although she'd tried to camouflage the reality, it was a baby that was going to be sucked through that tube.

"The whole procedure should only take a few minutes," she informed me with a smile. It seemed too brief a process. Shouldn't ending a life be a monumental undertaking? Shouldn't it require more than just ten minutes of my time?

Just as she'd said, the doctor was in and out of my room in about eight minutes. I lay on that table thinking about what homework was due the next day. Not wanting to think about what the doctor was doing.

"You'll have some bleeding, sweetie," the nurse told me, as she gave me several Kotex, "and some minor cramping." She turned to my mother. "But call us if she has severe pain or bleeds profusely. And I would give her two Advil every four hours or so."

Take two pills and call me in the morning.

And then we were out the door.

I don't think I said two words the entire trip home. I was too numb. *How ironic that I will have my period right away,* I thought, or what amounted to it anyway. Right back to normal, as if none of it had ever happened.

"OK, sweetie. You can put this all behind you now," my mother told me when we got home. "I think you need to take your medicine and go to bed for a while. Do you have any homework?"

And that was how my parents dealt with their sixteen-year-old daughter getting pregnant. Just make like it never happened, as quickly as possible, and get back to normal.

But I wasn't so sure I would *ever* be *back to normal.*

It had all happened so fast, I didn't really have time to come to grips with it. It's since occurred to me that maybe my parents didn't want me to have much time to think about it. Get rid of it, and then pretend it never happened. Go on about my merry way. *Back to normal.*

Now Planned Parenthood requires counseling before they'll perform an abortion, especially if you're a minor. To make sure you understand what you're doing. To make sure your *parents* understand what they're doing. To make sure everyone will be prepared for the gaping void that is sure to consume you the next month, or year, or many years down the road. At the time, I thought I'd handled it O.K., and thought I was continuing to handle it.

Until Andrew was born. And then things changed.

Ten years later and the choice I'd made when I was sixteen had come back to haunt me, lurking in my subconscious until it knew the exact time to surface, to inflict the most pain. Andrew was the joy of my life. When they handed him to me for the first time, I couldn't believe what a little miracle he was. But soon after, I also began to think about the little miracle I'd eradicated from the world before it ever had a chance.

I'd finished high school, gone to college and gotten a dual degree in creative writing and journalism. I got a job editing a local magazine, assisting with a column entitled *In a Nutshell*, which spotlighted various residents of our community. I'd fulfilled the plan my parents had for me.

I was such a good girl.

One night, I'd gone with my friends to happy hour after work; there I met Drew. It had taken him two hours and three beers to finally build up sufficient courage to approach our table of five girls and tell me how beautiful I was. After a six-month romance, we'd gotten married. I became a stay-at-home mom when Andrew was born.

Had I not gotten that abortion, would I have had the same life, but with three children instead of two? Most likely not. How would I have gone to college, gotten my degree? I probably wouldn't have been working at the magazine or been in the bar after work. I probably never would have met Drew.

My intellectual self still tried to assure me that I'd made the right decision - correction: my *parents* had made the right decision. But my emotional self had been drowning in the murky waters of self-doubt.

I hate what I did. I don't care how young I was. It wasn't right.

I'd erased a little wonder from the world. For my own advantage, and for the convenience of my parents. Why would God give me a second chance? Don't miracles only happen to those who deserve them?

When Andrew was only two weeks old, I began having nightmares about the death of babies. My baby would die a strange and unusual death, and the next night he would die a different way. But all of the deaths were somehow tied to my negligence. I couldn't sleep, didn't want to sleep, dreading the silent video of doom that I knew would visit me during the night. I'd then obsess about my dreams during the day.

I was consumed by guilt, over both what I'd done so long ago, and having a perfect baby I didn't deserve. I was overcome with fear, waiting for the punishment I was surely still due. Paralyzed by anxiety.

After a year of struggling with the scattered pieces of my sanity, Drew finally forced me to see a therapist. I couldn't get out of bed in the morning, couldn't bear to face another day. He was worried about me, but also frustrated. He tried his hardest to take care of me and Andrew, and put in his time at the office as well. But he was saddled with a crazy woman, and an infant son who needed someone to take care of him. It was too much.

"Elaine, I'm going to call the Employee Assistance Program when I get to work today," he'd told me one morning, as he went to get Andrew, crying in his crib because I hadn't yet been able to drag myself out of bed. "You've got to go see someone. I'm gonna lose my job if I have to take any more time off," he stated as an absolute, with no room for negotiation. I'd always argued with him before. But this time I could hear the ultimatum in his voice.

I really had no choice.

So I went to my first session, and was told to journal my feelings. I think it was a good thing. My tears fell freely, making the pages in my notebook soggy. I guess that was part of the therapy, to see your mistakes on paper and cry them out.

I'd buried my feelings so deep that it took Andrew's birth to make them resurface, like a dormant virus waiting until just the right time to strike, knowing when its host was most vulnerable.

I truly felt like I'd lost my mind.

Chapter 7

Elaine

June 3, 2011

I begin the next day as if I'm jet-lagged, like I've just returned from a trip around the world. I don't remember if I dreamed during the night; don't remember anything at all. But I feel so tired, as if I haven't even slept. I sit down with a strong cup of coffee for a few minutes, hoping the caffeine will circulate thoroughly and chase away the stupor into which I've been plunged. I sit in the den and once again listen to the mantel clock ticking, my gaze drawn to the possessed laptop on the desk, just daring me to try the writing thing again.

But I'm afraid to, irrationally worried that it's not just a tool, but something bewitched, its purpose to push my mind over the edge.

The prickles of anxiety once again attack my body, like ants just under the surface of my skin. Why did I type that woman's name yesterday? Is it the name destined to be a character in my story? Did it come to me by chance? Maybe I came across it while watching TV and just saved it to memory for future reference. It was so very bizarre though.

I take my mug of coffee to my desk, pull the laptop from its cover, and power it up.

I'm scared to death.

Scared of insanity. Scared of failing. But I have to know.

I Google her name. *Eliza Genevieve Darling.* To my surprise, the screen is filled with a list of references, most citing a book written by a historian at The University of Texas, *A History of American Prostitution*.

> I click on the first reference.

Although there are numerous sources of information which detail prostitution through the ages, including the fate of turn-of-the-century prostitutes during the American Progressive Era and the Social Purity Movement, there is very little information available that details the lives of the individual prostitutes. However, one of the few references available to us is a diary kept by a former Dallas prostitute, Eliza Genevieve Darling, that is surprising in its detail. The diary gives us extraordinary glimpses into the lives of prostitutes during that era, and the struggles they faced when trying to become "redeemed" women.

> *My God!* I'm stunned. She was a *real* person.

> I click on the next reference. It's an excerpt from her diary.

May 15, 1903

Today Ms. Dixie informed us that she is closing The Orpheum. She'd asked a lady who ran a local shelter for women if she would consider taking in girls who wanted to leave the life of prostitution, and the lady had agreed. Ms. Dixie said she's thought long and hard about it, and she's decided that living life as a prostitute is not fulfilling God's divine plan for us. Yes, it is a living, but at what cost? The intensity with which the social purity crusaders are battling our profession is increasing so that it seems we might soon be the pariah of Dallas. Although it is my profound opinion that we provide a necessary evil, supplying the good men of Dallas with a suitable outlet for their sexual desires (surely supplying what their devout wives will not!), I understand that Ms. Dixie is trying to help us better our lot. After all, as she says, our profession is just that – a way to make a living, and at the same time, keeping us from the slavery of the mills and farms. If there were a better alternative, why not take it? Well, supposedly, now there is. Ms. Dixie has come to the conclusion that what she wants more than anything for her girls is to give them that chance. She's decided that wealth and fancy dresses aren't worth the cost. When she told me this, she gently touched her fingertips to the jagged scar on my cheek, as if her decision for our future could somehow take back the past. Next week, our small harem of the most desired women in Dallas will move to The Virginia K. Johnson Home & Training Center for Women. I guess it is truly saying something for Ms. Dixie to give up her beautiful House, and her sizable income, to help us all have secure and respectable lives. I trust Miss Dixie implicitly, and will most likely follow her until we both drop off the ends of the Earth.

Wow! Chills run a footrace up my back and back down to my stomach. Snippets of my hallucination, or daydream, or whatever the hell it was, come back to me. Bits and pieces. It seems I know these women. *But how in the hell is that possible?*

Chapter 8

Elaine

June 4, 2011

Wayward women.

The Virginia K. Johnson Home.

Eliza Darling.

I am totally enthralled with what I'm reading. She'd been a real person, and a real prostitute. The diary entry references the manuscripts kept in the Dallas Public Library's Archives Division. They are entitled *The Eliza Papers*, and amount to three boxes of documents. I must sheepishly admit that although I've lived in Dallas my entire life, I've never been to the main library downtown. It's a huge seven-story building which takes up a good portion of a downtown city block. For some reason, it's always been a little intimidating to me.

I keep pulling up references as I scroll down the list on the screen. Most are snippets written about the prostitution industry in the early twentieth century, and mention Eliza Darling. Her diary is apparently one of the few known detailed records describing a prostitute's life during that time. I continue to click on each reference; I'm drawn to her story, and desperately want to find another of her diary entries.

I have to know more.

I have quite a stake in her being real. After all, if she really lived, I didn't just conjure her up. Maybe my sanity has not been compromised. But I also feel drawn to her, like a strong magnetic force is pulling me closer, almost against my will.

Eliza lived almost exactly where I do now, in the heart of old Oak Cliff, one of the first areas in Dallas to be settled. I wonder about the Home she lived in. What is the name again? I scroll back up the screen to find it.

There it is. *The Virginia K. Johnson Home and Training Center for Women.*

I've lived in Oak Cliff all my life, and can't believe I've never heard of this place before. I type the name into my search bar, and references pop onto my screen. I open one, and it links me to a picture of a very large three-story red-brick house with four large white columns around the front porch. A third-floor balcony presides over the front of the structure. Sure enough, the name on the facade is *VIRGINIA K. JOHNSON HOME*. It appears to have been an impressive structure in its time, but without pretense. Massive, but modest, utilitarian instead of ornamental.

I don't remember ever seeing this building, and click on another reference in hopes of finding the address. There doesn't appear to be a wealth of information about this place, but more about the founder, Virginia K. Johnson. Then I come across an old conversation on a historical chat room site.

> *The home was first named The Virginia K. Johnson Home for Destitute Women, and was a shelter for unwed mothers, and for young prostitutes who wanted to leave the life of depravity and had no other means of support. Many of the girls there were either pregnant or already had children.*
>
> *The Home not only sheltered young women, but it also educated them, and provided vocational training. The girls were taught to read and write, if they didn't already know how, and were taught the basics of mathematics. They also received training in a vocation of their choice. Programs to learn skills in dressmaking, nursing, and millinery were*

offered. Later, when it was more acceptable for women to hold office positions, the program was expanded to include courses in bookkeeping, typing, and stenography.

Ms. Virginia Johnson had been the wife of a well-to-do attorney who never had it in her head or heart to look down on those less fortunate than she. After all, she'd spent a year in prison in Missouri when she was in her early twenties, the punishment for aiding confederate soldiers. Ms. Virginia's daddy had been a Methodist minister, so she was well-versed in the Methodist mission, and eventually became the president of the King's Daughters, the Methodist Missionary Society in Dallas. She was quite well known as a defender of people in unfortunate circumstances. Even though proper *ladies shouldn't even know about the prostitution problem, much less speak of it, Ms. Virginia wrote numerous articles for the Methodist newspaper that she published, The King's Messenger. One such article pointed out that our American society carried a two-faced attitude toward its* degenerate *women - can't live with'em, can't live without 'em. Ms. Virginia was quite the topic of conversation. After all, respectable women shouldn't have been carrying on about the welfare of those who lived life in disgrace.*

But the story hit its target.

One day not long after, Ms. Virginia was approached by a local madame who asked her quite sincerely if she would consider helping those young women who wanted to rid themselves of the sporting life. This madame also pointed out to Ms. Virginia that many of them had babies who would benefit from their mamas being removed from the life they were leading.

Ms. Virginia had never been one to shy away from a challenge or a heart-felt plea for help, so she chanced the ill-favor of polite society, and considered that madame's please as a call to action from God himself. She would no more have turned away that woman than she would have turned away the Angel Gabriel delivering her a direct message. In fact, she considered the madame an angel in disguise. Ms. Virginia, or Saint Virginia as she was called by some, knew that most of these women were just trying to earn a living; they were no more irredeemable than she had been while in the Union prison.

Wow, who would have thought such a place existed here at the turn of the century! I still don't know exactly where it was located. I continue to scan the articles in search of an address.

At the corner of Paige and Madison Streets.

But why have I never noticed it before? Maybe I've just always been in such a hurry to get where I'm going that I've neglected to notice things which are plainly in front of my face?

I continue to scan the chat-room conversation about this amazing place.

Oops. That's why I've never seen it. At least, not recently.

However, in the 1930's, the Virginia K. Johnson Home was bought by the Catholic Church, and turned into an orphanage, the St. Joseph's Home for Girls. This was the beginning of the Catholic Charities in Dallas. The orphanage was in turn torn down in the 1970's and replaced by a Catholic retreat.

I shake my head in dismay at the apparent lack of attention I've paid to my community. This place seems like it was such an important part of Oak Cliff back then, rescuing young ladies in trouble. How does a person who thought she was attuned to her town totally miss what was once such a significant part of her neighborhood? I slip my feet into my flip flops, and roll my chair away from the desk. I have a sudden urgent need to see where this Home had been. The site is only five minutes from my house, but my mind's eye can't focus on its exact location. I have no impression of it at all, and that bothers me. I grab my keys and wallet, and walk to the car. I feel compelled to see what I hadn't seen before.

I park the car at Paige and Madison, and admit these streets hold no significance for me. They have just been avenues to get me somewhere else, to take the kids from point A to point B. Just a part of the local landscape that's always been here, a motionless backdrop for the movement and action in my life.

The fenced-in compound to my right is filled with apartments and parking lots. A sign at the entrance indeed states it is owned by Catholic Charities. Of course, there is no Johnson Home or orphanage, only very modest housing for the elderly and a nursing home. Nothing fancy, or remotely quaint. Small shrubs grow along the fence, with some grassy areas around the edges of the building. Scraggly trees stand like weary soldiers, slightly bent from their combat against the heat and elements. The asphalt of the parking lot is cracked and weathered. The entire place seems tired and sad, as if it has just given up on life.

I'm on the edge of history, just peeking in. Peering inside a time capsule in which the priceless treasures of the past were buried before my time. I'm filled with an overwhelming sense of loss - this small slice of my town's past is totally gone.

I drive back home, park the car in my driveway, and just sit there, looking at my house. It was built in 1933. Not so many years after Eliza Darling lived five minutes from here. I wonder where she was in 1933, if she even still lived in Dallas then. If she even still lived at all. She would have been forty-seven, older than I am now. Did she marry? Did she have kids? It's possible she could even have been the first owner of this house. Who knows?

I know my mind is getting carried away, but I don't care. I return to my kitchen, make myself a cappuccino, and hesitantly decide I'm going to try to write again. I sip my coffee as I sit down at my desk, and press the power button, bringing my laptop back to life.

Eliza Genevieve Darling. Why do I feel like you're part of me?

I open *Word* and just begin to type, hoping that sudden inspiration will find its way to my fingertips.

> *I am a woman who understands the powers of her body; what she can do with it and what it can get her. I'd learned at an early age what power women have over men. An immense power that could bring down royalty and cause the ruin of the wealthy.*

I look at what I've just written. *Oh my God!* It's almost as if my fingers are possessed. I have no idea why I wrote that! Then it suddenly strikes me that my words sound as if I'd copied and pasted right from Eliza Darling's diary. Am I such a talented plagiarist that my brain is stealing someone else's work without even thinking about it? But on second thought, I don't remember reading an entry with those words. I pull up the diary excerpt and read it again. Sure enough, Eliza didn't write that paragraph. It was all me.

Very weird. I feel the goose-pimples rise on my skin. I almost wish Rod Serling would stroll out of my kitchen, bringing *The Twilight Zone* theme song with him. At least I'd know what is happening to me.

Then the charms on my bracelet catch my eye, like sparkles from elegantly-cut diamonds. I am drawn to it, mesmerized almost. The charms tinkle when I move my hand. I hear the beautiful melody again, like small chimes in a breath of perfumed air.

I feel as if I'm here but not here.

As I exhale a bewildered breath, all sound stops. Nothing makes a noise. I'm surrounded by total silence, almost a state of suspended animation. But then a small pattering announces itself, increasing in both volume and speed in the time it takes me to look to the window. Faster and louder. It sounds just like raindrops hitting the metal of our chimney flue. I'm always warned of a downpour right before it happens; the single raindrops giving me notice they will soon mingle into a torrent of water. Now I hear their united front, the sound of a downpour hitting my roof, running down the shingled slope and splashing onto the front porch.

It was so sunny just a few minutes ago! I lean back in my chair and crane my neck to look out the window. I see nothing. At least nothing but sun.

But I hear it! I hear the rain! And then thunder pierces the quiet of my house. *I hear a storm!*

I go to the window but see only blue sky, the sun filtering through our oak tree. It must be approaching from the west, I think, as I go out into my front yard to see if the darkness of a stormy day is approaching from the western horizon. But only billowy white clouds plaster the sky of another sunny, heat-filled summer day.

I am surely losing my mind!

I return to my living room in a state of confused anxiety. I don't understand this. Any of it.

Then another crack of thunder pierces my thoughts, and I hear the slapping of the rain against pavement.

I'm terrified. Am I having an anxiety attack, or an episode of random derangement? Through the years, there have been cases of mental illness in my family. Was my struggle eighteen years ago just a precursor to a more aggressive attack on my mental state?

I feel shaky, and sit down before I give my knees a chance to buckle.

I look at my laptop screen and see the words begin to blink. I am once again enchanted by their constant dance, mesmerizing me into rapt attention. The chiming of my small charms continues; that and the rain are all I hear. Then I'm plunged into darkness, except for my laptop screen. A tunnel appears, and somehow begins to draw me into it. I seem to be surrounded by angry clouds and darkness. I'm pulled closer and closer. I see a woman with wet hair, sitting at a small desk, in a small bedroom.

As if a switch has been flipped, my fear is gone, replaced by a peaceful tranquility. And curiosity.

The scent of cinnamon seems to be everywhere. I look down. My left hand caresses a golden locket at my throat, my right hand holds a pen. I'm writing in a small book, laying open on a desk, next to a dainty china cup filled with hot steaming tea....

Chapter 9

The Diary of Eliza Darling

My First Day at The Orpheum

1899

I've been shown to my new room, and sit at the writing desk in the corner, recording today's events while drinking tea.

From that jail cell, I trudged through the downpour until I arrived at The Orpheum. I'm told it's the most popular and most expensive of all the bordellos in North Texas. All shame has been appropriately tucked away into a secret place inside that I don't intend to open.

The Orpheum is a beautiful place, having the look and feel more of some up-and-comer's mansion that a house of ill-repute. It even has two parlors, one on the first floor, and one on the second. The furniture looks as if it were imported directly from Europe, made from fine silks and velvets. More like rooms found in a Queen's castle, a royal gathering place.

Ms. Dixie Aronsson is the madame here. A more sophisticated and elegant woman I've never met before. When she greeted me in the parlor, she was wearing a silk gown of colors pulled from a kaleidoscope, with her long hair worn up, the unruly red curls barely kept in their place by the pins and combs. A fine necklace of pearls, shimmering with the faintest of pink tint, encircled her throat.

Except for asking the house-girl to bring me a towel, Ms. Dixie did not appear bothered by my soggy hair and clothes. She sat me down on a small love seat and gave me a china cup filled with the most wonderful cinnamon tea. I was quite nervous, in spite of my desire to change the course of my life, and I caressed the locket my daddy had given me, hoping it would give me the courage I needed for my life's next chapter. Ms. Dixie asked me how I'd come to her establishment. I told her that my plan had been to work at the finest house on Emma Street, so here I was. With that answer, she considered me with those thoughtful emerald-green eyes that seemed to look right into a person, trying to find what was stirring inside. She asked me if I'd ever been a working girl before, and I honestly didn't know how to answer her question. In a way, I had. Bartering for my freedom. I wasn't especially proud of how I came to be here, but I also told myself I shouldn't be ashamed of it either. It was what it was – something that just happened. It hadn't been planned. It just was.

Chapter 10

Eliza

Evening

June 2, 1907

"Ms. Dixie, it was a crying shame. That girl I met at the mill was lovely. But it seemed to me she was working herself into being an old woman before she could even enjoy being a young woman."

Ms. Dixie and I sat in the parlor after dinner, I with my hand-sewing and she with her ledgers. Ms. Dixie was Ms. Virginia's *right-hand man*. Ha! Thinking about Ms. Dixie being a man *anything,* right-hand or no, was enough to send a tickly spasm of laughter from my throat. I was sure her curves and cleavage were famous from here to Oklahoma. Why, her Orpheum was the only house in Dallas that charged up to ten dollars. And even so, it was always packed. None of us girls were ever wanting for customers. *Ever.*

"Eliza, don't forget. I saw that every day. The beautiful young girls who came into my parlor wanting work. They're the bread and butter of the trade. You know that. Fate doesn't give them any extra consideration because they're beautiful and innocent. If anything, it wraps a strangle-hold on them even tighter." Ms. Dixie spoke those matter-of-fact words as if it were just a normal occurrence in an unfair world. Which it actually was. "You were one of those girls yourself."

I knew Ms. Dixie was right in what she said to me. My path to her door had really been no different. The girls of her house had carried on this discussion many times before. How most women were liable to sell themselves one way or another. If a woman married an old dried-up-prune-of-a-man just to make sure she'd be taken care of, wasn't that the same thing? Of course it was - any woman would understand the price for that kind of marriage. Crawling between his sheets once or twice a month to satisfy his cravings, and in turn, receiving a roof over her head, food on the table, and maybe some social status thrown in for good measure if she married the right kind of dried-up-old-prune. What was the difference between that woman and me?

And what about those poor women toiling down at the mills, like Mamie, or out in the fields picking cotton, working twelve and fourteen-hour days, just to scrape together wages that might or might not put enough food on the table. Weren't they essentially selling themselves to the mill bosses and farm foremen? Why was mill work and farm work considered *honest* work, but prostitution wasn't? Of course, as a prostitute, your ears weren't filled with the deafening noise of the spinning machines; a girl didn't have to brush the never-ending lint from her hair, or blow its remnants into her hankie. Even working half the time and giving Ms. Dixie half my pay, I still made more than ten times what a mill-worker made.

But it bothered me to think of Mamie Carroll being a slave to her family's need for income. At least working in a parlor house, a girl wasn't covered with cotton lint and the sweat from twelve-hour days standing on her bare feet.

As I saw it, they were both a form of slavery, but the parlor house at least offered luxurious rooms, and fine clothes, and time to dream.

Of course, the risks were different.

Chapter 11

Mamie Carroll

June 2, 1907

Dallas Cotton Mill

Mamie Carroll had always been just a slight little thing. At thirteen and a half years old, she was still barely fifty-five inches tall; one of the only spinners who still needed to climb up onto the frame from time to time, to reach the very highest bobbins. After hopping up there for the last five years of her life, she had it down to an art, no longer slipping from the slickness of the machine oil which covered its surface. Mamie was of the opinion that she could probably do just fine as an acrobat in the circus if she had a right mind too.

But none-the-less, Mamie was always scared to clean that dang machine. She had to swipe her metal hook under the rollers, inside the frame. Mr. Duffy, the spinning room foreman, didn't turn the spinners off for anything but bobbin changing, or when the perverted man wanted to *speak* with one of the girls behind his locked office door. The cleaning usually had to be done while they were running. It was a frightening task: the gears and rollers and spindles were constantly moving, claiming not only the cotton threads, but anything else that happened to put itself in the way. She was scared of the monster jaws with their sharp teeth of steel.

Mamie was always terrified that she'd lean in too close, and something on her would accidentally get caught between the rollers and sucked into that horrible, hungry mouth that required feeding twenty-four hours a day. A strand of hair loosened from her long plaited braids; the corner of her apron after catching the rare puff of breeze. It had happened before, when she was nine. A girl of eleven on the other side of the spinning room had fallen asleep and leaned into the machine, and her right hand had been sucked between the gears. The machine so hungry it had eaten two of her fingers before Mr. Duffy managed to get the dang monster shut down. He'd explained to the girl's mother that he always tried his hardest to catch any spinner on the verge of sleep, waking them up by pouring cold water on them. But he hadn't seen her head nodding that day. That girl came back to the mill only a week later, with two fewer fingers on her hand. Mr. Duffy told her to be thankful it was only her pinkie and ring fingers; she could still do the spinning.

Mamie looked at her tiny hands. She didn't want to lose any fingers.

Her hands were so very, very small. Her mother had always told her she had the hands of a princess. But all she saw now were the hands of a forty-year-old granny. Worn, with wrinkles and weathered skin. She frowned at the sight. According to her grandma, hands told the story of their owners. They testified to character and hard work; they spoke of grace and caring. What story would her hands tell if they could speak? No tale very interesting, she thought. Only stories of twelve-hour-days spinning cotton into thread, constantly watching three-hundred spindles to catch any severed threads immediately upon their breaking.

Mamie tucked a few stray tufts of cotton into her apron pocket. Her apron was an absolute necessity. She was forever picking up stray puffs of cotton lint which seemed to fly in every direction and land haphazardly over everything. Then into the pockets her cleaning tools would go until the next cleaning was due.

Mamie was there so many hours a day she felt like the mill was more her home than her real home was.

She watched the spindles and watched the thread, waiting for the bobbins to empty themselves and scream for replacements, waiting for the spools to fill. They were like needy little children, always requiring help from their mama, always demanding undivided attention, lest a wandering eye missed a broken thread or a spool's sudden nakedness. There was almost no time to even daydream. *Almost.*

Thank the Good Lord, Mamie's spools were finally full, ready to be picked up. When the machine stopped, she walked to the staircase, hearing her cleaning tools clanking in her apron pocket – her *mill music* as she'd often thought of it. The only jingle in her life. She always found herself wondering what it would be like on the outside. To not have the loud thundering noise of the machines blasting its way down deep to her bones. A vibration so intense that even when she left in the evening, her arms and legs still trembled from the strength of it. The noise so constant and loud, Mamie's hearing in her right ear had slowly faded away, like a little bit had been taken every day until there was nothing left to take. She'd been totally deaf in that ear since last Christmas. The price of her employment was steep.

"But to be expected; it was a common thing," Mr. Duffy had reminded her.

Life *outside* of the cotton mill.

No white fuzz sticking to wet and sweaty skin.

No buzzing vibrations attacking the body, from the skin to the bone.

No fear of being swallowed by a metal monster.

A girl could only dream of a life that fine.

Chapter 12

Mamie Carroll

June 4, 1907

Mamie walked to the mill with little anticipation for the new day. Her emotions had become flat, one day just running into the next. Monday was like Tuesday, and Wednesday would be the same. She'd given up on any hope of something different. Her eight-year-old brother Christian skipped at her side, still filled with little boy notions and playful innocence. Although he'd begun work at the mill this past month, his fragile childhood had not yet ended. He still loved to make-believe he was a dragon-fighting knight with a silver sword, or a Texas hero fighting off Mexicans at the Alamo. In most respects, he was just like any other eight-year-old boy. But she knew his carefree days would soon be swallowed by the ever-increasing demands of the mill, and the fatigue of their work would consume him. Just like it had her. Their daddy worked at the mill too; she didn't see why her eight-year-old brother had to work as well. Yes, she knew the family could use the extra income. But at what cost?

She looked at her brother, haphazardly swinging his lunch pail, and wished he were swinging a bat instead, or a wooden sword.

"Mamie, if you could wish for anything, what would it be?" Christian asked her. That was easy, she thought, but she didn't say what was really on her mind.

"I would wish for a beautiful new dress," she answered instead. "One with pearl buttons and ruffles at the bottom. Like the ones in the window at Sanger Brothers." Yes, she would love a new dress, one manufactured at a dress company, instead of the ones sewn out of rough cotton Lotus-cloth by their mother.

But what she really wanted was her freedom.

"Maybe I can buy you a new dress for your birthday, with the money I make at the mill," Christian answered with the sincerity of a little boy who loved his sister more than anything.

She smiled at him, and at his innocent misunderstanding of the reason for his toil and labor. "That would be nice, Christian," Mamie answered, knowing full well their papa would never let his wages be spent on something so trivial when there was food to be put on the table, and rent to be paid. She put her arm around his narrow shoulders and wished more than anything that his fate could be changed; that he didn't have to grow up so fast.

Mamie and Christian finally arrived at the mill, and each went their separate ways - Mamie to the spinning room, and Christian to the lunching room where the doffer boys waited until they were needed. Mamie's tools jingled in her apron pocket as she walked to the third floor to begin her long day.

After only an hour, the spinning machine stopped for a bobbin change, and Mamie quickly moved to the stairs en route to the fresh air outside, even though it already felt like a smothering wool blanket at only eight o'clock in the morning. But her escape had not been quick enough.

"Mamie, would you come to my office," Mr. Duffy instructed, without even looking in her direction. It wasn't a question. Her heart was heavy, although beating frantically. How could one's heart feel as if it were sinking while beating so fast it felt it would beat itself right out of her chest? She couldn't breathe, as if her breath had just been swallowed up, sucked right into a vacuum.

Not now, Mr. Duffy! Please don't now!

On the inside she was begging, while on the outside she followed the instructions she was given. She knew all too well what would happen if she didn't do as he asked. Even longer and harder hours, with fewer breaks. And now she had Christian to worry about too.

But she also knew what would happen if she *did* follow his instructions.

Mr. Duffy closed the door behind her, and twisted the lock. It's click the sound that locked her fate. Was Christian on the other side of the door, changing bobbins, not knowing what would soon transpire in the boss's small, dingy office? Mamie had the sudden, desperate urge to call to him, to anyone, for rescue. But instead she stayed as quiet as a field mouse, as was required.

"Mamie, you must be sure to keep your hair pinned up," Mr. Duffy whispered to her, as he stroked her hair, and pulled the stray wisps behind her ears. "And of course, your apron strings must be tightly knotted. I don't think you tied them quite right," he said from behind her, as he untied the bow in back of her waist. "I'll help you," he said quietly. "You wouldn't want a loose end to get caught in the rollers."

Mamie closed her eyes, trying to wish herself to another place. She tried her best to ignore the sickening smell of him - sweat, and hair tonic, and dirty clothes, all mixed together - but it invaded her every breath. A shiver attacked her body as his hands slid under her skirt and into her bloomers, a stark reminder of how vulnerable she was. Although today she hadn't heard the familiar fumbling sound, the rustling of the course material, she knew he'd already unbuttoned his trousers to free his lust for her. That was the pattern; it always happened this way. Always from behind. At least she never had to move, never had to look at him, never had to do anything but lean over his desk and let him feel her body under her dress, as he pulled her into him and rubbed himself against her, and then put himself inside.

Mamie forced herself to be somewhere else; she thought of the beautiful dress she described to Christian, the pale pink ruffles of taffeta surrounding her throat, and imagined how beautiful she would look in it. What would she look like with her hair curled and pinned-up on top of her head? And wearing dainty leather boots, instead of the black lace-ups with patches on the soles she usually wore?

Her daydreaming had mercifully allowed her to escape the worst part of the foreman's assault, but now his gravelly voice abruptly interrupted the pink-taffeta visions her mind had conjured.

"There now, Mamie, you're all tied up proper, and ready to go back to work. Get along now," Mr. Duffy said, patting her bottom, without so much as another glance toward her, and walking out of the office. Would he not look at her because of guilt or shame, or did he not consider her worthy to receive the same regard he'd give to any stranger on the street? She didn't know and didn't care. Duffy was a pig.

After the first time, she'd frantically told her father what the foreman had done, expecting him to defend her honor; expecting him to somehow avenge the gross violation of his daughter's chastity. But instead, her father had just looked at her, almost looked right through her to the other side of the room, as if he hadn't heard, and then said, "I'm sure you're mistaken, Mamie. Duffy is your boss; I'm sure he was just trying to help you." And that was that. No more was said. Ever. And no more was said by Mamie either. What was the point? It was crystal-clear where her father's loyalties lay. If her own father wouldn't stand up for her and protect her, who would? Mamie knew the family's employment would end if such an accusation were made. All three of them would lose their jobs because of it.

Mamie wished she had a looking glass. She wasn't one to pay much attention to vanities, but today she felt as if she were wearing a mantle of shame, and frustration, and anger, all rolled up together and spread over her entire body. She hoped no one else would notice, and if they did, she hoped they wouldn't ask her about it. She wiped away a stray tear that had somehow managed to evade her steely self-control, and opened the door.

What happened next surprised Mamie even more than it was sure to surprise everyone else. She kept walking, holding her head high as she made her way through the spinning room. Most of the girls were taking their breaks, since Duffy still had the machine stopped; she was thankful no one was there to ask her questions. How many of the other girls were taken to his office, she wondered? She wasn't sure, but guessed there were many.

Mamie walked until she reached the staircase, and without any additional thought, she descended the stairs. She wasn't thinking, she was just walking. There was no forethought, there was no plan. She just took one step after another after another, until her steps led her right out the side door into the bright sun of another suffocating summer day.

But *this* day was quite different. Mamie was beside herself with the sense of freedom that pulsed through her entire body, to the tips of her fingers. *What was she doing?* Mr. Duffy and the others would be wondering where she was. But she kept walking. One foot in front of the other. She couldn't stop herself. It was as if her body were possessed by someone else.

Someone else.

That's what she wanted more than anything. To be someone else. Her resentment of her life had taken over. Then and there she decided to become a different person. At only thirteen, Mamie felt as if her life had already become all it was ever going to be, and she hated it. And the liberties Mr. Duffy felt he could take with her at will - it disgusted her. She would just have to take care of herself from now on. If her body were going to be used for the pleasure of others, she might as well get something other than cotton lint from it.

Mamie knew then where she was going and what she had to do. *I may not be the prettiest or the smartest girl that inquires about work, but I'm sure one of the houses on Emma Street will take me.*

Then Mamie's dreaming was suddenly replaced with the image of her brother Christian, swinging his lunch pail. What about him? Would Mr. Duffy punish him for her sudden defection? She loved him dearly, and her heart ached to leave him. But she knew that if she stayed at the mill one more minute, she would lose her mind. She had to do this. *Maybe I'll make enough money to send to my family so Christian won't have to work anymore?* Mamie justified her leaving as a way to improve her brother's lot. It was not a disloyalty; a betrayal to his devotion to her. It was a way out. For both of them. She was certain of it.

Mamie saw the trolley making its way down Lamar to its Griffin Street stop, and she waited. Emma Street would be her next stop, and the beginning of her new life.

Chapter 13

Eliza

July 1, 1907

I held the babe in my arms as if he were my own, and fantasized what it would be like. Being a mama. When I was working for Ms. Dixie, it had just been natural for me to put all thoughts of having children and a family right out of my mind. After all, being a sporting woman didn't really lead one on the path to domesticity. What man would have asked me to marry him? At that time, I didn't even consider living the life of wife and mother, of being a *normal, dignified* woman living a *normal, dignified* life.

And the scar.

It stared back at me every day when I looked in the glass, making me thankful I was no longer totally vulnerable to men I didn't even know. Being a prostitute was very dangerous work. Yes, we wore beautiful gowns, and had more lace undergarments than we could shake a stick at. We got to sleep late in the morning, and eat meals that were prepared by a hired cook. It was all business expense. We were given all the niceties one could want; that was part of the lure. But they were also our *bonus wages*, our compensation for the dangers involved. Most of the girls had to suffer the rough and rowdy hands of clients now and again, but thankfully not many suffered disfiguring assaults that left a permanent legacy of her wayward life.

As always, my thoughts flew back to the night of my attack. No matter how hard I tried, the horrible memory had a way of sneaking up on me at the most unwanted and unexpected times. Regardless of how unwanted the remembrance, it always hovered at the edge of my brain, just waiting to make me relive it one more time.

We had argued over his payment that night. He was a new customer - the regulars knew the schedule of fees like the back of their hands.

But that man didn't know, and wouldn't listen. He said he was entitled to more for the payment I was requiring. I held my ground, and his eyes showed a hatred I hadn't noticed before that moment - call girls don't generally gaze into the eyes of their customers. I saw a fearful hardness that sent a shiver through me. He unbuttoned his pants a second time, and pulled his hardened organ right out.

He grabbed me by the arm, hard enough to leave bruises. "Well, if you're gonna charge me that much, you can certainly give me another round," he'd said, the venom in his eyes a palpable thing, filtering right through the frightening tone of his voice and the iron grip of his hand. He pushed my head down onto his erection. I struggled to resist, but he was quite strong. Much stronger than one would at first suspect. When I refused to open my lips, he yanked my hair so hard I thought he'd actually pulled the roots from my scalp, causing me to cry out, which had been his full intent. He then used that opportunity to force himself into my mouth. I couldn't breathe. I was filled with panic at being so totally overpowered. I did the only thing I could think to do. It was instinct.

I bit him.

I knew I drew blood, because I tasted it.

He pushed me away with such force that I landed hard on my behind, several feet away. I quickly rolled over, and began to scramble on my hands and knees across the floor, toward the door, at the same time screaming for help. I tried to stand and make my escape, but was once again yanked back by my hair.

"You bitch!" he screamed, as he fiercely jerked my head back.

I saw the glimmer of the razor right before it slid effortlessly down the left side of my face, from my eyebrow to the bottom of my jaw. Blood immediately poured from the hideous gash onto my camisole, and then to the floor. I remember being curiously captivated by its brightness, and vexed that my best camisole was ruined. Odd thoughts for one just sexually assaulted and mutilated by a razor. I suppose I went into a stupor; I was stunned.

The door opened, and just as Ms. Dixie and several of the other girls ran in, the client ran out, shoving them out of the way to escape before they realized what had happened. Their stares were glued to my face, so none of them even remembered what he looked like. But I did. The picture of his face, wearing its murderous grimace, was seared into my memory.

The man disappeared into the night, free as a bird.

It was the second worst night of my life, only trumped by the night my mama had given me away.

I shook my head to chase away the memory, looking down at the baby boy I now held in my arms. Such delicate features. Truly a wonder, and a blessing, though most of the girls here certainly hadn't thought of themselves as being very blessed upon first learning they were pregnant. After all, being with child has a tendency to get in the way of a working girl's ability to work.

Thankfully they hadn't chosen to rid their bodies of their tiny miracles. A pang of sorrow filled my breast as I stroked the baby's silky hair. Sadness for what I didn't have, and regret for the past.

"Constance, he's just beautiful! I do think he favors you; he has the same auburn hair and those blue eyes! Blue as ocean water, just like yours."

"Thank you, Eliza. And thank you again for watching him while I helped Taffy with her mending." Although all of us at The Home were undergoing training for ourselves, we were required to assist with instruction to the other girls as well. Doing something for someone else was not only a charitable act, it kept one's mind away from her own troubles, and gave us a purpose that wasn't centered only on ourselves. All of us at The Johnson Home tried to be good Christians, helping each other in our times of need. Ironically, and regardless of the opinions of some, prostitutes can be quite charitable.

Constance had come to The Home almost thirteen months ago, having been very popular with the clientele at The Palace, the other *exclusive* house on Emma Street, several doors down from The Orpheum. She was probably the most sought-after girl there, until she became pregnant and sought refuge at our Home. The madame at The Palace, Ms. May Singleton, wasn't nearly as understanding as Ms. Dixie had been. A girl had to protect herself against such things as getting pregnant, and if she didn't, she wasn't worth the lost income. The girls at Ms. Dixie's were more like a family; the girls at The Palace were just employees there to make the house as much money as possible.

"What are we reading today, Eliza?" Constance asked as she sat down, taking the baby from me to give him a warm bottle of milk.

"I thought we'd start *Little Women*." As was the case with many of the girls at Ms. Virginia's, Constance had never learned how to read, and since reading was my particular passion, I volunteered to tutor as many as I could. "I think you'll truly love this book; it's a particular favorite of mine."

After the reading session, Ms. Dixie and I made our weekly visit to Emma Street. As the Administrator at The Home, it was Ms. Dixie's job to go forth into the community and let the working girls know there were other options. Although our visits were sometimes met with suspicion and irritation, some madams viewing our efforts as an attempt to *steal* their girls, most understood we weren't being judgmental, like the social reformers. We were just providing options for the girls who wanted a different life. We wanted them to know there was another place to go; another alternative to feed and house themselves.

"Where are we going today, Ms. Dixie?" I asked as we lifted our skirts and boarded the trolley bound for downtown.

"We're due to visit The Palace today. I need to work on Ms. May Singleton again. Our last visit didn't go exactly as I'd intended," answered Ms. Dixie.

How curious that we were going to The Palace, after I'd just been thinking of Constance and her struggle there.

Ms. Dixie had been trying to crack Ms. May's steely and stubborn disposition since we started making these visits. And Ms. May hadn't budged in her consideration of what The Home had to offer. As far as she was concerned, her girls were doing just fine. I also thought Ms. May had always been so envious of Ms. Dixie's beauty and success that she just refused to give her the time of day. The Orpheum was always crowded with the male cream of Dallas society and politics. The men with money and power only wanted the best, and that's what they found at The Orpheum. Because of their favor of Ms. Dixie's, the funds she *donated* to the Police Department were lower than others on Emma Street, and the fines assessed against her were almost nil. It helped to know people in high places. Even the Reverend Upchurch, the leader of the local social reformers, couldn't stir enough vexation to deter the popularity of Ms. Dixie's house, being the favorite of the city's mightiest.

Ms. May was never able to attract the same caliber of clientele, and hadn't received the same *consideration* as Ms. Dixie. There had been a fierce competition between the two houses, at least as far as Ms. May was concerned. Of course, once The Orpheum closed its doors, The Palace was the only exclusive house left. To May's delight, the Dallas wealthy and powerful really had no better options than her establishment.

Ms. Dixie was bound and determined to get Ms. May to listen to her, and at least let the girls who were struggling know there was another place to go.

The trolley made its way over the Trinity River, and into the West End. Brown Cracker & Candy Company rose up as a sentinel, guarding the downtown streets on the west side. Not only did the brown brick structure lay claim to the corner on which it sat, but the owners, Mr. And Mrs. Horace F. Brown, were also the self-proclaimed guardians of this part of downtown. Emma Street sat on the West End's northern border, and had been a continual vexation for the company. The Browns were ultra-conservatives, who'd long been trying to rid Dallas of its vice district. They'd even gone so far as to condemn Linder's Pharmacy for catering to the wayward, and had sponsored a long-standing boycott of the store. Of course, Linder's made most of its money from the saloons and bordellos in the area, so it wasn't about to fold to the pressure inflicted by the Browns. And after all, even though wayward, didn't these people need medicine and care as well? But of course the conservatives generally felt that a person depraved enough to consort with the sinners should get what they deserved, be it Syphilis or the flu.

I wondered what Mr. and Mrs. Horace F. Brown would think of their only son, Horace Jr., spending almost every Saturday night in Ms. Dixie's upstairs parlor? I think some would call that quite ironic. And quite humorous, considering their close friendship with the Reverend Upchurch. (One privilege of being a whore was being privy to the secrets that could destroy the respectable citizens of our town, and that was a most powerful protection.)

But that's exactly the situation with so many of those who cast shame on the oldest profession. During the daytime, when one was expected to be an upstanding citizen, the reformers would denounce us as depraved. But at night, that was quite the different story. Those same men who spoke out against us and proposed city ordinances to rid the town of our likes paid visits to Emma Street after darkness fell. It was as if their beliefs and principles just disintegrated after the sun went down, as if without the light, they were lost to the darker side of life.

Or maybe it was all just an act to begin with?

Some argued that call girls were the *protectors of the home*, taking care of men's desires so that his attentions could be focused on his job and family. A necessary evil to create the balance between a man's sexual needs, and his wife's usual lack of interest. Prostitutes served to keep the peace in a marriage. At least, as long as everyone looked the other way. But *we* knew what was meant when a man said he was going to *The Club*.

As the streetcar rode down Emma Street, we passed what was once our beloved Orpheum. It had been bought by a real estate investor and turned into a rooming house. Ms. Dixie's fine furnishings had been moved to Ms. Virginia's home, so it was bare when she last said her goodbyes. Hopefully, seeing it caused good memories for her. I had memories of freedom, and family, of course until marred by the memory of my attack. As always.

The trolley stopped at the end of the street, and we departed. It was quiet at this time of day, of course; the saloons and bawdy houses came alive after the normal workday was over. The girls in the cat houses usually slept until well into the early afternoon, some later than others, depending on how busy the night had been.

We walked to the door of The Palace and rang the bell. We were met by a house-girl who seated us in the downstairs parlor, then went to fetch Ms. May. The drawing room was filled with rich carpets and velvety sofas, but not the richness to which we'd been accustomed at The Orpheum. It felt more like an attempt at being lavish than a true display of luxury. I imagined the power brokers of the city could detect its pretense as just that.

Ms. May soon entered with her usual air of exaggerated self-importance. However, I will admit that since Ms. Dixie's defection, she had, by default, assumed the role of preeminent madame.

"Good morning, ladies," she said as she made her way to the sofas, her satiny house-dress fluttering in the wake of her entrance. "To what do I owe this pleasure?" she asked, her question oozing with feigned cordiality. Our visit was neither a pleasure for her nor a pleasure for us, but regardless, each of us behaved as if it were.

"Why good morning, May." Ms. Dixie addressed her. "It's been a while. How have you been?" she asked.

A smile of superiority crept across Ms. May's face. "Why, I've been very fortunate - business has been excellent. It's almost as if the city's push to rid itself of us just serves to increase its need. Funny how that seems to work," she answered. "I certainly have no plans to shut the doors anytime soon." She glared at Ms. Dixie, almost daring her to suggest such a thing.

"Of course, I understand your position," answered Dixie. She surely knew that money and power were a potent combination that was difficult to give up by one's own choice. "I would never expect that to happen," she said, with a small smile. As if telling May in no uncertain terms that she was sure her greed for luxury and influence would never allow her to close her doors. And May responded with the look of one certain she would remain the queen of her kingdom. "However, I was wondering if maybe you knew of any girls in your employ who might be having difficulties with the life. I'm sure you'd be most concerned for their welfare, and would want them to know of their alternatives."

Ms. Dixie knew this was far from the truth, as did May, but the farce continued regardless.

"Of course I want what's best for my girls. However, the inmates here are more than happy with their present circumstances," answered May, with the satisfaction of knowing Ms. Dixie had no first-hand knowledge with which to contradict her. The Palace girls were known for being quite tight-lipped about their lives; otherwise, they'd be turned out without another thought. "And I've even arranged for you to speak with my newest girl. She will attest to her contentment here."

Under the scrutiny of Ms. May, I thought.

At that moment, the door to the kitchen opened, and a young girl entered, carrying a tray with a teapot, cups, and saucers.

Oh my lands! It's Mamie Carroll, from the mill. That beautiful, young girl is here!

"This is Honey, our newest addition. She came here almost a month ago, begging for a position. Of course, she's so young and had no experience, but she's been a very eager student," said May.

My insides knotted at the thought of what Mamie had surely learned here in the last month. Nothing is spared when initiating a girl who is new to the business, *especially* at The Palace. Mamie kept her gaze on the tray, until it was safely lowered to the table. She looked up at us, and was shocked to find a face she'd seen before. When the recognition registered, her eyes widened; a look of something between fear and shame flashed across her pretty face. Then she quickly looked away. Was she embarrassed that I'd found her in her present circumstance, with her name changed to Honey? I wasn't sure, so I didn't mention the fact that I'd already met her, in another world.

"Honey, why don't you sit down and tell these ladies how you've managed at The Palace this last month," instructed Ms. May.

Mamie looked as if she'd been asked to run down Main Street buck-naked. It was apparent she was scared to death. She sat quite still, just staring at the china teapot in front of her, as if it held a magic genie who would grant her the wish of immediate escape. But she eventually mustered the courage and gathered her wits about her.

"The Palace is a beautiful place. I have plenty of food and beautiful clothes to wear. And Ms. May has been a fine housemother," declared Mamie in the smallest of voices, almost as if she could avoid her impromptu performance by making herself so tiny she would just disappear from the sofa.

"As I told you," May announced to Ms. Dixie in her usual defensive tone, "my girls are quite happy here, and content to be eating fine meals and wearing fine dresses. What more could they want? Who would complain about such an arrangement?" she asked with feigned innocence.

What bally rot!

It was as if Ms. May were speaking to young, innocent school girls. As if she'd forgotten that Ms. Dixie and I knew the unspoken truths, the words that *weren't* being offered to us. We knew good and well what went on in these houses.

"Well, May, I'm sure you wouldn't mind if I spoke to Honey directly, would you?" asked Ms. Dixie.

Ms. May stiffened at her request, raising her nose in a superior posture. "Well, do as you will," she finally answered.

"Honey, dear," Ms. Dixie began, putting her hand gently on Mamie's small hands, pressed so tightly together in her lap, as if she were pleading for her life. "I'm Dixie Aronsson, and this is Eliza Darling. We're from The Johnson Training Center for

Women. A home for working girls who want to leave *the life*, to improve their situations by learning *another* trade. Eliza and I are former sporting women ourselves, and we know how difficult and dangerous this life can be."

At these words, Mamie raised her head and looked at me curiously. It had apparently never occurred to her that I'd been a *working girl* myself. I was not one of the judgmental upper crust. I'd been just like her.

And even though I always tried my best to cover it, she now noticed the scar that ran the length of the left side of my face, obviously drawing the conclusion that it was an unfortunate consequence of the danger of her new profession.

"The Johnson Home is a safe place to live, and learn a skill or trade, such as nursing or dressmaking," Ms. Dixie explained, nodding in my direction. "May I ask if you had employment before you came here?"

Mamie looked at Ms. May for permission to speak, and received the woman's resentful nod in reply.

"I worked as a spinner at the mill," answered Mamie. "I must say, compared to my previous circumstances, this is the life of luxury. I don't have to work twelve-hour days in the heat, and I wear beautiful dresses. I only earned six dollars a week at the mill, and now I make over one-hundred dollars. I find this work to be much easier, and I'm able to give my family so much more money now," Mamie said with an air of satisfaction, as if this were all the explanation anyone would ever need. But I sensed sadness hiding just beneath the surface of her words.

Neither Ms. Dixie nor I could argue with the facts she'd given us. We both knew them to be true. Even after the fifty-percent she was required to give Ms. May, her income from The Palace was like finding a stockpile of gold nuggets that she wouldn't be able to get anywhere else. It was hard to argue that life working in an exclusive club didn't have its tempting advantages.

"Well, Honey, I certainly understand your situation," answered Ms. Dixie, in all sincerity. "But of course, there's always, *always* the danger to consider as well."

Mamie and I locked eyes when she said this, mine pleading with her to reconsider her situation. Hers resolute to stay.

"If you change your mind, please come calling at The Johnson Home, and we can discuss your options. And if any of the girls here have had enough of *the life*, please tell them there's a place for them to go."

Our eye contact was broken as Mamie sat up straighter, with her head held high. "We're all happy to be here," she answered with resolve. And that was that.

Ms. Dixie and I stood to leave. There was no more to be said. "Thank you for the time, May," Ms. Dixie told her, as the house-girl showed us to the door. "And thank you, Honey."

"As I said, Dixie, my girls are quite happy here," May answered in reply. "Quite happy." Then the door was shut quite firmly behind us.

"That was the young girl I told you about, Ms. Dixie," I said, as I thought of the day last month when I'd met Mamie, covered in perspiration and cotton lint. I understood why she'd be happy there. I' be happier there as well if I'd been toiling at the mill. How could one argue with a choice like that? "She's the pretty little thing I hated to see ruined by the mill. And now she's being ruined by Ms. May!"

"It's unfortunate," answered Ms. Dixie. "I'm quite afraid to think of what her initiation has been like."

As am I, I thought sadly, watching The Palace fade down the street as the trolley took us back to our home.

Chapter 14

Mamie

July 1, 1907

"You did good, girl," Ms. May said. "You put those meddling women right in their places. They have their nerve, coming into my establishment, trying to talk my girls out of making a living. I doubt they'll be back for a long while."

Mamie placed the teacups back onto the tray, and carried it back into the kitchen. She was proud of herself for being able to carry on such a conversation when she was so nervous. She wasn't comfortable being the object of attention. As a matter of fact, she'd never really *been* the object of anyone's attention. Except, of course, for Mr. Duffy. But that kind of attention she could do without. Unless she was being paid for it.

Mamie had tried to be truthful when she spoke of her satisfaction with her present circumstances, living and working at The Palace. She was making so much more money than she had at the mill, her weekly salary more than ten times what it had been. And she *was* grateful she didn't have to toil in the heat, no longer tortured by the cotton lint sticking to every inch of her, or its filaments invading her nose and throat. She could sleep until noon if she was inclined, and her evening wardrobe included the beautiful camisoles and dresses she'd always wanted.

But it was also true that for every good thing at The Palace, there seemed to be a bad thing to offset it. Or maybe, to satisfy the debt for it. Mamie had come there that morning after Duffy had molested her. *For the last time*, she'd whispered to herself, and smiled. She'd knocked on the door looking much more bedraggled than she'd hoped, partially covered in sweat and cotton fuzz. She was taken to Ms. May, who'd inspected her like a cow being inspected at a stockyard sale. It had been humiliating. *But not as humiliating as being raped by her boss,* she reminded herself.

Mamie's first month as a prostitute was a disturbing education for her, the young girl who only knew how to do two things - look after siblings, and work at the mill.

She passed inspection, but only by a hair's breadth. She wasn't voluptuous or full-figured. After all, she was only thirteen, slight of frame and thin. Ms. May turned her around, and then lifted her skirts, inspecting all the while. "Well, some like their girls young and skinny," she pronounced. "You can stay, but only if you make money," she said, more as a warning than any kind of welcome. "You'll room with Candace, and she will handle your education," she said, and promptly left the room, without so much as a *glad to meet you,* or *nice to have you here.* It was quite evident that Ms. May was all business. She was not a housemother; she was most definitely a boss.

Mamie was shown to her new room. Even though it was dark, with the shades still drawn at ten-o'clock in the morning, she could see the clothes strewn about the floor and furniture. There were three beds, two made up and empty, and one still occupied with a woman who was snoring as loud as her Grandpa used to snore after staying up half the night drinking home-made whiskey. Mamie didn't know quite what to do, so she did nothing. She sat down on one of the empty beds, the one farthest from the snoring woman, put her hands in her lap, and just waited for the next phase of her new life.

Finally, at almost noon, Candace woke from her noisy sleep. She propped herself up on an elbow, and opened one eye in Mamie's direction. "Who are you?" she asked with a raspy croak that could easily have been uttered by a river frog. The wrinkles punctuating her eyes and mouth and throat led Mamie to believe her roommate must be a veteran of the house.

"My name's Mamie. Mamie Carroll. I'm new."

Candace flopped back down on the bed. "Wonderful. Just what I need. *Another* girl to take care of." She rolled over and pulled the pillow over her head, saying not another word.

So much for the warm welcome, thought Mamie, somewhat hurt. Well, at least she was here, and not at the mill. She chided herself for acting like a school-girl. She was in the adult world now, so she'd better start acting like one. Mamie lay her head down on the pillow and waited.

Later in the afternoon, Mamie tried to style her hair as best she could. She'd worn it in two long braids for as long as she could remember, but now she needed to look older, and more appealing. She'd never tried to look attractive for men before, and was afraid that she might not be able to make the transformation from mill girl to sporting woman. *What if I can't do this?* she wondered, panic suddenly rushing through her from head to toe. But she knew she had to; it was the only option left.

Candace regarded her with a shake of her head. "Girl, haven't you ever put your hair up before?"

"No," Mamie answered simply.

Candace walked to her and took the brush from her hand. Mamie looked at Candace in the glass, roughly brushing Mamie's long hair, and trying different twists. "Your hair is the color of honey," Candace said. "And I believe we just found your new name. *Honey.* It fits you. And it's a good whore's name too."

Whore. The word hit Mamie like a small spike driven deep inside her chest. *From now on, I'll be known as a whore. And I don't want to change my name!*

"I think we'll advertise you as somewhat of a schoolgirl. You're young, and skinny. And I bet still a virgin. Ha! Some of these men will beat down the door to have a go at an inexperienced thing like you."

I'm not a virgin, she thought. Mr. Duffy had repeatedly made sure of that.

Mamie's first night at The Palace included a visit from only one man - he paid for the whole night. He was almost as old as her grandpa, and it disgusted her to think of giving her body to such a shriveled-up prune. But then she thought of Mr. Duffy just taking what he wanted for free, and as far as she was concerned, no man was as disgusting as he was. Mamie found that if she just lay on the bed, and made her mind travel to a place far away, she could survive the recurring assaults on her purity.

Mamie survived her first week with surprising strength. Candace and Ms. May had decided to portray her as an innocent child who knew nothing about sex *(well, it was almost true, anyway),* and the men were practically waiting in line to get to her. Why were young, inexperienced girls so appealing to older men? She didn't know if she'd ever understand, but didn't think she even *wanted* to.

However, the second week almost broke both Mamie's spirit and resolve.

There was another large parlor in the back of the house; Mamie had never seen anyone go in there, and the bright red door was kept locked. It was curious to her, but she had better things to do than worry about a locked room in a brothel. Or so she thought.

Unfortunately, she found out that second week what the room was for, and why it was kept locked. The Palace Circus.

Mamie had never been to a circus before, and she was filled with an odd mix of curiosity, excitement, and trepidation when Candace told her that attending would be part of her initiation.

"Honey, I'm not going to make you perform after only a week, but you can surely sit and watch what makes The Palace famous," Candace told her with a wicked little smile. Mamie wasn't sure if Candace meant her ill-will, or if she was truly trying to educate her.

The show took place the next night, after most of the customers in the front parlor had already escorted their ladies upstairs. Ms. May herself was monitoring the back-parlor door. Mamie noticed that the men who were let through that door hadn't lingered at all after they'd arrived. No small talk in the front parlor, or drinks during chit-chat with the girls. These men walked right through The Palace's front door, straight through the house to the back parlor, into which they disappeared immediately. She'd even seen the chief of police going through that door, and was curious about how he could be a customer when he was sworn to rid the city of undesirables. Since prostitution was supposedly under attack, his presence here was quite the contradiction. But Mamie soon learned that as long as Ms. May paid her fees on time, the police would turn their eyes the other way. Mamie supposed that admittance to the circus was just part of the payment.

Then at midnight, Mamie was ushered into the back room. It had a small stage constructed at the far end. There were about ten men seated in plush chairs, upholstered in crushed red velvet, all turned toward the stage, the chandeliers casting a muted light throughout the room. Mamie was told to sit in a chair on the back row, for which she was grateful. Her natural instinct told her to be as inconspicuous as possible - an invisible spectator. There were a number of house girls sitting amongst the men, some with their hands on the men's knees, some whispering softly into their ears.

Then the show started.

The Victrola began to play, the room filling with music.

Two girls entered the stage in kimonos of the sheerest material that left nothing to the imagination, their breasts and pubic hair plainly visible under the thin robes. Mamie had met both briefly, Lilly and Brandy. They'd worked at The Palace for over a year.

They moved their bodies sensuously to the tune of the soft music, undulating to its erotic melody. Then Lilly reached over and slid Brandy's kimono from her shoulders, baring Brandy's large breasts. Brandy did the same. Their arms and legs began to intertwine in a dance that looked to be more for themselves than for the audience. Lilly then faced Brandy, and began to softly touch her breasts, rubbing gently until Brandy's nipples hardened. She then cupped them in her hands, raising them to her lips, first sliding her tongue over them in a teasing fashion, and then sucking gently on each, making Brandy elicit a soft moan.

Mamie sat in her chair as if she were made of stone, both mesmerized by the display on the stage, and mortified by it.

The women danced with their bodies pressed into each other, fondling as they moved, hands and mouths roaming and touching. Then Brandy led Lilly to the chaise, which was perched lengthwise in the center of the stage. Brandy pushed Lilly down and began to slowly lick her body, starting with her neck and breasts, then moving downward. Belly and navel. Hips. Thighs. Then Brandy gently opened Lilly's legs, and put her tongue between them, moving it slowly at first, over her genitals, and then faster once she'd found the perfect spot. Her tongue flitted spasmodically over Lilly's sex, teasing and taunting, until Lilly's back arched toward the ceiling, a groan of both ecstasy and release escaping from her upturned lips.

Mamie sat stiff as a statue. She couldn't move, in shock at the sight of what she was witnessing. She'd never seen two women making love to each other, if that's what it should even be called. Mamie had never even considered it a possibility. She looked around the room, at the other girls, some whispering into their *dates'* ears, some gently rubbing the men's thighs in a teasing fashion. The men seemed transfixed to the stage, and no wonder.

Mamie's insides were as confused as her thoughts, filled with both fear and excitement, and a peculiar tingling deep in her hips, all rolled into a jumbled-up chaos that felt both dangerous and exciting at the same time; she was perplexed by the push-and-pull of her feelings.

Then the music faded to silence, and the show stopped. The girls kissed each other, and made way for the next act. Candace then entered the stage, likewise clad in a sheer kimono, obviously not intended to cover her body, but only to tease her audience. Seductive music once again started, and Candace swayed her body erotically, in sync with the tune, her eyes closed and hands caressing her breasts. She seemed to be in her own world. She slid the kimono from her shoulders, letting it flutter to the floor, and reclined her body on the chaise. Candace lit a cigarette while she gazed at the ceiling, then took two long drags, blowing the smoke slowly through her lips, her neck arched and head titled back.

She then did something that Mamie couldn't believe was even possible - she spread her legs wide open so that the audience could see her lower genitals, totally visible with no trace of pubic hair as if she were a young girl, and she placed the cigarette into the orifice, the burning end sticking out as if her vagina were a cigarette holder. She moved her stomach in an undulating motion, and puffs of smoke rose from the cigarette. She'd made her vagina smoke a cigarette!

Oh my dear Lord! Mamie cried inside. She didn't dare let out a sound for fear that her shock would be heard down the block. Her brain was consumed with revulsion, the depravity of the act overshadowing any hint of stimulation left from Lilly and Brandy's carnal dance. Mamie once again looked around the room, and the men were all smiling, nodding their heads in admiration.

Candace spread her arms, signaling the end of the first act. Applause fluttered throughout the room, almost as if this act, although appreciated, was somewhat old news, and not nearly the epitome of her talent.

Act II began.

Candace was still reclining on the chaise. But this time, she lifted her legs and hips, and balanced herself on her shoulders and back. Her arms were at her sides, lying flat on the chaise, stabilizing her balance, her legs spread into a perfect *V*. The still-unclothed Brandy walked onto the stage, holding a gold coin up for the audience to see, teasing them as to its function in the feat to follow. Brandy flipped the coin into the air over Candace, over her wide-spread legs. As the coin made its descent, Candace moved her hips in a posturing motion underneath it, her vagina quickly swallowing it as it fell toward the chaise. Her legs snapped closed, legs and hips arcing down swiftly, and in one fluid movement, she rolled herself up from the chaise, and raised her arms in the air. The coin was nowhere to be seen, still hidden somewhere deep within Candace's talent. The male audience went wild with applause, as Candace took an extreme but graceful bow, as a juggler or acrobat would in a true circus. She was obviously the star of the show, so it was only befitting that she acknowledge the appreciation for her unique skills.

No doubt Candace would be quite sought-after when the show ended, but then again, arrangements had surely already been made for the man who'd be lucky enough to enjoy her obvious talents.

The house-girl then brought small glasses of whiskey into the parlor, and quietly distributed them to the clientele. Mamie didn't usually drink, but truly wished she had one as well. She was beginning to understand why the opium and cocaine were so popular with so many of the girls. She felt as though she desperately needed something to help numb the turmoil that was having its way inside her.

For the final act, Lilly entered the stage with a large male German shepherd wearing a diamond-studded muzzle. Mamie was filled with disgust at what she knew was about to happen - an act that was unnatural and loathsome under God's watchful eye. She'd never been especially religious, but she still waited with trepidation for the lightning bolt that was surely bound to strike them all dead at any moment. And in fact, she'd never known that intercourse with an animal was even physically possible.

Now she knew it was.

Lilly moved her hand over the dog's large phallus until it became quite erect. Mamie could then no longer bear to look, lowering her gaze to her hands that were clasped together so tightly in her lap that her knuckles displayed a strange combination of red and white. Although she refused to watch, she still heard what was happening in front of her: Lilly's low moaning, the shrill whines from the dog, and the lust-filled throaty growling from the men. She truly believed that if she watched it, she would retch right there in the parlor. She'd never imagined such a spectacle. It was revolting.

Then Mamie's revulsion quickly turned to bone-numbing fear.

Was this in her future at The Palace? Is that why Candace had been so insistent that she come? Was this a preview of what was in store for her?

Mamie sat as still as a cold, hard marble statute, and waited out the agony of the remainder of the show. She tried to imagine herself somewhere else, *anywhere* else. She closed her eyes tight, hoping to escape the images before her. But it was too late - they'd been forever branded into her memory.

At last the show was over, wild applause bringing Mamie out of hiding, back to her present circumstance. She rose slowly, as if to reclaim a fragile balance which had been totally turned off-kilter, the axis of the normal having shifted to a precarious, crooked angle.

Candace met her at the parlor door. "So, Honey," she began, with her head cocked to one side in a playful gesture, "talented, aren't we?" she asked with a wide grin. The shock on Mamie's pale face was all the answer she needed. Candace laughed, pleased with herself at having accomplished the intended reaction.

Mamie's initiation was quite complete.

Chapter 15

Elaine Dearborn

July 1, 2011

Depression.

Anxiety.

Insanity.

These scary words are lodged in the back of my mind, like nails driven deep into wood. Not budging.

I continue to visit Eliza, sitting at my computer every day until the mysterious tunnel swallows me right up, sucking me into the computer, and into another life and time. I can't explain it, but my captivation with the story that unfolds holds me hostage. Like taking a break to sit on the porch and read a really good book. You start looking for reasons to sit on that porch just so you can read more. And to make it even more enthralling, the tale is told in 4-D. It's hard to tear myself away from it. I hurry through my daily chores so I can sit back down at my computer, and when I'm not at my computer, I spend my time trying to figure out when I can return to it. An addiction.

I'm terrified this is all in my mind. My brain playing *make-believe*, a built-in entertainment system to fill the lonely spaces. But even though each day I warn myself to proceed with caution, the urge to be enveloped by another world is just too great. It pulls me in, and I let it.

I feel like I know Eliza intimately, as if we've shared many personal secrets on a rainy day. She almost feels like my other self.

My other self.

The words gently tumble around in my brain, like lingerie in a slow dryer.

I am drawn to you, Eliza.

Chapter 16

Elaine

July 2 & 3, 2011

For the past month, I've continually asked myself what it would take to be convinced I'm not hallucinating. What would be considered proof?

Someone experiencing the travels with me?

Bringing someone back from the past?

An evaluation by a psychiatrist?

And then I get my answer.

When I return from my visit today, I'm shocked to find a beautiful silver-colored thimble on my finger. It's etched all around with pictures of jungle animals - a lion, an elephant, a giraffe, and a snake, with vines twining around them. The base is raised with a small lip. It seems old, much heavier than the cheap, disposable kind they usually sell nowadays. I notice it right away, a new appendage to my body. At first, I'm terrified to see it on my index finger. I've never used one, but it fits me perfectly. Then it dawns on me that the small, intricately etched piece of metal is actually my validation that I'm *not* going crazy from some hormonal imbalance, that I'm *not* losing my mind.

The thimble is my proof that it's real! It's all real!!

The significance of this moment makes me laugh out loud in relief, and I close my eyes and say a small prayer of thanks.

I haven't told anyone about my experiences, my *travels*. Who would believe it? Hell, I can hardly believe it myself - a middle-aged woman who somehow travels back to the early twentieth-century through her computer? I think Drew would probably pick up the phone and make me a long-term reservation at the nut-house.

After all, it sounds totally crazy, even to me.

But now I have proof!

The realization is scary, and exciting, and comforting all at the same time.

But why me? Was I just in the right place at the right time, or is there something more? Is Eliza Darling connected to me in some obscure way? She would have lived only one or two generations before me. Surely if she were a relative, I would have heard her name spoken by someone in the family at some point?

Why do I feel like I know her so well?

"So, what's on the schedule for today?" Drew asks, giving me a gentle peck on the cheek as I make him a coffee for the road.

For some reason, I feel panic at the unexpected question. As if I've almost gotten caught having an illicit affair, having a secret life that only I know about. But isn't that about the gist of it?

"Umm... I think I might go to the library this morning," I answer, hoping that his haste to get to work will trump his curiosity.

There is also another errand I need to run, but I don't mention it.

"The library, huh?" Drew answers as he picks up his keys, heading for the door. "I don't recall you ever hanging out at the library before. But, whatever you want to do..." he says with a slight crinkle of confusion in his brow.

"Well, I thought I'd go see what books they have for writing the perfect novel," I add quickly. Totally believable, since I'm supposed to be writing one.

"Well, O.K." he answers, with a slight shrug and tilt of the head. "Good luck then," Drew says as he walks out the door. "Talk to you later."

And then I'm left to consider my next steps.

Before visiting the library, I need more information about the thimble. I decide to visit The Dallas Women's Museum. Surely, someone there will be able to help me.

I drive to Fair Park, where Dallas' older museums are located. I'm nervous about being asked questions I don't want to answer. But I've got to do this. I inquire at the reception desk, and am told that Dr. Jane Ansor, a professor of women's studies, would be the best person to talk to; she's supposed to be a leading authority on all things female.

Five minutes later, an older woman *(ha! - about my age, I quickly realize)* with reading glasses hanging from her neck approaches me and extends her hand. "Hello, I'm Dr. Ansor. How can I help you?"

"Hi, I'm Elaine Dearborn," I say as I stand, and shake her hand. "Thank you so much for seeing me. I'd like to learn more about an old thimble I've acquired."

"My pleasure. Let's go back to my office," says the doctor. She has a welcoming smile, with small wrinkles around her eyes and mouth, the tell-tale signs of a face accustomed to displaying happiness. I immediately feel comfortable with her.

When we enter her office, my compulsion to have everything neat and tidy almost overwhelms me. There are messy stacks of paper and books covering almost every surface. "Let me make room for you," she says, taking a wobbly stack from the visitor's chair. "Don't worry, I won't let you get buried alive." She grins, not in the least concerned about the chaotic mess. "So let's see your thimble."

I open the small, zippered section of my wallet - the secret place where I usually keep my personal spending money - and take out the thimble, handing it to Dr. Ansor. She turns on a super-bright viewing lamp, and the etching on the silver sparkles as if it's magical.

"Ah, very pretty!" she states the obvious, with an appreciative smile. "How do you like that for a professional opinion?" *Good, a professor with a sense of humor. I like her.* Dr. Ansor then holds the thimble under the magnifying glass which is built into the lamp.

"So, you've probably already guessed that it's made of silver. Well, at least the outer layer. What you may *not* know is that this is a Dorcas thimble. Back in the earlier nineteenth century, thimbles were usually made of *pure* silver, which is a very soft metal. After women had complained for years that thimbles didn't do squat to protect their fingers from the sharp steel needles, a man named Charles Horner decided he'd do something about it." She looks at me with a smirk. "Ha! - I'm guessing his wife probably did a bit of sewing herself, and the guy just got tired of hearing her complain about pricking her finger all the time," Dr. Ansor conjectures.

"So, Mr. Charlie decided that if he first made a thimble of steel, and then just *covered* it in silver, it would protect the dressmakers' fingers and be beautiful as well. The perfect solution." Ansor looks almost lovingly at the intricate etchings of the jungle animals and vines. "I've never seen one exactly like this. You know, these Dorcas thimbles are quite favored by collectors."

I knew when I first saw it that it was something quite special. It's more a functional work of art. I then ask the million-dollar question, butterflies in frenzied flight in my stomach, causing both fear and excitement. "How old do you think it is?" I ask her.

"Well, although I've never seen another one exactly like this," Dr. Ansor says, still studying it under the magnifier, "it looks to me like this is from the late nineteenth century. Sometime around 1890 or so."

Bingo!

I then release a breath of trepidation I didn't realize I was holding. More ammunition in the campaign to prove my sanity.

Her words are my proof. Validation that this whole thing is real, that I really *am* experiencing a different time, a different life. *Wow.* I'm scared and thrilled at the same time. I'm certain this thimble belonged to Eliza Darling.

"Thank you so much, Dr. Ansor," I say simply.

"My pleasure," she answers, turning off the light, and holding the thimble in my direction. "If you're ever interested in making a donation, we'd love to put it in the museum. We don't have many thimbles, and certainly none made with this craftsmanship."

"I appreciate the offer, but I wouldn't dream of parting with it," I say, as I take it from her and put it back into my secret pocket, closing the zipper to its little hiding place. Not only is it an antique work of art, this thimble is my only proof that I'm not a lunatic, and I intend to safeguard it along with my sanity.

Dr. Ansor walks me to the lobby. "If you ever need anything else, don't hesitate to come back," she offers with a smile and handshake.

I may just do that, Doctor. I certainly may need to tap into your knowledge again. "Thank you so much. I truly appreciate it," I answer, and walk to the car.

Next stop is the Dallas Public Library. The Texas Archives Division.

I emerge from the parking-garage elevator into a huge lobby, large and airy and filled with art work. There is also a used-book store to my left. In a normal world, I would head straight to it, my need for more books an obsession that I've never been able to get a handle on - books spill from every shelf in my house, and cover my bedside nightstand. But today I'm not in a normal world. My need for books is totally overshadowed by my need to uncover the life of Eliza Darling. I pass right by that used-book store, and approach the information desk.

I'm told the Texas Archives Division is on the seventh floor. The image of an attic spilling over with yellowed paper, old clothes, and other antiquities flashes through my mind.

The elevator door opens and my eyebrows instinctively rise. *Nope, not an attic. Not in the least.* I walk out into a large room filled with shelves and shelves of reference material, and reading tables. It's functional, and intellectual, and historical all at the same time, with not a trunk in sight.

I make my way to the counter, feeling as though I'm on an expedition. I guess, in truth, I really am.

"I'd like to see this diary, please" I inform the library archivist, and give him the catalog number that I'd copied from the internet reference. He disappears for a few minutes, and then comes back with a very old and weathered book, leading me to a table where I can lose myself in its contents.

The cover is a well-worn, rose-colored satin, the edges slightly frayed, small satiny fibers dangling from the binding - I imagine the by-product of many fingers stroking it through the years. A small electric thrill runs through me as I realize that Eliza's hands had touched this same book, and I imagine her seamstress's fingers gently caressing it as she poured her heart out onto its pages, her words now transcending the century between when it had been written and when it is now being read.

To my dearest Eliza on her thirteenth birthday.

October 8, 1898. With all my love - Papa.

The inscription causes me heartache as I realize that whatever happiness she had as a girl apparently died along with her father.

I open the journal to the first page, and see the entry from 1899 I'd read on the internet, in a flowery cursive that brought me even closer to the woman who was Eliza Darling. The tragedy of her mother labeling her a prostitute, and her journey to Emma Street. The details of a young life that was shattered before it had even really begun. Then I turn the pages and read more about a life I inexplicably feel I already know.

Chapter 17

The Diary of Eliza Darling

1903

I am finally alert enough to gather my thoughts about what happened almost three weeks ago. My attack. Ms. Dixie had administered laudanum almost constantly, to alleviate the pain as much as possible, and to minimize my movement.

Mart Waymond, the messenger boy who usually worked the bordello district, had been delivering Chinese food to Stella, another of Ms. Dixie's girls, so he was here when the attack occurred. He was commanded by Ms. Dixie to summon Doc Finley as fast as he could. The fight for my life had expended most of my energy, and the loss of blood from my wound had expended the rest. Ms. Dixie had done her best to stem the flow of blood, holding a clean towel over the left side of my face until the doctor arrived.

Ms. Dixie had learned enough about infection to know that boiled water would be necessary to clean the wound, so she'd immediately ordered Alta, our young house-girl, to put a pot of water on the stove to boil.

Doc Finley entered my room with his small black bag in hand. He was a kindly man who didn't much care what his patients did for a living; call-girls were still human beings who needed care just like anyone else. Just like the *upstanding* citizens he treated. At least those who would still seek his treatment; the ultra-conservatives of our town would no longer make use of his services. As far as they were concerned, his tending to the *depraved* of the city was proof that his moral character was certainly in question.

Doc Finley instructed Ms. Dixie to bring him the boiled water, clean towels, and as many clean cloth strips as she could provide. He then removed the blood-soaked towel from my face, and examined the handiwork of my deranged client. I remember thinking how bright and pretty the crimson color was, and how I might like to have a dress made of material with a like shade. Odd thoughts, but I imagine I was in shock from the attack, and in a hazy confusion from the laudanum Ms. Dixie forced me to drink as soon as I'd been lifted to the bed. I'd never been one to use opium, like some of the other girls. It's not that I'm judgmental about it. I've just always been able to do my job with the willingness that came from knowing that I'd chosen my profession, and this house was my home. But after the attack, I was thankful for the foggy haze that filled my head; my thoughts could get lost in it, instead of in the pain that had quickly consumed me.

I saw the small flicker of shock in Doc's face when he first saw my wound. I wasn't sure if his reflexes were slowing down in his later years, or if the damage was just excessively gruesome. My attacker sliced a gash in my face from my temple to just under my jaw, a raw and gaping slash, cut deep through both flesh and muscle. It was a shocking sight, and Doc Finley was worried that he couldn't repair it adequately.

He first cleaned the wound with rags soaked in the boiled water. Another dose of laudanum was administered, then Doc set to work with his needle and thread. I now have nightmares of being in a dark hole, bodies falling on top of me, one after the other. As if I were being buried alive. My body was pinned by the flesh lying on top of me, hands around my face. Unmovable. I couldn't breathe from the weight that crushed my chest. I have vague recollections of screaming as I tried desperately to free my body from the leaden heaviness that secured me to my bed. Ms. Dixie guessed that my nightmares hadn't really been dreams at all, but my remembrance of the girls laying themselves over my body, hands holding my head in a human vice, trying to keep me still as Doc Finley stitched the wound in my face.

Even after I was mended, the torturous *dreams* continued for what seemed an eternity. Although my body was finally free of its confinement, the dark tunnel still remained. I apparently believed I was back at Sanger Brothers, behind the counter. The girls told me I'd babbled about shirt sizes, and suspenders, and lollipops. I still had my mother, and had called out to her on multiple occasions, waiting for her kind words and warm touch, which of course would never come.

My opium haze.

The girls had all helped tear various pieces of cloth into strips. Doc Finley soaked a few in an antiseptic solution of acid and chloride, making a poultice to dress my wound. He'd done the best he could, but because the injury was on my face, it was difficult to secure the dressings in place.

Even though every effort was made to keep my laceration as free from germs as possible, it became infected nonetheless. Doc Finley surmised that the razor used for my disfigurement had been dirty, the germs embedding themselves deep within my flesh. Antiseptic on the surface would do nothing to rid me of the bacteria already traveling freely through my body. Not only did pockets of thick yellow puss rise around the angry red and swollen skin that had just so recently been my face, but my blood was poisoned as well. Septicemia. A fearful word for a very dirty and dangerous condition.

Ms. Dixie continued to administer the laudanum. I soon came to crave her arrival, knowing that a dose of the bitter amber liquid would let me escape my current circumstance, would let me float above the wincing pain to watch from afar, as if I were just a spectator and not the spectacle.

My body was consumed by high fever, a companion to the septicemia, a conspirator to my infirmity. More rags placed on my body - forehead, chest, limbs. Cold rags, soaked in icy water. My teeth chattered in a contradictory response - I was burning and freezing at the same time. Every effort was made to keep me as cool as the fever would allow. The girls took turns: Essie would dab my forehead while Stella tried to cool me with her oriental fan, and vice versa. Stella said it was as if I'd traveled far away from them, my eyes as vacant as if my soul had totally left my body. And quite honestly, I remember very little from that time, only vague and fleeting images of people coming in and out of my field of vision, what little vision I had.

Then there were the images I didn't understand, and would never understand, because they were just specters, visitors from a foreign land, caused by the powerful drugs that seemed to reign supremely over my beleaguered form. I spent those days of the fever either floating outside my body or buried deep within it.

Ms. Dixie later confided that at one point, she was sure I'd no longer have the strength to chase away the infection. My body and spirit had both been weakened almost beyond recovery.

Almost.

Mart, our messenger boy, had not only gone to fetch Doc Finley in a frenzied panic after my attack, he'd also spent much of his free time outside my room, worrying about my condition, and inquiring if there was anything he could get for me. It was true that we'd shared many a kind word between us, but I'd never realized that his heart was made of gold, as well as flesh.

One night, Stella and Essie were both ill with stomach pains, no doubt from some suspect culinary feast of which they'd both partaken. Consequently, Ms. Dixie allowed Mart to sit by my bedside during the worst part of the night - the wee hours. After his shift at Southwestern Telephone & Telegraph, he'd once again appeared, waiting outside my door. Ms. Dixie asked him if he didn't need to get home to his mama, but he just shook his head, saying that she understood when his work kept him out late.

"Ms. Eliza is special to me," he told her. He hadn't intended to explain, but Ms. Dixie continued to look at him, waiting to hear how I'd made such an impression on such a young lad.

"One night when I was deliverin' here, she seemed to know I hadn't had nothin' to eat that day. I don't know how she knew, but she did. She'd saved half her steak and potatoes for me, and a whole oatmeal cookie. I've never taken part of a woman's dinner before, but Ms. Eliza made me. Said she was so full her corset was about to bust wide open; she was likely to explode if she ate another bite. But I knew she was just savin' it for me."

So Ms. Dixie let him come in and sit with me. He was just as worried about me as my house-mates, standing guard at my bedside as if his diligent gaze would be the only thing that prevented me from slipping into a permanent sleep. He talked to me all the while, telling me about his family at home, his mama and the kids. He told me about his deliveries: which ones had been the strangest, and which had been the farthest. He finally worked up the courage to hold my hand, and sing an old Irish tune his mama used to sing him when he was a small boy.

Who knows? Maybe Mart's diligent guard is what pulled me out from under the heavy cloak of infection. The very next day, my fever began to subside, and my wound finally began to lose some of its raw, red anger. I could finally open my eyes to the daylight, shedding some of the constant opium fog that had continually surrounded me since the attack.

My laudanum doses grew further and further apart, until I was at least clear-headed enough to discuss my attack with the policeman who was investigating my ordeal. Thank the Lord Jesus that the bitter liquid hadn't become my best friend in a bottle, like it had for some of the girls I knew. They couldn't survive the day without their small brown vials.

The police here, and I imagine in most places, don't generally assign much urgency to crimes against whores. After all, they're not like attacks against *upstanding* citizens. Their general opinion is that, as prostitutes, we're all but asking for violence and criminal conduct. However, my assault was so brutal that Ms. Dixie demanded they try to find the man who had forever marked me with my own scarlet letter.

The officer's name was Otto Heinrich.

I could tell he hadn't been a policeman long, having not yet acquired the requisite swagger that most constables displayed as an order of routine, after they'd been on the job and learned just how powerful they'd become. Officer Heinrich was shown to my bedside, and of course, he immediately asked to see the awful flesh that had once been the left side of my face.

I'd never seen such concern in a pair of eyes before. Concern and compassion. As I watched him look at me, those dark eyes seemed to ignite with feelings above and beyond his call of duty. He gently placed his hand on my arm, as if to say *I'm so sorry for your pain and suffering;* when our gazes met, I was confused as to his true intentions. Then his furrowed brow and the pitch black of his irises seemed to overflow, the pain of his compassion quickly morphing into a palpable anger, almost a living thing. He tried not to show it, but I knew it was there, not just in my imagination. The brutality of my attack fueled a steely determination to find the man who had done this to me. I was quite surprised. Policemen only came to The Orpheum for two things: to collect the required fines and licensing fees, and to relax after a hard day's work. It certainly wasn't to find justice. But this man was different. He wore his outrage right next to his badge, as if it were a part of his uniform.

"Miss Darling," he insisted on calling me, "tell me exactly what happened, from the time he first walked into The Orpheum. I need every detail you can recall; something small you may remember might reveal who he was or where he was going." His brown eyes were pools of the darkest melted chocolate, looking right into my pain and suffering. The image of those piercing eyes has been forever burned into my memory.

I then recounted the horrible performance in which I'd played the star role, not realizing I'd been crying until I was almost finished, my cheeks wet with uninvited tears.

Officer Heinrich just sat next to my bed, not speaking, wearing his strong resolve like a weapon. "I will do everything I can to find the man who did this to you, Miss Darling," he said. "I promise."

And I believed him.

Chapter 18

Eliza

July 2, 1907

It was all I could do not to think about Mamie Carroll as I worked at my sewing on the day after we'd visited Emma Street. I was overwhelmed with frustration on that hot and humid morning. Not only was Mamie sitting on my shoulder, filling me with a peculiar sense of defeat, but I'd started the day not being able to find my thimble. It was a beautiful thing, made of silver, and etched with the wild animals and vines of the jungle. Ms. Dixie had given it to me as a graduation present of sorts, after I'd finished my schooling in dressmaking. "Every seamstress must have her thimble," she'd told me. "It will not only protect your finger, but will remind you of where you've been and where you want to go." And it had.

Now I couldn't find it. I always kept it in the small, velvet-lined box in which I'd received it, but it wasn't there. I'd looked everywhere with no success. My heart was aching from both the misplacement of such a beautiful gift, and the tainting of such a beautiful girl. I had two losses to grieve over that morning.

I did recognize the fact that when I was Mamie's age, I'd done everything possible not to work at the mill. Including becoming one of Ms. Dixie's girls. So I couldn't blame her for her choice. But I also knew of the dangers that came with *the life*, and the additional vulnerabilities that came with working at a place like The Palace. Although by all appearances, her new home seemed luxurious and safe, I knew for a fact that May's concern for her girls wasn't much greater than the concern shown for the women at the two-bit whore-cribs which existed not far from Emma Street. Mostly housing Negro and Mexican women, they were a far cry from the high-priced houses frequented by the prosperous. Drab and drafty buildings with *cells* instead of rooms, housing four times the number of girls living in a higher-priced house, where two quarters was all that was needed to buy five or ten minutes of carnal pleasure. The niceties at The Palace were just there to lure the customers, not to take care of her employees. I'd heard that May occasionally even hired *procurers* when her stable didn't provide sufficient selection for various tastes. *Procurers* was too kind a word. They were nothing but slave-traders, tricking young girls into thinking they would have respectable jobs, working as a house-girl at a resort or club, only to be forced into other services.

It was true that May did ensure her girls were free from disease, or she'd no longer have her upscale clientele. But that's as far as she went. The more money she spent on her girls, the less she could put in her pocket, and that was what she cared about most.

I felt a connection to Mamie Carroll. I knew how scared she must have been, all the while putting her courage before her fear, needing to be self-reliant. But she was still so young; still vulnerable. Still fairly innocent in her views of the world. It gave me great concern to think of that innocence being forever lost after experiencing the seedier side of life.

I had to do something to help her. I *had* to. I couldn't stop thinking about her long auburn hair, put-up in school-girl braids. She didn't even seem old enough to work at the mill, much less work at The Palace. I finally decided it *was* my place to meddle; after all, I was trying to save her life.

But how to go about it?

I was sure Ms. May wouldn't let me get within twenty feet of Mamie. *Honey*, to her. I pushed my needle into the material of the dress I was sewing, then pulled it through the other side. The repetitive motion was soothing to me, and helped me think. Like rubbing a worry stone. The smooth fabric and push-and-pull of the needle and thread was almost hypnotic, and put me at ease. Of course I had to be more careful with the push-and-pull, seeing as how my dang thimble was no- where to be found. Doing this routine task had let my mind wander in a carefree state many a time, and now it was searching for a solution to the problem of contacting Miss Mamie Carroll.

Well, if I were *a man*, I'd have no problem contacting her, I thought sourly. Then my mind ran away with that thought. What about contacting her at The Palace through someone else? A customer maybe? Did I know any men who would do this for me? Could I pull this off without embarrassing Ms. Dixie, or angering Ms. May?

Think, think, think!

And then a thin, freckled face popped into my brain. Mart Waymond! Of course! I was sure he delivered to The Palace all the time. No one would think much of him delivering something to one of the girls. To Mamie. Perfect!

I quickly put up my sewing and walked to the writing desk. Pen in hand, I thought about what I should say. I didn't want to cause her anxiety; she might be afraid that meeting me would vex Ms. May, and jeopardize her employment. But what if I just invited her to socialize? Just a visit between two almost-friends? After all, Fourth of July celebrations were already underway all over Dallas. It was the perfect reason to send her an invitation.

Dear Mamie,

It was so nice seeing you again yesterday, and I would truly like to get to know you better. Would you be able to meet me at Lake Cliff Park in Oak Cliff tomorrow, July 3, at 10:00 (before the sun gets too hot)? There is an Independence Day carnival there

I'm sure you would enjoy. The trolley on Emma Street will take you right to it. I hope you'll accept this invitation. I'll be waiting by the entrance archway.

Yours Truly,

Eliza D.

I folded up the note, and wrote the name *Honey* on the outside. I needed to get to Linder's early enough to catch Mart before he left with his deliveries.

"Good morning, Mr. Linder," I said as I entered the pharmacy. "So nice to see you again."

"Why Eliza Darling, howdy-do?" Mr. Linder asked me with a smile, his face crinkled with the proof of a thousand smiles before it. He was truly a man who always saw the best in people, and believed that good would win over evil every time.

"I'm doing just fine, Mr. Linder. Thank you for asking. I have so many dress orders I almost don't know how I'll get them all done."

"Well, glad business is good Eliza. Lord knows we need The Johnson Home to flourish. You ladies are doin' a fine job of takin' care of the girls you got, but I know there's no limit to the number who might be needin' your assistance. Why, my business just seems to get busier and busier, in spite of the purity crusaders," he said, shaking his head with the first-hand knowledge that human nature usually had a way of trumping human intellect and intention.

"You're doing a fine job of taking care of the girls yourself, Mr. Linder," I told him with sincerity. Linder's was one of the only pharmacies that still supplied medicines and other necessities to Emma Street. Mr. Linder's concern for his neighbors and fellow human beings was bigger than politics, or moral judgment. He had compassion for human life. Period. I've always loved him for that.

"Mr. Linder, do you have any deliveries for Mart Waymond this afternoon?" I asked. "I have something I need to ask him, and I thought this would be the easiest place to find him."

"Why yes I do, in fact. Just like most days. He should be in shortly. Just take a seat, and I'll make you a nice cup of tea while you wait," he offered.

It was hard to think of a nicer man, except of course for Mr. Gramercy. I'd been blessed to have a friend in each.

Not long after, the bells on the door jangled, announcing Mart's energy and enthusiasm. I didn't know how he could have such zeal for his work, but he did. He almost passed me right up as he hustled to the back counter where his deliveries were kept. Almost.

"Ms. Eliza!" Mart almost shouted, his smile greeting me with even more warmth than the sun outside.

He was dressed in knickers that appeared to be a size too small, a faded messenger cap, and worn and dusty black boots with a hole in the left toe.

"How've you been, Mart?" I asked. "I see you're making runs during the daytime now. And you must've grown about a foot since I saw you last!"

He grinned in the lopsided way that always made me smile, even on my worst days.

"Turned fourteen last week, Ms. Eliza. No one can call me *kid* no more!" he answered.

In truth, I didn't think Mart had *ever* been a kid. At least, not since his daddy died, when he was eight. Just like me, necessity forced him to leave his childhood behind to help feed his family. His mama still had three small children at home so couldn't work; it had been up to the three brothers, Mart being the youngest, to make sure their family had food on the table and a roof over their heads. He'd gotten the job of night messenger for ST&T, and I imagine has ridden that bicycle every day of his life since. He'd actually been the only messenger working The Orpheum; it was almost like we'd adopted him as our own child. Mart took orders for all the girls in the house, even picking up cocaine or opium for those who needed their *powders* to get them through the night. They just told Mart what was needed and gave him the money, then he handled everything from there. Why, some of the girls even used him as their personal secretary; he would set up their dates with clients. He'd been a street-smart thirty-year-old hiding inside an innocent eight-year-old's body. I just hoped that life had postponed his happiness for a later time, instead of robbing him of it altogether.

"Well happy belated birthday, Mart!"

We chatted for a bit about his family, and then I finally got to the reason for my visit. "I need to ask you for a favor," I told him.

Mart's expression beamed with even more happiness at my revelation. "Ms. Eliza, you know I'll do anything I can for you. Always," he said honestly, and I absolutely knew, without a doubt, that it was true.

"I need you to deliver a note to a girl at The Palace. It must go directly to her, no one else."

"Sure I can," he said, almost as if he were disappointed that I hadn't asked for more.

I handed him the folded piece of paper with the name HONEY printed on the front. He looked at it and furrowed his brow; I could tell he was trying to place her in his mind's eye.

"I don't rightly know if I've met a girl named Honey at The Palace. That's funny - I thought I knew all the girls there," Mart answered, confused as to how he hadn't yet met her. I assumed she was probably just trying to keep a low profile, staying in her room until it was time to entertain her clients. A girl is nervous about making much of a stir at first, not knowing what to expect. And especially at The Palace, a low profile was always best.

"Well, she's new," I told him. "If you could deliver it directly to her, and no one else, I'd be much obliged. Mart, it's very important that this message get to her," I told him with a seriousness that he immediately recognized.

"Yes ma'am, Ms. Eliza. Don't you worry. I'll get it to her directly," he answered, as he put it into his messenger bag.

I knew it was already as good as delivered.

Chapter 19

Delivery

July 2, 1907

Mart Waymond had always been a good son, a good brother, and a good employee. He tried to be good, period. After all, that's what he'd always been taught by his mama, and at church. *Do unto others as you would have them do unto you.* He tried hard to be friendly and kind to everyone he met. But when it came to Ms. Eliza, he would do just about anything.

When she'd worked at The Orpheum, Ms. Eliza had always been especially kind to him. He worked at ST&T to help support his mama and siblings, so he never had enough of anything. Never enough money, never enough food, and certainly nothing extra, like sweets or soda waters. Although he'd never told anyone, and certainly never complained, Ms. Eliza seemed to know how things were with him. She'd made him sit in her room for a few minutes with a hot cup of tea on cold winter nights. She'd given him part of her dinner on countless occasions, after correctly guessing that he'd had none. Ms. Eliza never made anything of it, never even acted as if it were any sort of charity at all.

But Mart knew the truth, and would always be grateful to Ms. Eliza for her kindness.

The assault on Eliza had left Mart off-kilter and shaken. It was as if his own sister had been attacked by a maniac. He'd been in such a hurry to get Doc Finley, he'd almost been hit by a car, and then had caused a horse attached to a carriage to rear up, almost toppling the buggy to the ground. But he hadn't cared; he was on a mission to save one of the special people in his life. One of his family.

He'd sat by her door for countless hours after work, listening to the other girls taking care of her. When she was burning with fever, and they weren't even sure if she'd survive, he felt like a part of him would have to die right along with her. Mart didn't want to bury someone else. He'd helped bury his baby brother, who'd died of the whooping cough at just three months old. They hadn't had enough money to pay for the burial, so an arrangement had been made: Mart would help the gravedigger with the shoveling. It hadn't been a very big hole - just large enough to fit the tiny box. But it felt as though a heavy yoke were sitting on his shoulders as he dug. Just the thought of what the hole was for made his arms heavy, as if they were made of lead that took twice the effort to move. Then shoveling the dirt on top of that small coffin, forever sealing that baby into the ground, had been a horror for Mart. It was like sentencing his little brother to forever darkness, the only thing that the cold earth could provide.

Mart was afraid he'd have to go through it again, and he'd cried quiet tears at the thought.

The day Ms. Eliza woke from her fevered sickness had been one of the best in his life, and now he'd do anything for her. Anything.

Mart propped his bicycle against the wall by the entrance, and knocked softly on the front door of The Palace. This wasn't within his usual delivery hours, so he was afraid of encountering Ms. May.

The door opened slightly and he saw the young face of Maude, the house-girl, peek through the crack. "Mart, what are you doin' here?" she asked with curiosity. "You never come so early."

"Is Ms. May downstairs?" Mart asked her, a hint of his anxiety peeking through the question.

"Not yet," she answered, "she's still in her room. But I wouldn't be surprised if she heard your knock. Her ears could hear a pin drop onto the carpet."

Disturbing Ms. May was the last thing he wanted to do. Although a good many of his deliveries were made to The Palace, he always cringed at the thought of her asking him about the tips her girls were giving. More tips in his pockets were less in hers. After all, he was no more to her than a street urchin on a bicycle. He didn't linger here like he had at The Orpheum; the one time Ms. May found him sitting with one of the girls in her room, she'd boxed his ears and told him her girls had no time for chit-chat with the likes of him. "What would my wealthy clients think if they happened to see their companion for the evening giving attention to a dirty little messenger boy?" she'd asked. His feelings were hurt more than his ears. In honesty, he was more comfortable delivering to the crowded and dirty saloons down on Wood Street than to The Palace. Ms. May scared him.

"Who you gonna deliver to?" asked Maude. "I'll take it for you," she offered.

"Nope, gotta deliver it myself," he answered resolutely, his desire to please Ms. Eliza greater than his fear of Ms. May.

Maude opened the door wider and let him inside. "Fine," she whispered, "but you better be as quiet as a mouse, or she'll hear you for sure. Then I'll get my hide tanned for lettin' you in," she told him, the concern in her voice an extra warning to him. "Who's it for?"

"Miss Honey," he told her.

"Oh, the new girl. Well then, you best be *extra* quiet, 'cause she shares a room with Candace, and you know she's almost as bad as Ms. May," Maude warned. "She's apt to throw somethin' at you if she wakes and catches you in her room. Unless, of course, you're a payin' customer. But I'm guessin,' even then, she'd be too grouchy to entertain much."

The two walked on tip-toe up the stairs until they reached Mamie's room; Mart prayed that the door wouldn't announce his presence with a loud and screeching creak.

"Honey's in the bed on the right side of the room. Good luck to you," whispered Maude as she scurried away from the door, clearly afraid that she'd be caught in the act of helping a lowly messenger boy sneak into the house while so many were still sleeping.

Mart was not to be deterred. He opened the door an inch at a time, just in case. Thankfully, the hinges were quiet. He crept into the room, one soft footfall at a time, hearing snores from the bed on the left. *The growling of the beast*, he thought. He moved toward the small form curled up like a baby on the other bed, facing the wall, almost hidden under her coverlet. The only part clearly visible was her long, flowing hair, the soft color of honey. Mart couldn't help a tiny smile - her name fit her well.

He approached the bed, bent over, and softly touched her shoulder, trying not to startle her. Trying to prevent any noise that would cause either Candace or Ms. May to assault him. Honey didn't move at all. Then Mart suddenly had an overwhelming urge to do something he just couldn't help - before he tried to wake her again, he gently caressed a lock of her hair, stroking it quite delicately as it lay on top of her pillow.

It's so soft, he thought. Like golden silk. Mart had never experienced much softness and beauty; his life was filled with rough edges and dullness. It seemed the only beauty he ever experienced was within the walls of these houses.

Mart stood there for a few more seconds, just looking at her hair, not wanting to disturb the picture in front of him. Then he gently nudged her shoulder again, causing her to turn around abruptly and rise up with a start.

"Ssshhhhh," Mart whispered, putting his finger in front of his lips. "It's OK - I'm just the messenger boy. I have a delivery for you."

But after getting Mamie through the initial shock of seeing him, he just stood there, almost stupefied. She was the most beautiful girl he'd ever seen, like an angel in the books his mother read to him when he was little. Later, when Mart would think of her image, he could swear there was a halo of golden rays around her head. He just stood there staring, so entranced he found it hard to speak.

"What are you delivering?" Mamie finally asked in confusion, bringing Mart back to the task at hand.

"This," he finally managed to croak, holding up the note from Ms. Eliza. He thought he might faint when her fingers slightly brushed his as she took it.

Chapter 20

A Meeting of the Minds

July 2-July 3, 1907

Dear Mamie,

It was so nice seeing you again yesterday, and I would truly like to get to know you better. Would you be able to meet me at Lake Cliff Park in Oak Cliff tomorrow, July 3, at 10:00 (before the sun gets too hot)? There is an Independence Day carnival there I'm sure you would enjoy. The trolley on Emma Street will take you right to it. I hope you'll accept this invitation. I'll be waiting by the entrance archway.

Yours Truly,

Eliza D.

Mamie read the invitation several times, not sure what to make of it. She'd now met this woman named Eliza twice, in totally different circumstances. Was she somehow destined to come to know her more intimately?

Mamie had been in a sound sleep, dreaming of beating her brother Christian at marbles, their normal Sunday game. A good memory which brought happiness to her heart and a smile to her lips. But a painful dream at the same time, knowing that she'd left her little brother behind, to his life at the mill without her.

But I'm sending my family more money. It's got to be helping him.

This was her mantra, but she truly didn't know if his life were any better.

Then her dream was interrupted by the tap on her shoulder. She'd rolled over, and was startled to find a young man peering at her. He'd quickly shooshed her, telling her he was just delivering a message, so she hadn't been scared. Just surprised. Although not especially handsome, the boy had an endearing quality to him, and his smile was warm, lighting up his freckled face.

It was odd - after she'd taken the note, he'd just stared at her for a few more seconds, as if he'd never seen a girl before. Then, without another sound, he just tipped his hat to her, turned on his heel, and walked very quietly out of the room.

It had been so curious; she didn't even know how he'd gotten in the house, much less found her room. She would ask Maude about it later. She and the house-girl had gotten to know each other somewhat, a surreptitious friendship away from the all-seeing eyes of Ms. May.

Mamie looked again at the note from Eliza D. *How very curious.* Not only did she want to know more about this woman, who'd supposedly been a prostitute like she was (she cringed at the thought - Mamie still had a hard time associating the word *prostitute* with herself), she also had a very childish desire to go to the amusement park. Although Mamie's family was kept afloat by their mill jobs, and they usually had enough food to eat after their other debts were paid each month, there was barely anything left for *extras*, like clothing or shoes. Her ma had made most of their clothes; she was able to buy defective cloth from the mill at a much cheaper price. There had certainly never been extra money to go to an amusement park. She couldn't even imagine what it would be like, and felt almost giddy at the thought. Mamie's little girl soul wanted to fulfill at least one of her childhood dreams.

Money wasn't the only thing that had kept the Carroll children from the amusement park. As many kids were taught from the time they were small, places of pure enjoyment were places to avoid. Movie houses, saloons, billiard parlors, and carnivals bred sinfulness. Places where the ways of the wicked could rub off on the young and innocent. Like prostitution. *Well, I don't need to worry of that danger anymore*, thought Mamie. She was already corrupted.

The thought of seeing what Lake Cliff was like brought a much needed smile to her face.

Mamie lay in her bed, her head filled with thoughts of adventure and Eliza and all things fanciful. But how would she go about it? Would she be able to sneak out of the house that early? Most of the girls didn't even wake up until after noon. Maybe she could rise early, get dressed, go for a quick trip, and then be back before anyone realized she was gone? Candace was such a sound sleeper, staying in bed even longer than the other girls. She didn't think her roommate would hear or notice anything. But what if she were caught? Would there be consequences? It wasn't as if she were a prisoner here; she should be able to come and go as she pleased. In truth, she didn't really know. But Mamie decided then and there that the adventure would be worth the risk.

The next morning, Mamie woke early, dressed, and tip-toed quietly down the stairs. As usual, Candace was sound asleep, her snoring so loud it could almost be heard down the hall. Mamie decided the noise would most likely cover-up any sound that her exit might make.

"OK, Maude," she whispered conspiratorially to the house-girl, "I'll be back by noon or a few minutes after. If Ms.

May notices that I'm not here, just tell her I had to run an errand, and I'll be back shortly." Mamie had explained her plan to Maude the night before, easily enlisting the girl's help. Mamie was not much older than Maude, and it seemed that Mamie was the only resident who treated the house-girl as if she weren't just a slave to her every wish. Only one step above the hired help, newcomers to The Palace were on the lowest level of the pecking order; every woman in that place was Mamie's boss, in one way or another, and they loved to let her know it. So she knew exactly how Maude felt, and wasn't about to add to her oppression.

Ms. Eliza had been right: the trolley car deposited her right in front of the entrance to Lake Cliff, after only a very short ride from Emma Street. Even after all her years of working downtown at the mill, Mamie had never been over the river into Oak Cliff before.

The park's immense entrance archway sat majestically like a lion king on its throne, guarding its magical kingdom. It wasn't just a simple curved arch made of iron, allowing a person entry by just taking two steps to get to the other side. This passageway was a massive structure of brick and stone, imposing in its height and solid structure. One had to journey through a tunnel to finally gain entry at the other end.

Mamie stepped off the trolley and looked toward the archway, set back a good way from the street. Peeking out from behind it, on the right, was a large and curious structure of dips and curves. *What an unusual place*, she mused. She walked toward the park and saw Ms. Eliza, dressed from head to foot in black and gray. Mamie hadn't really thought much about it the other day, but each time she'd seen the woman, Eliza had worn a dark shade. *How peculiar*. But the gloominess of Eliza's clothing was in no way an omen of the greeting Mamie would receive from her.

Eliza caught sight of Mamie and waved, a warm smile of welcome meeting her as she walked to the entrance.

"Oh, I was so hoping you'd come, and now here you are!" Eliza exclaimed with excitement, holding out her hand in greeting. A large, but soft and delicate hand. Mamie shook it gently, her own hand gloved in white lace. She'd taken to wearing gloves since she'd moved to The Palace, to hide the shameful consequence of her many years of hard work at the mill. Her hands betrayed Mamie's years of toil and struggle, and she neither wanted to be reminded of, nor wanted anyone else to notice, the disconnect between her lovely, young face and the hands of an old crone.

Mamie had been so terrified when she'd spoken to Eliza and Ms. Dixie at The Palace - *those damned Johnson women,* as Ms. May referred to them - that she hadn't really looked very closely at Eliza. But now she saw she was a curious sort. Not only were her garments the color of melancholy, but her hairstyle was so drastically different from the style of the times. Most women had long hair, which they wore pinned up on the top of their heads. Especially in the summer, the moist heat felt twice as hot if a woman's hair covered the back of her neck. But Eliza didn't wear her hair pinned up; she didn't even have long hair. It was cut short, to just under her chin, a little longer in front than in the back, and was parted in the middle, framing either side of her face, covering most of it. *How odd,* thought Mamie. *But she most likely finds me odd as well, to be wearing gloves in the blazing heat of summer.*

"Hello Ms. Eliza. Thank you for inviting me. My stars, I haven't heard my real name spoken in so long I almost forgot I had it," said Mamie, with a small shake of her head, as if she were surprised to remember she'd once been another person.

"Yes, I know you go by the name Honey now, and if you'd prefer I call you that, I certainly will," answered Eliza. "But I always used my real name with my family and close friends. After all, I was still me."

"It's been difficult to get used to my new name. Sometimes I almost forget just *who* I am," Mamie said with a hint of sadness that vanished before she really let it materialize. "What *was* your other name?" Mamie asked almost playfully.

Eliza looked into Mamie's eyes, and behind the curiosity, saw intelligence and wit. "It was Somber," she said. "Because as you can see, I wear only dark colors."

"Why?" Mamie asked.

Eliza was tickled at Mamie's directness. My goodness, she wasn't as shy as she'd first appeared. Not shy at all. "Because blacks and grays are the colors of shame and mourning. And lost innocence. When I started in the profession, I decided that wearing dark colors would be my penance for giving my girlhood up to *the life*."

Mamie listened to her explanation as they walked through the entrance tunnel. There was something very different about Eliza Darling.

As they exited the tunnel, Mamie couldn't help but suck in a short breath, not able to believe what she saw in front of her. It was as if she'd traveled to a whole other world, just by walking those few steps through the archway. *A magic archway*, she thought. The park looked to be just as amazing as Mamie had always imagined. Although it was daytime, there were small electric lights on cords strung around the trees and fences. Just in front of them was a small lake, with ducks and swans swimming peacefully, pruning their feathers, making occasional ripples in the water. Brightly-painted gondolas floated at the water's edge.

To their right was the huge structure she'd seen from the outside, made of metal rails and wooden poles and platforms. The rails wound up, down and around - Mamie couldn't imagine what in the world all those rails were for.

Eliza just had to smile. "It's amazing, isn't it?" she asked her.

"It's such a monumental thing," Mamie answered. "But what is it?"

"It's a roller coaster," answered Eliza, just as a small cart zipped over the rails and dropped from its highest point to the valley below, its wheels never leaving the railing underneath.

Mamie gasped, the noise scaring the amazement right out of her. "Oh my lands!" she shouted, putting a small gloved hand to her chest. "How in the blazes did that cart stay on the track?" she asked in disbelief. "I would've expected it to sail right off at the first curve."

"It *is* a wonder. And even more amazing to ride on one. I tried it once last year, and thought I'd die right there in that cart. As a matter of fact, I almost lost my stomach coming down the tallest of those slopes," said Eliza, with a small shake of her head.

"No ma'am," answered Mamie. "I don't think I'll be riding on one of those anytime soon. It liked to have scared the bejeebers out of me just watching."

The ladies walked onward, around the curve of the lake, and entered what the sign announced was an *Authentic Japanese Garden*. An ornate pergola made of wood flanked the entrance and stretched across the entire walkway, with unusual sculpted trees adorning either side of the path. Mamie wasn't used to being in such close proximity to many plants or flowers, and certainly none that appeared as if they'd been manufactured instead of grown, in shapes that Mamie never imagined trees could grow in.

"Those are bonsai trees," explained Eliza. "It's an old Japanese art form. They prune the trees so they take on different shapes."

Japanese lanterns of colorful paper hung from the pergola. Mamie felt like she were in a world of whimsy and magic. It was as if she'd been transported to a mystifying land.

Then a slight breeze blew around them, blowing the lanterns and riffling their hair and skirts, as if the garden were trying to be even more hospitable, giving them respite from the heat that had already begun to settle over them like a woolen cape. That's when Mamie saw the deep scar that covered the left side of Eliza's face, ravaging her youth and loveliness. It had been hidden under her hair, but now seemed to scream *look at me!!* She couldn't help but stare, as if her eyes had been lured by a force too strong to break. *That's why she wears her hair down*, thought Mamie. To cover the ugliness that had permanently inserted itself into Eliza's beauty.

Mamie's transfixed gaze did not escape Eliza's attention.

"My scar," said Eliza in an almost whisper.

"Oh, I'm so sorry. I truly didn't mean to stare," said Mamie in apology.

"No need to be sorry," replied Eliza. "It's part of me, and it's not going away. I've come to terms with its presence."

"How did it happen?" asked Mamie.

Eliza locked eyes with Mamie. "I think you can probably guess how it happened," she answered. "An angry client." Eliza paused, trying to gather the right words. "That's one reason why I wanted to speak with you. *Privately.* I understand everything you said during our visit the other day. I truly do. And I don't know how you worked at the mill so long. I'm sure there's more to your story than you'd even want to share; I know *I* couldn't have worked there. So I understand why you went into the business. I know what it's like to wear beautiful dresses, and live in a beautiful home, and make a fortune, at least compared to what you *were* making." She again hesitated, looking for the words to make the beautiful, young, innocent girl understand. "I also know what it's like when someone gets angry, and wants to hurt you. There's nothing to stop them. Of course, it's still a crime, but let's just say it isn't given much priority by *upright* citizens." Eliza willed her words to be heard, *truly* heard, by the girl walking beside her.

Silence while Mamie considered what she'd just been told. "Did they ever catch the man who did it?" she asked.

Eliza just shook her head, acknowledging the defeat she felt every time she thought about it. "No, they didn't." She seemed to think a moment before she continued. "The officer who investigated was truly dedicated to finding him. He worked on my case for weeks, following every lead he had. He promised me he'd find him. But then his Captain told him to cease his investigation." Eliza paused again in remembrance, anger seeping into her words. "He told the officer he'd '*wasted* enough time trying to find someone who'd disfigured a *whore*, not even killing her.' He was ordered to return to 'solving crimes that mattered.'"

Mamie considered Eliza's words, a deep sadness suddenly overtaking her. She'd never wanted to be one of the *unvirtuous*; it had been thrust upon her, by Duffy's unscrupulous attentions and her father's cowardly complicity. She'd done the only thing she could think to do. Her mind raced from her horrible mill apron, to the beautiful, soft gowns she could now delight in, to the extra money she sent her parents every month. Then her defenses unfurled like a flag of a newly independent nation. *Danger be damned*, she thought.

"The mill was dangerous too, in *many* ways," answered Mamie, wanting Eliza to understand her meaning, without actually having to speak the words. "I'm not afraid of danger," she said, stealing a furtive glance at the raised and jagged scar. "I suppose there's the risk of danger with many jobs." Even as she said it, she could feel she wasn't being totally truthful with herself; that this job probably *was* more hazardous than most. But she wasn't going to let that stand in her way.

The women had walked through the sculpted garden, and finally exited under another ornate trellis, covered in vines. When they emerged, they were again back at the water's edge.

"But like we were trying to tell you the other day, you have choices," Eliza said, suddenly stopping and turning to look at Mamie, taking her small gloved hands into her own. "Mamie, you could live with us, at The Johnson Home. I could teach you how to be a dressmaker. You could learn to make a living using something other than your body. I did. We all did."

Mamie listened to Eliza's words. They made sense, of course. She felt fear every night: as she sat in the parlor, waiting for the man who would choose her to go upstairs with him; as she slowly removed her kimono in front of him; as she struggled to give him whatever he desired; as she pretended to be entranced by him. As she struggled to be someone that she never in her wildest dreams would have imagined herself to be. And what if she wasn't successful in pleasing the man? What then? Would he slice her face with a razor? Candace had more than once complained of the brutality that some of her suitors had shown, the bruises clearly evident on various parts of her body. Mamie shuddered, knowing it could happen to her at any time, on any day, regardless of what she did or didn't do. It *was* a dangerous profession.

But then Christian's smiling face popped into her head, and she dismissed all thoughts of herself and her well-being. *What about his well-being? I have to make sure his burden is lessened by the money I send home. Surely my help would be minimal if I were to become a dressmaker.*

"Thank you, Eliza," Mamie said quietly, "but I need to stay where I'm at. I don't think the wages of a dressmaker will keep food on my family's table. Hopefully I can keep my little brother from having to spend every extra minute of his childhood working at the mill."

There was not much more to say. They continued to stroll through the park, around the lake, and past the opera house, the casino, and the skating rink. All wonders to Mamie, who had never happened upon anything so grand, such places never existing in her world.

"Step right up, ladies!" came the deep bellow of a man wearing a black bowler hat and a red bow tie. "Swami Aseem from India can read your fortunes right from your hand. A mystic of the most exceptional kind!" Eliza and Mamie looked toward the voice, owned by a carnival barker wearing a thin black mustache. "Just a nickel, ladies, to learn what awaits you, to learn what the future holds. No better deal have I ever heard," he announced with conviction, pointing his cane of shiny black wood and brass handle to the sign bearing the Swami's name.

Eliza looked at Mamie with no less than wonder in her eyes, like those of a young girl whose life stood before her, the possibilities endless. But whereas Eliza was filled with excitement, Mamie could only withdraw into herself, hiding her gloved hands behind her skirts, sure that the only thing any fortune-teller would be able to see in her aged and weathered hands was the hard work that had always come before, and the never-ending struggle that was sure to pave the path of her future.

"Oh, let's do," said Eliza with a look of childish delight and intrigue, pulling Mamie with her to the Swami's booth. Golden stars covered the worn wooden structure; stone elephants stood guard to the left and right of the deep red velvet curtain that covered the entrance.

"Just five cents and your future is yours," announced the barker, with a smile that reassured his customers they were no longer in need of their hard-earned wages.

Eliza thought of the fortune-telling booth in Atlantic City that her aunt had once described at great length. *The Amazing Zoltar*, it was called. She'd listened to every detail with rapt attention, filled with wonder that one's future life could be predicted.

Eliza opened her small handbag and produced two nickels. "One for each of us," she said with a smile of excitement. What Eliza meant to gain from this charlatan Mamie didn't know, except the promise of losing ten cents. "Maybe he can see who my betrothed will one day be, or that I'm in truth a princess, taken from her cradle in the black of night."

Now Eliza was just being foolish, Mamie thought.

"Eliza, no. Surely you don't think he can truly tell the future," replied Mamie, almost certain the woman was daft. And even if he weren't a fraud whose existence was solely to rid people of their money, her mama had always taught her to be wary of soothsayers, for they were the agents of the devil.

Eliza just looked at her with a seriousness that surprised Mamie. "But haven't you ever wondered if maybe, just maybe, our futures may not become what we'd expected at all? Even after the twists and turns our paths have already taken, maybe there are wonderful surprises waiting for us," she said thoughtfully, before quickly regaining the gaiety that had overtaken her demeanor. "But even if not, it's bound to be amusing nonetheless! Don't you think?"

"Maybe for you," Mamie answered, "but no, not me. I've come to believe that I'm quite in control of my future, and that is just how I want things to be," she said.

"Well, all right," answered Eliza, putting one of the nickels back into her handbag, and giving the other to the dandy in black. "But come with me to hear what the Swami has to tell me."

Eliza led Mamie through the curtain and into a small, darkened room, its walls shimmering with the dust of a thousand stars. It was as if they'd been transported into a mystical time and place. A small table lay in the center of the tiny room, on which sat a ball made of the most beautiful crystal either woman had ever seen. The light reflected from it as if the sun filled its center, the sparkle of its illumination almost blinding them as they entered. Behind the ball sat a short man of slight build, his dark skin and white beard glowing from the crystal's light, as if he were made from the same sparkling glass. His head was adorned with a turban of shimmering satin, the purple and blue colors dazzling in their promise of magic. Small clear crystals were embedded in the cloth, like tiny stars twinkling in a boundless night. "Come, come," he said soothingly, as he gestured for them to approach. "Give me your hands, and I will give you your future." His weathered face bore the knowledge of a thousand endless days, and his eyes the understanding of times yet to come.

Mamie sat at the small table, still determined not to give in to her sudden desire to trust him. But Eliza was mesmerized, sitting in front of the ball and giving him her beautiful, smooth hands as if he were a long lost uncle that she welcomed back to her acquaintance. There was something in the way he looked at her, almost through her. Eliza immediately felt that he was reading her mind, and even feeling her very thoughts. His hands were not those of an old and wizened man, but of a young and manicured prince who'd never had to use them to make a living. "Hands are the windows to the soul," he said softly, putting into words what Eliza was already thinking. She was shocked to hear her own thoughts repeated to her; a thrill ran through her as she bestowed her trust in this most unusual man.

"I am Aseem, teller of fortunes. Teller of misfortunes. Teller of lives," he said as he gently stroked Eliza's hands, all the while looking into her eyes with a deep probing gaze. Reading her thoughts, and reading her dreams. Eliza had never felt so overtaken; it was as if she and he were the only ones in the room; the only ones in the entire world.

"Do you believe?" he asked with mischief. Eliza could only nod in wonder. She truly *did* believe. She'd always felt there might be something else, and now her hopes might be fulfilled.

With a twist of his wrists, Eliza's palms were turned toward the crystal, which suddenly filled with a swirl of colors, and even brighter light. *Where in the world have these colors come from?* she wondered. But the rest of her brain, her entire being, was captivated by its glowing beauty. The mystic studied its depths as he held Eliza's hands, and made a small, gasping sound, ever so slight. But Eliza had heard it. "What?" she asked him. "What did you see?"

The expression on Swami Aseem's face changed from one of wonder and mischief to a deep concentration and struggle for understanding. Surprise and fear seemed to mix within his countenance. "You are one of the few," he whispered. "One of a thousand lives. A blessing or a curse, I cannot know."

Eliza felt no fear at this prophesy, only the thrill of intrigue. Could she be one of only a chosen few? But chosen for what? "What do you mean?" she asked. "What are you telling me about my future?"

"Your future *and* your past," Aseem answered softly. "You will live infinite lives. You've lived your life before, in a different age and place. And you'll live your life again. Over and over, until your soul is satisfied that you've met your destiny."

"But I don't remember any other lives," Eliza said in a mixed state of confusion and excitement. "Will I never know of what has come before? Or what will come later?" she asked.

Aseem placed her open palms on either side of the crystal sphere, holding them sandwiched between the smooth glass and his own soft palms. He gazed deeply into the light of the ball, concentrating intently, entranced by the glow deep within its sparkling glass.

The Swami raised his head and looked into Eliza's eyes, almost looked *inside* her, to her very depths, as if he were trying to decipher the intriguing mystery that her hands had revealed.

"You will not know who you've been before, and certainly not who you will become. But there is something else, something I have never before encountered. Another message. An intricacy I am not able to explain. But it is there. Your future intertwines with your present. Your future has revealed itself, and will come again. How, I do not know. And why, I cannot tell you. But it is so," he told her softly.

"Will I not know anything of the revelation?" Eliza asked with rapt attention.

"I can only tell you that a physical object will connect your present with your future. You will lose something that the future will gain," he said, closing his eyes.

Swami Aseem sat at the ball in perfect stillness, breathing evenly. When he opened his eyes, he declared, "The prophesy is done. I am honored to have met one who will be eternal." And with that proclamation, he bowed his turbaned head, rose, and walked behind another curtain, leaving the ladies alone in stunned silence.

Eliza looked at Mamie, and saw fear in her eyes. She herself wasn't afraid, only amazed and perplexed. A visit from the future. *I will lose something that the future will gain*, Eliza thought, contemplating the Swami's prediction. And then it dawned on her, as she almost felt the blood draining from her face, only to fill her stomach with excitement.

My thimble.

Eliza knew it had to be true. She *knew* it.

"Come, let's go," she said to Mamie as she rose, and pulled Mamie by her gloved hand. Neither wanted to speak of what they'd heard. They kept a mystical secret between them -

Mamie not wishing to discuss it because of both skepticism and fear. Eliza not wanting to talk of it because she knew deep within her heart that what he'd said was true. It was her own fate that seemed too unbelievable to speak of.

Eliza and Mamie exited the Swami's tent in silence, their eyes adjusting to the bright summer sun as they parted the red curtain, walking out onto the sidewalk, and continuing back toward the entrance. As they came full circle, Eliza and Mamie walked past the incredible flying machine, both enthralled with what could come from man's imagination, and each contemplating what their futures might hold.

Chapter 21

The Diary of Eliza Darling

September 24, 1903

I am finally strong enough to admit my grievous weakness and failure. The last two months have been as blurry as a bad dream, a nightmare that I lived through, but only marginally. It's as if I've been living just on the fringes of my own life, while mysteriously enacting another person's destiny.

I'd like to blame it solely on the opium, but I know that wouldn't be honest. My character must have a flaw, a weakness which allowed me to fall into the gaping hole that had swallowed me up and kept me prisoner for the past months. The time passing, but not passing, like moving in molasses. And strange images visiting me in my sleep.

I'd recovered from my attack, or so I thought. But my craving for tranquility overtook me; I experienced a very queer circumstance I'd never been in before. I'd suddenly find myself in a state of utter panic, and physically yearned for the peacefulness the opium had given me. I was rattled, unnerved with my life, and fearful in a way I'd never been before. What if another customer got angry? What if I were not so *lucky* next time? I couldn't stop my mind from obsessing on the possibilities. I was going quite crazy with the compulsion to think about it.

I needed calm, and the only way I knew to get it was the opium.

Ms. Dixie had discouraged her girls from using drugs at The Orpheum; years ago, she'd experienced first-hand their habit-forming nature. She didn't want her girls falling into the same powdered sink-hole. But one afternoon in mid-summer, I felt ants crawling just under the surface of my skin. Prickly, tickly, crawly itchiness all over me. I wanted to escape my own body. I finally left the house to go for a walk, foolishly believing I might be able to cure my jitters with some physical exertion. I let the front door bang closed behind me, and made my way down the dusty sidewalk of Emma Street.

As I neared a house called The Palace, I thought I might pass the time by visiting Chastity, a friend I'd made while waiting in line at Linder's one day last year. I'd immediately liked her entertaining sense of humor. After all, a prostitute with the name *Chastity*? Ha! I couldn't believe I'd heard her correctly! And as her name suggested, her demeanor was no less rebellious and unique.

My one hesitation for stopping to visit was the dread of dealing with their horrible madame, May-something-or-other. But I needed the distraction, so I knocked on the door. Of course, as my knuckles rapped on the wood, I couldn't know that visiting her would be my curse.

I sat in her room and laughed more than I had in many weeks, entertained by her quick wit and playfulness. She cheered my depressed spirit. But even as we chatted and joked, the tiny bugs still crawled just under my flesh, the itchy sensation unnerving me until I had to admit my suffering to her.

"Well Miss Somber," she replied. "No one ever said you had to *stay* somber, did they?" Chastity asked, rising from her chair and walking to her bureau. "Have you ever heard people say that you need a hair from the dog that bit you? Well, that means you need a little *medicine* to take the jitters away," she said, as she took a pipe from the drawer.

"Oh, no," I answered right away, shaking my head. "I don't smoke opium. I'm quite afraid of not being able to stop once I start. I don't want to become addicted," I added, quite naively.

"But Miss Somber," she said, shaking her head and smiling with a mixture of condescension and pity, "don't you realize? You already are!"

Her words hit me like a cold, hard slap to my face. *Already addicted?* I'd been so diligent in not using the drug; I'd tried so hard through the years! *How could I be addicted?*

"The laudanum's practically the same thing," Chastity said. "I know you didn't *mean* to become dependent on it, but from what you're sayin,' you most certainly are."

I realized what she said was true. I hadn't been the same since before my attack, and I craved the tranquility the laudanum had given me. Now I was living in a continuous state of panic that I couldn't figure out. Until now. Defeat pressed itself down upon my shoulders. "Maybe I could smoke it just once, just to get me over this skittishness," I answered in a hopeful tone, even with the certain knowledge that I was giving in to it.

"You'll be fine," Chastity told me. "Just lay down on the chaise, sideways on your hip. That's the best position to use the pipe - it's easiest to rest the end on the edge of the chaise, 'cause it's so long."

I laid on my side, as instructed, holding the pipe to my mouth while she lit it. I inhaled as best I could, and suffered through quite a fit of coughing. But once my lungs became acquainted with the sweet smoke, it was quite enjoyable. I soon felt better than I'd ever felt in my life, even *before* the attack. The smoke worked quicker than the laudanum ever had. My fears seemed to melt into nothing, my jitters disappearing into my past.

From that day on, I couldn't do without the pipe. The next day, I visited Chastity again. My body craved what she had for me. My mind needed it, my whole being, it seemed. I honestly couldn't help myself.

I began to need the smoke more and more, and Chastity suggested a way to pay for the expense. I was in a state of lost inhibitions when Chastity convinced me to perform in The Circus with her. I'd heard about it from other girls, but could never fully imagine it. It sounded outrageous and repulsive, not what a prostitute with any self-respect would engage in. But Chastity assured me it was akin to performing in a play. The erotic pleasure was all pretend, just for the audience. She told me to think of myself as an actress, giving a performance that would forever be scorched into the minds of the men who watched it. Customers who enjoyed the entertainment stayed at The Palace longer, and left very large tips.

"Somber, we'll just smoke our peace pipe before we go on, and the rest will come quite naturally," Chastity assured me.

I performed in The Palace Circus three times before Ms. Dixie discovered my moonlighting. She knew I wasn't the same girl she'd guided and nurtured at The Orpheum. She grew quite concerned about the cycle she saw playing out in my demeanor - anxious and discouraged before my afternoon walk, and quite the opposite after I returned. The look of my eyes had changed, and I had a continual struggle with the dryness in my mouth and nose.

Ms. Dixie was so troubled, she decided to follow me on one of my daily outings. She watched me enter The Palace through the back door, unsure of my intentions. She returned to The Orpheum and made inquiries of those she knew at The Palace, thus discovering my dependency on the white powder. Although I'd needed the laudanum to help me bear the pain of my recovery, she still felt partially responsible for my current state, and knew she had to act.

That night when I returned to The Orpheum, feeling as if all were right in my world, Dixie came to my room with three other girls.

"Somber, I won't even bother to ask where you go every afternoon, or what you've been doing. I already know. I've come to tell you that your opium use must stop. It will be painful, but only for a while," Dixie told me.

I tried to deny my use of the drug, but she was deaf to my words, as if I hadn't even spoken. Dixie proceeded to tell me what she was going to do, even though against my will. It wasn't a request.

"We're going to make sure you stay away from the opium until your body no longer needs it. I'm so, so sorry to say, the only way to do that is to keep you in this room, until your body is no longer dependent. I'm so sorry," she said softly, shaking her head with the empathy of one who'd been through it.

While I'd been gone that day, Ms. Dixie had installed a lock on the outside of my bedroom door. When she left, I heard the loud, almost thunderous, turn of the key as she left me to begin my suffering.

For five days, my body lapsed into a terrible state of illness, as if the flu had invaded every ounce of my flesh and would never loosen its grip. Slowly, the sickness began to subside and I foolishly thought I was over the worst of it. But then my brain became infected with such depression and anxiety that I thought I would go mad. I banged on my door for someone to help me, for someone to let me out of the dark hole in which I'd been buried alive. I banged so hard for so long that my knuckles and the palms of my hands turned an odd shade of violet. But Dixie had instructed the girls to ignore my cries for mercy, to just tune-out my pleadings and the sound of my fists beating my wooden cell door. As the house shook from my screams and pounding, they just went on about their business. They surely had nerves of steel.

I soon came to the conclusion that to end my suffering, I had to end my life. But Dixie had foreseen this as well, had removed everything I could use for this purpose. She knew all too well of the despondency that came over me as my body rid itself of its dependency.

I vacillated between screaming fits filled with anger and venom, and overwhelming loneliness, filled with tears of the hollow pain that filled my chest. I had no other options but to let this morbid cycle play out, until I had no more screams to shout or tears to cry. After almost two weeks of being kept as a prisoner, I was finally able to shed the white chain that had bound me.

After two weeks, I was finally free. Ms. Dixie had saved me from myself, and to her I will be forever grateful.

Chapter 22

Elaine

July 3, 2011

I now know what I'm going to write about: Prostitution in Dallas in the early twentieth century.

What I've been able to research so far has been so extremely interesting; I yearn to get my hands on more information, and what I've been able to find, I can't stop reading. Even after the North won The Civil War, and slavery of Blacks was abolished, there was still another form of slavery being practiced in the early twentieth century - what was referred to as *white slavery*. Young girls were tricked into prostitution, or even kidnapped into the profession. Some bordellos were above-board, hiring girls who willingly wanted to enter *the life*. Like Eliza Darling. But other houses made use of procurers, men who secured working girls for an establishment, by whatever means possible. Young girls from poor families were promised positions of maidservant or house-girl at a high-end *resort,* and were told that, in addition to room and board, they would earn wages of two to three dollars a week. Many were foreign-born, just immigrated to the United States, in desperate need of a position to earn money for food and lodging. Some were friendless girls, having no family and no support system, essentially starving on the streets. They were happy to find solid positions, even traveling many miles away from their families, only to find her place of employment a prison, on quite a physical level. On arrival, she had no choice but to remain, already indebted to the procurer for her traveling expenses, and having no money with which to escape her new surroundings. If she were lucky, she would arrive at an upper-scale resort, with fine furnishings, nice clothes to wear, and plenty of good food to eat.

But many poor girls weren't that fortunate.

There existed the prostitution tenements in the poorer parts of the red-light districts. Horrible houses whose rooms were actually small cells called cribs, with bars across the windows, and doors which remained locked until a customer turned the key to enter. Sometimes, up to two hundred and fifty girls in each tenement were kept as caged property, almost like animals. Poor working men would stroll the hallways, looking through windows in the locked doors until they found a girl who met their fancy. It was like touring an animal shelter, viewing the creatures on display, as they deliberated over which one could give them the most pleasure for their money. Turning the key in the door-lock gave them power over another human being, fueled by the sexual fire they'd brought with them. In the daytime, these men might toil at the mercy of an overbearing employer, but after nightfall they were the all-important masters at the crib house. It was they who were in control for the fleeting moments when a girl behind a locked door would do their every bidding, as long as the fee was paid.

The human chattel kept on display in these cages were scantily dressed, not only to appeal to their male customers, but to minimize the risk of escape. What young girl would run into the street dressed only in a thin kimono which left nothing to the imagination? Many crib inmates performed services for up to thirty men in a day, a fee of fifty-cents charged for whatever pleasure could be given in such a short time.

My fists clench in knotted anger as I read about the horror of the tenements.

My novel will be written about crib whores. I'm compelled to tell the story of their suffering, when most of the country believed that slavery was over. Slavery was *not* over - it just took the shape of a different monster, one made up of greed and sex combined. Greed for money is bad enough, but when fueled by sexual desires, it combusts in a firestorm of arrogance and power. Throughout history, wars have been fought because of sex; the magnetic pull of sexual attraction has dethroned kings, and felled the greatest of men. Sex and greed together are a formidable pair.

The crib-masters were devoid of kindness and concern for their fellow man, slavers of the worst kind. I'd never known of this part of our history, happening right under our noses. It was too risque for history books, never mentioned in school. And yet, I've driven down the very downtown street on which these warehouses of torture were located. *Can it be happening still? In the bowels of society, where middle-class citizens would never dare to let their thoughts wander?*

I continue to visit the library archives, and research as many books as I can find. There don't exist many first-hand accounts of the lives of these women, many not even knowing how to read and write. Eliza Darling's diary has still been the best source of information. I spend an entire day with it at the library copying machine, and now have the entire thing sitting on my desk. I catch myself laying my hands on top of its pages, as if I can pull inspiration right through Eliza's words, a sort of time-altered osmosis.

I close my eyes and will Eliza Darling to let me understand what it was like to be a prostitute. I rub my silver thimble, my charm from the past.

And once again the room is deathly still and silent.

Chapter 23

Mamie

July 5, 1907

Mamie woke earlier than usual, feeling like she hadn't slept much. July Fourth had been particularly busy at The Palace. She'd always heard that people celebrated the country's independence with picnics and fireworks, but she'd never actually attended any of these festivities - the managers at the mill never thought working-class people needed to waste their time on foolishness that didn't earn them their bread-and-butter. And while it was true that employees at the mill were people, just like the management, and would appreciate a rare respite from their labors, they welcomed even more the extra pay that working through the holiday would bring. After all, food on the table was more important than celebrating the freedom that most didn't even feel they really had. Freedom was only a word to most, not an actual state of being.

Mamie rolled over in her bed, and found herself staring at a very thin, young girl, sitting in a chair close to the bedroom door. Her skin was a light brown, the color of warm caramel, with hair the color of chestnuts. Mamie wondered what race she was - she was too brown to be a white girl, but too light to be a Mexican. And she certainly wasn't a Colored. Mamie guessed she had to have at least some Mexican in her, but she'd never known anyone who was a mix of two races, so she wasn't sure.

The girl said nothing, and was so still Mamie wasn't even sure she was breathing. Mamie then looked toward Candace's bed, and saw her prone form under the coverlet, the pillow over her head. More than likely, Candace would hear nothing of any conversation going on in the room. She generally slept as if she hadn't slept for days. Her nights were full of men and alcohol and opium or cocaine. She had to recover during the daytime.

"Hello," Mamie whispered to the girl, but received no response. She wondered if maybe the girl was hard of hearing, like herself. "My name's Honey," she said, the name still feeling quite foreign on her tongue.

The girl shifted slightly in her chair, and looked down at the floor, as if she were scared to move any more than absolutely necessary, for fear of a scolding, or worse. "My name is Rosa," she finally answered, still looking at her very-worn boots. Mamie saw that not only did they have scuffs and holes, but her dress looked as if it had been plucked right out of a pile of rags. She'd never seen such a tattered garment. Mamie's mill-clothes may have been worn and weathered, but at least they hadn't been full of holes. Mamie had no idea who the girl was, or why she was in her room, but she looked so forlorn that Mamie felt she had to offer her what comfort she could.

"Are you tired?" asked Mamie, and the girl nodded. Mamie walked to her. "Well, you best rest now while you can," she told her, taking her hand and leading her to the empty bed.

Rosa removed her boots, and lay down on the mattress, fully clothed. Mamie looked around the room and could see no valise which might contain Rosa's belongings. She guessed Rosa had come to be here the same as she had, as a last and desperate resort. Rosa laid her head on the pillow, facing upwards, looking at the ceiling. Her arms lay at her sides, and she hadn't even bothered to cover herself up. How strange, thought Mamie, as she raised the coverlet, and pulled it over Rosa.

Mamie had never thought of herself as outgoing, but in comparison to Rosa, she felt quite strong. Although she herself was new to *the life*, Mamie felt a compelling need to take care of this girl, who was no older than she, and maybe even younger. Of course, it was almost like one child taking care of another, but

Mamie hadn't thought of herself as a child since coming to The Palace.

Rosa's eyes closed and she was immediately drawn into sleep.

Mamie lay back down in her bed; it appeared most in the house were still asleep, and there would not be much to do if she rose early. So she didn't. That was one of the benefits of life at The Palace - not having to rise before the sun came up, or even before it was high up in the sky. Mamie wasn't sure she'd ever feel totally comfortable sleeping while the sun was shining brightly through the window, but at least she wouldn't have to wake up before the day birds.

For some reason, anxiety crept into Mamie's thoughts. She didn't know if it was Rosa's arrival, or something else that had nestled itself just under the outer layer of her brain. A peculiar restlessness invaded her privacy, and her thoughts carried her back to her outing with Eliza Darling at Lake Cliff Park. It had been quite an odd visit, almost like a fantasy manufactured by some internal need. She truly liked Eliza. The woman was most friendly and agreeable, and seemed to care about Mamie's welfare. She certainly wasn't the enemy that Ms. May had made her out to be. After all, Eliza and Ms. Dixie had walked in her boots, and were well aware of the risks and dangers. Eliza most of all. Mamie unconsciously shuddered when she thought of the horrible scar that had ravaged half of Eliza's pretty face.

Mamie knew perfectly well it was a dangerous job. She didn't *want* to be a whore; had *never wanted* to be one. What respectable girl in their right mind did? One day you were respectable, and then your mill foreman had his way with you just because he could, and the next day you were tainted. Maybe no one else knew, but *you* knew. You then decide that if you're going to be defiled, you might as well get paid for it. You might as well give your brother the benefit of your struggle.

Ms. May constantly complained about the social purity reformers who referred to prostitutes as *feeble-minded,* having no self-control over their sexual desires and immoral choices.

Bally rot, thought Mamie. Why should *she* be considered feeble-minded? Who was free from all mistakes, or poor choices, or transgressions? At least prostitutes weren't devious in their dealings - everyone knew what their job was. There was no deception.

But Eliza Darling was proof enough that the profession had its dangers and disgraces.

And what of the mysterious prediction made by the Swami from India? Mamie was covered in goose pimples at the thought. At first, she'd thought he was just a con man, humoring carnival-goers, and stealing their nickels at the same time. But the crystal ball actually glowed, the peculiar light reflecting images, as if they were actually floating inside. The ball was filled with magic. Mamie had been both afraid and mesmerized. She'd never before believed in psychic abilities.

But now she wasn't so sure.

Why did the Swami seem almost afraid when he told Eliza of her gift?

Eliza was eternal, *one of a thousand lives.* She would live over and over, and would be visited by her future. Mamie had never heard of such a thing, and certainly didn't know what to make of it. How could it possibly happen?

Mamie thought of what it would be like for a soul to be immortal, and wondered if it could be true? If it were really possible? She finally fell asleep thinking of another, future life, filled with happiness and innocence. A life in which she lived with virtue. *Wouldn't it be wonderful to live without shame? Wouldn't the world be a much better place without the Mr. Duffy's and Ms. May's to steal one's innocence away?*

Chapter 24

The Story of Rosa Robles

Fifteen Months Earlier

Rosa Robles was not quite thirteen years old, and small for her age. Her figure hadn't yet transformed into that of a woman. She was still quite thin, with no breasts to speak of, and her hips had not yet taken shape. Although she worked alongside her family in the fields of South Texas, both planting and harvesting crops at farms all along the Mexican border, her skin was not yet weathered, the light brown only made richer by the sun's rays. Rosa was the prettiest girl in the fields, her mama had always told her. Surely her future held more than planting seeds and picking cotton. Surely she was destined for something better.

Rosa and her brothers were different from most of the other migrant workers - her mama was White, and her daddy was Mexican. The Whites didn't take too kindly to a Mexican corrupting a young white girl by marrying her, and the Mexicans didn't see why one of their own would need to dilute the lineage with pale blood. But there it was - they'd fallen in love when mama was only fourteen, and she'd run away with her daddy. Rosa and her brothers had skin the color of creamed coffee, auburn- brown hair instead of black, and hazel eyes instead of brown.

In one of her normal fourteen-hour days, she could pick two-hundred pounds of cotton, at least if nothing slowed her down, like the cuts she sometimes got on her hands or feet from the dry, sharp cotton bolls, her skin just splitting right open. The gloves her family owned were reserved for her papa and brothers, so her fingers and wrists constantly wore the proof of her labor. And of course, they never wore shoes in the summer.

That was an extravagance her migrant family could in no way afford, reserving shoes for the colder winter months. Sometimes the hard, shriveled bolls would fall from the stalks and just sit on the ground, waiting to skewer any unsuspecting bare foot that might carelessly step on them. Rosa had learned to watch where she stepped.

To make the days pass faster, and take her mind away from the brutal sun constantly beating down on them, Rosa liked to invent contests between herself and her two brothers, one eleven and one fourteen. She loved to show them up by picking more pounds than they did, taking pride in her victories, especially since she was a girl, and one who had no gloves at that.

One late summer day, during cotton harvest season, a White man came to visit the foreman of the farm at which the Robles family was working. He wore expensive-looking clothes, the chain of his gold watch hanging from the pocket in his vest. There was no dirt under his fingernails, and no dust covering his countenance. He most definitely didn't work the farms. He sat with the foreman around an empty beer-barrel table just outside the barn, drinking beer and smoking cigars.

Rosa had been in the field since sun-up, but had returned to the barn several times that day to haul in the bags of cotton she'd picked. When she first saw the fancy man, she was getting a drink. As she lifted the ladle to her lips, she chanced a glance at the foreman and his acquaintance. It wasn't often that she came in contact with city people. Her world was filled with barns and dirt and cotton, and outside of this world, she was just plain invisible. Noticing the White man staring at her, Rosa quickly returned her gaze to the water pail. But she just couldn't help another quick flit of her eyes. The same mustached face under the same black hat was still looking at her. A mix of fear and excitement filled her chest as she felt the heat of self-consciousness rise into her cheeks. She returned the ladle to the bucket, picked up her sack, then turned and walked back out into the field. But she could still feel his eyes on her, his gaze piercing her cloak of invisibility.

The next day when Rosa brought her second sack to the barn, she saw that the man was back, just standing in the yard, with his arms crossed over his chest. Watching Rosa, studying her. She wasn't much of a sight - barefoot, with dirt covering her body and the light cotton work-dress she wore every day. She was ashamed to be seen by a man in such fancy clothes, and was quite uncomfortable with this new emotion. *Why does this bother me?* She tried not to think about him, and went back to the task of beating her brothers yet again.

Later that night, when the Robles family could no longer see what they were doing in the darkness of the fields, they finished for the day and returned to their small cabin for their usual supper of beans and tortillas. During dinner, Rosa noticed that her mother was considering her in a strange way, almost as if she were seeing her as a different person. *Why is everyone looking at me today?* she wondered.

Later, as they were cleaning up their dishes, Rosa's mama tenderly put her hand on Rosa's arm. "Rosa, come sit. I need to speak with you."

Rosa's stomach had butterflies and June bugs flying around in it. *Did I do something wrong? Is that why the fancy man was talking to the foreman? Is that why mama needs to talk to me now?*

Rosa's mother held both of Rosa's hands in hers. "Rosa," she began slowly, "Senor Gonzales had a visit from a man today, from up North." *And yesterday, thought Rosa, but she didn't interrupt.* "This man told Senor Gonzales that you caught his eye. He made Senor Gonzales an offer."

What kind of offer? A sense of dread began snaking its way into Rosa's head, as if it were an evil serpent.

"Rosa," her mother said, "the man from town, Senor Smith, has offered to take you up North, to Dallas, so you can attend school. He's from a school for girls, and it's his job to find girls working on the farms, and then make arrangements for them to go to school. It's the school's mission to give farm girls from the country an education."

Rosa listened to her mother, but didn't understand what she was trying to say.

"Rosa, he wants to take you to the school. You wouldn't have to work in the fields any more. Maybe you could become a school teacher," she said, pausing. "Or maybe even the wife of someone important, who would take care of you."

Rosa couldn't believe what she was hearing. "But mama, I don't want to leave you. I'd rather stay and pick cotton." Her fear was now overtaking everything else; she didn't care about being more educated, or marrying a rich man. She just wanted to stay with her family. She squeezed her mother's rough hands as if they were a life-line.

"Rosa, your papa and I don't want you to pick cotton all your life. We want something better for you than what we have," her mama said, tears filling her eyes. She didn't want to give her baby girl to a stranger, didn't want to do without her every minute of every day. Her heart was nearly bursting at the thought of losing her, but she knew it might be Rosa's only chance to leave the brutal life of farm work behind. "You have to go, Rosa," she said quietly.

Rosa cried herself to sleep, thinking of her brothers, and her mama and papa. *I don't want to be a teacher!* she insisted to herself over and over, the mantra that finally sent her into a fitful sleep.

The next day, Rosa packed what few possessions she owned into a small duffel bag:

An extra dress.

Undergarments.

A hairbrush decorated with mother-of-pearl, handed down from her grandmother.

But not her doll.

Rosa resisted the strong urge to take her childhood companion with her. It would be comforting to have, but she was beginning a new life, leaving the childhood that she'd known behind. She considered this omission a symbol of her growing up. She had to be strong and brave, or she might just go run and hide where no one could find her.

She tearfully kissed her mama and papa goodbye, and hugged her brothers. No one knew when they would see each other again; it might be never. She and her mama cried freely; the men and boys tried to control their emotions, but the task was proving more difficult than they expected. Rosa was everyone's sunshine, and now she was leaving them. Their days would now be filled with a gray monotony, the light taken away by a man from up north.

Mr. Smith and Rosa rode in a simple horse-drawn carriage, more of a fancy covered wagon than anything else. The trip to Dallas would take almost four days. Mr. Smith sat next to Rosa, and appraised her now and again. Rosa just tried to keep her head and eyes turned toward the floorboard. She was too afraid to meet his gaze, and too afraid to speak. She pretended she was hiding inside herself, and was invisible. Maybe if she didn't move or make a sound, her presence in the wagon would just evaporate. Mr. Smith didn't speak to her, and that was just fine.

The wagon stopped at several different farms, picking up three more girls for the journey. They appeared just as worried and scared as Rosa. No one spoke to the others, choosing to sit in silence, as if not talking they could somehow pretend they weren't being taken by wagon to a new life in a big city, without their families.

In the middle of the fourth day, the wagon finally reached Dallas. Hardly any of the girls had seen towns containing more than two or three buildings, so the bustling Dallas downtown was quite a shock to their senses. So many people crowding the streets, and so many big buildings. Rosa was amazed to see the motorcars rolling down the streets, inventions she'd only heard about, but never seen with her own eyes. The city was both amazing and frightening.

At last, the wagon stopped in front of a four-story building made of dirty-gray brick. The front door of nondescript, weathered wood wore patches, and splotches of mud covered most of the lower half, as if all the muddy boots in the city had gotten carried away when stepping over its threshold. Trash lined the sides of the grimy street - pages of newspaper and the unwanted discards of society. Horse manure had piled up on the dirty and neglected pavement, as if waiting indefinitely for stable boys who would never come. And most ominous were the building's windows, like eyes that warned of hardship and destruction. Cracked and broken glass peeked through the metal bars mounted across each window pane. Rosa briefly wondered if the bars were to keep the undesirables out or the students in. A thread of fear and worry again twined its way through her slight frame.

There were no signs of any kind posted in front of the building. Nothing whatsoever to indicate this was a school. It was nothing like Rosa had imagined a school would look like. The other girls appeared to think the same thing as they studied the structure's weary exterior.

"OK, girls," Senor Smith said with a smirk and a wink, "we have arrived at your *new school.*" The way he said the words made Rosa shiver. It was as if he'd made a joke that only he understood. He seemed to think it funny. The fancy man stepped down from the carriage and made his way to the door. "You stay put now, and I'll be back as soon as I've made the arrangements." Then he was gone, through that beat-up door as if it had swallowed him.

What arrangements did he have to make? wondered Rosa. Hadn't they already been made? According to her mama, it was just a matter of finding the right girls to benefit from the wonderful opportunity. The idea of jumping from the carriage and escaping Mr. Smith and the school altogether briefly flitted through her mind, but just as quickly vanished. She had nowhere to go; she knew no one. She would starve if she didn't stay right where she was. What other choice did she have? Rosa tried to smile at the other girls and await further instructions. After all, they were all in this together.

Rosa's intuition was accurate. What she couldn't see from her seat in the wagon was the transfer of bills from the proprietor of this place into Mr. Smith's greedy hands. He counted it to make sure he had been paid his due, and once satisfied, stuffed it into his fancy suit pocket with a wide grin of yellowed teeth. "Nice doin' bid'ness with you," he told the woman who'd handed him the money, then turned on the heels of his dusty boots and walked back through the door to the wagon.

"OK girls, you can get down from the wagon. Your *rooms* are ready. You each get your own. Now ain't *that* nice!" he announced.

Surely he couldn't mean there was a separate room for each girl! Why, Rosa had never heard of such a thing. Not only had she slept in the same room with her brothers, but in the same bed as well. Maybe the school wasn't as bad on the inside as it looked on the outside. After all, looks could be deceiving.

The girls jumped out of the wagon, and were handed their small bags. It was almost impossible to maneuver around the horse droppings, which were everywhere, but after many careful, well-placed steps, they finally reached the door, which opened with a slow creak. The entry was dark, the gloom on the other side of the threshold quickly eclipsing the one remaining ray of hope Rosa had felt just a minute before.

A large woman stood just inside, her heavy chest almost spilling from the bodice of her dirty red dress. Her unwashed hair was piled haphazardly in a limp knot on top of her head, and the sight of her missing teeth when she smiled was Rosa's confirmation that this woman was no school mistress.

As soon as the girls were all inside, the woman slammed the door, and flipped the deadbolt into place. "Well now girlies, welcome to yer new *school*," she croaked in a gravelly voice, followed by a terrifying cackle that brought tears to Rosa's eyes. "Let me show ya to yer rooms. Yer gonna love it here, if I do say," she said with an almost toothless grin. Rosa felt her nerves twitch, her body on high alert.

As they walked through the dirty foyer and up two flights of stairs, the small group had been joined by three men, none of the girls realizing their presence behind them until they'd reached the third-floor landing. As the girls proceeded down the hallway, they were accosted by the terrifying reality of their futures.

The corridor was floored with dirty wooden boards, covered with the mud and muck of who knew how many people over a period of who knew how many years. As they walked down the dim passage, the truth screamed out at Rosa. The doors on either side of them were closed, their small windows adorned with metal bars in lieu of glass. A large keyhole sat like a dare under each doorknob. The building looked more like what Rosa imagined a prison to be, instead of a school.

Rosa didn't know what this place was, but she knew it was no school.

She looked at the other girls walking beside her, and wondered if they'd yet realized they'd been brought here under false pretenses; that their families had been tricked? Was there anything they could now do? Would they get more than a few feet if they turned and ran as fast as their thin legs could carry them? The cold hand of fear tightly gripped Rosa's chest.

"Here is yer new room, girlie," the woman in the red dress said to Rosa with a wave of her hand, giving her a slight push through the doorway. "Time to start yer schoolin'!" Before she knew it, the door was slammed behind her, and a swift turn of the key locked her into the nightmare. Rosa felt the terror rise up into her throat. *What is this place?*

Mama, mama, oh mama! I want to come home!

Rosa looked around the room. There was a thin, dirty mattress on the bare floor, with a threadbare coverlet and small pillow on top. A white washbasin with a chipped edge sat in the corner on a small rickety table. A simple gas lantern sat beside the washbasin, a chamber pot beneath. There was nothing else.

Rosa walked to the window, the cracked glass grimy from a hundred years of neglect, the left- bottom pane totally missing. Metal bars stretched from the very top sill to the very bottom. *Did I see this very window when I looked up from the street?* she wondered. The dirt and grease encrusted on the glass prevented much sun from entering; only the missing pane allowed any light at all to pass into the room, a small square of it present on the floorboards, as if reminding Rosa that one solitary patch of sunlight was all the freedom she had left.

All Rosa could think to do was sit on the mattress and pray, the tears escaping from her beautiful hazel eyes, making round, wet splotches on the dirty floor beneath her.

Chapter 25

The Diary of Eliza Darling

July 6, 1907

I'm happy to finally have a chance to write about what's been swimming around in my head since my visit with Mamie. What happened on Wednesday was both wondrous and frightening. During our outing to Lake Cliff Park, Mamie and I visited a Swami from India, who called himself Aseem. I wasn't sure what to think about him - whether he was sincere or just a ruse for amusement's sake. Mamie was convinced his sole purpose was to relieve us of our coins, but I wasn't so certain. Maybe it was something in his eyes, reflecting a certain magical light from the glass ball. I don't think I can accurately describe my feelings when I looked at him. It was as if I were entranced.

Was I just gullible? I suppose I'm not certain. But I was drawn to this man - I almost felt I knew him. As if we were connected somehow.

One of a thousand lives.

He'd told me I was one of only a chosen few. I would live infinite lives, my soul surviving through the ages. He warned that soon, my future would intertwine with my present. I am still in shock at this revelation. I know I could just as easily dismiss the Swami's pronouncements as nonsense, mere entertainment for a carnival-goer wanting to believe in magic, looking for excitement. And I suppose, too easily willing to let go of a nickel. But there was something about him, and the glass ball, that I can't ignore. Instead of just looking into my eyes, he seemed to be looking right into my very thoughts. I have never felt that sensation before, and have a peculiar trust that he is real.

Who had I been before? Was I a woman or a man? Where did I live, and what year did I live there? I was daunted with the sheer wonder and intrigue of it.

And Lord knows, I wouldn't even begin to know how to envision myself in the future. *My future will reveal itself.* I've tried to determine if I've felt peculiar lately, but can't put my finger on a thing. And I've thought about the physical object that connects my present with my future. As I write these words, I am convinced - it is the thimble! I can feel the certainty of it through the prickles in my skin that move right down to my bone.

The future now possesses my favorite thimble. A physical part of me.

Will the future visit again, and how often? Will other things be taken?

Just reading these deranged thoughts on paper almost leads me to believe I'm going mad. Surely if anyone else were to read this, they would have me committed to the sanitarium!

But I know in my heart I'm not crazed. It's as if an eternal puzzle of the universe has just been revealed.

I wish I could talk to Ms. Dixie about this current turn of events. I can't get it out of my head, and feel so honored to be carrying this special gift. I refuse to even consider it might instead be a curse. However, discussing my fortune reading with anyone would cause either much amusement or much concern, not to mention the reaction I'd receive upon confessing my belief in it, a trip straight to the asylum. Any sane person would think me delirious, maybe suffering a long-dormant aftershock from my attack.

The only other person who knows of these prophesies is Mamie Carroll.

Mamie first thought the Swami to be a fraud. Does she now believe? Or did she return home thinking me twice as foolish as when I first gave up my hard-earned coin?

Now back to my initial purpose in going to Lake Cliff. I don't think my message was received by Mamie as intended. She saw my scar, and was concerned and aggrieved for me, but apparently not deterred. To a young and tired girl whose life has already worn her down, the danger isn't as real as the money she can send home to her family. I truly understand. But there *is* a better way. I'm living proof of it. I have no plans to give up on that girl anytime soon. Maybe she could visit The Johnson Home, and see what a wonderful place it is.

Could I could somehow arrange for her to see her brother? The Johnson Home hosts a Labor Day picnic for its residents, and their family and friends. Yes, it would be the perfect time to invite them. Perfect.

Chapter 26

Becoming Friends

July 30, 1907

The days came and went, Mamie staying up until four or five in the morning, almost until the sun came up, and then sleeping well past noon. As she acclimated herself to the routine of The Palace, she found that sleeping with the sun shining outside wasn't so difficult after all.

Mamie found herself wondering quite a bit about the new girl, Rosa. Her feelings of protectiveness towards her had been somewhat stifled by Candace's complaint that their room was barely big enough for two of them, much less three. She hadn't been very agreeable to even sharing a room with Mamie, so she certainly threw a tantrum when Ms. May tried to squeeze-in another girl. Ms. May relented, and moved Rosa and her bed to another room on another floor the very next day.

Mamie suspected that one of Rosa's new roommates, either Tawny or Belle, must have helped the poor girl fix herself up, much as Candace had done for her on her first day. At first, with the way she'd been dressed and the thinness of her tiny frame, Rosa had almost looked like a street urchin. Mamie wondered where she'd come from; maybe she *had* been living on the streets.

Mamie was surprised to see Rosa on her first night in the parlor - she hadn't even looked like the same girl. Her hair had been curled and pinned up, with coloring applied to her cheeks and eyes and lips. The girl had been dressed in a silk kimono, not quite transparent, her slender body hidden by the billowy material.

Mamie had tried to sit by her that first night, so that she might offer her friendship, and any help the girl might want or need. But almost immediately, Rosa was taken upstairs by a man who'd always chosen Candace in the past; Candace was nowhere to be seen. Mamie wondered if she were ill, but she'd seemed fine earlier. Maybe Ms. May had given her the night off, which didn't happen frequently, so was indeed a rare treat.

The next night, before Mamie could even approach Rosa, she was once again whisked away upstairs by a pair of men who were known to be quite rough in their sexual pleasures. Mamie had always been glad that Candace usually serviced them, and she was shocked to see Rosa between them, disappearing up the stairs. But *that* night, Candace hadn't been ill, or enjoying a night of leisure. She'd been right there in the parlor with them. The men had spoken with Ms. May as soon as they'd entered, and were led immediately to Rosa. Mamie noticed that Candace rose from her seat when she'd seen them enter, shock swiftly transforming her face when they were taken to Rosa instead. Candace wore an angry glare as she made her way to Ms. May. It was certain they had words, but then Candace returned to the sofa, obviously not mollified by whatever Ms. May had told her, but apparently not having recourse to change the outcome.

Over the next weeks, it became clear that Rosa was the first to be chosen for an evening, and usually by the clients who were known for their harsh sexual demands.

"That brown slut has no business bein' in a house as nice as this," Candace hissed to herself one night as they were getting dressed for the evening. Mamie hadn't known too many Mexicans - the mill employed mainly White people. The Mexicans and Coloreds were usually hired for more dirty work - cleaning stables, sweeping floors, and picking crops. But even so, Mamie had nothing against them. Although admittedly different from the other girls at The Palace, Mamie thought nothing much of Rosa working there with them. Her mama had taught her that people were just people, no matter the color of their skin, or the job they set about doing every day.

But to Candace, Rosa was an atrocity. "Why a man would want to poke such skin and bones is beyond me. The little bitch has skin the color of dirt, for God's sake. That little whore should go back to the cribs where she came from," she announced to her mirror, pursing her lips as she applied more color than usual.

Mamie didn't understand.

"What are *the cribs*, Candace?" she asked hesitantly, for Candace had such a short temper, she generally didn't like to be bothered with silly questions that a girl with any sense should already know the answers to.

Candace turned around with a look of disbelief. "In Frogtown, down around Wood Street, those crumblin' old brick buildings. Where they keep whores in cells until someone unlocks their door to get a quick poke or suck. *Jesus* girl, where in the hell have you been, not knowin' about crib whores? They're the filthy sort, only bathin' once a week, if that, and after seein' twenty or thirty men in a day!" she answered with impatient disgust, shaking her head. "Nothin' dirtier than a crib whore. And now we not only have one, she's doin' more men than anyone else. She even has an act in the Circus!"

Mamie's chest filled with the willies as she thought of the Circus. So far she hadn't been asked to perform in it, and she hoped she never would be. Doing a man's bidding in the privacy of a bedroom was bad enough, but doing the vulgar things she'd seen, and on stage in front of a room full of people, was totally different. Thinking of it made Mamie's blood run cold.

And Rosa was already performing in it?

Candace put the finishing touches on her face, and spritzed perfume behind her ears, and on her breasts and wrists, still shaking her head and muttering as she looked in the mirror.

"*Nothin'* worse than a crib whore." Then she turned and left the room, leaving Mamie to her thoughts.

Rosa had been a crib whore. She'd never heard of *cribs*, and until this moment, hadn't understood that the brothels lining Emma Street were not the dregs at the bottom of society's bottle. From the sound of it, they were the red light district's champagne, while the cribs were its homemade hooch. Mamie didn't understand how so many girls could be kept in such a fashion, and be forced to have sex with twenty or thirty men in one day! The thought made Mamie's stomach turn; she wanted to vomit, thinking of having sex with one man after the other. It revolted her to even consider it.

Mamie soon realized there were classes of prostitutes, just like every other form of life. The *have's* and the *have-not's*. The upper-crust and the lowly. And just like the social classes in the regular world, they didn't hold each other in the best regard.

Mamie was determined to get to know Rosa better. After all, with her past history, and having made an enemy of Candace, the poor girl definitely needed some form of friendship and support.

Mamie's opportunity to speak with Rosa came the next day. After lunch, Rosa was sitting by herself - it seemed that none of the other girls wanted much to do with her. Did they also know she'd been a crib whore? Candace had undoubtedly spread the word. She would make sure Rosa wore her past like a sign posted on her back.

Mamie approached Rosa and sat next to her on the sofa, holding out her hand. "Hi Rosa. Do you remember me? I'm Honey," she offered with a friendly smile. Rosa took her hand, but looked as if she were in a daze; she didn't seem to recognize her. "From your first night here. Remember? You spent your first night in my room."

Rosa considered Mamie more closely, and then squeezed her hand quite slightly, as if not wanting to bruise ripe fruit. "Yes, I remember," she said. "My name is Carmelle now," added Rosa wistfully, almost as an afterthought. "My skin is the color of caramel."

Even though it happened with everyone, and was expected, Mamie was saddened by the thought of Rosa changing her name. "We can share a secret, if you'd like. I'll keep calling you Rosa, and you can call me Mamie. My real name. It will be private, just between the two of us."

When Mamie saw the smile spread across Rosa's face, she knew she'd succeeded in striking up a friendship. "Nice to meet you, Mamie," Rosa answered.

"Remember, I share a room with Candace. She can be brutal, as I'm sure you've noticed. So I'd take care to stay away from her as much as possible," warned Mamie.

"Yes, I've been trying to stay as far away as I can," Rosa said. Almost as an afterthought, but actually in the forefront of her mind, added, "She's made of evil."

Mamie totally agreed.

Several days later, when summer exploded into the extreme heat of August, the girls at The Palace were told they were having a special contingent of businessmen visit from New York and Boston. They would be more sophisticated than their normal customers, even more so than the local political gentry and the North Texas moneybags who normally frequented their establishment. To prepare for the occasion, Ms. May had everyone dress in make-believe, all of them pretending to be someone else. The mocking irony of it wasn't wasted on Mamie. Every single day she felt like she were pretending to be someone else - a prostitute named Honey.

Rosa and Mamie were instructed to dress as very young girls. As disturbing as the intent appeared, the reality was that they *were* young girls. Nevertheless, they adorned themselves with bows and ribbons and frilly dresses, but wore no bloomers or underclothes of any kind underneath. Mamie was quite disconcerted with the understanding of why they were dressed this way - to satisfy the tastes of men who would rather have sex with little girls than with fully grown women. Mamie looked in the mirror and saw what the small girl of her childhood might have looked like, had she not been bartered to the mill. Her long hair fell onto her shoulders in curled ringlets, with large bows pinned to the top of her head. She'd never looked like this before - she'd had none of this finery in her family's home. This was the costume of a well-to-do.

Rosa was almost unrecognizable - the thin waif who had come into the house only weeks earlier now looked healthy and almost aristocratic, how Mamie would imagine a wealthy girl from Spain might appear. No one would've ever guessed that Rosa had been working in the crib tenements only a month before.

Mamie and Rosa were the first of the girls to finish dressing; they waited for the others in the parlor.

"I never wore such fine clothes when I was a little girl," Rosa said almost wistfully, "or the bows. This dress would never have survived cotton-picking. I didn't even wear shoes until the weather got cold, and they were usually the old boots that my brother had worn the year before," she stated, matter-of-factly.

"You were a farm girl?" Mamie asked.

"Yes," Rosa answered. "We traveled all over Texas, picking whatever there was to pick. But mainly cotton. *Before*."

Mamie understood the word *before*. It was the word that separated their current lives from the lives they'd lived with their families. Before they'd seen the ugly side of upright society.

Before they'd become prostitutes. *Before* was on the other side of the line that each had crossed, just a distant memory now.

"Cotton," repeated Mamie. "I worked at the mill, spinning what you picked into thread. We're both children of the cotton boll, just on different ends of the process," Mamie said, the coincidence not as great as one might think, since Texas seemed to revolve around cotton. "Well, I agree that this dress would have gathered a pound of cotton lint in the mill. I don't even think my apron would have saved this finery from being spoiled within ten minutes of working on the spinning machine, maybe even sooner," Mamie replied. "I'd look like a walking cotton puff," she said, looking down at her dress, as a giggle escaped her throat. She hadn't meant to laugh, but the thought of her spinning in that heavily petticoated dress of crinoline and lace was just too amusing.

Then Rosa smiled and laughed as well. "These petticoats are a far cry from the feed bags mama used to make my dresses. This fancy, ruffled skirt wouldn't have fit down the field rows. I'd have to lift them up to my chest just to be able to walk, never mind having any hands for picking," she laughed, as she imagined her brothers looking on in utter shock.

The differences between the two had quickly been replaced with a surprising familiarity that each felt for the other. Mamie considered Rosa, with her light caramel-colored skin and lighter eyes and hair. She couldn't help but ask. "Are you a Mexican?" she ventured, rather bluntly. "Your skin is such a beautiful color; I don't know that I've ever seen a complexion quite that shade before." Mamie meant no offense, and Rosa took none.

"My papa is Mexican, but my mama is a White lady," she answered. This fact was just a normal part of Rosa's life, but Mamie couldn't help but show her surprise at this news, raising her eyebrows and opening her eyes wide.

"I never knew anyone with different-colored parents before," Mamie replied. "I guess I wasn't even sure you could mix the two."

Instead of being offended at Mamie's naiveté, Rosa's giggle turned into an all-out laugh. "Mix the two?" she repeated. "It's not like we're mutt-dogs," she said, but then reconsidered. "Well, all right, maybe it *is* like we're mutt dogs."

Rosa had really never known any different. "People in the city aren't mixed?" she finally asked Mamie in pure innocence.

"Well, I don't rightly know if it *ever* happens. But *I've* never seen it with my own eyes," Mamie answered. "To tell the truth, you're the only girl I've ever known in the Houses to be anything other than white as snow."

Rosa considered this information, and realized she was indeed the only one at The Palace with any color to her skin. She'd never even thought about it before that moment. "At the last place I lived, there were all sorts of girls, but more Mexicans and Coloreds than White girls."

"Candace told me you came from the cribs," Mamie said somewhat hesitantly.

"I never heard that name before," answered Rosa soberly, her prior lightheartedness swallowed up by the memory of it. "I don't know if that's what it was called," she answered. "But it was horrible. I just called it prison."

Prison. Mamie had always thought of the mill as a form of prison. She understood quite well how Rosa felt. But then she considered the fact that the mill was instead an upscale establishment compared to the brutal truth of the crib houses. At least according to Candace.

"Did they really keep your doors locked until a customer came in?" asked Mamie, not yet able to fully envision Rosa's prior circumstances.

Rosa had a pained expression on her face, no doubt from remembering the trauma suffered there. "Yes, they did," she answered quietly. "And there were bars on the windows, and over the windows set in the doors."

"There were windows in the doors?" asked Mamie.

"Yes, that's how the men decided who they wanted to...*visit*. They walked down the halls, looking in all the windows, until they saw a girl they wanted. Then that horrible bitch, Fanny, would give him the key to unlock the door. He'd come in for a few minutes to have his way, then lock the door again when he left. That would happen over and over, all night," she answered. "And sometimes during the day." A cold shiver ran through Rosa as she pictured Fanny and Jimmy walking the halls, the keys on the large ring jingling away, as if they were bells announcing the time of day. Announcing what was expected of them.

"The bars in the windows were there to make sure we didn't try to escape. One poor girl jumped out her window on the third floor. When she reached the ground, her neck twisted clean around, and she died right then and there. Not that Mr. Pilcher or Ms. Fanny, the ones in charge, even gave one care about that girl. It was the police coming they were more afraid of. As it turned out, the police didn't care that much about what happened either. After all, it was just a crumbling old building in the bad part of town. But Pilcher and Fanny were still afraid that the girls would bang on the windows, or yell through the holes in the glass, to try to get their attention." Rosa paused, a sad and mournful look transforming her face. "But I don't know why they were even worried at all; the police never cared what went on in that building," Rosa admitted tearfully, and proceeded to tell her new friend what life had been like for the past eleven months.

Chapter 27

The Crib - Rosa's Tale

The first afternoon at her new *home* Rosa spent laying on her small, thin mattress. She was afraid of what the future held for her. What *was* this place? She knew it wasn't a school; she was a captive, not a student. But what was the purpose? Why was she there?

As the sun finally made its lackluster descent, Rosa heard voices in the hallway, then the jingling of keys. The lock in her door turned with a click. As the door opened with a loud creak, the oily fat woman with few teeth ambled into the room.

"Come on girlie," she said with a nod of her head. "Time fer yer inspection. Don't know why Pilcher agreed to take ya up front without no inspection first. Don't care *if* Mr. Smith was in a hurry. Lotta good it'll do me now if we find somethin' wrong with ya. Not sure what we'd do with ya then. Guess just return ya to Smith and get Pilcher's money back, next time Smith comes through here," Ms. Fanny said, pulling Rosa up by the arm. "Ok girlie, take yer dress off. If ya can even call it a dress," Fanny mocked with a slight laugh. "Don't matter, though. You won't be needin' it no more."

Both confusion and fear slammed into Rosa like a blast of North wind.

What is she going to do with my dress? What does she mean?

"Now take it off, girlie," Fanny commanded, "Let me take a look atcha."

Rosa didn't understand what this woman wanted her to do. Why would she need to take her dress off? It made no sense; Rosa just shook her head back and forth in stunned protest.

"Now, I told ya. I gotta inspect ya to make sure ya don't have no defects. We gave Smith a hunnerd dollars for ya; gotta make sure Pilcher didn't get cheated, though I don't rightly know that yer worth no hunnerd dollars. Too scrawny," Fanny announced with a shake of her head. "Now take it off, or I'm gonna have Jimmy paddle ya. He's just outside the door."

Rosa glanced fearfully at the door, and saw a man partially visible through the doorway. He was swinging some sort of leather tool against his leg, making a swatting sound, constant as a clock ticking down the time. She was afraid. Why did they pay money for her, and why did this woman have to look at her without her dress on? She was trying to be brave, but tears nonetheless escaped from the corners of her eyes, her small lips trembling at the thought of her future.

"I *said* I won't hurt ya," the greasy woman spat in exasperation when she saw that Rosa was crying. "But Jimmy might!" she added, with a phlegmy cackle erupting from her partially- toothless grin. "He already got a little carried away with the other one; had to stripe her legs an' ass. Course she was a-squirmin', an' he missed and got her on the back instead. Ha! That's one girlie who won't be sleepin' on her backside for a while," Fanny said with a giggle.

Rosa's whole body trembled with fear and dread.

"Now take it off!" Fanny screamed impatiently, harshly yanking at the neck of Rosa's dress, the material tearing in a jagged rip, the sound scorching Rosa's ears, as if the fabric of her life had just been torn to ragged pieces.

No! This is my best dress! Screamed Rosa in her brain, her current situation not yet taking hold in her thought process.

"Jimmy, git yer ass in here," Fanny commanded.

When Jimmy entered the room, the wild and crazy look in his eyes told Rosa everything she needed to know. Never mind his unshaven face, his crazy grin of brown and dirty teeth, his clothes the color of mud; his eyes warned Rosa not to provoke him. This was obviously a man who took much pleasure in hurting women. She now saw that the leather object he'd been swatting was a horse quirt. It was quite clear from the way he swung it against his leg that he took delight in using it.

Rosa finally did as she was told, removing her once-best dress, and cotton underpants. She tried to cover herself, modest not only in front of this horrible woman, but especially in front of Jimmy. She'd never undressed in front of anyone other than her mama, and her brothers. And not even in front of them since they'd gotten older. At the sight of her naked body, Jimmy's eyes seemed to bore holes in her vulnerability.

"Git yer hands away from yer body!" Fanny yelled. "How do ya 'spect me to look ya over if yer coverin' the most important parts?"

It took all of Rosa's bravery and determination to lower her arms down to her sides.

"Well, you are a skinny one," Fanny commented, turning Rosa around to look at all angles. "No tits or ass to speak of. Smith picked a young-un, he did. Raise the arms," she said. And Rosa did it. "Now open yer mouth." Rosa again obeyed, while the woman inspected her teeth.

"All righty, go lay down on yer bed an' spread those skinny legs. Gotta make sure ya don't have no case of the drips."

Rosa couldn't believe what this horrible woman was asking her to do. She felt the burning flush of humiliation cover her, as if a veil to hide her nudity and shame. She'd never done such a thing before, for anyone. She didn't even know what *the drips* were, but she was sure she didn't have them. She couldn't make herself move toward the bed; her body just wouldn't go.

"Jimmy," the woman called in exasperation, "help the girl." Fanny's face wore the sour expression of the terminally disappointed and frustrated.

Rosa's entire body shook, but she just couldn't make her feet move. Jimmy's face twisted into a threatening grin, as he came toward her. "Don't wanna follow Ms. Fanny's orders, do ya? Then ya gotta get yer whoopin'!" he said, his smile growing larger as the horse quirt arced sideways and lashed Rosa on the upper thigh. The sound of the thick leather thongs and the sting against her skin made Rosa jump, crying out in pain. "Wanna 'nother?" Jimmy asked, raising his eyebrows and grinning maniacally, as if he lived for these moments. Which, as it turned out, he did.

"No, no. Please don't. I'll do it," Rosa cried, through the tears of her shock and desperation. It was to be only the second of a thousand humiliations Rosa Robles was to suffer in this place. She just didn't know it yet.

As she spread her legs and felt the grotesque woman roughly inspecting her genitals, Rosa made herself think about picking cotton as fast as she could, two rows at a time, filling two sacks instead of one. She refused to accept what was happening to her; there was nothing she could do in her present situation, so she might as well disappear from it altogether, at least in spirit anyway.

Rosa would once again pick more cotton than her brothers. In her mind's landscape, the sun was going down, a huge orangey-pink globe above the never-ending fields of white puffy cotton.

"No drip," announced Fanny. "Looks like Smith made us a deal, even though she's almost just skin 'n bone. Well, I'm sure some a them men who love young and scrawny will come through here."

Fanny usually liked the new girls to be more on the plump side, that way better able to handle the immediate loss of weight after coming to her place. Pilcher wasn't one to be generous with the food; each inmate was fed twice a day, but as little as possible. And, as Rosa would soon learn, feeding the girls only very small amounts was *quite* possible.

As soon as the horrible woman was finished inspecting every part of her, Rosa covered her body with the thin coverlet that lay across her mattress. She was already in a semi-state of shock from being looked-over like a cow or pig at auction when she was slapped with the terrifying knowledge that her plight was far from over.

"OK Jimmy, she's all yers," announced Fanny as she turned and made her way toward the door. "I 'magine she don't know nothin' 'bout what she's s'posed to do, so ya best teach her best as ya can," she said with another cackle. She was out the door in no time, turning the key that would control Rosa's entire life from that point forward.

Rosa heard the loud click of the lock moving into place as she looked into the crazy eyes of the man called Jimmy. Enforcer and initiator. "OK girl," he said through lips upturned in a crazy, wide grin. As he moved closer to her, Rosa could smell the stench of his dirty clothes, and dreaded the filth of both his body and his mind. She shrank back on her small mattress, but there was nowhere left to go. "My job to 'nitiate the new girls. Don't you worry none - it won't take long. You don't have to do much; them men come through here by the tens, and in 'n out they are," he declared with a laugh.

Jimmy unbuttoned his pants, letting them fall to the floor, the thud of his belt punctuating the dropping of Rosa's heart. She'd never seen a naked man before; only her brothers as they washed in the communal washtub at home, or while skinny-dipping in a stream. But she'd never seen the parts of a grown man, and didn't know anything about the change that came over the male species when excitement for a woman welled up in their bellies. His pecker was long and thin, and stood straight up, out of the mound of dark hair covering his groin. "Don't you worry none 'bout Ms. Fanny fussin' 'cause you're so young 'n skinny. I like the young 'uns the best," he said, coming toward her.

Rosa could think of nothing to do but jump from her mattress and run to the other side of the room. Her flight was just instinct. Of course, as far as Jimmy was concerned, this only added sport to the job at hand. "Oh, ya wanna' play 'catch-me-if-ya-can', do ya?" he asked mischievously with a brown, stained-tooth smile. "That'll just make the suck all the more delicious when I catch ya!" he announced.

Jimmy considered Rosa's flight from the bed as a form of foreplay. That is, until he couldn't catch her. She proved to be quick on her feet, moving faster that her pursuer, who moved in a rather shaky, unbalanced way, as if he'd had ale for dinner, and not much else. But liquor also has a way of heating anger that much faster. After trying twice to catch her and failing both times, Jimmy's face morphed from that of a demented maniac to one of a dangerous predator. "God-dammit girl, ya best stay still if ya know what's good fer ya," he shouted, horse quirt in hand. "Might be yer gonna need another whoopin', 'n I'll be happy to give it to ya," he warned.

Rosa knew she couldn't keep jumping around the room - he would eventually catch her, or get help from others who would. She just stood still in the corner, eyes on the whip. She'd now made Jimmy angry, and no telling how violent he might get. Rosa finally had no choice but to resign herself to the inescapable, taking a deep breath and moving toward the bed. Jimmy grabbed her by the arm and pushed her down roughly. "Stupid bitch," he spat at her. "I outta wear out yer hide, and give ya some stripes to decorate that skinny ass," he said. "But might be as ya can make it up another way," he added, laughing with the rough and gravelly sound of the cruel and vicious.

He grabbed a handful of Rosa's long hair and forced her head down onto him. Rosa struggled against him, her instinct again propelling her to fight, regardless of whatever punishment might befall her. She'd never heard of anything so disgusting, and couldn't believe what he was forcing her to do. Whining noises involuntarily escaped her throat as she tried to keep her lips closed tight. Until she simultaneously felt and heard the sharp slap of the leather thongs against her leg. Rosa cried out, just as Jimmy had planned, and he pushed himself into her mouth. He smelled of sweat and dirt and the underside of society. With the horrible stench, and the revolting thing forced into her mouth, Rosa couldn't help but gag. But that only resulted in another sharp slap of leather on her skin. Jimmy pushed her head down further, her tears escaping from eyes closed tight against the horrible picture taking place in the room.

Rosa gagged again, and once more received the painful lash of the quirt, this time across her back. She cried and winced, but kept her head down on him just the same. It was obvious she would have to do this, or her poor, thin body would end up covered in red stripes and welts.

Rosa willed herself not to think about the vulgar act she was being forced to do. Instead, she again thought of things that had always made her happy. Racing her brothers down the dirt road and back. The way her mama had patiently braided her long hair when she was small. The kitten named Mew who'd purred around her feet when she'd put her bags of cotton in the barn. Her favorite doll with the brown yarn hair and missing eye; the doll she'd ignorantly left at home because she was beginning a new life and wanted to be grown-up.

Finally, Rosa's escape to cherished memories was interrupted by Jimmy pulling on her arm so hard she unintentionally cried out. "Now turn over for the rest of yer lesson," he growled at her, pushing her face down into the mattress, which smelled of urine and sweat and other nauseating odors she would soon become quite familiar with. Jimmy's rough hand spread her thighs apart; they felt like sandpaper rubbing away the last remnants of herself, burning her smooth and tender skin. Then he hovered over her. Rosa was scared to death. She knew what would happen now - she'd seen the animals in the barn sometimes. She was unable to control the utter terror that filled her, her bladder emptying right there on the mattress. But Jimmy didn't seem to notice, or if he did, he didn't care.

Jimmy had his way with her. Rosa couldn't help but scream out - the pain was so horrible she thought she might faint. She could swear she felt something rip inside her. Tears flowed freely down her soft and innocent cheeks, and her nose was running, dripping onto the mattress. She didn't care. She prayed to God for help, prayed to Him to deliver her from this horrible place. But it was more out of habit than anything else. At that point, she wasn't sure there was anyone listening to her anymore.

Jimmy finally finished her initiation, slapped her on the backside for good measure, pulled up his pants and buttoned them closed, then left the room. The click of the lock in the door was the sound of Rosa's life ending. She lay on the mattress for a long time, doing nothing and thinking of nothing. Her body and mind were both numb from the ordeal. She finally noticed the blood stains underneath her, on the place her hips had lain, and feared that her spirit might rip right along with her body.

Rosa Robles remained in her small room behind the door that was forever locked. It was a cell, she knew, just like a prison. Her clothes had been taken and traded for a thin shift, more like a nightgown. Even though her old clothes were far from fancy, and even frayed in some places, she wished she could at least keep them on; they were her only connection to her prior life. As far as her parents knew, she was at a wonderful school for girls. Even if they wanted to find her, and take her home, how would they even start looking? There was nothing to trace her here, nothing at all. Except for the lying Mr. Smith, and even if they found him, there was no way he would ever admit to taking girls under false pretenses, kidnapping them.

Rosa cried most of the night. She was so afraid to close her eyes, but eventually realized that no one could come into the room without the sound of the lock opening and waking her up. She finally shut her eyes and fell dead asleep.

The next morning, Rosa dreaded what awaited her this second day. She was brought meager portions for breakfast, but no lunch. No one spoke to her. She willed the door to remain closed. Closed forever. Maybe God would have pity on her and let her strong desire to just vanish take her away from this awful place.

But she knew that wouldn't happen. After bitterly accepting the fact that this was where she would remain, she made an important decision. These horrible people couldn't make her do anything she didn't want to do - she would just have to suffer the consequences.

At what seemed like late afternoon, Rosa heard footsteps coming down the hall, and voices. She just lay on her mattress, and looked at the small, barred window in the door. Heads floated past, with voices floating down and around the corridors, disembodied from the mouths that uttered them. Other locks clicked open; doors opened and shut. Occasionally she heard a cry or a whimper from some other girl imprisoned in some other room. But thankfully, her door remained closed, and her lock remained latched. The sounds of her new life continued far into the night, long after Rosa had finally willed herself to sleep.

The next morning was quiet, as it had been before. It seemed as if the whole world were far removed, while Rosa waited for something to happen. Waiting and wondering and worrying - Rosa's silence and apprehension continued for days. Then on the fourth day, when the sun was making its way downward in the Western sky, something did happen.

Rosa heard voices, at first far away, but then getting louder as their owners proceeded down the hallway. They became clearer, and this time, instead of seeing the profile of someone's head pass by, she saw eyes peering at her through the barred window, their owner sporting a dirty face with scraggly whiskers.

"That one. I'll take that one," the disheveled man announced.

The lock to her room clicked open, and an older man walked through the door, limping in his dirty boots. His hands were covered with the grime of a thousand dirty jobs, the tattoos of his labor through the years. She could smell his sweat-soaked clothing from where she sat.

"Only paid for five minutes, so you best hurry up," the man said, unbuckling his belt as he walked toward her. "Two bits'll get me all I need today. Ain't got no more to spare; need to go buy beans and rice for suppers this week," he said. He talked to her as if he were talking to a long-known acquaintance instead of to a twelve-year-old girl who'd been snatched from her family.

Rosa thought she would vomit.

"Come 'ere girl," he instructed, as he lowered his pants and underclothes, revealing his desire.

But Rosa didn't move.

"You're tryin' my patience, girl. I work hard for my wages, and I ain't gonna waste 'em," he said gruffly, moving toward her.

But Rosa had already made her decision. She wasn't going to do it. What Jimmy had done to her made her feel so dirty; she wasn't going to do it again. Rosa jumped from the bed, and ran to the other side of the small room.

"I'd usually like a little sportin'," said the man, "but not today. I ain't got no more money or time to spare. Now git yourself over here and let me have a poke!"

Rosa just stood where she was, daring him to catch her. He didn't seem like a violent man, just someone you might see walking down the street, going about his business. Rosa had made up her mind. She would *not* give him what he wanted.

"Goddammit!" he shouted, shaking his head, and pulling his trousers back up. "I'm gonna git my money back." He turned and walked toward the door. "A waste a Goddamned time, and with nothin' to show for it," he swore under his breath as the door opened and closed. The lock clicked back into place.

Rosa breathed hard, glad that some of the stench of human toil and hardship had left the room. At least she could breathe now. She closed her eyes and was happy that she'd stood her ground. She would not let herself be violated again.

But Rosa's self-satisfaction didn't last long, quickly being replaced with a paralyzing fear. Only minutes later, the lock clicked, and the door flew open into the room, hitting the wall with a thunderous bang. Fanny and Jimmy stormed in, Fanny with an angry scowl on her face, and Jimmy wearing the wide grin that told the world he was crazy as a rabid dog.

Fanny went directly to Rosa and slapped the girl's face so hard she was knocked to the ground.

"Refusin' customers are ya? Think yer gonna jist git away with it? Ya better think agin, girlie!" she screamed, droplets of spittle spraying over Rosa's arms and legs, which were still splayed on the floor. "Jimmy, come here and teach this little bitch what happens when a girl don't do what she's spose to do!" she yelled, her face the color of raw anger and rage, as if she'd been holding in her wrath for a very long time, and was now ready to explode from the fury of it.

Jimmy was more than happy to oblige. He lashed at her with the horse quirt until her legs wore the red stripes of a Christmas peppermint cane. Rosa could do nothing to protect herself from it; the only thing she knew to do was to make herself as small as possible as she lay on the ground, thinking of her brothers, and the kitten in the barn, and her mother's warm and protective arms around her.

"Now, Jimmy, let's make sure this little whore won't give us no more problems," instructed Fanny. "Just a lashin' ain't gonna do it," she said. "Hold 'er down while I give 'er the drops." Knock-out drops - Fanny's insurance that the occasional stubborn girl would learn to do as she was told, one way or the other.

Jimmy tried to roll Rosa over onto her back, grabbing her wrists and prying her arms loose from the rolled-up ball into which she'd put herself. The only thing Rosa could think to do was bite him on the hand. She bit down hard, tasting the dirt and sweat of a thousand lashings that Jimmy seemed to wear on his very person. It was only sheer will, and fear, that kept her teeth locked into his flesh until she drew blood, the taste of metal replacing the flavor of his violence.

Jimmy cried out in pain and anger. *The skinny whore was not going to get the better of him!* "You little bitch!" he snarled through teeth clenched with his determination to dominate. "You WON'T fight me NO MORE!!" He raised the short leather whip into the air, then brought it down onto Rosa again and again, the snapping sound of its thongs filling the room. He had no concern for where it landed. "How do ya like that!?" he spat. "Teach ya to bite me!"

Rosa was long past crying, and yelling out. She was in her faraway place. It was far easier to just retreat within herself than physically fight the monster who relished hurting the defenseless.

This time when Jimmy placed his hands on her to roll her over, she didn't resist. He stuck his grimy, bloodied hands into Rosa's mouth, and pried her jaw open. She then saw Fanny's creased and puckered face hovering over her own, her personal hobgoblin floating above her. "This'll teach ya to behave yerself," she hissed, as she squirted a bitter liquid down Rosa's throat. "You won't *never* do that agin!"

Rosa tried not to swallow the drops, but the horrible woman had squirted the liquid into the back of her throat, and they just went down of their own accord. Jimmy and Fanny sat there with her, Jimmy's hand over her mouth to prevent her from spitting the vile liquid onto the floor. When they were sure the drops had reached their destination, they left Rosa sprawled out on the floor, limp with exhaustion and covered with red welts from the thrashing.

"Little bitch," mumbled Jimmy, looking at his injured hand, as he walked through the doorway.

Then Rosa's vision began to blur. Instead of one filthy mattress, there were two, instead of two hands, she had four. She tried to raise herself, but her balance had somehow left her, and she fell back to the floor. The last thing Rosa remembered was the blurry shape of a small, dark smudge crawling across the floorboards in front of her.

Chapter 28

Funk

"Git up girl! Git up!" the voice commanded Rosa as he nudged her thigh with the toe of his work boot. He looked with pity at her thin, naked form, lying on the small cot in the shed. Dark red welts, tinged with the blue of bruising, covered most of her body, especially her legs. *Holy God*, she couldn't be any more than twelve or thirteen. He felt bad about using his boot to try to rouse her, but his sensibility didn't allow him to touch a young girl with no clothes on. He didn't even want to *look* at her when she was naked, much less use his hands to wake her.

But the girl hardly even stirred. Her eyes opened slightly when he prodded her, but closed again just as quickly. He knew she wasn't merely asleep; he was certain she'd been drugged.

"Oh Lord," said the burly black man, shaking his head back and forth. "Quinn asked for a whore, and they send him a drugged-up child. What the holy hell am I gonna do with that?" John William Funk was the foreman of a Colored work crew who'd been paving streets on the outskirts of Dallas, those roads that the planning people assumed would come into more use in the coming years.

Funk's work crew had been out this way for the last three weeks, working to pave these roads so they wouldn't become impassable with sticky, wet mud during the fall rains. His men were good men, at least most of them. One or two had joined up later, after learning that Funk offered as much work as any hard-working man could want. Funk had probably taken on some he shouldn't, but he didn't want to stand in the way of any man trying to earn a living for himself and his family. Colored or not. Notwithstanding the few men who hadn't yet earned Funk's respect, they were a good lot.

The crew slept together at the work-site for weeks on end, many of the men living on the other side of Dallas, not having the transportation to get back and forth every day. Although Funk supposed he could get home if he wanted to, he was more comfortable staying with his crew. They were his responsibility, and he didn't aim to let them down, or act as if he were the king of their world. As long as they knew that he was boss, he was content to live on an even plane with his men.

John Funk cared about them. He cared about people.

That was why he'd agreed to let Quinn get them a prostitute. Funk had never been one to need sex as much as some men did. Sure he loved it, just like any man. But he was content to be with a woman five or six times a year. Of course, if he were truly interested in a woman, he would be more than happy to oblige her if she wanted to bed down with him more often. He'd just turned forty, and was no closer to getting married now than he'd been when he was twenty. He wasn't averse to the idea; he just hadn't found the right one yet. Maybe never would, he supposed.

But his men were a different story. A few days before, Funk's work leader, Avery Quinn, a man he'd known for quite a long time and thought he trusted, had told him that the men were restless. They were here night and day. Some of them had greater needs of the flesh than others, and those needs were beginning to make themselves known. The men were getting so jittery with sexual tension that small fights had broken out here and there. Nothing major, but enough to convince Funk there was a problem that needed tending to.

Avery Quinn's suggestion had been to get a whore from town delivered to the work-site. He'd learned from other work crews that this was quite a common practice. He could make all the arrangements; Funk would only have to provide the payment and the place - any empty shed would do just fine. Early that morning, Quinn had told the men they'd have some recreation time added to their lunch hour, and they were surely happy men today. Quinn had met the wagon from the whorehouse, and told the driver to place the girl in the shed. Funk hadn't seen the girl delivered, and didn't know a thing about her until he opened the shed door to peek at the woman inside.

Now he didn't know *what* in the hell to do.

"Quinn, where's Quinn?!" Funk barked as he walked around the lunchtime camp.

"Think he's over at the water barrel, boss," one of the men said, through a mouthful of grits and bacon.

Funk didn't even respond, just redirected himself and marched onward.

"Quinn, what the hell happened with the whore? There's only a naked little girl covered with strap marks in that shed! How you expect the men to have their way with her? She don't even look old enough to be away from home by herself, much less service a bunch a horny Colored men!" he bellowed. "And she's unconscious, for Christ's sake!"

Quinn looked up with worry plastered over his face, walking away from the lunching men who sat under the nearby trees to protect themselves from the late summer sun. He motioned Funk to follow.

"I din't know they was gonna send a girl that young," Quinn responded. "I jus' tol' 'em to put her in that shed, and they done that. I ain't even been in there yet. Some a the men was askin' me how far they had to pave on one side, and I din't pay no attention when they took her from the wagon," he answered in a low voice, almost a whisper. He knew his men were anxiously awaiting their time with a woman, and he was afraid of what might happen if any of them happened to hear their conversation.

"Well, even if you don't consider her age, that little girl's covered with strap marks, and drugged-up. Won't even open her eyes for more than a few seconds. It would be like beddin' a corpse," answered Funk. "Can't do this," he told Quinn.

Quinn glanced at the men with a worried expression, his weathered face creased from both sunlight and distress. "Don't know that we got a choice," he answered. "The men ain't gonna be none too happy if we tell 'em they cain't have their time."

"Goddamnit, don't tell me what we can and can't do!" yelled Funk. His raised voice captured the attention of the lunching men. The argument replaced the cold grits and bacon as the focus of their noontime meal.

Again Quinn looked around, worried. "Look boss, I know most a the men would understand. They'd wait 'til we could make other 'rangements. But a couple of 'em won't stand for no waitin' till next time. They already think we took too long in tryin' to make sure they was satisfied."

The crew put down their pails and sauntered closer to Funk and Quinn.

"Well, they're just gonna have to wait! No other choice in the matter!" Funk had never really given a situation such as this much thought. What prostitutes did day in and day out was their own business. If they wanted to earn money by spreading their legs for horny men, that was their choice. And he supposed someone had to hire and maintain them. The brothels. He hadn't given them much consideration either, but he knew they served a purpose. What went on there really wasn't his business, as far as he was concerned. But this - *this* was just a disgrace to everyone. To the girl, to the brothel, and to his men. *To humanity, for God's sake.*

One of the newer crewmen hovering close-by, Harris, jumped into the conversation. In the past, he'd certainly proved that his mouth was sometimes more aggressive than it should be, his voice not always overruled by his brain's warnings. "What's goin' on, boss?"

Funk looked at him as if he'd materialized out of nowhere, but Quinn had known they'd eventually draw a crowd.

"Nothin' Harris. We were jus' discussin' some bidness. Nothin' you need worry 'bout," answered Quinn with the naive hope that Harris would just let it drop.

"Well, it *is* somethin' he needs to worry about. At least if he was expectin' to have some time with a woman today!" Funk yelled, looking at the men whose presence had added an extra layer of tension in the yard.

"Whatcha mean, boss?" Harris asked, squinting at Funk as he slightly cocked his head to the side.

"What I mean is that there ain't no woman here today. Only a girl young enough to be your daughter. Won't be no fun and games today," he told them.

"Now hold on," said Harris, shaking his head. "I seen them bring her in here. Whores don't care nothin' 'bout no age limits. And we don't neither. We was promised a woman today, and I aim to get her!" Harris answered with a raised and resolute voice, looking at the other men for confirmation. He turned and began walking toward the shed, the others following his lead as if he'd suddenly taken the place of both foreman and work leader. They liked what Harris had to say better than the crap coming from Funk.

"I *said* there won't be no sex today, Harris. And I *mean* it!" shouted Funk. He was normally more of a gentle giant, but not today. Today he wore the mantle of protector.

Harris just kept on walking, his followers right behind him. He made it to the shed in no time flat, and began to open the tin door. Then out of nowhere, a huge fist attached itself to Harris's shirt collar, and wrenched him away, the door clanking as it bounced back into place.

"Goddamnit, I said *not today!*" Funk could feel the resistance in Harris' body as he yanked him from the door handle. He was a big man, but Funk was bigger. Funk spun Harris around, and just as the man regained his balance, another huge fist arced through the heat-laden air, like a warm knife through a cold slab of butter, and made contact with Harris' left cheek. At the moment of impact, a sickening crack filled the ears of all present, and all eyes watched Harris fall to the ground, no longer interested in anything, least of all the shed. He was out cold, his slack left jaw hanging lower than the right.

The air became still and quiet as the men all looked between one and the other. Time and space froze for those few seconds, a flash-point in the afternoon sun.

"Boss, we was *promised* we could be with a woman today! We been workin' hard boss. Thought we could take your word for it. Now you gonna go back on it? Ain't right! Ain't our fault they brought some young whore in here!" Jepson, another of the crew, who'd been eating his lunch next to Harris, screamed at Funk, looking at his friend still unconscious on the ground. His hands balled into fists as he faced his foreman, a detail that hadn't escaped Funk's notice.

The two men squared their shoulders, the other workers encircling them like a boxing ring, sure a fight between the two was imminent. But then Funk surprised everyone. He didn't throw a punch, he didn't even make fists. He drew up close to Jepson, his face a mere inch from Jepson's eyes. Funk wore a mask of simmering rage and fury, fear nowhere to be seen. "I said you ain't gettin' no whore today." Funk's voice was a mere whisper, its hush scarier than a bellow.

Jepson looked into Funk's eyes, and recognized something there that sent a chill through his bones, something deep that was barely contained, trying to get out. He shivered in the almost-unbearable heat. At that moment, Funk's soft and dangerous words made more of an impression on Jepson that any shout or yelled curse could have. He lowered his eyes to Harris, who was finally emerging from his unconscious state, then just turned and walked away, shaking his head. Jepson wasn't as smart as some of the men, but he was surely smart enough to know when to let things be.

"*Goddamnit!*" was all Funk could think to mutter as he walked away, leaving Quinn and the other men to look after Harris. By God, it had been close. He shouldn't have hit Harris, but what was he to do when threatened with a mutiny? Sometimes a well-aimed punch was the only choice. He was just glad his fist hadn't caused another tragedy. The image of that boy so long ago flashed through his mind, the small trickle of blood running from his nose as his life had run from his body. The boy's lifeless form splayed on the ground with no hope of revival. Funk involuntarily shook his head, clearing the image from his mind. That was long ago. What was done was done.

The men returned to their work.

Through her state of drug-induced fog, Rosa was roused by the commotion outside. She heard the tin door to the shed creak open slightly, then bounce back just as quickly, followed by the sound of angry men. She couldn't collect her thoughts, couldn't force herself to wake enough to even sit up. She knew she was at the mercy of the men outside, instinct causing her to be afraid of what might come at any minute. Rosa knew she had no power to stop it, whatever *it* turned out to be. The knock-out drops had seen to that.

Later, after the angry voices had died away into the heat, the shed door opened, and the large colored man from before came toward her. He had a light blanket in his hands, which he put over Rosa to hide her nakedness, to hide her vulnerability. He said nothing, just covered her and left. She heard the door creak once more, and he was gone.

"Quinn, where's the muthafucka brought that girl here?" Funk demanded, through clenched jaw, his anger still saturating him like a sweat-soaked shirt.

"He's over there, with his wagon. Under that tree yonder, in the shade," Quinn answered, motioning behind him with his thumb.

Funk pushed past him and made his way across the work site, toward the ramshackle wagon. At first, he saw no one. But as he got closer, he heard the sound of sleep, a raspy snoring coming from a bedraggled man snoozing in the wagon's bed. Had he not known better, he would have thought the man was a beggar instead of a panderer. Dirty hair and clothes, and no telling how many days worth of whiskers. Another sharp blade of sadness stabbed him as he thought of the girl being controlled by this pathetic excuse for a man.

"Get up!" yelled Funk, as he gave the wagon bed a kick with a large booted foot. "Get the hell up!"

The wagon jerked with a groan; the dirty man startled awake. "What the hell!" Jimmy yelled in anger, before he remembered he was currently in someone else's castle.

"You the one brought that little girl here?" screamed Funk, as he grabbed Jimmy's grimy collar and pulled him out of the wagon. Jimmy looked like a child himself next to Funk, cowering like a damned two-year-old.

"You ordered a whore, so I brung her," Jimmy answered, in a pitiful attempt at self-defense.

"Don't take no genius to see she ain't but a little girl! How you gonna give her to a yard fulla horny men who haven't had a woman in weeks!?" Funk yelled.

"She had a lesson comin' to her. And we paid for 'er, fair 'n square. Too much, if ya ask me. She's been nothin' but trouble ever since she came," answered Jimmy, shaking his head.

"I don't give a good Goddamn if you paid for her or not. She don't belong in no work yard fulla men! Take her back!" commanded the foreman.

"No sir. Cain't take her back yet," Jimmy hesitantly replied, shaking his head back and forth slowly. Although fearful of Funk's size and anger, he knew how harsh his bosses at the tenement could be, and he'd bet their punishment would probably be a good deal worse than what he might suffer here.

Almost before the words were out of Jimmy's mouth, Funk wrenched his collar and pushed him back hard against the wooden slats of the wagon bed. "I. Said. You. Will. Take. Her. Back. NOW!" he screamed into Jimmy's face, staring into the weaselly man's eyes until he was certain he saw surrender.

"Fine," mumbled Jimmy grudgingly, "'though I ain't gonna be responsible fer this."

"That's fuckin' plain as day," answered Funk. He felt like he needed to go wash his hands after touching the filthy man, and being involved in this filthy mess. "I'm givin' you five minutes to pack up and leave, or I'll put your face into that ground," he shouted. It wasn't as much a threat as just a sure fact of what the future held for Jimmy if he didn't disappear from that work site in a flash.

Funk told Quinn to make sure Jimmy got the girl and drove off within the next five minutes, then he went to the campfire to pour himself a cup of coffee from the pot they'd brewed for lunch. He walked toward the back of the work site and into the tent he called his office, sitting down on a cane-backed chair he kept there, and rubbing his eyes, trying to rid himself of the frustration that bubbled up inside his head. For the life of him, he couldn't figure out how such a young girl had come to work in that whorehouse, being a slave to that scum-laden-no-excuse-of-a-man who'd brought her.

Was that human ferret her only taskmaster? Probably not; he surely had a boss too. Funk briefly wondered how the others treated the girl, but then knew the answer before he'd really even asked himself the question. He was hyper-sensitive to anything even remotely close to sounding like slavery. His mama and daddy had been slaves, until the war justly ended their deplorable bondage. All men belonged to God, and only to God, his mama and daddy always told him. He'd always believed this. How could one man own another?

"Don't never let no one tell you what to do in this world, or act like you're one a their possessions, like a piece a livestock, or a piece a furniture," his daddy had warned him early on. "You belong only to God. No one else," he'd said, many a time. His daddy had been a slave all his life, born right on the same plantation where he'd spent most of his days, until the war ended his incarceration some thirty years later. He'd become an expert cotton-picker at the ripe age of five, picking that cotton, and working the fields until he knew everything there was to know about tilling and planting and harvesting.

Funk had heard the stories of his parents' hardships throughout his childhood. One in particular still brought tears to his eyes when he thought about it. His mama had gotten pregnant. This in itself was not a worry to their master, as every new baby just added to his workforce without costing a penny. But when his mama birthed the baby, a girl, the master was told right away that she was defective, born with only one leg, and a small stump where the other should have been. An hour later, his mama held her newborn, admiring the tiny nose and eyes and ears that peeked out from the swaddle in which she was wrapped, when the master entered the slave quarter that had been used as a birthing room.

"Lollie," he said to her, "I was told your baby isn't whole. Is that right?" he asked her quietly, as if he might actually be concerned about the child's welfare.

"She's the most beautiful thing in the world," answered his mama, for in fact, even without two legs, she *was* the most beautiful baby Lollie had ever seen. Of course, she'd have her challenges ahead, for Lollie would have to figure out how her baby would make due with only one leg, but she knew she could make it work.

"But Lollie, you know there's no way a child with only one leg can work on this farm. And besides, she'd need extra care that would take you away from your chores in the house," he said. Lollie was in charge of the kitchen in the main house, and even without looking out for a baby, a crippled one no less, she was already running around in circles, trying to keep up with all the work there was to do.

"I'll manage just fine, sir," Lollie answered her master resolutely. She didn't know *how* she'd do it, but she would. She *knew* she could.

"Lollie, you know as well as I do what needs to be done," he said, as he reached out for the baby. "Now let's don't make this any worse than it has to be."

How could it be worse? Having your baby taken away! "No, mister! No!" Lollie answered emphatically, tightening her grip on the infant, and shaking her weary head. "You cain't have her. She's mine." She wasn't hysterical, just firm in her denial of his command. Lollie thought that if she stubbornly just held her ground, she might win out, and get to keep her crippled child.

But her master wasn't in the habit of negotiating. He'd already made up his mind. The baby would take too much time away from what needed to be done in the house, never mind the child not even being able to work her fair share later on. The mistress of the house would never be able to accommodate Lollie caring for a damaged infant.

The master left the room for a few minutes, but returned with two of the men who worked the fields with Lollie's husband. "Hold her arms down," instructed the master, "but don't hurt her," he said, almost as an afterthought.

Lollie's mind raced then. She felt like a rabbit trapped in a cage, about to be grabbed and slaughtered. She held her baby tighter than anything she'd ever held onto in her life. "No!!" she screamed. "You cain't have her!! She's mine!!"

Lollie frantically looked into the eyes of each man who had come to restrain her. She willed death to those who would conspire to take her child. But those men only looked away, conflicting emotions battling for control. Their guilt at what they were doing clashed with the fear of what would happen if they didn't. Fear won, as it usually did.

"No!!!" she screamed again, to ears that refused to hear a mother's worst agony.

"You can have another," said the master, as he picked up the swaddled form. "One that's whole," he said, as if that were all the comfort Lollie would need, as if that explained everything.

Lollie never saw her baby girl again. She never asked what had become of her. She knew the answer, and also knew she couldn't bear hearing the actual words, words that would be more like iron nails pounded into her heart. Her sweet girl was gone from this world.

Funk's daddy told him that Lollie liked to not get over losing her baby girl. But somehow she'd managed to make it through one day, and then another. Life went on. Then when the North won the war and all the slaves had been freed, she insisted on getting as far away from that plantation as fast as they could. They'd traveled west and settled in Texas. In Dallas, where Funk was born.

"Don't never let no one take your freedom," his daddy had warned. "Your freedom is the most important thing you got." Funk's belief in those words had never wavered.

He cringed when he thought of that little, naked girl being taken back to whatever hell-hole she'd come from, and wondered how he could just sit back and let her return to a life that was akin to the slavery his parents had suffered. He left the tent, and walked with determination back to the shed. He'd made up his mind.

But the shed was empty and the wagon gone.

Whatever good intentions Funk had mustered in his office tent had been swallowed-up into the stifling afternoon heat. He'd acted too late.

The girl was gone.

Chapter 29

The Past

Funk swore he'd never do it again; never get carried away with his fists in a blur of rage. No matter who it was on the receiving end, or what the reason. They may deserve it plenty, just as that boy had so long ago, but that didn't mean he could afford to lose himself in fury, bringing the wrath of his strong body down on the unlucky recipient. He couldn't afford to get carried away in the passion of his anger. Funk's soul would be quite lost. And someone might die.

Back when he was a teen, Funk had worked as a field-hand at a nearby cotton farm during the summer. The heat and physical exertion had never bothered him; he'd actually favored it. Sweating all the time built up stamina in a person, and the farm work built up his muscles. By the time he was seventeen, he had a reputation for being the strongest mule within ten miles, with the endurance to match. He could pick cotton for twelve straight hours in the hot Texas sun, and still have energy left to walk the three miles home and eat dinner after.

It was his anger that got the better of him. If he felt it was truly justified, the rage was like a runaway train, beginning in his brain, and traveling straight to his fists where it exploded in furious passion. He couldn't help it, he'd always told his mama. It would just *happen*. Then one hot summer day, Funk found out what the consequences of his anger could be, warranted or not. He'd always thought of himself as the protector of those treated unfairly, of those who couldn't protect themselves. And that was true on the day that would change his outlook for the rest of his life.

Funk had been working the field, just like he always did, but he'd stayed a bit later than usual that day - he'd had a bet with Franklin Ayers, another boy working the farm, that he could sack more cotton by the end of the week. Funk was walking past the second barn, where the tilling machines were kept until needed in the spring, when he heard a whimper that sounded almost like a kitten trapped in a bramble bush, trying to find its way out, but being poked by thorns with every move. Funk stopped to listen, and heard it again, but this time it was more muffled.

He entered the dim barn and paused, trying to give his eyes time to adjust. The only light he saw was what remained of the daylight coming in through the open door, and the cracks in the wood caused by weather and wear. "Where are you now, Kitty?" he called softly, looking around to see where the little critter might be stuck.

Then he heard shuffling, and one small creaking sound. But no more whimpers. Maybe it wasn't a stuck kitten after all? As the inside of the barn came into focus, he saw a small room in the back, to the left of the tiller, most likely a storeroom. He stared at the open door to that space, but saw nothing. He could *swear* he'd heard something. No, he *knew* he'd heard it. Funk walked toward the storeroom to investigate.

He expected to see a cat, or raccoon, or other small animal that normally inhabited small hiding places on a country farm. But John William Funk had never expected to see an eleven-year-old girl with her dress pulled up to her chest and drawers pulled down to her ankles, being held down by a teenage boy with his hand over her mouth, his drawers down around his knees. The girl's eyes were as big as full moons, and when they spied John walking near, she made loud mewling sounds behind the boy's hand. The only cry for help she could manage.

A red film coated Funk's vision, his entire brain. The rage he felt when he saw that young girl being violated caused him to turn into someone else, whether a defender or avenger he didn't know, but the only thing that person could do was exact justice. Funk's sight narrowed into a tunnel through which he could only see the boy, now as terrified as the girl, as well he should be. He picked the boy up by the strap of his overalls, and held onto that strap as an anchor. Funk threw a right hook which landed on the boys left cheek, wrenching his head to the side, spittle flying out of his mouth as if it were trying to escape.

"Run!" Funk shouted to the little girl, as she pulled her drawers up and crawled on hands and knees past them, and through the door.

"Didn't do nothin'!" the boy yelled between blows. "Didn't do nothin'!"

But Funk could no more stop his fist from pummeling that boy's face than he could stop a locomotive moving down the rails. It had been put into motion. An upper cut, followed by another hook. Up and across, up and across. His brain told him he'd better stop, but his heart directed him differently. *He was rapin' that little girl!*

After what seemed like an hour, but was only a minute, Funk somehow registered that the boy no longer moved. He stopped punching and just held him by his overalls. The boy's head hung slack, his face quickly swelling, blood trickling from the split flesh caused by Funk's huge hand. Funk just stared down at him, then let go of his hold. The boy's body crumpled into the pile of straw on which he'd reclined not two minutes before. Funk just stood there, in a daze, looking at his right fist that was covered with the boy's blood. He couldn't bring himself to move one inch.

Then men running in behind him. He heard their boots beating the earth floor of the barn, heard them shouting, felt the rush of their bodies entering the storeroom. He backed out of the way as they ran to the boy. "He ain't breathin'!" one of the men yelled, as they knelt on the ground by the boy.

He ain't breathin'! He ain't breathin'!

Funk's brain could process no more than that. "He was rapin' her," was all Funk could manage to whisper.

Even after the little girl, Lessie Tate, told her story, the father of the dead boy, Lester Fouts, the foreman at the farm, demanded justice for his son. He was so devastated that he even accused the little girl of lying about what happened, causing her parents outrage. But they hadn't much recourse. Although the girl's mother helped with the washing, cleaning, and cooking at the farm, the foreman's wrath overshadowed any argument she could make. So Funk remained in the jail cell, waiting to hear his fate.

His mama was the only reason Funk was eventually released. As it turned out, Lessie Tate's mama went to the same church as the Funks, so Lollie Funk decided to use their church as the catalyst to win John's release. Lollie and Ms. Tate had organized the church-women to protest John's incarceration, and held a vigil at the farm, all day, every day, until the owner was damned tired of the whole mess. Tired of hearing about the Colored boy locked up because he was trying to protect a little girl. Tired of the foreman busting his balls about it. Tired of the Colored ladies on his property every day, singing hymns. He finally just threw up his hands, and retracted his statement to the police, allowing John Funk to be freed.

Upon Funk's release, Lester Fouts up and quit as foreman, leaving the same day. No one ever heard his name again.

Funk was so grateful to have his life back. But his mama sat him down at their kitchen table, and admitted she thought she'd lost him for sure, tears streaming down her worn face.

"You lucky they let you go, John," she told him. "I was beginning to think they was gonna keep you there." Lollie wiped away her tears with the hem of her skirt. "But the good Lord Jesus saw fit to answer my prayers, and now you're back," she said. She took his large hands inside her small ones. "You gotta realize how powerful you are. I know you didn't mean to kill that boy, only punish him for what he done. But between your strength and the anger that takes a hold of you when you get riled, you gotta make sure nothin' like this *ever* happens again! *Ever!*" He'd never seen his mama so upset. "You just 'bout killed me, boy," she added quietly. "I lost one of my babies; I cain't go through losin' the other," she murmured in quiet desperation.

Funk looked at his mama's tired face, knowing what she'd gone through as a slave. She knew how it felt to be someone's prisoner, having to answer to their every command. How they'd ripped her little girl from her arms. He regretted putting her through so much extra sorrow, and vowed to himself that he'd never put her through that kind of pain again. "I promise, mama," he'd said through the hoarse voice of regret, as he hugged her to him. "I won't ever lose control like that again." And he meant it.

Chapter 30

Rosa's Return

Rosa felt as if she'd been thrust into a nightmare, images swirling around her like specters in the dark. The knowledge that she wore no clothes, that she needed to move, to bolt into action to save herself. But her brain and limbs just wouldn't cooperate. It was as if her arms and legs were made of lead, and her brain was working in slow motion. At last, the bumpy ride back in the wagon, hearing Jimmy mumble and curse as he steered the horses back downtown. He'd then picked her up roughly, throwing her over his shoulder like a sack of flour, then tossing her onto her mattress in a heap.

An eternity later, Rosa finally woke, her head pounding as if she'd taken a fall from a horse, and landed top-side first. She opened her eyes, and found herself in the same room in which she'd spent every second since coming to Dallas. *Was it all a dream?* she wondered. A grotesque fantasy that her weary mind had conjured? But what about the large Black man? She hadn't seen many Black men in her short life. If it were a dream, how had she come about the details of his face, and large hands, and work boots nudging her legs? She couldn't be imagining; she was remembering something real. She *had* to be.

Rosa lay still as a statue, trying to will her head to stop throbbing, when she realized that her hands were tied together, hidden under the blanket, along with her nakedness. From the same dream-scape, images of Jimmy entering the shed and tying up her hands, carrying her to the wagon, and roughly plopping her into its bed. She wasn't sure what she was supposed to do, or what she *could* do, at this point. So she did nothing but lay there and listen.

Not long after, Rosa heard the familiar sounds of food being delivered to the rooms:

The click of locks.

The slamming of cell doors.

The muffled half-conversations between jailer and inmates.

Bread and beans, and sometimes rice, if they were lucky. The sounds soon neared, but then just as quickly moved farther from her room. The doors on either side opened and closed, opened and closed. But not hers. *Did they just pass her up?*

At last her door did open, but not until the following evening. She was so hungry, her stomach hurt just to breathe. She generally stayed in much of a state of hunger. But this was different - it was as if a great hole had been carved from where her stomach should have been. She hadn't eaten since sometime before she'd swallowed the knock-out drops. Had that been yesterday? Two days ago? She wasn't even sure.

"Well, if it ain't the lucky little girlie who got outta her punishment," announced Fanny with a sneer, her haggard face appearing above Rosa's bed. "Servicin' that work camp woulda taught a snotty little bitch like you that you gotta do what I say. Pilcher 'spects me to make sure every one-a the girls in here services at least twenty men a day, more if there's enough men wants it. You ain't serviced one yet," she snarled, spittin' a glob of brown, tobacco-laced phlegm onto the floor of Rosa's room. "You think you're better 'n any other whore in here? You think you're better 'n me? I even have to put-out ever' now and then. You definitely ain't no better 'n me!" Fanny yelled.

"Goin' to that work yard was yer punishment for not puttin' out here. *Now* yer punishment for not puttin' out at the work yard is no food. You can starve yerself for all I care," smiled Fanny. "Ha! And I don't care. Not one lick!" she said laughing.

Rosa was almost caving in on herself she was so hungry. Just hearing Fanny's words made the pain growl even louder. "But it wasn't my fault," Rosa pleaded. "I don't remember turning anyone away. I don't think anyone ever came in!" Rosa yelled. At least no one except the big Black man, prodding her with his boot. Then another image of him throwing a blanket over her glided into her mind. But she wasn't going to mention him. He hadn't wanted to touch her.

"Don't matter none," answered Fanny in return. "You didn't bring in no money. Same thing as turnin' em away. Same thing," she proclaimed. "You *will* learn to do as yer told! Think you're a *Goddamned princess* in a hole like this? You damn well'll learn you ain't no better than no one else in here!" Fanny screamed. It was obvious to Rosa that she should say nothing, or risk getting slapped or even worse. Jimmy wasn't in the room right now, but Rosa was certain he was lurking somewhere close by.

Panic and despair fought for control of Rosa's entire being as she lay still on her mattress, listening to the horrible woman spew her horrible words. Her stomach hurt, and her wrists hurt. All she could do was lay as still as possible, and just let the tears silently escape from the corners of her eyes, rivulets of despair making their way down her still-dusty cheeks.

"Are ya hungry?" Fanny asked her, her voice at an almost-normal level.

Rosa nodded her head. "Yes," she answered hesitantly, not sure why Fanny would ask about her hunger while in the middle of a tongue lashing.

"Well, good!" she yelled, "'cause that's the way yer gonna stay! At least 'til ya decide to make Pilcher some money. Someone's gotta pay fer this food. Good riddance if ya just withered away, and starved yerself to death, I'd say. But I'd have to tell Pilcher, and then I'd get my own lashin'"

Fanny turned and walked to the door. "When yer ready to eat, you just let me know Princess, and I'll start lettin' the Johns come 'n visit ya," she said over her shoulder with a vicious laugh. She slammed the door behind her, with the familiar click to follow. The click that Rosa had come to associate with a life sentence. She turned over, lying face down on her mattress, and cried herself to sleep, all the while praying for salvation from a God she wasn't sure even cared anymore.

The next morning, Rosa woke up feeling as if she were going to vomit. But vomit what? Her stomach was empty. Suddenly loud voices and high-pitched screams filled the hallway. Fanny yelling something for all to hear.

"Wake up and see what happens to any little bitch who tries to leave us!" she yelled. "Look what we got here! Get up and see! Lookie, lookie!"

Her words filled Rosa with dread, but she couldn't stop herself from getting up and running to the door. She looked through the barred cut-out of the window and saw Fanny and two men, pulling a young woman along in between. The woman was dirty and quite bedraggled, looking almost like Rosa had sometimes looked after a long, hot day in the fields. One man pulled her by a rope tied around her waist while the other dragged her along by her hair. The woman was trying to fight them off as best she could, kicking and punching, but the men were just too big to injure, and they had straps. The man who held the rope swung his strap, and it landed with a loud slapping sound on her bare legs. The woman's frantic face happened to turn in Rosa's direction and for a split second, their eyes met. Rosa was shocked to see one eye swollen to the size of an orange, the lump a violent shade of red. But more disturbing than her injury, she saw fear and pain. And hopelessness.

As they passed, Rosa plainly saw the red strap marks that were quickly covering the woman's arms and legs, some of them so deep they trickled blood, dribbling down her body like silent little rivers. Rosa guessed there were even more marks hiding under her clothes. A small red stain had even sprung up on the part of her shirt covering her back. They'd beaten her, and beaten her badly, by the looks of it. Who had done it? Jimmy? Or one of the two men who held her? But it didn't really matter. A beating was a beating.

"This stupid bitch thought she could just leave when she saw the chance. But it don't work like that!" Fanny screamed. "You all belong to us. We bought ya, fair and square. And we aim to keep ya. If ya run away, Eddie and Henry here'll find ya, and drag ya back where ya belong. But not without givin' ya the beatin' of yer life! There's nowhere to run, just remember that!" Fanny yelled, as Rosa watched the group continue to the other end of the hall.

Nowhere to run. The words kept echoing inside Rosa's brain as if they were the new mantra she was meant to live by. She guessed that's exactly what they were. That was the purpose for dragging that poor woman down the hall. An example for every other woman who lived in this horrible place.

Even with escape, there was nowhere to go and nowhere to hide. The devastation and hopelessness was more than Rosa thought she could bear. Since she'd been here, it seemed her life was always at its bottom, but then something more horrible just weaseled its way in to make her understand that things could always be worse. At least she was alive. But that thought alone brought very little comfort to her. She'd been sentenced to misery, so did being alive really matter that much after all?

After the question ran itself through Rosa's mind for most of the morning, she finally came to the conclusion that being alive *did* matter. After all, Rosa's mother had taught her there was always hope. But Rosa's mother had never seen a place like this, she was sure.

After one more day of being bound and starved, Rosa surrendered. Her will to survive was stronger than her desire to be pure, free from the disgusting things men were trying to do to her. She had to eat, and if she didn't eat, she would die. It was a simple truth. She wasn't sure how she would feel next week, or next month. But today, right now, she knew that she still wanted to live. She would do what was necessary to survive.

"I'll do what you want," she quietly told Fanny the next time the greasy woman barged her way into the room after delivering food to the other girls. The girls who were doing their jobs. "Please give me something to eat," she said quietly, in the beleaguered tone of defeat. She hated to surrender, but she was starving to death. She didn't know what else to do.

Fanny cackled as she made her way over to Rosa, producing a knife to cut the rope which still bound her wrists. "Ha! I knew you'd change yer mind, girlie! They all do. Here's yer food. Be expectin' the johns this afternoon," she instructed, as she pitched Rosa her clump of bread, a piece of beef, and a soft and bruised apple. "You've got a lotta makin' up to do!" she called over her shoulder as she left the room.

Rosa barely heard her as she stuffed the bread and meat into her mouth. The sound of the door lock clicking was now just a familiar background noise that had lost its hold on Rosa's soul. It was just another part of this new horrifying life that she would now have to own.

And she did.

Chapter 31

Eliza

August 30, 1907

The months of July and August passed relatively quickly, thank the Lord for small favors. This summer was one of the hottest on record, some days getting to one hundred and five degrees or better. But just as the heat elevated to insufferable levels, it tapered off just as quickly. The Farmer's Almanac called for a colder-than-usual winter, and I wondered if, maybe by chance, the cool weather was starting off quickly, now that September had almost arrived.

I've been very busy in the last weeks, not only with my dressmaking and instruction to the girls, but also with getting ready for our Labor Day barbecue on Monday. Not only is it an event that everyone at The Johnson Home looks forward to every year, but it's also part of our community outreach program. Seeing as how many of the Madames don't especially appreciate me and Ms. Dixie trying to inform their girls about the other life options available to them, our message most times falls on deaf ears. We had to devise a less obvious way to let them know of the opportunities The Johnson Home could provide, and decided to invite as many girls as possible to our socials. Mr. Linder agreed to help spread the word by including invitations in the parcels delivered from the pharmacy.

During the month of August, a group of the younger girls and I spent several afternoons making pretty little invitations out of paper and lace. We will deliver them to Mr. Linder, who'll put an invitation into every package that goes out to Emma Street in the following weeks. Of course, we have no way of knowing who will or will not show up, but we're hoping that attendance will be high.

I also made a special invitation for Mamie, with dainty onion-skin paper and scraps of antique lace, left-over from dressmaking. I planned to ask Mart to deliver it directly to her; it worked so well the first time, surely he'll be able to do it again. But what about Christian, Mamie's brother? I want him to come, so that Mamie can see him. Maybe if she sees he's doing well, she might consider coming to live at The Johnson Home.

I once again found myself waiting for Mart at Linder's. And true to his normal schedule, I heard the bells on the door jingle as he walked in to start his day.

"Mart Waymond, how are you?" I asked, as I got up from my chair to give him a hug. "I haven't seen you since the beginning of July. How are your mama and the kids?" I asked.

"Well, howdy, Ms. Eliza!" he exclaimed, through a grin that I didn't think could get any bigger. "I'm doin' fine, and so are my mama and the young-uns," he answered.

"Glad to hear it," I answered. "Listen, remember when you delivered a message to The Palace for me in July? To a girl named Honey?"

With the mention of Mamie's new name, I could swear I saw a rosy crimson make its way up Mart's neck and over his cheeks, until his entire face, to the tips of his ears, was the color of a ripe tomato.

"Yes ma'am," he answered with a small hitch in his voice, as if his words had gotten caught up in a sticky spider's web on the way out of his throat. "I remember." Was that a look of enchantment that suddenly fell over his face like a magical spell? His eyes had an extra twinkle that I hadn't noticed before. I wondered if he'd been smitten with the young beauty who'd taken her life into her own hands.

"Do you think you'd be able to deliver something else to her? Directly to her, like you did last time?" I asked.

I could see the gears turning in his brain. Would this be a risk for him? Or would it be a treat instead?

"Yes ma'am, Ms. Eliza. I'll be able to deliver it just fine," he answered with something that sounded like determination.

"Well, it's not an urgent matter or anything. I just wanted to extend an invitation to her for our Labor Day celebration. Of course, I've also got one for you, Mart," I told him, taking the two cards from my bag, and handing them to the boy. "We'd love it if you could come, Mart. I know the girls would love to see you again," I told him. Everyone had always loved and trusted Mart. And of course, I trusted him more than anyone.

Mart's eyes teared up upon taking the notes from me. He pocketed his invitation, but just held the one for Mamie, tracing his finger over the lace, as if he were touching a girl's petticoat. "I'd be honored to come, Ms. Eliza," he answered. "And you can count on me to deliver this to Miss Honey," he said, carefully placing the invitation into his worn messenger bag. "I'll get it to her today," he said with a certainty that I knew meant it was as good as already delivered.

"Thank you so much Mart. Now you take care of yourself, and I'll see you on Labor Day," I told him, giving him a hug that let him know he was still my favorite boy in the world. My *very* favorite.

I left Linder's and walked to the trolley. Next stop, the mill. I would deliver Christian's invitation myself.

Chapter 32

Mart

August 30, 1907

Mart left Linder's in a strange state of both panic and giddy happiness. Another delivery to Honey. Her face had regularly appeared in both his waking thoughts and in his dreams. She was the most beautiful girl he'd ever seen, and now he had a chance to see her again. So many times he'd practiced what he'd say to her if he ever again had the opportunity, but for the life of him, all the versed words escaped him when he needed them most. He'd been given another chance, but felt as if he were a chicken on the slaughtering block. He thought the cornbread and beans he'd eaten for dinner last night might just up and leave his stomach.

Mart looked down at his breeches as he got on his bicycle, and saw the dust and dirt he'd accumulated the day before. Had he known this day would be special, he'd have washed himself more carefully. The better part of him was still covered with the evidence of his hard work, and he was sure his hair was an uncombed mess under his hat. He couldn't let Honey see him in such a dirty state, and decided he should fix himself up as best he could before he rode over to The Palace. Mart propped his bicycle against the side-wall of the store, and walked back in, the bells chiming as he opened the door.

"Did you forget somethin' Mart?" asked Mr. Linder, as he saw the boy walk toward him with his hat in his hands.

"No sir. But could I use your sink to wash up a bit?" Mart asked.

Twenty minutes later, with skin washed and hair combed down, Mart Waymond rode up to The Palace. His previous anxiety was nothing compared to the panic that now bound him like straps. He just prayed he didn't lose his voice. He propped his bicycle against the rail near the sidewalk, and just stood next to it, shuffling his feet, trying to calm his nerves to take care of the business at hand. But he was petrified. What if he made a fool of himself? What if this were his last chance to ever talk to Honey again, and he made a mess of it?

Mart took a very deep breath and held it in; *One, two, three, four, five,* he counted, then let a long breath of hopefulness float out into the afternoon. He did feel somewhat calmer and more able to think, instead of feeling as if his brain had been attacked by a band of crawly ants, making it twitch wickedly under the pressure.

How should he go about this?

Maybe just like last time. Just march right in there and go up to her room. But if Ms. May were anywhere near, she'd most likely demand he give the delivery to her, and then there might be trouble. He knew that Ms. May didn't like Eliza being friendly with any of her girls; she was bad for business.

Suddenly, the front door opened with a massive creak, interrupting his thoughts. Mart jumped nervously, hoping it wasn't May, but preparing for an ear-boxing all the same, his sure punishment for just standing around on her porch, detracting from her establishment's sophistication.

He let out a relieved breath as Maude, the house-girl, walked out with a broom in her hands. They'd been friends for as long as Maude had worked there.

"Why Mart! What are you doin' just standin' around on the porch?" Maude asked, so used to Mart just coming through the door to make his deliveries that she was temporarily stunned to see him standing there, just shuffling his feet. But Ms. May was mighty watchful over exactly which rooms he visited and how long he lingered. She knew he'd gotten a good wallop in the head from Ms. May the one time he'd unfortunately stayed too long.

"Howdy, Maude. Uh, I was just about to come in. But I gotta favor to ask ya'" he answered hesitantly. "I got somthin' to deliver to Miss Honey, and I gotta give it directly to her. Do you think you can ask her to come out here? It'll just take a minute." Mart paced back and forth, as if he were worried the sky might begin to fall at any second, preventing him from delivering his message. "I don't wanna make Ms. May upset by goin' up to Honey's room myself," he added.

Maude looked at him as if he were suddenly a person she didn't know, wrinkling her brow as she tried to figure out why a sudden fit of nervousness had overtaken the boy who was usually so casual in going about his business. "I guess," she answered somewhat hesitantly. "I just saw her a few minutes ago, eatin' her lunch. I'll go and fetch her," she said, curious as to the circumstances, but nevertheless turning around and going back the way she'd come.

Mart's cheeks flushed a bright cherry-red, as the rest of his body went cold with fear. He swiped his messenger's cap from his head with one hand, and smoothed his hair down with the other. His mouth suddenly went as dry as the sun-baked earth, and his stomach felt as if it were doing cartwheels.

Oh Lord, please help me get through this!

He didn't know how much longer he could stand on that porch, and had the fleeting idea of just jumping on his bicycle and peddling away as fast as he could. But then the door opened, and the girl of his dreams was suddenly standing before him, a sweet mirage shimmering in front of a man lost in the desert. He wasn't even totally convinced that she was truly there.

"Yes? Maude said you had something for me?" she asked, quickly recognizing Mart as the boy who'd delivered Eliza's invitation way back in July. She knew he routinely delivered other things to The Palace, but she wasn't in the habit of ordering anything herself. Mamie smiled at the boy who held his hat in his hands, almost crushing it under the death-grip of his fingers.

For some reason, no words came from Mart's mouth. He willed them to, but they just didn't. He realized he was sweating profusely, and hoped and prayed that his shirt wouldn't soak up the evidence of his affliction. "Hello, Miss Honey," he finally managed to stammer.

Her eyes were full of warm molasses, beckoning him to carry on a conversation. Suddenly, he realized they both had something in common.

"I been friends with Ms. Eliza for a long time," Mart told her. "She was always real nice to me," he said.

"I don't know her very well," answered Mamie, curious as to why he was talking about Eliza, "but she seems like a very nice woman."

Mart considered her words, knowing they were quite the understatement. "She knew I was hungry half the time I was workin', so she always shared her food with me. Lunch, or dinner, or just a small somethin'. It didn't matter. And she always made up an excuse of not bein' hungry, and not bein' able to finish her food. I know she just didn't want to embarrass me," he said with the tenderness of someone who'd been wrapped in the loving arms of a person who cared what happened to the rest of the world. "She made me feel like her little brother, with the way she always looked out for me and all," he said, with evident love and admiration for the woman they both knew.

"Didn't the Madame at her house mind you hanging around, and sharing food with her girls?" asked Mamie, having only May to compare any Madame to.

"Naw. The Orpheum wasn't like The Palace, and Ms. Dixie sure wasn't like Ms. May. Ms. Dixie was almost as kind as Ms. Eliza. That House was my second home," he answered fondly.

Mart suddenly remembered why he'd needed to see Mamie, aside from the pure and simple fact that he wanted to lay his eyes on her smooth and milky-colored skin again. He opened his messenger bag, and took out the invitation. "Ms. Eliza asked me to deliver this to you. It's an invitation to The Johnson Home's Labor Day barbecue. They have it every year," he told her. "I got one too," he added, hoping that Honey would hear the almost-pleading in his voice, and would decide to go. Hoping he'd get another chance to see her, if only briefly.

Mamie took the pretty card, holding it gently so as not to crinkle the delicate paper. An intricate cream-colored lace adorned the edges, making it look more like an invitation for a princess's ball rather than an outdoor barbecue. She'd never received an invitation so beautiful before.

"I've only spoken with Ms. Eliza a few times. She's trying hard to convince me that working in a brothel is too dangerous, that I can do something else with my life," said Mamie.

Mart winced at the thought of the dangers Miss Honey risked, putting herself in harm's way every day. Not to mention subjecting herself to the sexual whims of her customers. An odd combination of jealousy and anger filled his veins as quickly as a shot of whiskey, making him almost drunk with his longing for this girl. He didn't want to think about other men putting their hands on her. He was surprised at himself - he'd never felt this way before. After all, in his line of work, he knew full well what was required of these girls. It was just their job, no more. That's the way they thought of it, and that's the way he'd always thought of it too. Until now.

"Miss Honey, if you'd been there after Ms. Eliza was attacked, I reckon you might change your mind," Mart answered her quietly.

"I saw her scar when I met her back in July, and I must admit, it did make me think more about the risks I'm taking," Mamie said, thinking of Eliza's damaged face, and how she wore her hair down to cover it. "It does scare me to think about it."

"That's not even the half of it," Mart said. "Right away, the cut filled with poison, and Ms. Eliza fought the delirium. She was so sick for so long, I thought she was most likely gonna pass on," Mart told her, remembering his fear and sadness when he'd been quite positive he was going to lose her.

Mamie had only to look at him to know that Eliza's ordeal had affected him deeply. Their eyes locked, and for a few strange seconds, it was as if they were connected somehow. Then she blinked, and the moment ended, the unexpected ease of their conversation giving way to concern that she was staying on the porch too long.

"Well, thanks so much for delivering my invitation," she finally told him quietly, a sudden punctuation to their trance-like gaze. "You've brought me two notes so far, and I don't even know your name?" she finally asked him.

He smiled his lopsided grin, filled with the warmth of her question. "It's Mart. Well, Martin. Martin Waymond. But most folks just call me Mart for short," he told her with the self-consciousness of a schoolboy.

"Well, nice to meet you, Mart," she said sweetly, holding out her hand.

Mart was sure he felt an electric current pass between their palms and fingers as he shook her hand.

"You take care, Mart. Maybe I'll see you at the barbecue," Mamie said, as she backed herself toward the door.

"You take care of yourself, too, Miss Honey," Mart almost whispered.

Mart would make sure that she saw him again soon. He only hoped that he'd be able to steel himself until Ms. Eliza's barbecue.

Chapter 33

The Barbecue

Labor Day, September 2, 1907

Except for the very tiniest, all occupants at The Virginia K. Johnson Home had spent the weekend preparing for the Labor Day barbecue. It was the biggest gathering they would have all year. In addition to inviting girls from the brothels, they'd invited many people from the community, not only to stay connected to their neighbors, but to thank them for their hard work and charitable contributions throughout the year. The Johnson Home not only accepted donations for the girls they educated, but also for distribution to others in need. It was a way to teach the girls about caring for others. Although most of the girls at The Johnson Home were well aware of the graces bestowed upon them, it was important to reinforce the lesson that it was better to give than to receive.

As promised, the trolley dropped Mamie and Rosa off right down the street from The Johnson Home. After Mart had delivered the invitation to Mamie, she'd read it over and over again. It sounded quite enjoyable, but Mamie also had ulterior motives for going. She was hoping that Rosa would like The Johnson Home, and the women there. If so, she was going to convince Rosa to stay. Because she'd come to The Palace as payment of a debt, she wasn't earning a single nickel yet. Rosa was pleasing those men every night for free, and it turned Mamie's stomach to think about it. She would discuss it with Ms. Eliza, and then ask Rosa what she thought. Truth be told, she would love to stay at The Johnson Home as well, but it wouldn't pay her family's bills, and it wouldn't help Christian.

Mamie was also going to ask Ms. Eliza to help bring justice to the girls who worked in the cribs. Maybe Eliza and Ms. Dixie already knew about them, and maybe their outreach work was already being done at the cribs, but she didn't think so. If people knew what was truly going on, she didn't understand how the tenements were still operating. On the other hand, after seeing Ms. May's reluctance to speak with Eliza and Dixie, she was sure the crib-masters would not even let the ladies through the door. Why would they care about the welfare of their girls? Their business was more like slavery, or keeping animals in cages at the zoo. But something had to be done, and she was going to do everything possible to change it.

Mamie and Rosa walked along Madison Avenue and quickly saw the large red brick house, set back from the street, the porch decorated in red, white and blue for the occasion.

"I'm quite nervous to be going to a place like this," said Rosa rather timidly. It had taken them an hour to put together an outfit for Rosa that would be appropriate for a barbecue. She didn't yet have many clothes for wearing about town, so Mamie had loaned her what she thought might work. They'd finally been able to compose a suitable outfit for Rosa's tiny frame.

"It will be fine. You'll see," said Mamie. "Most of the girls here came from the brothels. They know what it's like. They're just like us," she said. But in fact, she wasn't at all sure they were just like Rosa. Had any of them been caged like an animal, starved and beaten if they didn't cooperate? She guessed probably not, but she certainly wasn't going to confess that to her friend.

Mamie and Rosa strolled up the walk to the front porch. As they ascended the stairs, Ms. Eliza came through the door in a flurry of activity, giving instructions to one girl, and then the next, about where to set up the lemonade pitchers, and what decorations should go where. When Eliza caught sight of the girls, her face lit up like a burst of sun. "Mamie, it's so nice to see you! I'm so glad you could come!" she said, as she gave Mamie a hug.

"This is my friend Rosa. Rosa Robles," said Mamie, nodding in Rosa's direction.

"So nice to meet you, Rosa," answered Eliza as she extended her hand. Rosa took it timidly, looking at the ground as if seeking refuge.

Eliza led the girls into the parlor. "I knew Mart would get your invitation delivered right away!" said Eliza.

Mamie thought of Mart, nervous as all get-out on the porch of The Palace. He wasn't sophisticated like the men she knew, but then again, that was what she liked about him. He seemed nice, and considerate. "Yes, he delivered it right to me. We even had a conversation right there on the porch. But I must say, he seemed a might discombobulated," said Mamie.

Eliza smiled. Mart was almost certainly taken with Mamie.

"Well, hopefully he'll be here later today," Eliza told her. "He can usually take time off from his delivery schedule when something important comes up; he makes up the time later. Why, I've never seen a boy with so much determination to do his job well."

Mamie felt a smile spread across her face at the thought of seeing Mart again. There was that small spark in the pit of her stomach that lit up as they'd talked on the porch. It felt warm and comfortable. "That would be nice," she said. "I like talking to him," she told Eliza.

"I'm so glad you could come too, Rosa," said Eliza, noticing that the girl had taken a small step back from them as they'd carried on their conversation. Rosa still wasn't sure she belonged there, in that grand house, with those pretty city girls. She was just a country girl, who'd never known anything about the finer things in life. She carried that feeling with her like a pack on her back; it was always there, even at The Palace. She usually thought of herself playing dress-up, in a costume, pretending to be someone she wasn't. But wasn't that, in fact, the truth? Coming here was just a continuation of the make-believe.

"Thank you," Rosa managed to answer.

"Rosa lives at The Palace too, and we've become good friends," announced Mamie.

Rosa couldn't help but smile when she heard Mamie's pronouncement. *Good friends.* Nothing sounded so sweet to her ears. After all she'd been through, having a friend was the most important thing in the world to her. She'd lost so much. It was nice to have finally gained something.

"Welcome to The Johnson Home, Rosa," Eliza said, as she smiled at the quiet girl. "I hope you enjoy our celebration. We look forward to it every summer."

"Ms. Eliza," interrupted a girl who was carrying Constance's infant boy, now eight months old. "Can you hold him while I help in the kitchen?" she asked.

"Of course I can," Eliza answered, holding out her arms to take the chubby and ruddy-faced baby. "Horace, you've even grown since I saw you yesterday," she announced, as she balanced the white-blond bundle on her hip. "Constance named him after her granddaddy. It's a name you hardly ever hear anymore."

Eliza noticed the confusion on Rosa's face, and explained. "Rosa, some of the girls who come here are pregnant. As you can imagine, most girls are out of work if they get pregnant. Especially at houses like The Palace. I know most of the girls use sponges and the bag to prevent it, but that doesn't always work. And then, we're blessed with little angels like

Horace here," she said, smoothing the hair back from Horace's elfin face.

Rosa and Mamie both knew what was required to prevent pregnancy, or at least *try* to prevent it. They packed their vaginas with sponges to keep the men's spunk from invading their insides. Then when the work night ended, they pulled out the sponges and used a bag to squeeze vinegar-water up inside, to clean out whatever of the men still remained. They'd wash their sponges, and let them dry for the next day's use. Invariably, one or two of the girls would get infections of their female parts, and would require the creams and rinses from Linder's to rid them of the nasty irritations.

Mamie also thought of the story Candace had told her, after Candace had drunk some fancy champagne that "made her mouth want to wag". Apparently, even after doing everything she knew to prevent it, Candace had gotten pregnant several years ago. There had never existed a woman who wanted a baby less than Candace, so she set about to rid herself of it. She contacted the doctor Ms. May used for such purposes - it certainly wasn't Doc Finley, who didn't believe in getting rid of babies. The doctor had given her the black pills; she'd taken one each day for three days, along with a scalding-hot bath, and sure enough, on the third day, she'd miscarried that baby. The tissue just ran out of her insides and down the drain, as if it were just part of her dirty bath water. Candace had said she'd never been so happy and relieved in her life. Mamie couldn't see how disposing of what would become a beautiful child could in any way cause happiness, and she was sad just hearing the story.

"Can I hold the baby?" asked Rosa timidly. Other than offspring from the animals on the farms she'd worked, she didn't have any experience with babies. "He's the cutest thing I've ever seen," she said, as Eliza handed him to her, and showed her how to position him comfortably on her hip.

"Why, he's almost bigger than you are," said Eliza with a grin. "You sure you have him?" she asked.

"Oh yes," answered Rosa. "I know I'm small, but I'm strong as an ox."

"Rosa worked on the farms picking cotton," explained Mamie. "She's got quite a few muscles under her sleeves."

It was evident that Rosa was totally taken with Horace, so Mamie thought this might be a good time to speak with Eliza in private. "Rosa, why don't you and Horace sit on the sofa here and play a game of pat-a-cake?" she suggested. "I need to speak with Ms. Eliza about a few things."

Eliza was taken aback by Mamie's suggestion. Had their talk at the park in July made an impression after all? She was certainly going to find out.

Eliza led Mamie up the stairs and into Ms. Dixie's office, where they could close the door for privacy.

"Ms. Eliza, I wanted to come to your celebration today to enjoy myself, and also give Rosa a treat. But I've got to confess that I've also come to ask two favors of you. *Huge* favors," Mamie added. Mamie sat down and put her hands in her lap, squeezing them together nervously. She wasn't quite sure why she was so anxious. After all, if Ms. Eliza turned her down, things would be no worse off than their current situation, so no harm done. But she'd grown to hold Rosa very dear, and wanted the best for her. She'd thought quite often about Ms. Dixie and Ms. Eliza, and their mission here, and, even though it wouldn't serve *her* purposes to stop working at The Palace, Rosa certainly didn't need to be there.

"I want to ask if Rosa can stay here at The Johnson Home? She's such a sweet girl, and she only came to be a prostitute by trickery. More like pure treachery. She doesn't deserve the life. I chose it, but she never did. Would it be possible to take her in? Now? Today?" Mamie pleaded, suddenly so afraid that Eliza's answer would be *no* that tears began to well in her eyes before Eliza even had a chance to say anything.

"Of course she can stay here," said Eliza, taking Mamie's hands in her own, and squeezing them to give the girl some reassurance. Mamie looked as if she would break into sobs any moment. "What's happened to her, Mamie? How did she come to be at The Palace?" asked Eliza.

Mamie explained how Rosa had been kidnapped from her family, and sold to a crib tenement on Wood Street. "It was horrible for her, Eliza. They beat her, drugged her, and starved her, until she finally did what they demanded - *sleep with twenty to thirty men every day!*" Mamie knew her depiction was very brief compared to the story Rosa had told her, the very ugly truth. A horror story. Yet she knew it had really happened to her friend. She didn't even understand how Rosa had kept her sanity this long. If it had been her, Mamie thought she'd surely have already lost her mind, or ended her life at the first opportunity. Rosa was the strongest person she'd ever met, and she loved her dearly.

"My good Lord Jesus," answered Eliza quietly, thinking of the young girl in the parlor playing with the baby, almost a child herself. How horrible that she'd already suffered a lifetime of abuse at her young age. "How old is Rosa? She couldn't be any more than fourteen or so," said Eliza.

"Not even. Not yet. She won't be fourteen until next month," answered Mamie.

If there was anyone who needed rescuing, Eliza knew it was Rosa Robles. But she wasn't quite sure how Rosa would be received - there had never been a Mexican girl living at The Johnson Home before. Nor Colored, for that matter. It wasn't that they'd been denied the opportunity, but none had ever asked to live there, and no one from The Home had ever done any outreach to any of the non-white houses. The races had always been separated - it was just a fact of life. But she really couldn't even consider that now - the girl was here and she needed help. "We're happy to have her here," said Eliza, hoping the slight hesitancy she felt couldn't be heard in her voice. "She can most likely help with the infants until she decides what trade she wants to learn. She seems to be quite taken with babies; I think she'd work very well in the nursery." Rosa was still a child herself, Eliza thought.

"Do you have any extra clothing for her to wear?" asked Mamie. "Rosa couldn't risk leaving the house with a valise, and she really doesn't own much anyway."

"Why, of course," answered Eliza, with a reassuring smile. "Don't you worry about Rosa. We'll take good care of her."

Mamie felt she could trust this woman, so she proceeded with her second request. "And there's something else, Ms. Eliza. Something I think needs to be done most urgently," explained Mamie as she looked Eliza in the eye. "Can you help shut down the crib houses?"

Eliza just looked at Mamie as if she'd spoken in a different tongue. At first Mamie thought she hadn't heard her, but then she could see that Eliza had. "Shut down the crib houses," was all Eliza said in reply.

Eliza's eyes welled with tears, her mind filled with a thousand terrible images, and the knowledge that neither Virginia Johnson, nor Ms. Dixie, nor she had done anything to save the girls living as slaves to the crib-masters. Eliza had never been to a crib house, but knew they were there. They all did, but they tried not to think of them, she supposed just as the upper social crust of society tried not to think of the brothels on Emma Street. If they didn't *consciously admit* their existence, then maybe they just *didn't* exist. If truth is neglected long enough, it seems to magically disappear. Totally illogical, she knew, but what else could the human mind do to protect itself from anguish that just couldn't be erased? Some things just *were*, and they couldn't be helped. At least, that's what Eliza had convinced herself. Now, the truth of their neglect had swallowed up a thirteen-year-old girl; used up as much of her childhood as it could, and then flaunted itself in front of Eliza's complacency.

"So you know about the crib houses?" Mamie asked her. "What is being done about them?"

Eliza just shook her head, as if shaking away the injustice of the world. As if it *could* be just shaken away. "Nothing," was all she could answer.

"Nothing?!" asked Mamie in disbelief. "I know you and Ms. Dixie try to help the girls working on Emma Street. And I know you're going to help Rosa. But what about all the other girls, the slaves in the tenements? How can you ignore them?" Mamie didn't know what to think. The Johnson Home was just making its mark on the surface, not even touching the lowest forms of inhumanity.

"There is only so much we can do, Mamie. We try to help who we can, but there are just some people who can't be helped," Eliza answered in defeat, knowing that her argument sounded superficial and inept as soon as she said the words. At that moment, Eliza felt as if all the good works done by The Johnson Home were merely symbolic, hiding the most horrible conditions under a cloak of good intentions.

"Had Rosa not been sent to The Palace, she'd still be in that horrible place, with those horrible people," Mamie said quietly, once again shuddering at the tragedy of it all. "They're kept like animals in cages, Eliza. They're beaten and starved, and some girls even die. I don't understand why anyone puts up with it? Why don't the police do anything about it?"

It was evident that Mamie was still innocent to the way the real world worked. Even though she'd lived through her share of adulthood at the mill, and had taken her life into her own hands at the tender age of thirteen, she was still idealistic about what the world should and should not tolerate.

"I agree with you, Mamie," said Eliza. "It's a horrible, horrible part of our society. But it's a part that the people in power just don't want to consider. They turn a blind eye to it, as if hoping it would someday just vanish of its own accord." Eliza paused, trying to explain it.

"Like my attack. Officer Heinrich tried to find the man who did it. He tried most valiantly, working as hard as he could. But investigations take time, and his superiors ordered him to stop. The police devote the most effort to protecting their *deserving* citizens. As far as they're concerned, and as far as *most* people are concerned, prostitutes have made their beds themselves, and they must suffer through what they've asked for, what they've chosen."

"Why that's ridiculous!" shouted Mamie. "Prostitutes are people too. They live and breathe just like anyone else."

"But most people fancy themselves to be above us," answered Eliza. "And those people are the ones who elect those in power, and pay the salaries of the policemen trying to enforce the law. The wishes of those people are given more weight, and the weight of their opinions and desires is heavier than the weight of justice." Eliza felt the familiar fire once again flow through her veins. Why was the world so unfair? Why did it matter who of them had more money, or power?

Mamie looked at Eliza with tears in her eyes, and felt the heaviness of the indifference that kept them from doing more, an oppressive chain wound around them by those more fortunate, shackling any efforts to correct a horrible wrong. Eliza's eyes were filled with tears as well, the result of the frustration that was part of not being able to do enough.

Eliza hesitated, then said, "Of course, the cribs house mainly the Coloreds and Mexicans, and we can't rightly expect the police to devote as much time and energy to them. They're paid to protect the rights of the people who pay their taxes, and the majority of taxes are paid by Whites." She said it as a matter of fact, not opinion.

Mamie couldn't believe what she was hearing. "I thought you were concerned about the safety and well-being of the girls in this city? What difference does it make what color their skin is?" She was barely able to remain civil, instead of screaming in outrage. "So *that's* the *real* reason no one is doing anything about it!" It was not a question, but the logical conclusion.

Eliza looked calmly at Mamie before she spoke. "It's *both* reasons, Mamie. The police don't generally want to invest time in crimes against working women in the first place, and if they're not light-skinned, the importance of justice drops another notch."

Both women just stared at each other, neither quite knowing what else to say.

"Obviously, with the police turning a blind eye, it's very dangerous to even approach the crib tenements. Please don't fancy that you'd be able to change anything by trying to do something yourself. They're apt to capture you, and keep you locked up," pleaded Eliza.

"Do you hear yourself, Eliza?" Mamie asked incredulously. "Do you hear what you're saying? Young girls are just snatched and forced to work as slaves, all right under everyone's noses!

For God's sake, the North winning the war was supposed to end slavery. But it's still here! People are ignoring it, hoping it will just go away! But it will *never* go away, not unless someone *does something* about it!" Mamie was so distressed she'd turned red in the face, her arguments spewing like steam hissing from a tea kettle. Rosa had been a victim, and by luck she'd been freed. But how many other hundreds of girls had not been so lucky, and were still suffering at the hands of those greedy and ruthless people?

"I understand Mamie. I truly do. I've felt the same way many times, but now understand there's only so much we can do. I decided that it's better to help some than none, and that's what we've done here," explained Eliza. "But of course you're right. It's disgraceful," she said, trying to shake the image of imprisoned young girls from her mind. "How did Rosa escape?" asked Eliza.

"She didn't," answered Mamie. "The crib-master owed a debt to Ms. May, so they gave Rosa to her. Since she herself was a repayment, Rosa hasn't even received any wages yet. But of course, moving to The Palace was quite a step up from where she came," Mamie said.

"You don't care that Rosa's Mexican, do you?" Mamie suddenly blurted, almost holding her breath. She realized the question had been needling her brain ever since Eliza had spoken of society's unequal treatment of the races, and her acceptance of the situation as just a fact of life.

Eliza was taken aback by the question, feeling as if it were an insult to her sensitive nature. "Why certainly not," she answered, almost offended. But then it occurred to her that Mamie's question was perfectly logical, considering what Eliza herself had just minutes before told the girl. And it was true that she wondered how Rosa would fit in as the only non-Anglo there.

Their conversation was interrupted by a knock on the office door. "Excuse me, Ms. Eliza, but there's someone here to see you. He's in the parlor waitin' for you," said Constance, who had retrieved Horace from Rosa, and was balancing the happy baby on her hip.

"Thank you, Constance," said Eliza, with a small smile. She knew who it had to be, and he would be a most welcome interruption at just that point in their conversation.

Mamie misunderstood, thinking it was a suitor. "Thank you, Eliza," she said rather briskly. "I guess there is only so much that can be done. I know Rosa will love it here," she said, almost ruefully. It was true she longed to stay as well, but she wasn't going to let her mind dwell on that fact.

"Mamie, I think you're going to want to visit with my company as well," said Eliza almost playfully. "Let's go to the parlor together."

As they descended the stairs, Eliza saw a small boy sitting on the sofa, across from Rosa, with a glass of lemonade in his hand. His hair was the same color as Mamie's - thick honey squeezed from the comb. As they approached, he turned his head and it was as if she were looking at Mamie's face - skin fair and spattered with light freckles.

Mamie let out a squeal. "Christian! Christian! Oh my Lord! Is that you? What are you doing here?" She ran down the rest of the stairs, and took her brother into her arms. Arms that had sorely missed hugging him for the last three months.

"Mamie!" Christian cried. "I've missed you so much!" He hugged her back as if he had no plans of letting her go again.

"I *thought* you'd be happy to meet my company," Eliza said with a smile so wide one might actually notice the slight crookedness of her incisors.

"Let me look at you, Christian," Mamie said, taking his cheeks between her palms. "You seem to have grown since the last time I saw you. Where are those chubby cheeks I used to squeeze?" she asked.

"I'm almost grown, Mamie," he answered with all sincerity. Eliza guessed that was probably close to the truth, maybe not physically, but for the heavy burden of responsibility he carried.

"Sit down with me, and tell me everything that's gone on since I left," instructed Mamie. "Are you still working at the mill?" Mamie asked, hoping the answer would be *no*.

"Sure I am," he answered proudly. "I work more now than I did before you left. Papa said I'd have to take up the slack from you being gone," he answered casually, as if this were just the logical mathematical result.

Mamie couldn't believe what she was hearing! Her father made Christian work more, instead of lightening his load! What was he doing with all the wages she'd sent him? Mamie was livid that her father hadn't done the right thing. The realization that he had fewer morals than she'd even suspected hit her like a slap, and anger flamed up inside her like a newly-lit furnace.

"Where did you go, Mamie? Why did you leave us?" Christian asked quietly, not really sure he wanted to hear her answer. He'd always thought that maybe he'd done something wrong, something to drive her away, and he was scared to hear her say it out loud. "Did I do something to make you mad?" he asked with the voice of the small boy that he truly was.

"Oh, no, Christian, you didn't do *anything*," she answered tenderly, tears threatening to spill over as she saw his eyes fill with the loneliness and guilt that had plagued him since she'd gone. "I *had* to leave. I had to get away from the mill." She couldn't tell him the brutal truth, that Duffy's hands and their father's indifference had caused her flight. "Mr. Duffy was treating me unfairly, so I just had to leave," she answered.

"Why didn't you tell Papa?" he asked. "He would'a fixed it."

How could she tell her sweet brother that their father knew full well of her violation, and he'd done *nothing* to fix it. He'd been more concerned about the family's employment than the abuse she'd suffered at Duffy's hand. "I did tell him, Christian. But he didn't think he could make it better," she answered. Mamie didn't want her innocent brother to know how their father had thrown her over for the mill. One day she'd tell him the truth, but that day hadn't yet come.

"Where did you go?" her brother asked. "And how come you don't visit me?"

Mamie couldn't tell Christian where she'd gone, and what she'd become since she last saw him. No matter that her motivation was to make his life easier. She was still a prostitute, and she couldn't tell her brother. "I live at a house close to downtown. I make more money now than I did at the mill, and I send most of it to ma and papa," she told him. "I was hoping that you wouldn't have to work anymore if I sent them enough," she added wistfully, understanding that reality was far from her good intentions.

"I go in with Papa now, and stay all day 'til he leaves," he answered. "That way I can do the work of two doffers instead of just one."

No, no, no! It wasn't supposed to be this way!

"I miss you something terrible," Christian told Mamie. "I'll probably get a good licking for missing work today, but I had to sneak away to come see you," he said, looking into his sister's eyes with the longing of a lost puppy. "I miss you so much Mamie."

Mamie took him to her breast and hugged him with the fervor of a drowning woman, desperately clutching the solitary tree branch that would save her from the swirling waters of despair. "I miss you too, Christian! You'll never know how much," she whispered tenderly into his ear as she kissed his head, wishing she could hold him like that forever. Tears of both anger and sadness overcame her as she thought of the risk he'd taken. She couldn't bear to think of him being punished, just for wanting to see her, but it was most likely inevitable.

Eliza's heart went out to Mamie. She'd wanted this to be a joyful occasion, not sad. Maybe she could occupy her mind with happier thoughts if they took a break for lunch. Eliza didn't know if Christian ate sufficiently for an eight-year-old boy, but she was certainly going to make sure he got his fill at *this* picnic. "Why don't the three of you go out back, and get some lunch. We have barbecue," Then looking right at Christian said, "And for dessert, we have apple and cherry pies, and a chocolate cake."

Christian's eyes lit up as if he'd just been handed a pound of peppermints.

"Yes, let's go get something to eat," Mamie answered, standing but not letting go of Christian's hand. She only then noticed Rosa, and was ashamed. The shock and happiness of seeing Christian after all this time had made her forget her manners.

"Oh, Rosa, I'm so sorry. I got carried away. This is my brother, Christian," Mamie said, introducing him.

"Christian and I already got to know each other," answered Rosa. "We were sitting here, drinking lemonade, and talking about dogs and cats." Well, that certainly sounded like Christian, thought Mamie. Her brother loved all animals, even though he had no pets at home. When it was already too hard to feed the family, there was nothing left to spare for feeding pets.

"I think Eliza has a good idea," said Rosa. "Let's go eat. I'm hungry."

"Me too," said Christian.

The three walked out to the lawn where lunch was being served.

Chapter 34

Labor Day

Late Afternoon - September 2, 1907

The Palace

Mamie boarded the street car for her ride back to The Palace. Her heart was heavy and happy at the same time. Seeing Christian after so many months was the best gift anyone could have given her, and she'd be forever grateful to Eliza for arranging it. But leaving him again had been horrible; the anguish she'd felt in June had returned twofold. She hadn't made his life easier, and she'd missed him more than she realized. Who knew when she'd get to see him again? But at least she knew how she would get in touch with him - Mart offered to handle the communications between the two. He said he could make deliveries to the mill just as easily as he could to The Palace.

Mart had arrived at the barbecue midway through the afternoon, after his messenger shift had ended. Several times Mamie had caught him looking at her, as if studying her face. After the third time catching him stare, she decided to go talk to him. The least she could do was thank him again for being so diligent in delivering Eliza's messages directly to her. After all, he was taking quite a risk, knowing how Ms. May didn't allow delivery boys the same liberties he'd been used to at The Orpheum. Had she not gotten Eliza's invitation, she never would have seen Christian, or arranged for Rosa to stay.

Mamie made her way to where Mart was sheepishly standing, and just like the last time she'd seen him, his face bloomed with the pink hue of rose petals, small beads of his suffered anxiety glistening on his forehead. After all the time she'd spent with confident and powerful men, Mart's embarrassment and hesitation when he spoke to her was most endearing. It was quite obvious he truly cared what she thought of him, as if his life might be hanging by the thread of her spoken *hello*. Other than her brother, she was sure no one else had ever cared so much about her feelings.

"Why hello, Mart! May I join you?" Mamie asked, as she met him at the bottom of the front-porch staircase. He was so discombobulated that he dropped his cap, bent to pick it up, and spilled his lemonade in the process.

"I'd be honored, Miss Honey," he told her, as he tried to pretend his hands weren't twitching, his nervous reaction to the sound of her voice.

Mamie smiled at his sweetness.

Christian only stayed at The Johnson Home for a few hours; Mamie had convinced him to at least work part of the afternoon at the mill. Maybe his punishment could be stalled or avoided by hard work.

Hard work, she thought. He should be playing with his marbles and balls, not doffing at the mill. The thought of her father punishing him with her absence disgusted her. She sent him money weekly, but where was it going? She didn't know, but she was resolved to find out.

Saying goodbye to Rosa had been harder than she'd imagined. She was Mamie's one true friend at The Palace, and she realized she'd come to depend on their sharing of confidences. It helped when a girl had someone to talk to. The frustration and fear and anger didn't build up inside, like a pressure cooker building up its steam, and then escaping in a torrent of resentment and rage. Talking about one's troubles every day was more like a slow leak which was just absorbed into the atmosphere, without ever doing any damage.

Now Rosa wouldn't be there to listen anymore. Even though she was only a short trolley-car ride away, over the river could just as well be on the other side of the state. But although it would be hard on both not to have each other to lean on every day, at least Rosa would get a new start, and not have to sacrifice her small body. Rosa had been so happy and grateful when Mamie told her that she'd made arrangements for her to stay at The Johnson Home. Rosa knew how to speak Spanish, and thought that maybe she could become a teacher of some sort, helping local Mexican kids whose English was lacking. Mamie didn't think that any Coloreds or Mexicans lived at The Johnson Home - most of the non-White people she'd met in her lifetime lived in the west part of Dallas. She hadn't seen any at the barbecue, so was fairly certain that only Anglo girls lived there. The houses on Emma Street had no folks of color that she knew of - Rosa had been the first at The Palace, and that happened just by chance. But Rosa could read - both English and Spanish - her mama had seen to that. So if she could learn to be a teacher, maybe she could someday work in West Dallas teaching Mexican kids. Or maybe someday the Mexican kids would be living in Oak Cliff?

Then Mamie thought about the way Eliza had almost dismissed the injustices suffered by the *non-White* population, and she felt her skin prickle with anger. How dare she talk as if certain people were not as important as others, and shouldn't necessarily expect justice? Couldn't Eliza see this was the same view that high-society people had of prostitutes? Mamie was still stunned by the woman's hypocrisy.

Mamie prayed that Rosa wouldn't be treated as a lesser occupant, just because her skin was brown. Ms. Eliza hadn't seemed to hesitate when asked if Rosa could stay, so Mamie hoped it didn't matter. Nonetheless, the whole discussion had been quite perplexing and unsettling.

Mamie contrived to sneak back into The Palace in the late afternoon. Not that she wasn't allowed to leave, but she didn't want to be questioned about Rosa. Most everyone knew they were friends. Even though they'd left that morning at different times and walked in different directions, it would be reasonable to assume that Mamie would know where she was, and why she hadn't yet returned. Mamie would just try to keep as low a profile as she could, and hope for the best. She decided to enter through the rear hallway door, and use the back stairs. At this time of day, Ms. May was readying for dinner, and then the arrival of customers immediately after, so she'd most likely be in the front of the house.

Mamie held up the hem of her dress as she gingerly climbed the stairs. She mentally prepared herself to act like this was just a normal day. At least until they questioned her about Rosa, and then she'd feign surprise and distress that her friend was gone. Actually feeling distraught wasn't very far from the truth anyway. She opened her bedroom door and saw Candace sitting in front of her mirrored powder-table in her dressing gown, pinning her hair up. Their eyes met briefly by way of the glass, and Mamie could swear that she detected a hint of poison in that glance.

"Why *there* you are," Candace announced slyly to the looking glass. "We were wondering if you'd left as well?" she asked with a catty smirk.

Pinpricks of fear traveled quickly up and down Mamie's spine, as if she'd been stuck with a Chinese needle. "What are you talking about?" she managed to ask as innocently as she could, trying to cloak her anxiety in a veil of normalcy.

Candace's full lips turned upward into the all-knowing, close-to-evil grin of someone who's sure she holds another's fate in her hands, and could easily cause destruction, or not, depending on her mood. "Why, your visit to The Johnson Home, of course. Isn't that where you've been?"

Mamie was caught. She would tell the story she'd contrived for just this circumstance, although she'd foolishly hoped she wouldn't have to use it. "I was visiting my aunt. She's taken ill, and I wanted to make sure she's being cared for," Mamie lied.

"Your *aunt*! That's what you call those old whores at The Johnson Home? *Aunts?*" Candace chuckled. "And was the little brown bitch concerned about your auntie as well?"

Mamie forced herself to remain calm. Unless one of the girls had followed them, and she was certain no one had, Candace had no proof of anything. All Mamie had to do was keep up her ruse. "What are you talking about, Candace?" she asked, furrowing her brow in fabricated perplexity.

"Just so happens the little Mexican bitch you keep chummy with left about the same time you did, and as far as anyone knows, she's still not back," said Candace. "I'm guessin' she *won't* be."

"Rosa?" asked Mamie. "Rosa left?" She was trying her best to sound shocked, as if the rug had just been pulled from under her feet.

"*Really?*" asked Candace in mock surprise. Mamie guessed that she was quite enjoying her inquisition. "You didn't go to the The Johnson Home, and you didn't go with Rosa? *Hmmm.* You know, you're fairly good at actin' like you're better than the rest of us, but I wouldn't quit your day job yet. Ha! I mean night job!" she said, laughing at her own joke. "Oh, and Ms. May wants to see you. Since you didn't see her in the parlor, I'm assumin' you snuck in through the back way." Candace's malignant snigger attacked Mamie's sensibilities like an unwanted virus. Mamie hated her.

Ms. May. Damn it to hell! Mamie had prayed that Ms. May wouldn't notice she was missing. But even if she hadn't, Candace would've been sure to let her know. Mamie was sure her roommate was responsible, now certain that Candace had overheard her and Rosa discussing their plan. Candace would have done nothing to stop them. After all, she'd like nothing more than for Rosa to leave The Palace, so she could reclaim her position as the most sought-after whore of the house.

Mamie said nothing more, but turned and walked resolutely down the hall, then descended the front staircase to the parlor.

"Ah, there you are. Decided to come back, did you?" Ms. May asked with a small grin that served to deepen the crevices on her aging face. "We weren't sure if you would or not. But I take it you need the money." May studied Mamie's expression. "Where is your *friend*? Did she come back as well?"

Mamie prayed the right words would come, and that her nerves wouldn't fail her. "You mean Rosa? Candace told me she wasn't here."

"You mean Rosa?" Ms. May mocked with a knife-sharp edge to her voice. "Playing the little fool, are you? Where is she!?" May demanded.

"I don't know," answered Mamie. "I didn't know she was gone. I went to visit my aunt who's ill with the gripe. I haven't seen Rosa."

"Really," May answered with exaggerated skepticism, appraising Mamie with the hungry look of a bear about to attack. "Well, we'll see if she returns before the evening is over. And if she doesn't," Ms. May paused, smiling with the vengeance of one who's allowed to use it, "then you'll just have to take her place in the circus tonight."

No, no, no! Mamie's soul screamed. So far, she had evaded performing in the circus - she was terrified of it. She hadn't guessed that this might be her punishment for Rosa's flight. But she'd do anything for Rosa, and now she was going to pay heavily. *At least Rosa has escaped her nightmares*, she thought. *I'll just have to satisfy the ransom.* "I'm sure she'll be back before then," answered Mamie, her voice quivering with both the joy of knowing she'd helped her friend escape, and the paralyzing fear of knowing that she'd have to trade herself to pay for it.

Chapter 35

Eliza

September 3, 1907

Although everyone seemed to enjoy the barbecue, the conversation I'd had with Mamie plagued me all day and well into the night, infringing on my sleep. Her words and my insufficient responses kept replaying themselves in my brain, and my conscience decided it had to interject its opinions as well. I've never thought of myself as not treating all people equally - after all, I would think the fact that I was a prostitute would disqualify me from passing judgment on others. But talking with Mamie about the crib-houses made me finally admit to myself that I *hadn't* treated everyone the same. Or at least, thought of everyone in the same light.

I tried very hard to determine where these beliefs came from; they were certainly not mingled with my conscious thoughts, but buried deep within myself. So deep, in fact, that I didn't even realize they were there. Until Mamie shoveled them up to the surface. Now I had no choice but to consider them. It wasn't as if I'd made up my mind that Coloreds and Mexicans didn't measure up to Anglo's. It wasn't that at all. I wouldn't think the slightest thing about talking to any one of them on the street, or helping them if asked. After all, they were the same children born of Adam and Eve, and Jesus loved all of us the same. But Mamie saw through my self-deception.

I *did* think of people with colored skin differently.

I was filled with shame at the realization that I was just like the judgmental hypocrites I'd always loathed so much, and had fought against for so long. *Lord bless me, I was virtually the same.*

Mamie was right - something had to be done about the crib-houses. What went on there right under our noses was a horror! I was quite distressed to realize it, uncontrolled tears just spilling down my cheeks. Did I think I was better than a Mexican girl who'd been kidnapped, and forced to give her body and soul to a place like that? I was no better. No better!

My job was to help young girls escape prostitution, escape the streets, and the madams, and the men reeking of tobacco and whiskey. I then understood that it was also my job to try to help those in the tenements. *Damn-it, they deserved better too.*

But what could I do about it?

I sat for a long while thinking, trying to devise a plan of action. I'd never been one to just wait for something to happen. I had always *made* things happen. Now it was time to make things happen again. The thoughts swirling around in my brain finally began to settle into somewhat of an organized strategy. Not a perfect plan, but at least I knew where to start. At least I wouldn't be ignoring the problem, doing nothing. At least I would be doing *something*.

Later that morning, I once again found myself sitting on the streetcar, and once again, I was lost in thought.

I hadn't even discussed my decision with Ms. Dixie yet; this one errand I had to do without discussion. Without permission. My conscience was demanding action.

The trolley took me across the river and downtown, to the police station on Harwood Street. Officer Heinrich's station, as far as I knew. I was going to ask, no *beg*, for his help. He'd been quite vigilant in his efforts to bring justice to the prostitutes in this city once; hopefully, he still felt the same way.

But a niggling thought kept tumbling around in my head - maybe Officer Otto Heinrich hadn't been concerned about the fate of sporting women; maybe he'd just been concerned about *my* fate. I'd at one time thought he might have felt affection for me. He'd looked at me with those tender brown eyes, and seemed to truly care what happened. Or had that been my imagination? Just my secret hope?

I finally arrived at the intimidating stone structure that was Dallas' police headquarters. I walked up the huge stone staircase and opened the door to see a flurry of men in blue uniforms, all with an apparent purpose in their hurried activity. I made my way to the desk where an older man with a large handle-bar mustache was sitting with a pen and notebook. *Sergeant Manning* was the name pinned to the breast-pocket of his coat.

"Excuse me," I said to him, with as much authority as I could muster, "I'd like to speak with Officer Heinrich please. Otto Heinrich," I said.

The sergeant looked at me with a confused expression, as if he were considering why a woman would be inquiring after one of his officers. And then he noticed my scar, and I could see his mind working even harder to deduce my intentions. Women weren't generally involved in police matters, so why was I standing in front of him, asking to speak to one of his own? A woman who had obviously suffered from malice at some point. His discerning gaze considered me a moment longer, until he finally turned to a young officer behind him and quietly gave him instructions. "*Detective* Heinrich will be right down," he told me. "I've sent for him," he said, as I saw the young officer disappear up the inside staircase. "You may have a seat if you'd like," he added, nodding to an area across the room.

I made my way to the bank of wooden chairs along the far wall, and looked back at the counter. Sergeant Manning was still looking after me, as if I were an enigma that he was bound and determined to figure out. His gaze made me anxious, as if chastising me for being there. *But I had every right to be there*, I told myself. I was an upright citizen now. Although possibly out of the norm, dressed in black, my attire was conservative, my demeanor subdued. I thought that possibly my anxiety was playing tricks with my thinking. I was no less entitled to assistance than anyone else. But the shame from once being a working girl momentarily overtook me, as a cloak that somehow always covered me, one I was not able to remove. But *no*, that wasn't me anymore! I had *changed*, for the good!

Then an attractive man in a double-breasted gray pinstripe suit made his way down the stairs. He was so much more handsome than even my memory of him. Light brown hair slicked back in the current style. He still lacked the swagger of those in charge, but that was such a very good thing. He stopped to speak to Sergeant Manning who pointed in my direction, and then he turned my way. The surprise on his face upon seeing me was almost comical, and I had to smile in spite of the reason for my visit.

"Miss Darling," he said gently, holding out his hand to me as I stood. "You're a stunning sight," he said with a small smile, which was quickly replaced by the face of embarrassment. He'd apparently said the first thing that came to mind, albeit not quite appropriate. But of course, I loved his compliment, and was filled with the nervous fluttering of a school girl.

"Officer Heinrich. Oh, I'm sorry. *Detective* Heinrich," I said, blushing from feelings I hadn't known could still affect a woman of my experience, tingling with the excitement of it.

"What a nice surprise," he said, his hand still holding mine, as if he had no intention of letting it go anytime soon. "But I'm sure your visit is not just social. What can I help you with?"

I was momentarily tongue-tied. I just stood there, letting him clasp my hand between his. Those chocolaty eyes held even more liquid warmth that I'd remembered, as if there were so much depth to them they didn't ever end, like looking down into a bottomless abyss. But they also spoke to me, the crinkles around them as he smiled a telling sign that he *was* truly happy to see me.

I finally got my wits about me, and regained my hand. Not wanting to pull it away from him, but knowing I had to. It was then blatantly obvious to me that maybe I had an ulterior motive for coming here, but I was not going to let that get in the way of my larger purpose. "Detective, I need your help," I stated simply.

I was seated in Detective Heinrich's office, with a cup of hot tea. Otto Heinrich halfway sat on the edge of his desk. "So, to what do I owe the honor of your visit?" he asked, his voice like smooth, warm molasses. He *is* happy to see me, I thought, but then just as quickly wondered if it was instead my overactive imagination playing its favorite tricks on my thinking. I felt the blush blooming up from my chest, then over my throat and cheeks.

"The crib tenements," I blurted. "I need your help in shutting down the crib tenements." I stated my intention as if it were just the slightest of requests, as if fulfilling it would take only the snap of his fingers, and then it would be done.

Upon hearing my appeal, he raised his brows and emitted a slight laugh, as if I'd just asked him to rope in the moon for me. "Miss Darling…" he began, shaking his head.

"Please call me Eliza," I answered, although I had to admit the word *darling* coming from his lips filled me with a thrilling excitement.

"All right. *Eliza*," he said, "that is quite a request. You've surprised even me! I truly *was* hoping this visit might be just a social call."

I had to smile - *a social call!* Maybe my imagination had *not* conjured the spark I'd always felt by his presence! Lord, how I wished it *were* just a social visit, but my mission took precedence over my attraction to this man. "Detective..." I began.

"Oh no, call me Otto," he insisted. "It won't do for only one of us to be on more familiar terms."

My face couldn't help but reflect my pleasure, mission or no. "Otto," I began. His name when spoken sounded like the ping of crystal when it touched my ears. "I realize my request sounds flippant, as if I don't know that what I'm asking is a huge undertaking. But I assure you, I know how massive my request is."

He looked at me as if I'd just escaped from the sanitarium for the insane. He even laughed kind-heartedly. "Eliza, I know the problem exists, but you know as well as I do that it would take a huge amount of manpower to do what you're asking. And quite frankly, all that time and money and energy spent on saving Colored prostitutes in the slums in not something my bosses would consider."

I knew that what he said was true, and I'd expected him to say it. But he was also trapped within the apathy of our culture, just as I'd been. I continued. "I know the police department has diligently worked to shut down many of the parlor houses on Emma Street. The Reformers have demanded that vice be reduced, and you've done it. Can't you take it one step further? Can't the police department try to shut down the *truly abhorrent* vice that lives just below the surface? At least the girls working in the houses on Emma Street have a choice in the matter, and are getting paid for what they do. The girls in the tenements are kept like animals in cages, treated like slaves. If this city truly wanted to rid its streets of vice, I should think it would shut down the slave traders in the tenements." I was getting upset just discussing it - I could feel the heat spread across my cheeks as I argued my position.

Otto considered me and my lofty plea. "Eliza, even if I *could* get the approval, which I doubt I could mind you, we can't just go to every dilapidated building in Frogtown, knocking on doors, demanding to walk through the hallways to look for girls being kept as slaves. We'd need a warrant, and without any specifics to support our request, no judge in his right mind would sign a warrant order for us."

I met his gaze head on; I was not going to give up easily. "What if I could give you someone who'd been kidnapped, and sold to a crib tenement, then was drugged and starved and kept under lock and key? What if she could take you to the exact building that was her prison? Could you at least search that one tenement, and do what was necessary to shut it down?"

Otto looked at me with what seemed to be a strange mix of frustration and kindness, considering such an enormous task. "What's happened, Eliza?" was all he asked then.

"There's a girl who just came to live at The Johnson Home yesterday. She's Mexican and only thirteen years old. She was essentially kidnapped from her family, and sold to one of the crib-masters. She was beaten, starved, and drugged, until she finally did what they required." Sadness filled me as I thought of Rosa's struggle, but quickly turned to both anger and fear as I thought of the other women who were imprisoned there, for how long one could only guess.

"Otto," I began softly, "do you remember what it was like to be thirteen? Did you have a loving family, and a good childhood? Did you go to school, and pass your summers in the luxury of innocent amusements?" I regarded him, and wondered if possibly I'd been mistaken to ask. After all, he might have suffered hardships as a boy, I didn't know. I was taking a chance with this tactic.

Otto studied my face, now filled with the pain of hundreds of wasted childhoods, my eyes glittering with the tears that should fall for each one of them. "Yes," he answered softly.

"I remember what it was like being thirteen. I had wonderful parents who let me grow up without a care in the world, and allowed me to get my education." He seemed to be suddenly lost in memories of that golden time, and smiled. "One summer, I took my dog Max down to the banks of The Trinity at dawn, and I sat there and fished all day long. Didn't put my gear up until it was getting dark. I caught twenty perch and four catfish that day, and my mama cooked them up for dinner. My father was so impressed that I'd caught so many fish and provided dinner, he gave me a quarter to spend as I pleased." He was wrapped within the happiness of that far-off time, his smile lingering on his lips until he returned to the present. Then it was obvious that his thoughts turned to what it must have been like being kidnapped and sold as a sex slave at that age, his expression growing steely, his eyes now reflecting anger instead of joy.

Otto drew in a long breath, and exhaled slowly, tapping his fingers on the desk, his thoughts skittering in all directions. Then he looked at me with those deep brown eyes, and I knew that I had won his help. "Let's just focus on the *one* tenement right now, O.K.?"

Our crusade had begun.

Chapter 36

Elaine

September 2011

It's been a very strange summer.

My life has changed, at first glance so slowly I really didn't even recognize the movement. But today, in early September, I look in the mirror and see someone who wasn't there back in June:

1. I've grown my hair out a little, letting it enclose my face, my cheeks barely visible, as if I'm trying to hide.

2. I no longer wear make-up, letting my skin just reflect its natural glow.

3. My clothing has changed. For some reason, I'm drawn to the colors of melancholy - hues of grays and blacks. Somber colors. The style of what I'm wearing hasn't changed much - still the same Danskin skorts; still my stretchy *easy-fit* jeans. But now instead of cheery pinks and blues, they inspire a shadowy darkness. As if I'm in mourning for some reason I can't even fathom.

4. Mystery has somehow intertwined itself into my reflection. A hidden part of me that I haven't quite been able to put my finger on.

Drew loves my new look. Although he hasn't remarked on the dark colors of my clothes, he said the haircut makes me look ten years younger, and is *sexy as hell*. It felt so great to hear him say that. I smile, remembering how he tried to fondle me right there in the kitchen when I walked through the door. I mentally give myself a *Go Girl!* - my husband still thinks I look hot!

The summer has certainly been an evolution. Rayce's high-school graduation was a proud moment for us, another family milestone achieved. But since then, his preparation for college has been bittersweet. I'm happy for him, and of course proud, but I'm sad for myself. He's my baby, and now he's leaving me, starting his own life. I guess I've done my job, but I've come to the realization that my life will never be the same. Change is inevitable, I know. But that doesn't mean dealing with it is any easier.

Drew tells me not to worry, that we'll see Rayce all the time. And we can now live our lives almost selfishly. We can travel, and do things we weren't able to do after we had kids. It can almost be like a long second honeymoon.

For my birthday in August, Drew tries so very hard to make it special. We spend the night at a four-star hotel downtown, and go to the kind of fancy, *everything-is-separate* steakhouse that we usually don't indulge in. Then during dessert, my totally self-indulgent Creme Brulee with a cup of espresso, he slides a small box across the linen-covered table top.

"You've still got *me*," he tells me quietly, our intimate phrase that reminds us that no matter what happens, or how bad something is, we've still got each other.

I remove the lid from the box to find a quaint, antique gold heart locket gleaming in the light from the candle. On the front, my initials - E G D - are inscribed in ornate cursive letters. There is a tiny picture of each boy inside.

It has become a touchstone for me - I find myself caressing it with my fingertips without even realizing it. More so when I'm nervous or worried. This morning its image sparkles in the mirror as I straighten out the chain, moving the clasp to the back of my neck. The locket seems to take on a sort of magical quality; how had I never realized before that gold could be so mesmerizing? But here I am, just staring at its loveliness, almost entranced by its shimmering beauty. Touching it now I almost feel a strange energy that seems to give me strength.

Last week, Drew and I took Rayce to college. He's always dreamed of going to the University of Texas, in Austin, and now he's there. An official Longhorn. Driving back to Dallas, I couldn't stop the tears from running rampant down my cheeks. They were even dripping onto my lap, their little wet blotches on my blue jeans a testament to my suffering. I never realized how much I could miss an almost-grown child. I was so sad when Andrew left for Navy boot camp, realizing that he would really never come home again. But at least I'd been comforted by the fact that I still had one more child in the wings.

Now my one child left is gone too.

My appearance is not all that's changed. I've become sexually anxious, as if constantly waiting for the feel of Drew's skin against mine. Of longing and pleasure, and erotic feelings I haven't had since we were newly married. I'm a middle-aged woman, and I thought my time for crazy passion and desire was just about over. But now it's like I'm *starting* over, like the want and lust I have for my husband is brand new. That thrill of newfound romance; the excitement of sex. I wonder if it results from doing so much research on the prostitution trade; I don't know. Or maybe it's because we're living alone again, the first time in twenty years we haven't had kids in the house. We can finally have noisy sex without worrying whether we heard the front door open, or the shower turn on. Whatever sounds our love-making causes is no longer a concern.

Or maybe it's because of the erotic dreams that keep assaulting my brain as I sleep, and affecting other parts of my body as well. I haven't told anyone of these strange dreams, or maybe more accurately, *visions*. It's almost like the experience is real, like I'm truly participating in a sex show. I'm on a stage which is draped in red velvet, surrounded by an audience of men dressed in old-fashioned clothes, formal and stiff, and women only wearing thin negligees that reveal their nakedness, leaving nothing to the imagination. Images from a different time.

I do what I'm told on the stage. I lay back and let the show take me in and have its way with me. But it's as if I can *feel* what's being done to me. A sexual fantasy on steroids.

And I like it.

My body remembers these dreams throughout my days and nights, and in real life, craves the deep desires that I experience while I sleep. I seem to be constantly aroused. Just the thought of those dreams makes me want to attack my husband wherever he may be. Needless to say, Drew's noticed the change in my sexual appetite, and can't seem to get enough. I think most of him feels like he's been sent manna from the Gods. But I also think a small part of him worries about where this has come from, that maybe I've been having an affair and he's receiving the residual effects of the burning embers.

How could my life have changed so drastically in a mere three months?

I feel as though I'm not in control of what's happening; I'm just along for the crazy ride.

Chapter 37

Elaine

September 10, 2011

I've been diligently working on my novel, gathering as many facts as I can find about the history of the prostitution trade, especially in Dallas. Writing a novel about a crib whore is unsettling. Although my book is fiction, I know that the atrocity of the crib tenements existed in the real world, not too far away, and it is disturbing to think about.

As I write about my character, the desire to help young girls in trouble is almost overwhelming. I have to keep reminding myself that I'm a mother, and wife. And I'm a writer. I'm not a social worker. It's a hard urge to mitigate. It leaves me tense and feeling like I've got something more I'm destined to do. I consider contacting a battered women's shelter, or a homeless shelter, to speak to the working girls taking refuge there. Get their first-hand thoughts and feelings. Ask them how they got to that point, and what they need to quit the life for good.

But then what? Try to fix everything for them? Befriend them until their struggles burn a hole in my heart and incinerate my good intentions? I close my laptop, and the list of shelters illuminating my screen vanishes. If I act on these urges, I will surely enter a fight I won't know how to win, and that scares me. So I resign myself to doing nothing, and feel like a failure.

I've become friends with Jane Ansor, the professor at The Women's Museum. She's helped me tremendously with my research. She's quirky, funny, and compassionate. After my second visit with her, it was obvious our personalities just clicked. She *gets* me.

"Hi Elaine," she says, giving me a hug as I enter her office. "I've found something I think will be very helpful for your book," she tells me, as she walks to her desk and begins digging through stacks of papers, her office a cluttered mish-mash of interesting articles and research materials. Her propensity for clutter is a balance to my near-compulsion for neat and tidy. Ying and Yang. "Here it is," she says, and hands me a photocopy of what looks to be a very old newspaper. "It's a copy of *The King's Messenger* from September of 1907. It was a Methodist publication in the late eighteenth/early nineteenth centuries. A Dallas woman by the name of Virginia K. Johnson published it. She was a social reformer who tried to rehabilitate prostitutes into productive, law- abiding citizens. She took them in and gave them job training so they could earn an honest living."

Of course, Jane's not aware that I already know of Virginia Johnson, and oh so much more.

I take the document from her hands, and look at the type. It's of an older style, very formal, almost elegant. The date of this issue is September 10, 1907. The article on the front page is entitled *Slavery in Dallas Still Lingers*, and the author is listed as Eliza Darling. I am gripped by an icy cold, as if the chilled fingers of the past have suddenly wrapped themselves around me. I am intimately connected to this woman, and again hold the proof of her existence. Another concrete piece of history that helps prove I'm not losing my mind.

I fleetingly feel the carved initials on my locket as I rub it between my fingers. I haven't told Jane of my odd travels, nor of my spiritual connection (if you can call it that - I'm not sure *what* to call it) to Eliza and the others in Dallas at the turn of the century. I'm still quite terrified that anyone I tell will truly believe I've lost my mind, and have me committed to a psychiatric hospital. I have finally convinced myself that my visits really happen; however, just because *I* believe it, there's no guarantee that anyone *else* will. Once again, I consider confessing my secret to Jane. I truly want to tell her. It's almost frightening to realize that not another single soul in the world is aware of what's been happening. *Someone* should know. Just in case. *But in case of what exactly?* Being drawn through my laptop to disappear into another realm? I still don't know if my body is somehow transformed, or if it's just my soul traveling all those many years away. But even if someone were to know, what could they do about it if something goes awry? The million dollar questions.

"This article is about one of the particularly nasty crib tenements in 1907 Dallas. A thirteen-year-old girl, who'd been kidnapped and sold to the crib, provided the details. It was a call to Dallas residents to join in ridding the city of sex slavery. It even helped spur a police investigation. Very interesting stuff," she informs me.

You have no idea, Jane.

As much as I feel compelled to tell her, I just can't form the right words in my brain, or on my lips. Words that might actually sound believable.

So my secret remains.

I return home with the documents Jane has given me. Ten minutes later, I boot up my laptop, and sit at my desk with a hot cup of cinnamon spice tea, contemplating the next chapter in my book, and how I should unravel my plot. I look at the screen and watch the round cursor rotate on top of a picture from our family vacation last year, my desktop background, when it's suddenly replaced with a typewritten document. Even after everything that's happened since June, I'm still unnerved each time something from another era, from another dimension, pops onto my screen.

A shiver attacks me as I stare at the words glowing at me like neon. *The same article from* The King's Messenger *that Jane had just given me!*

Holy hell!

I am once again pulled into the past.

Chapter 38

September 10, 1907

The King's Messenger, Quarterly Issue 32

A Publication of the King's Daughters' Methodist Missionary Society

Dallas, Texas

Slavery in Dallas Still Lingers

By Eliza Darling

The Virginia K. Johnson Home & Training Center

The North won the war, effectively putting an end to the slavery of Colored people in the United States. All of us know this, and believe that justice has finally come to pass for all people, we think. But we are wrong.

There is another form of slavery still hovering in the dark and ignored corners of our country, in our own city, right in front of us, and most don't even realize it. Those who are aware of it justify it in their consciences, telling themselves that it is the inevitable end to a wayward means. After all, prostitutes have chosen their profession, so come what may. It is not the responsibility of the upright in society to ensure justice for those who aren't seeking it, for those who may not have the same standing in our fair city.

But I say, it is.

It's the responsibility of each and every one of us.

There are girls caged in forgotten tenements, on streets that our city tries to erase from memory, as if doing so would erase their existence as well. Girls kept behind lock and key. Beaten, starved, drugged, and raped. These girls are the ones the Social Purity Movement has overlooked. Yes, this goes on in our city. Yes, we have all turned a sightless eye. Including those of us who've tried so hard to give the inmates of the brothels a new trade, a new life. I am just as guilty as the rest. I'd convinced myself that we are doing all we can, that everyone cannot be saved.

I was wrong.

Turning a blind eye obscures the crib tenements from our thoughts, but in fact, the hard, cruel truth of the tenements lives well, most happy to be overlooked. They are there, in Frogtown, lying in wait for the unsuspecting unfortunate women who find themselves kidnapped, or tricked into debauchery. A zoo of humans, kept hidden from the righteous, locked in their cells with very little chance of escape. A prison of misery.

It is called White Slavery. Should this bondage be differentiated from the slavery of Colored people, which was just so recently ended by the Union? I say it should not; CANNOT!

Slavery still continues, just disguised as a whisper that no one wants to hear.

A young girl has recently come to live at The Johnson Home. She is now only thirteen years old, but in the last year has lived through brutality that most of us will fortunately never experience in our entire lives. This young girl was kidnapped from her family in South Texas, her parents made to think she was being given a scholarship to attend a school for girls here in Dallas. Instead, she was caged and starved and beaten. As punishment for her lack of cooperation, she was drugged and taken to a Colored work camp on the outskirts of Dallas, thrown naked onto a cot in a work shed, to be available for the pleasure of the workmen there. A disgrace that was brought to a merciful end by one of the men there, one can only conclude someone with the authority to prevent the rape and molestation of a young girl. I give a heartfelt thanks to you, whoever you are, for saving this girl from what would surely have ended her sanity. Thank you from the bottom of my heart!

Yes, the girl is Mexican, and her protector is Colored. But aren't they made of blood and flesh and bone as any of the rest of us? Don't they have souls and feelings and beliefs like those of us with pale flesh? Should the color of one's skin dictate what we will and will not tolerate in our society?

It cannot. Not ever again.

I call on all who read this article to insist that the abomination of the crib tenements of prostitution be ended. I call on the Christians of Dallas to insist that these women be freed. I call on all of us to end our apathy toward the wayward of this city, to free these women from the bonds that hold them. We must insist that it be stopped now!

Chapter 39

John William Funk

September 17, 1907

At least the brutal summer heat had abated somewhat, now that Dallas had begun its slow crawl into autumn. Funk always begged the summer sun to give way to clouds and wind that would at least provide some protection from the vicious temperature. He'd always loved the fall - when the air finally felt like you could breathe it fully, and the skin wasn't seared from the sun's burning rays. Funk walked into his office tent to have a bite of lunch, with his jar of sweet tea, and a newspaper to read. Sometimes he felt used up from the hard work that was his life, and he looked forward to the quiet of his mid-day break. He didn't subscribe to the Dallas Morning News; he'd never been all that concerned with what the city council had or had not approved, what the police were or were not doing to rid the city of vice. As far as he could tell, none of it really concerned him much. His life would be just about the same whether or not the City decided to place a surtax on liquor sold in the saloons. But he always read *The King's Messenger*, a local Methodist newspaper.

Funk's mama was a Methodist, ever since the slave days had ended. The plantation from which she was freed had been pure Baptist, and she swore that once she'd left that life behind, she was leaving the Baptist church behind as well. After all, the Baptist church hadn't done much to bring her closer to God. It had only seemed to bring her owners closer to hypocrisy. Lollie Funk had decided she was going to be a Methodist, and that's the denomination in which she'd raised her son John. She was an avid supporter of her church, and relished the news she received every quarter about the goings-on of her Methodist kin-folk. Although she'd never learned to read, her son John had, and he would read the paper to her as soon as it arrived. It was a special time for both of them, sitting on the front porch, drinking sweet tea, and reading that paper. After Lollie's death, Funk couldn't bring himself to cancel her subscription, so the paper just kept coming, four times a year. And he always read it upon its arrival, just like he did when his mama was alive. He'd always thought of it as his small tribute to her, and felt a calming peace as he turned its pages, as if she were sitting next to him, just drinking her tea and listening, savoring every word.

Funk took a big gulp of his halfway-cold tea and opened *The King's Messenger,* spreading its front page over his makeshift desk. *Slavery In Dallas Still Lingers.* The words hit him between the eyes like an errant bullet. What the hell?? *This* he was not expecting. He read the article quickly, as if it might disintegrate between his fingers before he had a chance to finish. "I'll be damned!!" he said out loud, shaking his head. The article was about the girl!

Funk had known down deep in his bones that she was in trouble, and he'd beaten himself up ever since for not doing more to help her. Yes, he'd protected her from his men, but in the end had just sent her back to whatever hellish place she'd come from. His guilt had plagued him like a lingering virus. He'd done *something*, true, but not nearly enough, and that knowledge had eaten at him for almost a year now. But what more could a forty-year-old Colored man have done for a young Mexican girl? Other than adopt her, which he knew he absolutely couldn't do, he just didn't know. At the time, he'd half-heartedly convinced himself that he could do no more; making that slimy man drive her off in the wagon was the only possible solution. But in truth, he knew that it had been only a very temporary reprieve for her; he was sure she'd just returned to the whorehouse to be abused by someone else. His conscience kept reminding him that his arguments were lame, even though he still couldn't figure out what more he could have done.

Now he knew where she was. She was safe. That was truly a relief for Funk. But the article in the paper was more like a call to arms instead of just a story. It begged for action, for the enactment of justice. Whoever wrote that article had called it what it truly was - slavery. His mama would be outraged had he read her the story. Discovering what was happening to young girls and women, only a few miles away. But Funk was wise enough to know that for some things, a few miles might as well be a few *thousand* miles, for all the good a body could do.

Surely, this story in a Methodist newspaper would raise both eyebrows and disgust. How could it not, being distributed to good Christians all over Dallas? Good White folk. If they'd ignored the truth to this point, and they most certainly had, surely it wouldn't be so easy from now on, with the reality of it in black newsprint staring a person right in the eye. Funk's guilt quickly turned to outrage. Slavery was slavery, no matter who was suffering. So many men and boys had died to rid the country of it, and yet it was still alive and well, lurking in the dark recesses of the city. By God, he couldn't just stand around and wait for something to happen, for someone else to fight the battle. He had to do something. He owed it to his parents. And he owed it to that little girl dropped onto the cot in their shed, defenseless in her nakedness.

Funk left his office and walked out to the grassy area where his men were eating lunch under the shade of several large pecan trees, a few men shelling the pecans they'd picked up from around their feet. Quinn saw the look in Funk's eyes, and knew that something wasn't right. As Quinn stood, Funk cocked his head, motioning him away from the group.

"Quinn, you 'member that little girl you ordered from that whorehouse last year?" he asked, as if such a humiliation could be easily forgotten. Quinn nodded hesitantly, afraid of where this conversation was leading. "Well, you think you could take me to the man you made arrangements with?"

Quinn just looked at him like he'd lost his mind to the gremlins. *What in God's name was his crazy boss gonna do now?* He didn't rightly know, but he sure wasn't about to ask him. "Yeah boss, I can take you," he answered reluctantly, not wanting to be involved in whatever crazy thing Funk thought he was going to do, but at the same time, not having the courage to refuse.

"Let's go then," commanded Funk.

John Funk sat on the trolley, crossing the Trinity River into Oak Cliff. He'd made Quinn take him to the street of crib tenements from which he'd ordered Rosa's services. But Quinn had just made arrangements with a Lighthouse, the teenage kid who stood on the corner and conducted business for all the houses on the street. Funk had always known about them, but hated to see them with his own eyes. Young teenage boys involved in the sex trade, working for the crib bosses, describing services, taking orders, and keeping look-out for the police, as if it were a street lined with high-end brothels. He knew that the tenements didn't have to worry much about police raids, or even a single policeman patrolling the streets - they just didn't care. At least now he knew which street that tenement was on. He could at least provide that much help.

Funk got off the streetcar at Bishop and Madison, and walked two blocks down until he stood in front of a large, stately building made of red brick, almost like a mansion, with a huge whitewashed porch to welcome its visitors. *The Virginia K. Johnson Home* was carved into the stone above the entrance. This is the place, he thought. He looked up and down the street, and didn't notice a single person whose skin was darker than a white daisy. He wasn't sure how he would be received, a Colored man in the White part of town. Hopefully no one would mistake him for a rapist or a robber. Hopefully they'd think he was just a Colored man applying for a janitor's job or the like.

Funk made his way up the concrete walk, climbed the stairs to the porch, and clanked the brass knocker three times. *Lord, what have I gotten myself into?* He removed his hat, and held it in his hands as he waited for the door to open.

The lock finally turned, and the door opened just a bit, enough for him to see a woman peering out, and for her to see him. Funk was briefly paralyzed, as if hypnotized by a magician. She was stunningly beautiful. Her flaming red hair was pinned to the top of her head, with small ringlets of curl escaping to hang free by the sides of her face. Her green eyes were like the emeralds described in the books he'd read as a boy, about pirates and their buried treasure. Although her dress was modestly tailored, and in no way revealing, he could still discern the voluptuous figure underneath, with curves like he'd never before seen on a woman.

"Yes, can I help you?" she asked politely, surely wondering why a Colored man was standing on her Oak Cliff porch.

"Yes, ma'am," Funk answered self-consciously, looking down at the hat he'd twisted between his nervous hands. Not only was he apprehensive about the purpose of his visit, but now he had to deal with the effects of this gorgeous woman. A *White* woman. She was most definitely taboo. *Oh Lord, maybe this wasn't the best of ideas.* But he cleared his throat, and steeled his nerves. "I read the article about the crib tenements in *The King's Messenger.* I might be able to help," he said rather quietly, half expecting to be chased back down the stairs.

Ms. Dixie regarded him with a curious look, as if she weren't quite sure what to make of him. He expected to be turned away, but instead she simply said, "Please come in," as she opened the door wider, and led him into the drawing room. "I'm Dixie Aronsson," she said, extending her hand.

"Pleased to meet you, ma'am. My name is Funk. John Funk," he replied, shaking her hand with the most delicate of squeezes, afraid of marring its softness with his rough-as-sandpaper workman's hand. As his skin touched hers, electricity seemed to ignite his flesh, as if he'd just squeezed the body of an electric eel.

"Please have a seat," said Dixie. "Do you drink tea?"

"Yes, ma'am," Funk answered. "I'd be much obliged for a cup."

"Well then, I'll be right back," she said, and left the room.

Dixie didn't know what to think of the man who sat in their parlor. There weren't many Colored people who ventured this side of the Trinity, except those who worked on construction projects, or as cooks and janitors. She felt a little light-headed, and her nerves tingled as she thought of him sitting out there on the sofa. She was impressed by his sheer size and muscular stature, but confused about the effect they had on her. How few rules the law of attraction seemed to contain. Having been in the sex business for more years than she could count, she wasn't one for letting desires cloud her judgment. But however odd and unseemly it might be, this man was stirring feelings inside her that she hadn't felt in years, since she was a teenage girl. She'd had suitors through the years, but none had even come close to producing the sensation she now felt in the pit of her stomach. *Good Lord*, she thought. *What in Jesus' name is going on here? I'd best get my wits about me before I go back out to that drawing room, or I might just spill tea all over the floor.*

Ms. Dixie finally returned to the parlor with two cups of tea on a tray. She felt a flush rise up past the top of her dress to her cheeks, and hoped that the man wasn't apt to notice. "So you read the article? Eliza Darling wrote it after the young girl, Rosa, came here three weeks ago. She's quite a girl, being kidnapped from her family, and then suffering through the horrors of the crib-house. Not to mention what she was required to do at The Palace," she explained, regarding him with much curiosity. *How in the world could this man assist them in righting the wrongs against Rosa?* "Do you know her?" Ms. Dixie asked tentatively.

"Well, ma'am, only in a manner of speakin'" Funk answered. "I'm a foreman for a work crew puttin' in new roads in the north end of Dallas. I'm ashamed to admit that I agreed to have a prostitute brought in for my men," he said sheepishly, the guilt from the incident having built up in him over the last year, like a wall that grew taller each time he thought about it, harder and harder to climb. "You see, they don't go home for weeks on end, so it was more of a perk, just to be able to let off a little of the steam that builds up when you get so little rest and relaxation," he explained, as he looked down at his cap being crushed between his large and calloused hands.

"Mr. Funk," interrupted Dixie, "you certainly don't have to explain to me. I was a madam for the most popular house in Dallas for over ten years. I know a little bit about men's needs," she said, with a glance that Funk thought looked mischievous and seductive as a cat's gaze. Flirtatious almost.

Did Funk really just see what he thought he saw? He was shocked that the beautiful woman sitting across the table from him had been a purveyor of prostitution, and was so forthcoming about it as well. But the shock quickly served to elevate his desire for her.

Dixie laughed slightly, her full lips turned up at the corners, showing small wrinkles that only come with time. "I can see you're surprised," Dixie admitted. "I closed The Orpheum almost four years ago, deciding there were better, more meaningful and, of course, less dangerous ways for the girls to earn a living. That's what The Johnson Home is all about - changing these girls' lives," she explained. She smiled again at him as she felt the electricity that seemed to connect them somehow.

"So what do you know about Rosa?" Dixie finally asked.

"Honestly, I didn't even know her name 'til you said it after I walked in. But unfortunately, she's the girl who was brought out to our work site," he told her with the shame he'd borne for so long. Funk explained what had happened that summer day.

"So you're Rosa's hero," said Dixie, not asking but stating an obvious fact.

"No ma'am, nothin' hero to it," he answered quickly. "I just had to put a stop to a terrible wrong."

"Well, believe me, Rosa thinks of you as somewhat of a savior," she said. "And so do I," she added quietly, looking into dark eyes that told a story of hard work and honesty, and the toils of his life. Dixie felt an odd connection to this man, honor radiating from him like an aura. She was so curiously drawn to him.

"After I read the article, I tried to track down the house she was brought from. I don't know exactly which building but I know it's on Wood Street." He seemed to consider something thorny that was stabbing his conscience and memory. "Ms. Aronsson, I had no earthly idea that the woman they were gonna bring for my men wasn't gonna be a woman at all, but a little girl. And then not to do nothin' but put her back on the wagon, still half drugged, and chase it and the slimy man drivin' it away was a disgrace. If anything's to be done against the monsters runnin' that place, I want to give whatever help I can," Funk answered quietly. "My mama and daddy were slaves, Ms. Aronsson. All their lives, until the war did away with that horrible sin to the human race. I grew up hearin' 'bout what they suffered, and no one should have to bear that cross. Especially a young girl, who didn't do nothin' to nobody," he added.

One doesn't often meet a man with this much character, thought Dixie. At least *she* hadn't. Not only was his stature formidable, but his integrity as well. She was surprised at how much she already admired him, and she'd just met the man. She hardly knew him. But he touched her in a way that not many others had. Not to mention the spark that she thought might just burst into flame any second.

"That's noble of you, Mr. Funk," she said.

"Please call me John. And no, Ms. Aronsson, not noble. It's just the right thing to do, what one human bein' should do for another," he answered.

"And call me Dixie, as well," was all she said in return.

They sat and regarded each other quietly, drinking their tea, and looking up occasionally to consider what was before them. "I believe Eliza has gotten the cooperation of the police department," said Dixie. "Officer Heinrich has agreed to try to close the tenement Rosa came from. He was quite convinced that the department would not agree to stage a purge of *all* the tenements, but at least he thought they might be able to close the *one*. Since Rosa is willing to speak about what happened to her there. And now we have you," she added.

"Yes ma'am, you do," he answered, the tone of his voice a guarantee in itself.

Dixie smiled at him, knowing that although this black knight in shining armor had come to help with their crusade against the crib tenements, to her personally, he was both very, very welcome, and very forbidden.

Chapter 40

The Palace's Revenge

September 18, 1907

The last two weeks had been such a struggle for Mamie. She hadn't had any close friends prior to Rosa. Their friendship meant more to her than she'd realized, and without her she was at quite a loss. Since Rosa had become her confidante, their friendship was the only real pleasure Mamie had at The Palace. Seeing Christian at the Labor Day barbecue had been both joyous and disheartening; Mamie could no longer convince herself that his life was better because she'd left the mill. She was more conflicted now than she'd ever been, and she had no one to talk to about it. Mamie wanted so badly to take the trolley to Oak Cliff, to see Rosa. But she didn't dare.

Mamie was also walking on eggshells at The Palace. She hadn't yet suffered the punishment from Rosa's defection, but she was sure it would come. She struggled through her days in a state of nervous apprehension, waiting and wondering. Not wanting to think about it, but not being able to stop her mind from the disquieting thought that she'd not yet paid for her disloyalty.

Then not long after, her fears finally materialized.

"Well aren't you the lucky little girl today!" Candace announced when she came to the dining room for lunch. Mamie tried to ignore her; Candace had been taunting her for weeks. "Don't you wanna know why sugar? Or *Honey*, I guess I should say," she mocked with a gravelly snigger.

Mamie made no response as she ate her soup, trying to concentrate on calming her quivering hand, willing the broth not to spill over the sides of the spoon. She was determined not to give Candace the pleasure of seeing her fear.

After a moment of quiet, Candace stopped smiling and just stared at Mamie, Candace wearing the shroud of jealousy, her personal demon she'd gotten to know quite well. A frequent visitor ever since youth had deserted the aging prostitute, leaving her with both withering body and soul. The wrinkles around Candace's eyes and mouth were even more pronounced now than they'd been at the beginning of summer. The punishment through which she'd put her body was revealed more and more every day. "That's fine, *Miss Honey*. Ignore me now if you'd like. But you certainly won't be ignoring me in the circus tonight!" she almost spat at Mamie, laughing again in the vengefulness that seemed to give her life purpose.

It was all Mamie could do to keep the damned spoon in her hand. She felt her whole body trembling, but she tried to keep it in check. She couldn't let anyone see the absolute terror which had assaulted her every muscle upon hearing Candace's announcement. She tried to focus only on getting the soup from the bowl to her mouth without spilling it down the front of her dress. But trying to steady her trembling hand was like trying to calm a violent storm. Mamie had never been more scared; on the inside she screamed, while on the outside she quietly ate her lunch. Maybe she should just walk right out the front door and keep walking. She could go live at The Johnson Home with Rosa. They'd have a place for her.

But every time she let the thought even wiggle into her mind, the sweet face of her brother popped right into her head, and Mamie just couldn't do it. Taking care of him was more important than any concern of hers. Even more important than her fear, or the violation she would surely suffer. Even though Christian hadn't yet received the benefit from her hard work, she was going to figure out a way to make sure he would, and two-fold.

As the afternoon melted into evening, and seven o'clock then slowly wore its way to eleven, Mamie's stomach felt like it had been assaulted by the gripe. Her soup from lunch was the only thing she'd eaten all day. After Candace's mockery, she hadn't been sure she could even hold *that* down; she knew she couldn't tolerate anything else. When Mamie thought of the circus, a cold perspiration covered her skin, and her insides felt like they'd jump right out of her body. She'd been terrified of it since last summer when she'd been forced to attend, the one and only time.

Mamie was given a sheer negligee to wear, with nothing underneath. She thought it ironic that even being a prostitute, she was still mortified to think of a room full of people seeing her nakedness. She supposed she should've become used to it by now, but she hadn't. It was as if she'd still been a mill worker, asked to prance around naked in front of strangers.

Candace had told Mamie she had a surprise for her at the show that night, and her taunt was almost more terrifying than the thought of having to perform. Candace was evil incarnate, disguised in a woman's body, and she was most certainly reveling in Mamie's fear and suffering.

Mamie stood behind the curtain to the left of the stage. The provocative music began, and the crowd stopped their talking. She peered around the edge of the velvet curtain, and saw the men sitting in chairs, smoking their cigars and drinking their liquor, watching the stage with provoked interest. The other girls from The Palace were perched at their sides, sliding their hands up and down the insides of the men's suited thighs. Mamie's gaze was brought back to the stage as Candace entered, totally nude, her body undulating to the music, her hands stroking her breasts in a mesmerizing dance.

Mamie was then startled as Brandy came up behind her, holding a long, wooden pipe in her direction. An opium pipe. Brandy knew Mamie never used the opium that was always available to them. Mamie fervently shook her head.

"Ms. May says smoke it or we'll have to *make* you smoke it," Brandy instructed with a mocking smile. Mamie pressed her lips together tightly and again shook her head. Then seemingly from nowhere, an invisible hand grabbed her by the hair and jerked her head back. As she cried out, a rough-skinned hand covered her mouth, and dragged her away from the stage. As she tried to get her wits about her, she stared up into the face of an ugly older man she knew only as The Palace's handy-man; she didn't even know his name. Mamie's eyes were wide with both surprise and fear, and she almost gagged at the smell of the dirty, unwashed flesh that covered her mouth.

"The lady said smoke it," he croaked through brown and decayed teeth, as he gave her the half-smile of one who enjoys power over another, regardless of the circumstance.

Mamie tried to free her hair, thrashing like an animal caught in a trap. "No!" she cried, her yell muffled by the press of his hand.

In answer, the man yanked her hair again as he jerked her around, then slapped her face with such force that she felt as if her head would just fly across the room, had it not been for her hair being wound within his fist.

The tears spilled from Mamie's eyes; she couldn't help it. But she nonetheless kept her lips sealed, along with her resolve. To open them would create a spiritual perforation through which her self-respect would just leak right out, like water through a rusting pipe.

Then another jerk, another slap.

"I said do it! And do it now, before I have to beat the livin' hell outta ya!" the disgusting man growled into her ear, trying not to cause a scene that would disturb the audience.

Mamie was trapped, and she knew it. What could she do but comply? Defeat bore down on her like an iron weight. She would finally lose her personal battle to keep her body as chaste as possible. Mamie was well aware this was an ironic goal for a prostitute, but she'd convinced herself that achieving it would somehow keep intact what little self-esteem remained.

Mamie now had no choice in the matter. Her cheek stung from the blows; she didn't want to be beaten by this grotesque man. Mamie knew she had to do it.

Once again Brandy held the pipe up to Mamie's mouth, and this time she didn't resist. "Take it in deep," Brandy instructed.

Mamie sucked in the smoke from that long wooden pipe until her eyes blurred from the sting of it. Her lungs felt like they were on fire, and she coughed violently. Mamie thought she might vomit; she'd never smoked anything before. She smelled the unmistakable scent of the opium, and then felt herself being wrapped inside a strange fog, as if she'd been removed from her body and hidden by the seductive mist. *Very strange.*

"Take another, and hold it in" Brandy said, once again lighting the pipe and holding it to Mamie's lips. Mamie inhaled the sweet smoke, this time not coughing as much.

"Have fun," was all Brandy said as she walked off with a smile on her lips.

The horrible man then dragged Mamie by the arm, and practically pushed her onto the stage. She blinked at the audience, not knowing exactly what to do. Certainly not dance or sway or stroke. Her body felt almost numb, as if she were having trouble making her muscles move. It seemed she could only take tiny steps to nowhere. Candace smiled menacingly at her, and grabbed her hand, pulling her to the front of the stage, then putting her hands over Mamie's breasts. Mamie was at first unnerved - she'd never been touched intimately by a woman before. Then Candace pulled her close, their breasts touching, Candace's hands stroking Mamie's buttocks. Candace pulled Mamie's head toward her shoulder, and leaned close to her neck, whispering in her ear. "You'd better pretend you're enjoying every minute with me, or these men won't be satisfied. Ms. May will be furious if she has to refund their money. Best act like you're dyin' to be with me, darlin'. Your punishment is about to start," she said quietly, then bit the lobe of Mamie's ear.

Mamie couldn't help but gasp at both the shock and pain of the bite. But oddly, Candace's words didn't panic Mamie. For some reason, all she felt was a strange calm. She seemed to have been somehow transported to a magical, happy place, her fear and confusion from before replaced by a euphoric tranquility, displacing any care she'd ever had in the world. The strange ecstasy was really quite wonderful. Why had she been so fearful of the circus? Why had she been so determined not to use the opium? Her self-esteem was just fine the way it was. She giggled at herself for being so scared all day. Scared of what? Everything was fine.

Candace then grabbed Mamie's wrists and backed her away so that each of their bodies could be seen in profile by the audience. She took one of Mamie's gloved hands and raised it to her mouth. With her teeth she bit the end of the glove on each finger, and gave a little tug. When she got to the middle finger, she tugged harder and jerked her head to the side, pulling the glove from Mamie's hand and letting it fall to the floor. As she menacingly stared into Mamie's eyes, she bent her head slightly forward, never taking her eyes from Mamie's, and put her lips around Mamie's middle finger, sucking on it gently. Mamie again thought about how odd it was that she wasn't upset, the strange calm wrapping itself around her like a security blanket.

As Candace sucked the finger, she took Mamie's right hand and rubbed it against her left breast. "Feel me," she whispered to Mamie.

Mamie did as she was told. Candace's breasts were large and rounded, slightly sagging from age and weight. But what was most seductive about Candace's breasts were her nipples. They were big and dark red in color, as if they were large plums, ready to be eaten. Candace continued to suck on the finger as Mamie rubbed her fingertips over the hardening nipple.

Somehow, Mamie had forgotten about being on stage. She could only focus on those huge breasts, and the plums hanging there. She couldn't help herself - she lifted a breast and put the plum to her lips, licking its redness. She then put it in her mouth and sucked. Mamie felt the tingling between her legs, the arousal. She then stopped sucking the left breast and lifted the right to her lips. As she licked the nipple, it grew harder and harder, as Candace's breathing quickened, and Mamie's became ragged and almost desperate. She could feel the wetness between her legs. Somewhere in the back of her mind, a very faint voice reminded Mamie that what she was doing was wrong, but she just couldn't help herself.

"*Now* you're ready," Candace whispered to her with a slight smile, then laying on the chaise and splaying her legs wide for the audience to see. "Come stroke me," she invited playfully.

Mamie followed her instructions like a slave, not thinking and not worrying - just obeying. Doing what she was told. She dipped her fingers in the bowl of warm oil, and stroked Candace between the legs. Soft moans came from both of them; it was impossible to tell who was enjoying it more. Then Candace raised her arms and pushed Mamie's head down, guiding where she wanted Mamie's tongue to venture. "Faster, faster!" Candace screamed raggedly, until finally her back flexed and arched, and a loud cry came from her as she climaxed, surprisingly more for herself this time than for the audience.

Mamie closed her eyes to the cries and gave herself in to the desire. Her stomach clenched with the ecstasy of it, and then she felt the throbbing as she climaxed along with Candace, throwing her head back, still on hands and knees. She'd never felt such lustful need before, and would have done it all over again if only she'd been asked.

Mamie vaguely heard the faraway echo of applause as she walked from the stage in a dream-world.

Mamie fell into a deep, opium-induced sleep as soon as she laid her head on the pillow. After strange and magical dreams, she awoke many hours later, the afternoon sunlight streaming through the window. Her brain felt as if it were covered in cobwebs. She'd never been so listless. And then she remembered why. The opium, and the circus. The show with Candace. Mamie tingled with the memory of it, but the weight of shame swiftly bore down on her.

This can't be, this can't be!

She shook her head as if doing so would eradicate her actions of the night before. Her eyes filled with tears of regret as she tried in vain to erase the vision that was her new reality. The degradation of it invaded her very being - not only the disgrace of having sex with a woman, with Candace no less, but most of all the humiliation she felt at remembering how much she'd enjoyed it.

Mamie was changed, debased in a way which could never be altered.

The Palace's revenge was almost complete.

Chapter 41

The Past Does Follow

September 18, 1907

"Rosa, are you sure you can go through with this?" Eliza asked, as they readied the parlor for their guests. The young girl looked pale and shaken, as if she'd recently been accosted by a specter.

Rosa nodded her head, agreeing to a fate she knew might bowl right over her, leaving her sanity in scattered pieces.

"I'm going to make you a cup of tea," said Eliza. "I'll bring more later for the others."

Eliza left Rosa on the parlor sofa and went to the kitchen. They'd been discussing Rosa's experience at the tenement. Eliza told her that Detective Heinrich was willing to investigate, and hopefully shut down the crib, if Rosa could show him which building it was. Her statement would serve to secure a warrant so the police could raid the crib-house. Otto said he'd most likely use other girls to testify in court, so Rosa wouldn't be shamed in public any more than she'd already been.

Eliza also told Rosa that the man who'd saved her that day at the work-yard had come forward, willing to help with the investigation in whatever way he could. He'd also provided the name of the street on which the tenement was located; that was the information Rosa was missing. She hadn't paid attention to the street signs when she'd first arrived, and then had been blindfolded the other times she was taken from the building. Upon hearing that she'd meet her hero, Rosa couldn't help the tears of gratitude rolling down her cheeks. She so wanted to meet the man who'd saved her, to thank him. So Eliza had contacted John William Funk, and made arrangements for him to be there as well.

Eliza took the tea to Rosa just as Otto and Funk made their way onto the front porch.

"Detective. Mr. Funk," Eliza greeted them with a slight nod of her head, shaking the hand of each. She showed them to the parlor. "I'd like to introduce Rosa Robles," she said.

Rosa stood and shook Otto's hand, but when she turned to Funk with glittering eyes, she was compelled to hug him. She wanted to feel the security of his strength and compassion, and she wanted him to know how thankful she was. Funk hugged her back, his eyes wet with both the happiness of knowing she was safe, and his regret at letting her return to that house of horrors.

Ms. Dixie entered the room. "Detective, you remember Dixie Aronsson," said Eliza.

"Of course. How are you, Ms. Aronsson?" he asked, shaking her hand.

"All things considered, I'm doing very well. Thank you," she answered.

"Ms. Aronsson," said Funk softly, holding out his hand.

Dixie looked into Funk's eyes as she held out her hand, once again feeling a slight shock when their flesh touched.

"Mr. Funk, thank you so much for coming," she said, as she held his gaze. Her eyes said more than any words could have conveyed, and his seemed to answer in return. She knew she should just break the connection, just look away, but the nervous tingling running through her body wouldn't let her do it.

"I'll go get more tea," said Eliza, leaving the room.

"So, Rosa, why don't you begin by telling me exactly what happened to you. How you came to be at the tenement, and what happened while you were there," Detective Heinrich instructed.

Rosa took a deep breath, trying to steel her nerves. She wished Mamie were there to hold her hand, but knew she had to continue nonetheless. She knew she had to do this, to save the women who were still imprisoned at that horrible place.

"It was the summer before last. My family was in the south part of Texas, picking cotton, when a man came to the farm. I noticed him watching me." Rosa continued with her story, not a sound in the room other than her tiny voice recounting the nightmare which had been the last year of her life.

Eliza left the kitchen with the tray of tea cups and tea pot, but stopped abruptly as the parlor came into view. Otto was in her line of vision; she took pleasure in secretly watching him. He was certainly handsome, but the strongest attraction for her was the integrity he lived each and every day. She'd admired him when he'd investigated her attack, but she respected his dedication to justice even more now. The goal of closing the crib tenement was not a job which would promote his rise in the police department, but more a thorn which pierced his respectable standing with his fellow officers. She only hoped the small hole caused by that thorn would not become a gaping tear that was beyond repair.

His pursuit of justice aside, Eliza also entertained the idea that his investigation of the tenement was being done for her, because she'd asked him to. Because he wanted to please her.

Eliza's fists gripped the tea tray with such ferocity that her knuckles turned white. Watching him listen attentively to a young teenage girl, she considered the possibility that she was in love with this man. She felt almost giddy at the thought that he might just possibly love her back. Eliza smiled anxiously, and made her way back into the parlor.

Otto Heinrich interviewed Rosa for more than two hours, writing down every detail of her ordeal. His request for a warrant had to contain as many facts as possible, and Rosa was a fountain of information. She was shy at first, ashamed of what had happened to her. Mortified and embarrassed, as anyone could understand. But as she continued to relay the horrifying conditions of the crib and the abuse of the girls there, her courage grew stronger in direct proportion to the anger that rose within her small body. Rosa hated those people, and she wanted to see them suffer. She wanted the girls to not only be free of them, but to exact some sort of revenge against them.

A warm and cozy prison cell would be just that.

Eliza and Dixie listened to the young girl with both sadness and anger, the truth of her struggle even worse than they'd known. But oddly, it seemed the person most upset by her suffering was Funk. He couldn't bear to look at Rosa as she told her tale; he either stared at the floor or at the teacup sitting on the table in front of him. Every now and again, one could hear deep, measured breaths coming from him, as if he were fighting to calm the anger pooling just beneath the surface.

Dixie considered John Funk with perplexity. A strong and honest man. *And Colored.* She was most definitely attracted to him, in a way she'd never before experienced. He seemed to her a tender man, but she could swear she also detected a current of violence underneath. He obviously managed to control it, but she knew it was there, way down deep, lurking below his kindness and reason. The man was an enigma, just like her feelings for him. Dixie knew full well that John Funk should be considered *off-limits*, but this fact just seemed to fuel her desire for him, not diminish it. At one point, he looked up and met her gaze, and she felt a current somehow connecting them, as if she were being drawn by a magnet, a force she couldn't seem to break. They just looked one at the other, neither wanting to break the odd spell.

Rosa finally finished her tale of atrocities, answering Heinrich's questions as best she could.

"Well, ladies," Otto said, "I'm going to take Rosa's statement, and draft a warrant to search the premises. Of course, a judge has to sign it before we raid the place, but with this much information, I don't think I'll have to twist any arms. Rosa, I *will* need you to go with me to Wood Street and point out the building," he added.

The prospect of again laying eyes on that foul building unnerved Rosa, but she knew it must be done. At least she'd only have to look at its ugly face from the outside, instead of seeing its bleak hopelessness from the inside. She shuddered at the images and sounds and smells that would be with her for a lifetime.

"Yes, sir," was all she said in reply. What more could she say?

"Eliza, would you mind accompanying us?" Otto asked, the corners of his lips pulling upward just a tad.

Eliza knew she would go to the North Pole with this man if he were to ask. Maybe he felt the same way about her? Wanting to be near her. Eliza would prolong their minutes together in whatever way possible. Had he only asked because of Rosa? Did she have a chance with him? Even just a sliver of possibility? Before, after her attack, she'd fully understood that a policeman could never court a prostitute. But now? Would he consider romancing a *former* working girl? Eliza didn't know, but regardless, she was going to keep his company.

"Of course," Eliza answered.

"Funk," Otto said as he stood, stretching out his hand to shake, "it was a pleasure meeting you, and thank you for the information. If I need any more facts, maybe to identify the man who brought Rosa out to the sight, I'll get in touch."

"My pleasure as well, Detective," Funk answered, shaking the man's hand. "You shut that place down. Ain't gonna sleep right 'til I know they won't be stealin' more girls and lockin' 'em up in that God-forsaken worm hole," he answered, the anger worn on his brow like a war shield.

"Mr. Funk, I have something to discuss with you," Ms. Dixie announced quite formally. "If you would be so kind as to stay a few more minutes, I'd certainly appreciate it," she said.

Funk gave her a profoundly confused expression. *What in the hell?* "Surely," was all he said in reply.

Heinrich led Rosa and Eliza out the door and down the steps, on their way to Wood Street. Dixie hoped the young girl's courage would steel her when she was forced to once again look upon the place of her nightmares.

Dixie closed the door, along with her eyes, willing her own courage not to abandon her in what she was about to do. She was throwing her normally-cautious self up into a strong wind, and prayed that she wouldn't be blown into a no-man's land.

Funk waited patiently, not knowing if Ms. Dixie Aronsson were going to offer him a job, or lecture him on the dangers of a Colored man showing himself in Oak Cliff on too many occasions. He honestly didn't know.

Dixie turned around and looked into John William Funk's eyes, which looked back at her in curious and cautious expectation. He still had his hat in his hands, gripping it as if it were his lifeline. Dixie was filled with both excitement and fear as she stepped to a small table in the foyer, and withdrew a pen and paper from the drawer. She quickly wrote her message, then turned back to Funk.

"Meet me," was all Dixie whispered, as she handed him the note. But her eyes told him more than any piece of paper could have, and her smile, encouraging him, wanting to make certain this would not be goodbye. She opened the door, and then closed it immediately after he'd walked over the thresh-hold. It was clear she wasn't waiting for an answer, or for him to say anything at all.

Funk stood on the porch and read the script covering the small piece of paper in his hands, the words just about causing his stomach to crush in on itself with anxiety. *Jesus, she wants to meet me at a hotel!*

Nothing could have prepared Funk for this invitation. Nothing! As he walked down the front steps, he wondered if the hue of his skin had somehow faded, transforming him into a man who wouldn't cause suspicion as he walked down Madison Avenue. He was baffled. It was bizarre! He held out his hand and studied it. "Nope, still Colored," he mumbled, as he walked away from the strangest meeting of his forty years. But all he saw as he walked down the street was Ms. Dixie Aronsson's full figure in the rose-colored dress she'd been wearing. "Lord help me," he whispered to himself.

Eliza, Rosa and Heinrich turned onto Wood Street, Heinrich parking the car against the dusty curb. Eliza hadn't been on this street for many years, and she knew why. The buildings looked as if they might crumble at any given minute, like age-old statues left to battle the elements, but losing the fight. Their facades were covered in grime, windows brown like huge dirty teeth. Pages of newspaper littered the gutters and sidewalks, sticking here and there to piles of horse manure that hadn't been removed. This place was a far cry from Oak Cliff, even a thousand miles different from Emma Street, although Eliza knew it lay only a mile or so away.

Rosa sat in the car with her hands in her lap, willing herself not to burst into tears. She remembered the first time she'd driven down this street, with *Senor Smith,* excited but nervous, searching for the building which housed her new school. Then the sinking feeling and internal warning bells that had overtaken her when they'd parked near the ancient structure. It now seemed so long ago, a lifetime. She was suddenly overtaken by the anger of one whose childhood had been stolen, and she wanted justice. Rosa took a deep breath and raised her hand, pointing. "It's that building, the third one on the right," she told Heinrich.

"Three-twelve Wood Street," Otto said to himself. "That's all I need."

Otto wondered how many other buildings on this street were housed with female prisoners, slaves to men's greed for sex and money. He wished he could raid every one of these places, but knew that wasn't possible. Not now. But at least he'd be able to bring justice to the girls at three-twelve. "I have a daughter," he finally said, "and it turns my stomach to think of her here."

Eliza looked at him as if he'd spoken a foreign language, not knowing if she'd understood him correctly, filled with confusion. "You have a daughter?" she blurted, before she'd even thought about it.

Otto looked as if he'd just confessed a crime. "Yes," he answered slowly, looking at her with hesitation. "She just turned two." He paused, not sure how much to say. "A lot has happened in the last four years, Eliza" he said.

Yes, it has, she thought, watching him avoid her gaze.

Eliza felt the bottom of her stomach drop away, as if someone had pulled a plug and her insides had just slid right out, leaving a hollow pit in their place. She tried to smile, but knew it most likely didn't come across as one. "You got married," she stated, for it really wasn't a question. She surely knew the answer.

"Yes, three years ago," Otto said, in a voice that was so low she wondered if maybe he hadn't spoken at all.

"Congratulations," Eliza whispered. She tried again to smile, but her chin quivered. *He was married!* Embarrassment and humiliation invaded her every pore. *How could she have entertained the dream that he fancied her?* A former prostitute. Her shame shredded her self-esteem like a paring knife, making slit after slit until any respectability she'd felt had been cut into tiny, unrecognizable pieces.

Did Eliza just imagine the look of pity on Otto's face as he turned toward her? *The poor, poor wayward woman who thought she was changed!* The pitiful woman who thought she could become respectable with a change of living arrangements! Eliza felt foolish at the thought of it. How could she have been so naive?

"Thank you," Otto responded quietly.

The world was quiet until Otto started the car's engine. "I should be able to get a warrant without any problem," he said. "As far as I know, Judge Jenkins only frequents the houses on Emma Street," he quipped, trying to interject humor into the airless vacuum that had filled the car. But no one laughed.

Yes, Eliza thought, the Judge *does* frequent Emma Street. Or at least he had. He'd been a regular at The Orpheum - she'd entertained him once or twice herself.

Eliza sat back in her seat as they drove away, letting her somber clothing swallow her in the humiliation she thought she'd shed when she moved to The Johnson Home. But it had followed her nonetheless.

Chapter 42

A Longing in Secret

September 18, 1907

Dixie sat on the Queen Anne chair, upholstered in a shimmery silk of gold and burgundy. She shook her head as she considered her spontaneous decision to initiate this rendezvous with John William Funk. She wasn't worried so much about *her* reputation as she was about that of The Johnson Home. After closing The Orpheum, she'd tried her hardest to live with as much propriety as one could. She'd given herself to the girls at The Home, and had resigned herself to being a conduit of education for the remainder of her life. She'd come to terms with the belief that her days of romance were past her.

Until John Funk had knocked on her door.

Dixie's stomach was filled with butterflies that hadn't visited since the long-ago days of her youth. How had the excitement of life escaped her, slipping by so unnoticed? She didn't know, but was sure of one thing - the feeling she had now was no mistake, and she didn't intend to waste the opportunity.

Yes, Funk was a Colored man. And yes, she'd surely have to deal with the consequences, however unjust they might be. But she'd never been one for following society's rules - that had been evident when she'd opened The Orpheum. Why should she worry about the world's opinion of her now? She knew who she was, and didn't plan to let anyone else's judgments stand in her way.

But what about Funk? Was he attracted to her? And if so, was it enough to withstand what others might say? Dixie knew how the Anglos felt about Coloreds, and what they should and shouldn't be able to do, and where. But she wondered if the

Coloreds had the same misgivings? Why wouldn't they, after suffering through two hundred years of slavery? Would a romance with her hurt Funk in some way? Dixie honestly didn't know, but she'd find out soon enough.

It was almost seven o'clock, the appointed time. After everyone had left The Johnson Home, she'd gone upstairs to freshen up, the excitement of what she planned to do welling up inside her like it would burst right out of her corset any minute. She'd pinned her red curls to the top of her head, and adorned herself in a dress of mint-green satin and vanilla-colored lace, with a conservative string of pearls around her neck.

As a madam, Dixie knew people from all walks of life; she'd decided to make use of one of them tonight. A man she knew, a former customer, was manager at The Exeter, the posh hotel at Lake Cliff, and his discretion could be trusted. Her note had given Funk the hotel name and address, and instructed him to ask the desk clerk for the room of Rose Lee, a name she'd used on occasion when necessary.

So Dixie sat in Room 117, in a chair by the window, nervously twisting the strand of pearls between her fingers as she waited to see what the evening would bring.

As he sat on the trolley after leaving The Johnson Home, traveling back over the river toward downtown, Funk decided he needed a glass of beer to calm his nerves and hopefully get his head to stop spinning. He looked through the open window, but the only scenery his mind saw was the pale skin of Ms. Dixie, with her fiery-red curls and luxurious green eyes. He shook his head as the wind blew in, somewhat cooling his close-to-fevered skin. Funk rubbed his face with his rough and weathered fingers, and it bothered him to think those fingers might just roughen her beautiful, soft skin, like sandpaper touching a fine piece of silk.

Funk got off the streetcar, and walked to his favorite beer joint, in the Colored part of downtown, over near the stockyard. Lord, he needed to think this through. This was the strangest decision he'd ever had to make in his whole life. He'd looked at Dixie longingly when he'd visited that first time, and he thought he caught a similar look in her eyes as well. But then he'd just as quickly talked himself out of that foolish thought, and went about his business, chalking his infatuation up to that of a crazy, lonesome fool who hadn't been with a woman in way too long.

But now. *Now* things were so different. Dixie *was* attracted to him.

A *White* woman. *Shit!*

Funk made his way to The Exeter Hotel, and asked the desk clerk for the room of Rose Lee, as instructed. He received stare after stare from the stately men and women who frequented the fine establishment - he felt as out of place as an alligator at a picnic. But he couldn't bring himself to just get back on that trolley and go home. He was drawn to this woman.

Funk knocked hesitantly on the door of Room 117, almost expecting a policeman to greet him with a pair of handcuffs, punishment for indecent thoughts about a White woman. But when the door opened, his eyes were treated to a lovely sight. The woman he hadn't been able to stop thinking about for the last twenty-four hours. She was wearing a gown that accentuated her full figure, even more than the dresses he'd seen her in before. Its light green color brought out the deep green of her eyes, emeralds that sparkled as if they were the most precious gems on the earth. Her flaring-red hair was pinned up on her head, small ringlets escaping and hanging around her face, her eyes. A string of pearls hung between her breasts, almost getting lost between the cavern within her luscious flesh.

"Hello, John. Please come in," she said with only a hint of a smile, almost as if she were unsure of herself. She opened the door wider for him to enter. "Thank you for coming," she said softly.

"My pleasure," he answered just as softly in return. "You're a sight for tired eyes."

"Well, let's see if we can't bring those tired eyes back to life again," she teased, looking up into his eyes and putting her hand on his weathered cheek. "I think I know just the thing to do that. You just leave everything to me. Tonight, there are no worries," she announced. Funk assumed she was referring to the social hurricane their relationship would surely cause.

Funk submitted freely to her soft touch - he couldn't help himself. And neither could she.

John Funk had never lain with a White woman before, had never even seen one unclothed, and had *certainly* never seen one with the lush figure that unveiled itself in front of him. Dixie had been right; she certainly *had* known what to do to bring the sparkle back into his exhausted eyes. She was confident in what she knew would please him, and also knew exactly what she wanted in return. All while being gentle and loving.

Although Dixie knew what she was doing, she'd never done it with a Colored man before. She pulled his breeches down and was momentarily taken by surprise, a quick gasp escaping her. "Well, it appears the rumors are true then," she said with a taunting gaze as she ran her fingernail down the considerable length of his erection. She definitely knew how to drive a man crazy out of his skin. After that, their tryst was more a blur to Funk than anything else. He almost felt like this woman's hostage, but one most willing to submit to her commands. He was totally at her mercy, and he loved it.

After what seemed like both days and then no time at all, in a vacuum of both passion and tenderness, they lay together on the bed, he on his back and she snuggling up against him, her left breast resting on his chest. It was a blissful calm. They were each entranced with the other, against all social reason. But even so, it felt right, as if they'd always been this way, as if the color of their skin wasn't as different as night and day.

"John, believe it or not, I don't think I've ever felt this way about a man before," Dixie said quietly, as her finger drew invisible circles on his muscled stomach. Funk knew it was the same for him.

"Woman, you best stop with the finger, or you might just start things goin' again," he cautioned.

Dixie smiled at his inane warning, knowing that he wouldn't mind a bit if she did in fact cause the spark to flame. Even though it was she who'd been the most experienced of the two, both the strength and gentleness of his lovemaking filled her with such happiness that she thought she'd burst. In the past two days, this man had caused her such surprise in herself that she wondered if she'd traded lives with someone else along the way but just hadn't been told yet.

Dixie hugged him hard, and nestled her nose into his neck.

Funk felt totally connected to this woman, like he'd know her all his life. "Dixie, I don't believe I've ever felt this way about a woman either," he said, as he hugged her back, and kissed the top of her tousled hair.

As of that night, both were truly color-blind.

Chapter 43

The Raid

September 25, 1907

Detective Otto Heinrich stationed his men at both the back and front entrances to the building. Except for the windows, there were only two ways out. But if the slave-masters who ran this abhorrent place wanted to jump right out of a window to their deaths, that was fine with him. It would save the taxpayers money in the end. He didn't anticipate too many needing arrest. The majority in the building were the girls and women held captive there. The mistreated.

From the information Rosa had given him, *mistreated* was way too kind a word.

Heinrich had brought as many vehicles as he could commandeer to carry the multitude of women he knew were caged inside. At the suggestion of Dixie and Eliza, he had arranged for several local churches to serve as temporary shelters. The Johnson Home would eventually take as many as possible, but most of their beds were already occupied. Dixie and Eliza had promised to help care for the women, to work on returning them to their families, or helping them find a new place to live. Since most were probably unskilled and *all* were poverty-stricken, it would prove to be a massive undertaking, but it had to be done.

Heinrich gave the signal - they were ready - and pounded on the scarred wooden door. "Police, open up!" he yelled. *One, two, three.* "Police, open the door!" *One, two, three*, he silently counted again. After he'd given them sufficient time to open, Heinrich and two of his men picked up the large battering ram, and ran it into the gray weathered wood. It only took one time. The old and worn-out entry gave way without a fight, surrendering into a hundred splintered pieces. The men rushed into the building, not surprised that not a soul was there to greet them. Heinrich guessed they'd most likely already attempted escape through the back.

The detective made his way upstairs with a group of officers, two carrying piles of dresses, if you could call them that. Most of them were really just simple shifts, collected hodge-podge from as many places as they could find which provided clothing for the poor. Eliza had warned him that most of the girls would be close to naked, and would need something to wear. This was a detail he hadn't considered, and he was grateful for her suggestion. Imagine the spectacle of collecting and transporting a hundred totally naked women!

The men had been told what to expect, but nonetheless were not prepared for what they saw. Heinrich walked down the dirty halls, the floor stained with the filth of thousands of dirty shoes which had carried their grimy owners through these corridors. The smell surrounded him wherever he went, the stench of unwashed bodies and soiled clothes, of urine and other bodily fluids he didn't even want to consider. He looked through the small windows as he passed each door, seeing only scantily clad women and girls, most lying on their thin mattresses. Only a few seemed to hear the noise of the raid, the multitude of footfalls running down the hallways. The rest made no movement. He guessed that most had heard his men, but had been stripped of hope so long ago that they just didn't care what was going on around them. Life behind lock and key had eradicated their desire to even contemplate what happened beyond their doors. After all, why would it matter? None of it had ever affected them before. They had only to concern themselves with pleasing the men who entered their rooms. If they did that, they could be reasonably certain they would escape a beating, and that eventually food would come.

As his men continued to make their initial inspection of the building, Heinrich made his way to the back entrance, where he found his men handcuffing a haggard, obese woman in a disheveled, grimy dress; an older man; and three dirty, unshaven men whom he assumed were the hired help. The bedraggled woman in the dirty dress cursed and screamed as she stood glaring at the officers. Her hair was a greasy mess, piled upon her head. Her face wore the wrinkles of a hard-lived life, her missing teeth a testament to struggles lost.

"Git yer God-Damn hands offa me!" screamed the woman. "I didn't do nothin' wrong!"

The men were also cuffed and standing near the woman, one clearly bearing a higher countenance than the others, wearing clothes that weren't covered with the grime of poverty. Heinrich presumed he was the owner, or at least the tenement manager. Well, they'd get the facts worked out soon enough at the station.

"Have any of you men recovered a key ring?" he asked.

"Yeah, here it is, Detective," one young officer called, as he pulled the bundle from around Fanny's neck, and tossed it to him.

Heinrich considered the different keys on the ring, one larger than the rest. "Is this the master?" he asked Fanny, holding it in front of her.

Instead of a word, Fanny brought forth mucus from the bottom of her throat, and spit the brown glob in his direction. He moved just in time to prevent the grotesque missile from landing on his coat, but not fast enough to keep it from hitting the ring of keys.

Heinrich just glared at her as the slimy mess slowly dripped onto the floor. "Take them to the wagon," he ordered, as he fished in his pocket for a handkerchief that would be thrown directly into the trash bin after wiping down the keys.

Heinrich made his way back to a corridor of rooms, and opened the first door with the large skeleton key, and then the second. He systematically walked down each hallway unlocking doors. After each creaked open, one of his men then entered the room, explained to the inmate that they were being freed from the tenement, and asked that they put on the dress provided. They should then wait in their room for further instructions.

As he turned the key in each lock, he peered through the small viewing windows in the doors, and cringed at what he saw. A bare room. A thin, dirty mattress on the floor, on top of which lay a thin and dirty girl. The windows seemed like sad, painted pictures hanging on the doors, all telling the same story. But in truth, Heinrich knew, each of those girls had her *own* story, had lived her *own* life, once upon a time. After settling the girls into their temporary shelters, each one would be interviewed, and statements taken.

Room after room was unlocked. But the room he now looked into was different from the others, the floor covered in trash. And the female lying on the mattress didn't move at all. Heinrich walked in and was overcome by the stench, an odor so terrible it wrapped itself around him and seemed to enter his body like an unseen virus. He covered his nose in a vain attempt to keep the noxious air from attacking his senses, to no avail. As he walked closer, he saw she was quite young, but in physical age only, for her ordeal must surely have aged her soul to that of a wasted old woman. Both the mattress and her skimpy frock were covered with the testament to the battle she'd lost. Her bowels had released when her body gave up its fight.

Tears welled in the detective's eyes at the sight of her body, curled into a small ball, her thumb in her mouth; no doubt she'd tried to return to a time of security and trust. A time of innocence. His own daughter took up the same position each and every night. What had this girl thought of in her last hours? Her parents? A beloved pet? Had she ever been doted upon as he doted on his own daughter? Most likely, never.

Flies crawled over a face that at one time might have been pretty. He winced at the sight, his stomach turning at the thought of her last struggle, the final of many. *No one should have to die like this, and die alone. Covered in their own filth. No one.*

Heinrich clenched his jaw in anger. At least they would end the sickening enslavement that had gone on in this building. At least he could save these few.

But how many more were out there? Next door? Down the street? He didn't want to think about it, for he knew there was nothing he'd be able to do. His brass had already told him this would be it. Just this one house was such a major operation they almost weren't able to make accommodations for the *victims* - his boss had said this word with a slight laugh, letting Heinrich know what he thought about the indigent whores being rescued. Heinrich knew the only reason they'd approved this one raid was because they had such a willing witness, whose ordeal was now in the public's eyes, thanks to Eliza and *The King's Messenger* article. And there was also John Funk. It sickened him that the police department wouldn't do its job and put the sex slavery business right into the ground - they were satisfied to turn the other way and pretend it didn't exist, as long as taxpayers made no complaint. Why waste time and money on non-White whores whom no one cared about?

But Rosa and Funk were real people just like anyone else.

And then there was Eliza. Heinrich had such a soft spot for her, he would never have been able to resist her request. He sighed as he thought of her. He knew he'd shocked her when he announced he was married, with a child. At one time, he'd thought about having a romantic relationship with her. She was beautiful, despite the scar, and charming - he was drawn to her. But in the end, he couldn't bring himself to do it. He loved police work, and he'd ultimately put his career before his other passions, including his attraction to Eliza Darling. If he were courting a prostitute, he'd have no chance of advancing in the police department. So he'd steeled himself against his desire for her, and let his life roll on without her. He'd finally found Lanette, from a well-bred old Dallas family, and married her. They were happy enough he supposed, but their marriage lacked the flame that Eliza always lit deep down inside him.

Nonetheless, romantic passion was one thing, but preserving his career was quite another. He'd chosen the career. He'd hurt Eliza, he knew, but there was nothing more to do about it, except of course to carry out the raid to the best of his ability.

Heinrich knew he didn't have any more say-so about raiding other tenements, so he was going to do his damnedest to shut this one down. He left the dead woman curled in permanent sleep to be carried away by his men, and proceeded down the hallways, unlocking one door after another after another until all who resided there were freed.

Jimmy had gone to fetch food from the market, one of his weekly chores for the tenement operation. The market vendors knew to expect him every week; he would buy the leftovers they hadn't been able to sell. Stale bread, and fruits and vegetables well on their way to rot, the poorest cuts of fatty and gristly meat that no one else wanted to buy. All for a much-reduced price, of course. Good for the vendors, since they would just throw the food away once it had gone to spoil, and good for the tenement master, who could feed a whole building full of women with very little money wasted on them.

Jimmy was driving the wagon back to Wood Street when he saw a very strange sight. Very odd indeed. From several blocks away, he spied large wagons and trucks lining the street, and there, in front of his building, a group of men were gathered. As he drew closer, he saw they were policemen. He stopped the wagon in fear and confusion, his innards beginning the shaky little dance they did whenever he was afraid. He just sat, wondering what would happen. But deep down, he knew. He knew exactly what he would see.

The police rammed the door down, and ran into the building. Jimmy just sat silently and watched. Five minutes, ten, twenty. He just sat. Finally, he saw the police escorting Fanny, Pilcher, and three of the other workers out the front door, with hands cuffed behind their backs. 'Course Ms. Fanny would be spewing every filthy word she'd ever learned; he knew her well enough to know that. They were loaded into a wagon; the truck's back doors were closed behind them. Then came the girls, line after line of them, coming out the front door single file, squinting from the sunlight as if they'd never set foot outside before. They wore an odd assortment of dresses that Jimmy had never seen. None of them had any clothes to speak of, only thin flimsy things that served not as protection, but as invitations to their customers. He guessed the police must have brought them. After all, they couldn't very well take all those girls out of there buck-naked.

Jimmy just watched as his whole life was led from the building and packed into the wagons. Most of him was thankful that he'd been away at the market, and had escaped arrest. Yes, that was a miracle, really. But the other part of him was scared of what his future held. Most likely nothing, as he'd worked for the crib-master almost longer than he could remember, and lived there as well. But now he was alone, wondering where he would sleep that night, and all the nights to come. At least he still had the horse and wagon, and the vegetables in the back, going soft and wrinkled, but edible nonetheless.

Jimmy shook his head, trying to will the fear away. *At least I ain't in jail*, he kept repeating to himself.

At least I ain't in jail.

Chapter 44

The Irony of Avarice

Early November, 1907

Mamie opened her eyes to blinding sun streaming through her window, already early afternoon. It was now her custom to sleep past lunch. It was difficult to begin the day, her head feeling like it was filled with lead, her stomach queasy with any thought of food. She rolled over and looked at the long porcelain pipe sitting on her nightstand. Her mouth was dry and her sinuses hurt, burning every time she took a breath. Now, Mamie never even got up from her bed until she'd taken two or three puffs from her pipe. Her journey from spinner girl to prostitute to opium addict in such a short time was astonishing to her. *How did I come to this point so quickly?* The question which rose up in her brain every chance it got. Even though a prostitute, she'd always prided herself in being *different* from the others, only doing what was necessary to earn a living, never partaking in anything that might be remotely pleasurable.

But now she was the same as the other girls. No different at all.

Mamie lay on her side and lit the opium, inhaling deeply, and feeling the rush of pleasure shoot through her body, her aches and pains and anxiety replaced by the feeling of well-being that could only be delivered by the fine white powder.

Another day, another dollar, she mumbled to herself as she shuffled through the room, not caring about the downhill-slide of her life. *Now everything was fine.*

Since that first night Mamie performed in the circus, she and Candace had been the main attraction, their show getting rave reviews. Ms. May was happier than a vulture at a slaughter.

After the show, most of the gentlemen in the audience requested two girls for the night, instead of just one. Hoping for a similar show in the privacy of a room upstairs, and doubling the profits for the house.

And the opium. Mamie hadn't been able to resist. It was not only what she needed to perform, but her body now required it to get through each and every day. At first, she smoked it for the extreme pleasure and sense of well-being it gave her - and courage. But now she needed it to survive. Although the dry mouth and sinuses, and chronic constipation were quite aggravating, they were only minor obstacles compared to the headache and belly ache she got after four or five hours without it. She kept telling herself she'd use it only for that night's show, but when she awoke the next morning feeling like a horse and buggy had run her over, she smoked just a little to get over the worst of it. But the worst always seemed to return, more demanding than the day before, and Mamie needed the white powder to come back to herself again. Every few hours, it seemed. Mamie was caught in a vicious cycle of overwhelming calm turning to pain and anxiety. Over and over again.

Mamie and Candace had just finished their best performance yet, every seat in the back parlor taken. Word of their show had spread through The Palace's clientele like an ocean-tide, rolling off the tongues of happy customers to the ears of others. Even bringing in new clients. That night a very wealthy merchant from New York City would be in attendance, and Ms. May had given them instructions to treat him like a king.

After the show, Candace and Mamie were told to meet the man in the large third-floor bedroom. The man who opened the door and motioned them in was brawny, his muscular build evident through his fitted shirt and fine silk suit. He was clean-shaven, but with a hint of stubble peeking through the surface of his chin. He was handsome in a rugged way; one would never guess he was *worth millions*, as Ms. May had reminded them several times. *Give him anything he asks for*, she'd instructed. *Anything.*

"I'm Candace, and this is Honey," Candace introduced.

"Just call me John," the man instructed, to the laughter of Candace who complimented him on his wit, even though he'd said it without any trace of humor. Mamie just looked on with a hint of foreboding. He was handsome, she admitted, and quite virile, the muscles of his arms clearly visible under the smooth cloth of his shirt. But there was also something else - his eyes had a hardened, dangerous look to them. When his lips turned upward at Candace's laughter, his eyes didn't smile with them. Those eyes sent a frosty shiver of fear through Mamie.

John opened a bottle of champagne. "Ladies, in anticipation of another fine exhibition," he announced, as he filled their glasses to overflowing, the foam of the expensive drink spilling over the sides of the goblets. "And here is something to put everyone in the proper mood," he said, as he removed the lid from a small porcelain jar sitting next to the champagne bottle. It was filled with the powder of Mamie's addiction. "This is extra special," the man said, as he produced a long pipe covered with black enamel and silver Oriental characters that winked at her in the chandelier's light. "Here's to a most memorable night," he said, as he handed the pipe to Candace, then turned to remove his shirt and tie. "A *most* memorable night."

Mamie and Candace made love in the dim glow from the candles scattered around the room. Curiously, he'd kept his trousers on, but had unbuttoned the fly to free his erection from its constraints. Then he'd done something Mamie had never seen before - he'd slipped a silver ring over the top, and slid it down to the base of his cock. He leaned back in a chair, spreading his legs out in front of him, holding his penis with both hands, one on top of the other. He'd applied oil to make it slick and easy to move his hands up and down, at first slowly, and then with more speed, matching the quickening of his ragged breathing. As his organ grew harder and harder, the ring had disappeared somewhere in his pubic hair, and his erection had taken on a reddish-purple color, looking as if it might explode any minute. But it didn't. Not then.

After Mamie and Candace were done, Mamie looked at the man, and saw that he hadn't climaxed. Far from it. He had the largest erection she'd ever seen. It was protruding from his lap like a deadly jungle snake, waiting for the right time to strike. John rubbed more oil over the snake's head and sprinkled white powder over it, then put more into the pipe.

John looked at Mamie with those cold, hard eyes. Eyes that spoke of malice lurking just under the pleasure, or maybe intertwined with it. "Honey, why don't you come over here and see what I've got for you," he instructed quietly, still stroking himself with one hand as if it were a pet. She just looked at him as if he were speaking in a foreign tongue, not wanting to move. Not wanting to discover what he had in store.

"John, why don't you let me," Candace suddenly interjected, glaring at Mamie with the resentment of one too soon replaced with a newer, improved model. "*She's* just learning, but *I* know how to give you everything you've ever dreamed of," Candace said, as she walked to him and touched her breasts to his erection, causing it to respond on its own. He then put his hands on the back of Candace's head and pushed her down on him.

As Mamie watched Candace's head bobbing up and down between the man's legs, he took more powder from the trinket jar and put it into the bowl of the pipe, but this time added a tiny bit of something from a small envelope he'd removed from the pocket of his shirt. *A most memorable night*, he'd said. She had no idea what the small envelope held.

Mamie moved to the shadows of the room, no longer invited to join after Candace had volunteered. But that was quite a good thing - she didn't want to. She just stood and watched, and for a reason she couldn't pinpoint, became quite disturbed by the play unfolding in front of her.

"Now it's time for the *real* fun to begin," the man said, as he raised Candace's head up and lit the pipe. But there was no smile in either lips or eyes. The way he said *real* sent a current of anxiety through Mamie as she stood as still as she could, trying to make herself invisible.

Candace took a deep puff, and almost instantly began shaking her head, as if trying to clear it of fog, or cobwebs. But then just as quickly, her body became still; a dazed, almost dead expression on her face. The man led her to the bed, and easily pushed her over, almost like blowing a feather out into the air. Just a tiny tap and she fell onto the pillows.

Then the man produced his toys, the straps appearing out of nowhere, like in a magic show. But if this performance had anything to do with magic, it was the black kind. Mamie didn't like what she was watching. She'd never been much involved with the men who liked their sex rough - that had always been left to Candace and Rosa. She assumed this was a normal part of the game.

Wrists and ankles all tied to bedposts.

The man kissed Candace's breasts gently, almost tenderly, as if he revered her, worshiping her body. Then he raised his head and picked up the candle which flickered on the bedside table. He tilted it over Candace's breasts, letting the hot wax trickle over them as if it were water. Candace let out only a small sound as the wax hit her nipples and ran down her voluptuous curves.

Was this a normal part of the performance? Did Candace normally allow herself to be burned?

Mamie didn't know what to do, so she just stood as still as she could, willing herself to be unnoticed. She knew the opium helped rid the fears and inhibitions that normally restrained her, but even it was not enough to quell her fear that night. *Something wasn't right.*

John bit each of Candace's nipples, then got onto the bed and straddled Candace backwards. Mamie herself had serviced many men who preferred their sex this way. But this man was doing something different. He rubbed his erection between Candace's breasts as he removed a long shiny cylindrical object from under the mattress. Was it made of metal, or porcelain? She didn't know, but saw that it was shaped like an engorged penis. She knew that some of the girls used such an instrument to pleasure themselves while their clients watched, but she'd never used one herself. The man covered it with oil and rubbed it between Candace's legs, as he continued to rub his erection between her breasts. Then he thrust his penis into Candace's mouth as he inserted the cylinder between Candace's legs, moving himself up and down, and the cylinder in and out. Mamie didn't know how Candace could handle such a large thing being pushed down her throat.

John then shoved himself deeper into Candace's throat, no longer moving up and down; his penis just stayed down deep. Mamie didn't want to watch this anymore; she quietly moved behind a wooden screen that covered the area used for washing. She closed her eyes and tried to calm her breathing, wanting only to disappear. Then she heard a peculiar noise, not quite gagging, but more of a moan combined with a low whine. Mamie peered around the screen and saw Candace's eyes become wide as silver dollars. The whine became louder as Candace's face turned purple. John seemed not to notice.

Mamie stood behind the screen, with her eyes shut tight. *I don't want to see any more, I don't want to be here.* For a reason she never totally understood, she didn't flee, or try to stop what was happening. Her ears filled with the sounds of Candace's asphyxiation.

Candace's desperate whine was now frantic as the man's moans became more insistent. Mamie once again peered around the edge of the screen, and watched Candace's face fade from purple to a light shade of blue. She knew she should do something, but as much as she willed herself to step forward, or yell, her body was frozen. *Why couldn't she bring herself to do anything?*

The man's penis remained in place, not moving, blocking Candace's airway, causing the pale blue to darken into a cold, deep-frozen color.

Mamie closed her eyes as she stood behind the flimsy screen, wishing it were a concrete wall that sealed her within, removing her from what was happening beyond it. She knew it was only an obstruction to her line of sight. Reality was still on the other side.

Finally, the man known as John groaned in climax; a faint gurgling sound came from somewhere deep in Candace's windpipe.

Mamie slowly peeked at the scene. The man just lay on top of the naked prostitute, weary from his passion. *Why doesn't he just get up, remove his weight from Candace, let her catch her breath?* But Candace's eyes were frozen in that silver-dollar stare, her skin a shade of blue that Mamie had never seen before.

John rolled off and began to remove the bindings from the bedposts. Only then did he notice the sightless stare, the open mouth that wouldn't close, and the hue of Candace's skin.

"Fuck! Not again!" he cursed, almost under his breath, at the same moment looking up and catching a glimpse of Mamie peering around the screen. "Come here!" he commanded, in a voice quite used to giving such orders.

"No!" Mamie screamed. The sound of her own voice seemed to break the spell that had overcome her; she finally willed her body to move, running for the door, barely reaching it as John grabbed the edge of her kimono. But Mamie didn't stop, leaving her garment behind, puddled like a statue of red wax which had melted onto the floor.

Mamie ran naked down the upper hallway of The Palace, finally reaching Ms. May's door, pounding as hard as she could on the thick wood. The last thing she remembered was the smoothness of it under her fingers as her vision darkened, her body sliding into unconsciousness at the threshold to Ms. May's room.

Chapter 45

Senseless

Mamie woke sometime later. She was in her bed, under the covers, light once again streaming through her window. Her head throbbed and her stomach felt as if she would retch any minute. She noticed that her hand shook slightly as she raised it to her brow. Another day. She couldn't even recall getting into bed the night before.

Then she remembered, and bolted upright. *Candace!*

Mamie looked across the room to Candace's empty bed, fear clutching her like the claws of a monster. She jumped out of bed and ran downstairs, not stopping to make sure she was presentable. Not caring. Her head felt as if it might explode any minute, but she had to keep going.

Mamie ran to the parlor. Most of the girls sat around the table, eating their lunch and gossiping about the previous evening, no doubt discussing experiences with their various customers, comparing notes. She'd heard them every day. Ms. May was at the head of the table, her usual spot, drinking a cup of tea.

"Ms. May, what about Candace?" Mamie exclaimed, breathless from both fear and her run through the house. "What did you do with Candace? Was the man arrested?" she blurted in urgency.

Ms. May hardly blinked as she looked up at Mamie, raising her teacup to her lips as if Mamie had just asked her about the weather, the day just like any other. "I'm not sure what you're talking about, dear," May answered calmly. "Yes, Candace did leave early this morning. She was invited to accompany her client to Europe; he was in need of a companion for a month or two," she stated matter-of-factly. "Nothing more," she added, gently wiping her lips with the napkin that was stationed in her lap.

"No, that's not what happened!" Mamie screamed, shaking her head. "He killed her! I saw him!"

Ms. May pushed her chair back and rose as she held a hand out to Mamie. "Come dear, we'd best get you straightened out before these hallucinations get the better of you."

Mamie narrowed her eyes, and looked frantically around the table, from one girl to the other. No one seemed concerned with anything she'd said; it was as if she'd told them Candace had just overslept. Then it occurred to her that the girls around the table thought *she* was crazy! *How could this be?* She felt as if she were in another space in time and place, only a specter here, with no one able to see or hear her.

"I'm not hallucinating!" she screamed. "Didn't any of you hear what I said? Candace died!"

But other than displaying a minor irritation, none of them seemed the least concerned. Had Ms. May warned them not to listen to her?

Ms. May pulled Mamie away gently by the elbow. "Come dear, we'll work this out," she said, leading her up the stairs toward the upper parlor. Ms. May had never called her *dear* since she'd met her. That in itself told her something was very, very wrong.

Once they entered the room, the slam of the door punctuated the immediate change in May's demeanor. "I think you need a good huff on the pipe," she spat at Mamie with a sneer, holding the long instrument out to her.

"No, I don't want it," replied Mamie, in only half-truth. Her body was screaming for it, but she didn't want to cloud her mind, didn't want the fog to shroud her memory.

"Suit yourself," said May.

"That man. That rich, important man we entertained last night. He killed Candace! I saw her. She *was* dead! What did you do with her? Did you call the police!?" Mamie screamed in frantic desperation, her head pounding as if it were an anvil being struck by a hammer.

"You forget you ever saw anything," May snarled. "You even forget you were there last night. Do you understand?" asked May, through an unyielding, almost deadly, expression. Ms. May's wiry fingers digging into the flesh of Mamie's left arm.

"What do you mean?" asked Mamie incredulously. Her brain just couldn't process what May had said.

"I *mean* that you need to *forget* about Candace," growled May through clenched teeth, her talons squeezing Mamie's upper arm as tight as a vice. "That man has enough money and enough political power to shut this place down if he wanted to, and I'm not going to provoke him into doing any such thing," she answered.

"But he killed Candace! She was dead!" screamed Mamie in horror and disbelief. "He needs to be punished! And what if he does it again? What about the next girl?"

May leveled her gaze, boring holes into Mamie's eyes, her stare almost hypnotic. "It was an *accident*," said May. "He explained what happened; he'd had no intention of hurting her. It was just one of those things. Besides, Candace was just another whore with no family; she can easily disappear without question. There's nothing more to do or say. As far as everyone is concerned, she left with a client. She'll eventually let us know that she won't return."

"How can you just ignore her death!? I thought you were supposed to take care of your girls!? I thought that was your job!?" screamed Mamie.

The next thing she knew, the palm of a hand flew across Mamie's left cheek, propelling her head sideways. Her neck hurt from the force of it, and her cheek burned as if she'd been stung by a hive of bees.

"Don't you *ever* talk to me that way again, you little bitch," growled May in the voice of a demon. "My job is to make money. If you girls can't take care of yourselves, so be it. That's *your* problem," she said. "And if you continue to insist that Candace was killed, I'll have you put in the sanitarium so fast your head will spin." Ms. May spit her venom, then walked to the door, dismissing Mamie as if she were just kicking an old shoe out of her way.

"Wait!" yelled Mamie, as she grabbed May's arm, preventing her exit. "He paid you off, *didn't* he? He *paid* you to pretend it never happened!" Mamie didn't even need to ask the question; she knew it was the truth.

Ms. May just laughed. "Yes *dear*, he gave me quite the incentive to just consider the whole situation an *unfortunate accident*," May not only admitted without remorse, but with pride in her extreme business acumen. "Candace had no family. She was getting up in years anyway, her value decreasing. No one will miss her," she stated matter-of-factly, as if that were the only measure of a person's worth.

Mamie couldn't believe May's callousness in considering the death of another human being. Even one as hard-hearted as Candace.

"I was very close to hating Candace, but even *I* can't understand how you could just ignore her death! She may have been hateful and uncaring, but *you're* an evil *bitch*!" Mamie screamed as loud as she could, winding her arm back and hitting May across the face with the force of a hurricane that knocked the woman to the floor.

Mamie then bolted down the hallway. She knew she had to leave before May gathered her wits about her. She ran to her room, stripped off her shift and wiped her wet face with it, then threw on the first dress she laid her hands upon. She stuffed her few belongings into a carpet bag, and ran down the stairs to the street.

Chapter 46

Refuge

Early November, 1907

It should have been me! It should have been me!

Mamie's brain screamed the words over and over as she ran down Emma Street with everything she owned in that one carpet bag. The mantra of both her fear and thanks. But for only a small twist of fate, the girl tied to that bed should have been her. The fear of what *could* have been assaulted Mamie's senses. The knowledge that she'd eluded death by only a hair's breadth made her weak in the knees.

Candace was the reason Mamie had escaped. She now thanked God for the other woman's pride and jealousy. Had Candace not insisted on servicing that vile man, she wouldn't be dead. It was *her own* damn fault!

But soon enough, her fear invited its old friend guilt to the party, seeping into Mamie's consciousness without her realizing it, making a surprise attack. She'd done nothing to stop the actions in that room.

Her emotions were a roller coaster of fear and guilt and anger, all having their turns with her sanity.

Mamie continued her trance-like journey down Emma Street toward the trolley. Her head pounded and the insides of her stomach felt as though she were at sea. Sweat gleamed on her forehead, not from the temperature outside nor her exertion, but because there'd been no opium in her body for the last nine hours. Tears streamed from her eyes and stickiness ran from her nose, but she really didn't even care.

Mamie boarded the trolley that would take her to The Virginia K. Johnson Home, where hopefully she could once again start a new life.

The last month had blown by in a whirlwind for Eliza. Not only did she have her duties at The Johnson Home, but she was trying to care for the tenement women in whatever way she could. There were over a hundred of them, scattered throughout Dallas in various churches. Most were Colored or Mexican, the majority not even able to read or write. Eliza's plan was to arrange for most to take on jobs as live-in maids or cooks for the Dallas well-to-do. She was counting on Ms. Dixie's considerable connections with the Dallas elite to help in her efforts. After all, who'd be more able to afford hired help than Highland Park society, whose men had visited The Orpheum so many times she was surprised their families still recognized them at all.

And of course, several of Ms. Dixie's personal clients had been the most prestigious of the powerful - the Mayor, the former Chief of Police, the owner of the largest portion of commercial real estate downtown, and several judges. The secrets Dixie had kept over the years had given her a sort of *carte blanche* for special requests. She could generally expect attentive ears to not only hear what she had to say, but to act on it. Up to a certain point, of course. Dixie had met the current police chief, but he'd never been her customer, and would never shut down all the tenements, preferring to just ignore them in the hope they might one day just implode. In this regard, her influence did not carry the weight of Otto Heinrich's desire to please Eliza.

Eliza knew it would be a long while before all the women were placed, requiring extra work and longer hours from her every day. But she was actually very glad for the distraction. Ever since the raid, when Otto had told her he was married, she'd felt as if her life had taken on a new course. It was obvious her destiny was not to marry and have a houseful of children, but to care for the girls who had gone astray. She didn't know how she'd fooled herself into thinking it could be otherwise. Some days she could swear she'd built her respectability up so high she'd have to climb a ladder to see it, but she now realized it had only been a temporary structure, doomed to topple in destruction with the slightest breeze.

That breeze had been Otto.

Eliza had told herself time and again that a romance with him was beyond reason. But when she saw him at the police station, and then again when he came to The Home, she could swear he'd longed to hold her. He'd stared into her eyes with a spark she knew only came from one place, way down deep where the fire resided. Twice she'd stolen a glance his way to find him already staring at *her*, as if it were just the two of them in the room. Before, she'd flush at the thought of his attentions, filled with the warmth of hopeful romance. But now...now she flushed with shame, the voice inside her head mocking her foolishness in thinking she'd ever be more than an ex-prostitute in a man's eyes. *Especially a policeman's eyes.* She'd tricked herself into thinking she was worthy of marrying a respectable man. *How completely daft to have believed such a thing!*

Eliza was tainted, and always would be.

Once a working girl, always a working girl. At least inside.

Ex-whores may get a second chance at some things, but not this.

As Eliza considered her folly, she happened to glance out the upstairs window and was shocked to see Mamie Carroll walking down Madison from the direction of the trolley stop, carrying a carpet bag. Eliza jumped from her seat, and ran to fetch Rosa from her room. They hurried down the stairs and flew across the foyer. When they opened the front door, the shock of Mamie's appearance rendered both women speechless. She was only a shadow of her former self. Mamie looked at them with misery in her desperate smile, and collapsed right there on the front porch.

"Mamie!" they both screamed as they tried to catch her.

"Rosa, go get Ms. Dixie!" yelled Eliza, as she cradled Mamie's head, trying to prevent injury. Rosa ran for help.

The woman lying on the porch hardly resembled the vibrant girl who'd visited on Labor Day. Dark blotches had invaded the skin under her eyes, and her lovely face had been swallowed by thin, hollow cheeks. How many pounds she'd lost, Eliza didn't know, but bones protruded from the neck-line of her dress. Mamie's face was covered in a slick sheen of sweat, her hairline wet from it. This wasn't perspiration caused by walking down the street on a fairly cool November day. This was the sweat of fever.

The women carried Mamie into the house, and temporarily laid her on the parlor sofa, not sure if even between them they had the strength to carry her up the stairs to a bedroom. One of Eliza's students was sent downtown to get Doc Finley.

As Eliza and Rosa held cold compresses to Mamie's face, trying to cool her flushed skin, she regained consciousness and began to cry. "I need help," she said over and over again through her sobs, as Rosa held her.

"Shhh, everything will work out," whispered Rosa softly. "It did for me; it will work out for you too. I know it," she said as she gently rocked her friend, like a mother comforting her child after a nightmare.

"What happened Mamie?" asked Eliza.

Mamie stared down at the floor, wishing she could just crawl under the carpet and vanish like dirt swept under the rug. But she knew she had to look the woman in the eye when she answered. Had to try and push aside the humiliation that had swallowed her, admit her failure, and finally admit to herself that she was just like all the other whores.

Mamie looked up at the two women. "I'm an opium addict," she confessed as she pursed her lips, willing herself to hear the words; turning them over in her brain as if they were foreign objects that had nothing to do with her, but trying to claim them anyway.

Rosa just hugged her more tightly, while Eliza took her hand, looking at it soberly, as if she were trying to give herself strength. "Mamie, you knew we had *something* in common, but I bet you didn't know we had *this* in common as well," Eliza told her gently.

Mamie looked at her as if she were speaking in another language. "You used opium too?" she asked.

"I didn't intend to," answered Eliza with remembered shame. "But my body grew accustomed to the laudanum I was taking after my attack. Then rather quickly, I realized I just couldn't go a day without it."

Mamie was stunned, but also comforted by the fact that Eliza knew first-hand what she was going through.

"How did you stop?" asked Mamie.

"I had help," answered Eliza. "My guardian angel stepped in and put a stop to it, until my body was free of its influence. Ms. Dixie. That woman has saved me from myself more times than I care to admit."

A guardian angel, thought Mamie. How wonderful to have someone to watch over you, making sure you didn't fall so hard you couldn't get back up. Maybe the woman holding her hand was *her* angel. It was finally time to find out.

"Ms. Eliza, something terrible happened last night," Mamie began, not wanting to speak about it, or think about it.

Just wanting to erase it from her memory altogether, along with the last two months. "Rosa has probably mentioned Candace to you," Mamie said, looking in Rosa's direction, who shook her head slightly. Mamie should've known her friend would just keep it to herself. "Candace was the most experienced inmate of The Palace. She was very jealous and very mean. And greedy. We were entertaining a very important man from New York last night, and she insisted on being with him first, even though he chose me. I watched him hurt her, then kill her. He told Ms. May it was an accident. But I think he knew he was doing something that could hurt her, something that he'd done before.

"Ms. May didn't call the police; he paid her to keep quiet. After all, who really cares about a whore who dies in the line of duty?" she asked with muted sarcasm.

"It should have been *me*. He'd chosen me, but Candace's ego just wouldn't let well enough alone. She insisted he take her first," she said, shaking her head. "It really should have been me."

Eliza listened to the poor girl in front of her, as Rosa held her. Together. Friends. "What do you want to do?" asked Eliza. "Admittedly, the police should've been called. But they weren't. And it probably wouldn't do much good anyway. As you know, they don't like to *waste* their resources," she said. Eliza unconsciously rubbed the golden locket which lay just under her throat, as if it had the power to console if only touched the right way. Her involuntary reflex to guilt, and confusion, and frustration throughout the years.

"Leave it alone," answered Rosa unexpectedly. "Candace was mean and vile; she didn't deserve to die, but she didn't have the right to be hateful either."

"But Rosa…," Mamie tried to interject.

"No, Mamie! Leave her death alone!" Rosa yelled, quite out of character. "It won't bring her back, and it won't do any good anyway. Just leave it."

Mamie was shaking again, perspiration returning to her forehead. It was a pathetic sight - this young, beautiful girl with her whole life in front of her, reduced to a trembling prisoner of the powder.

"Eliza, do you have room for me here?" asked Mamie, not knowing what she'd do if Eliza said no.

"Of course we do, Mamie," Eliza answered. "I've been trying to convince you to quit the life ever since I met you. I wouldn't give your spot away - it was an open invitation."

"I'm so happy, Mamie," said Rosa, hugging her friend tightly, afraid of letting her go. "But I'm worried for you; how will you stop craving the opium?"

"Unfortunately there's only one way to stop, and that's abruptly," Eliza said, remembering the terror of being locked in her room while sweat poured down her face and tremors overtook her body. "It's painful, and horrible, but it's the only way. Your body has to cleanse itself, and that can only happen if you take no more at all."

Mamie's body continued to shake. "I'll do it. I *have* to. I can't live like this anymore," she managed to whisper through her chattering teeth.

"I'll help you, Mamie," Rosa said as she stroked her friend's wet hair. "I'm here for you."

Eliza made up a bed for Mamie in Rosa's room, and the two girls made their way upstairs. Doc Finley would arrive anytime to make sure Mamie's body could handle the withdrawals. Eliza regretted the struggle that awaited Mamie, the battle against the enemy that had taken her body hostage.

But at least Mamie hadn't been left addicted *and* pregnant, as Eliza had been. Eliza had never admitted it to anyone, not even wanting to admit it to herself. She'd gotten pregnant during the time of her drug-induced escapades at The Palace. Ms. Dixie had discussed her options with her, and when Eliza made the decision not to have the baby, Dixie had arranged for a trusted midwife to cause Eliza to miscarry. Dixie had probably saved her life *that* day as well; so many women had died from unsafe and unsanitary procedures used to rid women of their pregnancies. Thank the Lord Ms. Dixie had known whom to ask for help.

But although her body had recovered, Eliza came to understand that she should have listened to Ms. Dixie with a more open mind. Dixie had told her to think long and hard before getting rid of her child; it would be a decision she could never change. And Eliza *had* thought about it. She'd been scared out of her mind just considering the prospect of raising a child, especially knowing she couldn't even take care of herself. She'd been terrified.

What Eliza *hadn't* considered was the extreme grief and guilt that seemed to overtake her very soul whenever the image of a smiling baby girl popped into her brain, or the satisfying thought of rocking a sleeping baby boy in her arms. Eliza had made many mistakes through the years that she'd managed to make up for. But *that* mistake she would never, *ever* be able to forgive.

Never.

Chapter 47

Elaine Dearborn

Early November, 2011

I sit in stunned surprise and sadness.

Eliza committed the same sin. *My* sin.

Getting rid of my baby, before it ever had a chance.

The violation I will carry with me forever; the offense that can never be undone.

And Eliza committed the same act against nature.

I feel the guilt from her transgression; her devastation and regret. Feel her yearning to undo the wrong.

Once again, I'm overcome with the familiar heartache, and longing, and shame.

I understand her. Completely.

Chapter 48

Elaine

November 15, 2011

The last thing I remember after I turn on my laptop is the tinkling of the charms on my bracelet, like glass beads moved by a slow breeze. Gentle at first, then getting louder and louder, filling my head with music. The telltale sign that I would be transported to another life. Now I'm *back* - once again sitting in front of my computer screen. Of course I realize my body has been here at my desk the entire time. Or at least I *think* it has. How am I to know, really?

I'm exhausted, physically and mentally, as if I've just fought a long and drawn-out battle, my strength and energy depleted. The weight of the entire world seems to bear down on my shoulders, daring me to move under its burdensome load. A strange anxiety has wrapped itself around my nervous system, causing worry, and fear, and anger, all at once. I've just experienced the death of a young woman, and the horrible addiction and violation of another, knowing that no one but a few former prostitutes even gave a damn.

My whole body's shaking; my hand instinctively makes its way to my locket. The touchstone that helps settle my nerves. I've tried to spend most of my time working on my book, but of course, I'm so often *transported*, then suffer from the weird jet-lag after my return. Drew frequently tells me I'm preoccupied, and the only thing I can do is apologize. I can't argue with him; I agree. But who *wouldn't* be preoccupied after traveling over a hundred years into the past?

I put my palms flat on the table and take a deep breath. I decide once and for all that it's finally time to share what's happening with someone else, loony bin or no.

I've *got* to tell someone; it's driving me crazy. I feel as though I'm the only person traveling to the North Pole to see Santa's workshop. It's lonesome, keeping such a secret. Not getting to share one of the most amazing experiences of my life.

Drew is out of town on business. I'm going to tell Jane.

Today.

Before I once again lose my nerve.

"Hey, what brings you here? Wanna have lunch?" Jane asks with her usual smile and perkiness, as she gives me a quick hug. She's now my closest friend. I feel like I'm betraying her every day I don't share what's been happening to me, for fear she will reject me.

Her friendship is too important to lose. But on the other hand, aren't best friends supposed to share everything?

"Well, maybe," I answer, hesitating, "but that's not the reason I came." I'm honestly not sure how to begin. I can't help but think my revelations will wipe that cheery smile right off her face, and send her running to the phone.

911 - what's your emergency? A woman who's hallucinating about being blasted into the past. Send someone with a straight-jacket right away.

Even best friends can slip now and then.

"I have something I need to tell you. Can we just sit down?" I ask.

"Well, sure," she answers with a puzzled, almost worried, look, as she moves a stack of journals from a chair so I can sit. *Boy Jane, if you think you're puzzled* now, *just wait a few minutes. Your face is about to turn into a thousand-piece jigsaw.*

"I don't quite know how to explain all of this, but…" I begin, pursing my lips together, just looking at the floor. I'm scared I'll chicken-out if I look her straight in the eye. *Shit, there's just no good way to say this.* So I just blurt it out. "I've been researching turn-of-the-century Dallas because it seems…" I stall. But now or never. *Oh God, please don't let her think I'm crazy!* "It seems I've been experiencing 1907. Here in Dallas," I spout quickly, as if speed might somehow lessen the shock.

There is no laughing - that's a *good* thing. But Jane's eyebrows almost lift right off her face. "Whooaaa…." she says slowly, drawing the word out as if its length will somehow help her process what she's hearing, giving her brain more time to think. I'd tried to speed the conversation up, and she's trying to slow it way down. "You mean, like a *Back-To-the-Future* thing?" she asks with a skeptical look.

"Kind of," I answer, nodding. I don't think Jane really expected that answer. "I'm not really sure."

"So do you have a DeLorean with a flux capacitor in the parking lot?" she asks playfully, glancing around the room as if searching for either Christopher Lloyd's car, or a hidden camera. She's apparently still waiting for the punchline.

"Jane," I answer firmly, about to knock the fun right out of her attitude. "I'm serious, and I have to talk to someone. I have to *tell someone* what's been happening," I insist, my eyes tearing up at the weirdness that's been my life for the last five months. "I need to talk to you about this."

Then total silence, my friend mulling over my words, narrowing her eyes in thought. The gravity of my tone overshadowing the audacity of my statement. *"Oh shit.* You're *serious!"* Jane states as she studies the worry in my expression. She can't help but look at me as if I've lost my mind, and I *totally* understand.

Been there.

"It started in June," I begin, and for the next thirty minutes, explain how my life has been totally turned upside-down and inside-out.

After I finish describing my latest experience, Jane just sits quietly, not saying or doing anything. I assume thinking, but hopefully not thinking about turning me in to the psyche hospital. "So, what do you think?" I finally ask her. I truly need her to believe me, to validate I'm not loony-toons.

"Can I see the bracelet?" Jane asks, and I hold my wrist out to her. She touches it softly, as if the charms are large diamonds instead of sterling and glass. "I've actually read about this happening, and thought long and hard about it. I was pretty sure I didn't believe it. But now...I guess I'm changing my mind," she answers with a small smile, understanding and acceptance reflected in her eyes.

It feels like the big boulder that's been sitting on my back is suddenly rolled away. *Thank you, Jesus, for letting her believe me! Thank you!*

Jane is still lightly running her fingers over my charms, slightly pursing her lips while she considers it. "The accounts I've read always involve some sort of talisman that acts as a kind of conduit to the other time. For *your* travel, I'm guessing it's your bracelet," she says. "But I've never heard of a laptop being involved. *That's* certainly a new twist for quantum physics."

No freaking kidding!

"I've learned so much about this person, Eliza Darling, I feel like I know her inside and out," I tell her.

"So the thimble?" Jane asks, once again raising her brows. I fleetingly think about the extra wrinkles I might give Jane by causing her expression to change so many times.

"I think it was hers," I answer. "I somehow brought it back. From...*old* Dallas. It was on my finger when I came back from one of my…visits." Jane's face now wears the look of total confusion. I just shrug my shoulders. "I have no idea how it works. And believe me, I've wondered if maybe I were a crazy loon. But I think the thimble proves I'm not."

Jane processes for a minute. "So, you start writing a book about turn-of-the-century prostitutes in Dallas, and you suddenly find yourself living it," she states, trying to organize the jumble of thoughts assaulting her brain. *I know the feeling exactly.*

"Well, you've actually got it backwards," I tell her. "I went back *first*, and *then* decided the novel would be about prostitution and white slavery."

"Hmm," Jane thinks, tapping the desktop with her fingertips, her mental metronome. "What if the past is actually trying to make its story known through you? As you found out from your research, there's not a lot of first-hand information about hookers from that time. At least not from *their* point of view."

I'm intrigued by her suggestion. The past is speaking to me through my computer, letting me experience it. It's like being given the gift of living another life, walking in someone else's shoes, but with flashes of the past involved. What Jane's suggesting is both fascinating and freaky.

"Your novels could be more like history on steroids, with up-close-and-personal lessons for your readers," Jane says. "It seems like the past is just screaming to have its story told. And the best way to do that is to have you live the experience yourself, so your book can be accurately soul-piercing."

"Wow, *soul-piercing?* I never thought about my novel being *soul-piercing.* " I answer.

Jane continues with her run-away-train thought process. "You know, you could write the book in first person, as being lived and told by Eliza Darling. How much more of a historical novel could it be?" Jane asks.

Well, she's got a point, I think. I've never considered writing my book from Eliza's point of view, telling her story. But why not? I feel like she's almost a physical part of me, my emotions so entwined with hers that it almost seems like I'm living her life. Or her *former* life, anyway.

Jane's right - how much more of a unique perspective could a person have?

"I think you may be onto something," I tell Jane, as I think about it. "I certainly *seem* to feel what Eliza must have gone through. And my laptop has given me the story, first-hand it seems." I continue contemplating this odd scenario. "But isn't it cheating to take a story that's already been told?"

"But it *hasn't* been told; it's been *lived*. There's a *huge* difference. How can you plagiarize something that's never been put to paper before?" she asks. "I know Eliza kept her diary, but that was just a chronicle of her thoughts and feelings. Not an autobiography. And *certainly* not a novel. Think of it like you're writing a biography about Eliza, or maybe a memoir through her eyes.

"You know," Jane says, cocking her head to one side, studying me, "your look has really changed since I met you. Would that have something to do with your travels?" she asks.

I look at Jane sheepishly, almost feeling like I've done something wrong. I feel guilty for something I can't even put my finger on. "I know. I realized it myself. I didn't consciously change anything. It just sort of *happened*," I tell her. "But I think it's Eliza. She wore her hair down, to cover the scar on her left cheek. And always dark colors, like she was in mourning. As if she were trying to atone for her mistakes," I say. Knowing exactly what she was trying to make amends for, and thinking how appropriate the dark colors are for me as well. "I think her guilt was always with her." I know I could be speaking about myself. Regret is a virus that never seems to die; once it's almost wiped out, it just seems to adapt.

I stop and wonder if I should tell her about the sex dreams and their effect on me. *Why not?* I ask myself. Of all the people I know, except for Drew, she's probably the only one who might understand this weird craziness.

"And there's another very freaky thing that's been happening to me," I start, and proceed to tell her about my erotic dreams, acting in the sex shows and having sex with whorehouse clients. And how my sexual relationship with Drew has hit an all-time high. Jane listens with rapt attention, again the eyebrows raised. Her nonverbal answer of *Wow!*

"It's almost as if Eliza and I could be the same person. Of course, if you don't count the hundred years in between," I consider. *Wow.* "But what I don't get is…why me?" I ask rhetorically.

It's apparent that Jane truly believes in this stuff. She truly believes me, and I am so, so grateful.

"I don't know, Elaine. But we're going to try to find out."

Chapter 49

The Diary of Eliza Darling

November 16, 1907

My days are bittersweet.

Mamie and Rosa are now both safe at The Johnson Home. Mamie still struggles to end her addiction to the opium, but she's been quite courageous in her determination. Each day, we locked her in her room with Rosa, where she remained in a state of illness. Headaches, tremors, nausea and horrible sweating were her constant companions for at least a week. But she never once tried to break out of her room; never once pounded on the door, screaming for escape. I think we have Rosa to thank for that. She has proved her devout friendship to Mamie tenfold, and I have the utmost respect for her fierce loyalty.

I am also grateful for Otto's fulfillment of his promise to shut down the tenement house. He did what he vowed to do. At least for *that* house.

After all of the girls were gathered and taken to various churches and ministries around the city, the final count was one-hundred and thirty-two women, mostly young. They were all starved, and most had bruises from various beatings, or sores that wouldn't heal. Most acted as if they'd been living in a cave. They'd been made timid from the torturous treatment they'd received, and reminded me more of wounded animals rescued from the streets, kept like wild things, recoiling from hands extended to help them. They must now relearn how to trust others, how to receive acts of kindness without demand for repayment. They must come to understand that there *are* still generous hearts left in the world.

I know Otto is still in danger of suffering repercussions at the police department, but I hope that won't be the case. Although it was the just and moral thing to do, he did it at my behest, and I would be heartbroken to think that I had interfered with his professional advancement. Otto's past choices have made it perfectly clear that his career means more to him than anything.

No romantic involvement with a former wayward girl, to be sure. That would have nailed his coffin tightly shut.

I grit my teeth as this thought runs through my mind. Even though I've convinced others that a person can improve themselves and their station in life, can make the changes that would transform them into someone totally different and respectable, does that really happen? *Once tainted, always tainted* is what it feels like on the inside. Maybe I'm the only one who can't overcome her past? I'm not sure. But the truth remains that I'm still here, alone. Still struggling with the remnants of my prior life, while Otto is happily married, with a child. How could the message be any clearer?

I've tried to stay so extremely busy that my mind won't stray to the happy pictures that live only in my brain, never in my reality. My life is here, at The Johnson Home, helping these women escape from the holes into which they'd dug themselves. *Working women.* Just like me.

Fallen.

But trying so desperately hard to raise ourselves back up.

Chapter 50

Convergence

November 16, 1907

Jimmy decided to take what few cents he had left and buy himself a beer and a plate of fried chicken. He couldn't remember the last time he'd eaten fried chicken. "Shit!" he said to himself, shaking his head. The crib was the best job he'd ever had. The only job where he'd gotten any kind of respect. And of course, he got a roof over his head, food (such as it was), and *rec-re-a-tion* time, as Pilcher had always put it.

But the respect was the best part. Well, he guessed it wasn't really respect, more like fear. Weren't they about the same thing? Yep, he knew those ladies feared him somethin' terrible. They knew what was going to happen if they didn't do exactly what he said. Although he wasn't exactly the king of the castle, he was damn sure close. Can't beat a job like that!

But now that job was gone, and he hadn't yet been able to find another. He'd been shuffling back and forth down Wood Street, trying to inquire, trying to make himself available should a position suddenly need filling. And since he had no job, he had no place to sleep either.

So far he'd had no luck, unless you counted cleaning out horse stalls for a quarter a day. *No thanks.* Jimmy was hungry all right, but not hungry enough to pick up horse shit all day, every day. He wasn't countin' on keeping that job, but somehow he'd managed to do it enough to feed himself, and sometimes they let him sleep in the stable. *I ain't no horse*, was the last thing he always thought before sleep took him on those nights.

"Another beer here!" Jimmy yelled to Jeb, the man behind the greasy bar.

"Jimmy, you ain't been here in months, and now you're gonna drink my tap dry?" he asked through browned teeth and the stubble of an unshaven face.

"Ain't been able to," answered Jimmy, the sharp edge of his anger cutting the air like a dagger. "Lost my damn job when the cops shut down the crib; haven't been able to do nothin' but look for another place to work." *And shovel horse shit!*

"Pilcher ain't opened another place?" asked Jeb.

"I 'magine Pilcher's still in the jail cell, 'long with Fanny," Jimmy answered, taking another swig of beer. "Still don't know what happened; why the cops got interested in the place all of a sudden. And only *that* one. Whore-cribs all up and down this street, and that's the only one gets busted?" asked Jimmy, shaking his scraggly head. "Don't make no sense."

"I know what happened," announced Jeb. "We was talkin' 'bout it one day after they closed the place. Fella come in here with the paper, readin' a story and talkin' to hisself. I asked him what it was he was mumblin' 'bout, and he told me."

Neither Jeb nor Jimmy had ever read or written a word in their lives.

"What'd it say?" asked Jimmy, his attention perking up as much as it could after three beers.

"Said a Colored man told the po-lice what street the crib was on, then one of the whores pointed out the buildin'. The po-lice listenin' to a Colored and a little Mexican whore! Can you believe that crap? Never heard nothin' like it before!" swore Jeb, shaking his head.

A little Mexican whore and a Colored man. God-damn! It had to be that little whore he took out to the Colored work camp!

Jimmy had always hated that little bitch, but now… Now he despised her! It was her fault that his job and his meals and his bed had been taken away from him.

She should pay for what she done! That little bitch should pay!

"Did he say anything 'bout where that little whore went?" asked Jimmy, almost sure that Jeb wouldn't know.

Jeb squinted his eyes and looked out the window, thinking so hard Jimmy thought his brain might explode. "Yep. Yep, he actually did say. Some home for ex-whores over 'cross the river. In Oak Cliff, I think he said," Jeb announced almost proudly.

"Did he mention the name of this place?" asked Jimmy hopefully.

"Uh…lemme think." It was almost painful watching Jeb think. "It was *somebody's* name. The James Home. Or The Johns home. I 'member thinkin' that I'd knowed a guy with that name," he answered, again through squinted eyes. "The Johnson Home! That's it! The Johnson Home," he yelled, satisfied that his memory hadn't failed him again, as it was apt to do more than not.

Jimmy once again felt the anger boiling up inside him, the pressure mounting like the steam in a tea kettle, waiting to blow itself out of his body. And he knew just how to let that steam go!

He might as well live like a king today; he may never have the chance again. "'Nother beer, Jeb," Jimmy ordered.

Then Jimmy just smiled his brown, crooked-toothed smile, waiting for Jeb to slide another mug of courage down the bar-top. "Thank you for that information, Jeb. That's all I need to know," he answered.

Rosa was so happy to finally resume her thwarted education. She spent most mornings on her studies, then the rest of her days helping teach the other girls. There were some who didn't even know how to read and write, much less do sums and numbers, and she was more than anxious to do what she could to teach them.

Rosa felt a strong satisfaction from the closing of the tenement on Wood Street. She hoped that dirty, disgusting woman, Fanny, was comfortable on the more-than-likely paper-thin mattress that furnished her jail cell. Rosa hoped it was just like the one that had soaked up so many of her own tears all the months she was there. And most especially, she hated Jimmy - the way he made the girls follow his orders or suffer a beating. Especially when he was breaking in a new inmate. It was clear that he most loved the power he could wield over them. Rosa was disappointed in herself for not having the courage and forethought to just bite his small dick right off and be done with it. He would never again have been able to stick it where he pleased.

Nasty bastard.

With the tenement closing, The Johnson Home had taken as many of the women as they could provide for, most of them Colored or Mexican. This was something new for The Home, as its color had always been pale, as if only White girls had been prostitutes in Dallas. Although that wasn't the case, it *was* true that only White prostitutes were employed at the fancy houses on Emma Street. Rosa didn't think it was something anyone at The Home had consciously *tried* to do. After all, they *were* taking care of women who were otherwise ignored by *decent* society. Women no one else wanted anything to do with. She guessed it was just Ms. Dixie and Ms. Eliza's upbringing. And probably Ms. Johnson's as well. They hadn't intended to discriminate. It was just something no one consciously thought about. Well, until Mamie had talked to Ms. Eliza at the barbecue. When Rosa had taken up residence here. When shutting down that horrible crib had brought girls of Color under The Home's roof, and integrated it.

The different perspective in itself was a triumph that Rosa was proud of. Both Rosa and Mamie.

In addition to helping the girls learn to read and write, Rosa was the new English teacher. Many of the girls freed from the crib could hardly speak or understand English. *The method of communication used at the crib was understood by everyone - it didn't matter where you were from, or what language you spoke*, Rosa thought. *Violence was universal.* Rosa was the only one living at The Johnson Home who could converse with the Mexican girls. She'd started out just speaking Spanish, but then began incorporating some English words into their conversations. A few here, a few there, and before anyone knew it, they were already learning English. Rosa was so happy she could make a difference. It seemed being a teacher was her calling.

"John, just put that trunk on the third-floor landing," instructed Dixie with a smile. Funk didn't think he'd ever get tired of seeing those lips turn upward into sparkle and sunlight.

"Yes, ma'am," he answered, happy to be of service to her.

Since their tryst two months ago at The Exeter, Funk couldn't keep his mind off the woman. Former madam or no, he'd never met anyone like her, and didn't think he was bound to in the future. What he'd learned in his forty years was that when you came across something special, snatch it right up, or it just might escape and never come back.

So he had. He didn't think he could live without Dixie, even with the obvious problem that the rest of the free world probably had with their relationship. *If it didn't bother the two of them, it shouldn't bother anyone else*, he thought. But he knew this opinion was too naive; the world was what it was. Maybe it would get better through the years to come, but right now, Colored and White didn't usually come together unless it was as employee and employer. But since that mid-September day, Funk had spent most of his free time with Dixie at either The Exeter or The Johnson Home. Since there were no men at The Home, he'd labeled himself official handyman, helping with anything that required muscle or strength, or a wrench. And even if it didn't, he was more than happy to help Dixie with whatever might need doing. Lord, he didn't know how the woman did all she did. *She was amazing.* Not only was she in charge of taking care of these women and children at The Home, but she was doing her best to ensure the care and placement of the women rescued from the crib. No small task.

Funk wasn't exactly sure what his mama would have thought of his relationship with Dixie, having been a former slave to the White world. But somehow he didn't think she would mind all that much, knowing her son was in love the way he was.

Funk smiled to himself as he hefted the heavy trunk full of second-hand dresses onto his shoulder and up the stairs.

Jimmy rode the streetcar across the river to Bishop Avenue. He'd never needed to pee so bad in his life. After four beers, it was all he could do to hold it in until the trolley stopped. He walked to the nearest tree and relieved himself right there on the trunk, in broad daylight. No one was looking, he made sure of that. But what would it matter anyhow?

Jimmy squinted at the street sign, comparing it to the piece of paper in his hand. He'd asked the trolley-man to write down the name of the street where The Johnson Home was located. M A D I S O N. Although he couldn't read or write, he could damn sure compare two printed names to see if they were the same. The streetcar conductor pointed him in this direction, and told him he couldn't miss it - it was the biggest house on the next few blocks. Big red brick, with a big whitewashed porch at the top of a large set of stairs.

Didn't sound like where a bunch of ex-whores should be livin', but nothin' made sense to him anymore. Who woulda guessed?

Jimmy made his way down the sidewalk, making crunching noises as he stepped on the brown and brittle leaves that had begun to fall from the huge trees lining the street, and acorns that the squirrels hadn't seen fit to gather yet. *There are a lotta trees in this part,* he thought. He'd never been across the river to Oak Cliff before. It was nice. *Too nice for a bunch of whores. 'Specially when I have to sleep in a horse barn.* That thought alone added fuel to the raging fire filling his insides, and gave him even more determination to do what he needed to do. He thought he might just explode any minute.

There was the house, across the intersection, to his left. Just as big as the streetcar-man said. He turned onto the walk and made his way toward the large brick building, all the while keeping his hand in his jacket pocket, stroking the small pistol he'd brought with him. It was a loaner. But that was OK - he only needed it this one time. One time should do it.

Jimmy didn't have much of a plan; actually, no plan at all. He was just going to walk up to that front door and try to get to that little bitch, by whatever means necessary. He'd never been one to over-think things. Really never been one to even think things through much at all, his ability to properly link action to consequence almost nonexistent.

Jimmy ascended the front steps with determination, and for a moment, just stood on the porch in front of the door, looking around to take in his surroundings. *Nope, no place for whores.* Then he pounded on the door with his left hand, keeping his right in his pocket. Feeling the cold, smooth metal gave him a certain confidence; he once again had power.

A pretty girl of about sixteen years opened the door. Jimmy's first impression was that she was beautiful, but he quickly remembered that she'd been a bitch-for-hire, just like the others. He looked at her through bleary, watering eyes. Eyes that were used to seeing fear, but had only seen homelessness and hunger in the last two months.

"I need to see that Meskin girl," Jimmy grunted at her.

The young girl just looked at him with wary eyes, as if he were a beggar or a thief. *He wasn't no beggar or thief.* He just had to give that little whore what was comin' to her.

"Eliza?" she blurted. "Could you come here?" she called, a trace of fear in her voice now.

Yeah, you best be scared of me, girl, Jimmy thought, savoring the moment.

Then another woman, a little older, came to the door, scooting the young girl back inside the house.

"Can I help you?" the woman asked. "What do you want?"

Jimmy's hand was still in his coat pocket, stroking the gun as if it were a charm, giving him the courage to do what he was there to do. "I jus' need to see that Meskin girl!" he said again, this time with more force. "The one came from the tenement on Wood Street!" he demanded.

Eliza glared at him. "You must be mistaken. There's no one here from Wood Street," she answered, as she began to close the door.

Hell no! No one was going to close a door on him! Jimmy quickly jutted his foot into the open space by the door jam, preventing Eliza from closing it all the way. *No one's closin' no doors in my face!* he thought. *Not today!*

Eliza opened the door wider, anger replacing her dismissive tone. "Now look here! You've got the wrong address. Go away! Go away now, before I send for the police!" she yelled.

Just as Eliza spoke, Ms. Dixie had walked into the parlor, hearing her words. "Eliza? Who's there?" she asked, as she made her way to the door.

The po-lice. There won't be time for no police, he thought, as he pulled the gun from its hiding place and pointed it at Eliza, trying to hold it steady as his hands shook from both anger and the after-effects of the ale he'd downed. "You bitch! Get outta my way!" he screamed in a voice hoarse with hard living, as he tried to push his way over the threshold.

Eliza's eyes went wide with surprise and fear when she saw the gun, but then her protective instinct took control of her body as she pushed him back out onto the porch, Ms. Dixie now behind her.

Now there were two women guarding the door. Jimmy pointed the gun at one, then the other, not knowing which was of more concern to him. He guessed the only way to get through was to shoot both of them.

The next seconds were a blur, as if Eliza's eyes saw everything moving at high speed and slow motion at the same time. She smelled the stench of an unwashed body mixed with liquor, as she shoved the dirty, drunk and disgusting man away from the door. She'd be damned if he were going to get past her to any of those girls, gun or no. She was vaguely aware of Dixie beside her, outstretched arms pushing him away.

They're crazy bitches! Jimmy thought as he slightly stumbled backward on the porch, trying to look as menacing as possible. *Who ever heard of women tryin' to fight someone off with a gun pointed right at 'em? I'll show 'em how stupid it is to do that!*

Jimmy wasn't even sure at which woman his gun was aimed, but didn't see how it made much of a difference. Even if he didn't actually hit anybody, the noise of it alone would cause them to get out of his way.

Jimmy pulled the trigger.

The sound was deafening, silence suddenly filling Jimmy's head, replacing the clamor of the struggle.

Funk was on his way down the stairs when he heard a commotion at the front door. Both Eliza and Dixie were talking, from the sound of it. Then raised voices, shouting. He ran down the steps two at a time; something wasn't right. There was trouble.

Then so many noises at once - the deafening bang of a gun firing, a scream, the breaking of the etched glass in the front door.

The door flew open, and with it a woman, reeling from the impact of being shot. Landing in the foyer, the sound of her head hitting the floor a sickening thump.

It was hard for Funk to process what he was seeing and hearing. He almost jumped down an entire flight of stairs, so desperate was he to get to the doorway. And then he saw the bedraggled and dirty man standing on the porch, the man who'd taken Rosa to the work camp. He was holding the gun in his hand and blinking at it curiously, as if it were a foreign object he had no idea what to do with.

Instinct took total control; Funk's eyes saw nothing but the man who'd just fired the gun. He pounced, a panther making its kill, his muscular legs propelling him through the doorway and onto Jimmy's skinny frame. They both landed on the front porch, Funk on top, and Jimmy lost somewhere underneath his bulk. Without even a thought, Funk raised himself as he twisted the collar of Jimmy's shirt in his fist, getting a good hold on him so he wouldn't fly away until Funk was through with him.

Funk's left fist held as his right swung, his massive hand a war hammer which bludgeoned Jimmy's head time and time again. One swing after another after another. The spray of blood flying in all directions - the steps, the porch, the railing. Funk's face and clothes. He heard no sound, his focus and rage replacing all else.

Funk had returned to that dark and treacherous place he'd visited all those years ago, the path indelibly etched into his brain.

Time seemed to both stand still and reel away at lightning speed.

Funk heard nothing as the right hook once again made contact with Jimmy's unrecognizable face. And then just as quickly as the rage had filled him, his senses returned, and his left hand released its hold from Jimmy's shirt collar. He heard the thump of Jimmy's limp body falling to the porch, and saw the bloody pulp of Jimmy's head lying on the white-washed boards. Funk remembered looking at his hands, the left one black as the day he was born, but the right one covered in the blood of a White man. *Don't matter, Colored or White, their blood looks the very same on my hand*, he thought curiously.

Funk had kept his promise to control his rage for the last twenty-three years. Until now. His mama was gone, and if the swine from the tenement was dead from the force of his fists, so be it.

Then Funk looked through the doorway, at the women kneeling on the ground over where she lay, amid the blood and shards of glass. "No!" he cried, as he ran to her.

or movement. Ms. Dixie held a towel to Eliza's stomach, pressing down hard, the bloom of a horrid red flower blossoming on the carpet under Eliza's back.

"Oh my Lord!" Mamie cried, not believing the truth she saw with her own eyes. "Who did this?! Oh my God!"

"I don't know who he is, but he's on the front porch," Dixie answered, almost absentmindedly. Her thoughts were focused on Eliza; she didn't even want to give the grimy bastard the honor of a thought or word. What he wanted and why he hurt Eliza was a mystery to her. Thankfully, John had stopped him from running.

Rosa had a sinking, sick feeling that Eliza had been hurt because of her. She said a prayer for the woman who had saved her, then backed away from the crowd and went to the doorway, just as John Funk was coming through it. His face was covered in a wet sheen, and his right hand was covered in blood. He seemed to not even see her as he ran into the house and over to Eliza. Rosa slipped out onto the porch, and saw him. Or at least she *thought* it was him. *Jimmy*. That horrible weasel of a man who'd plagued her life for so many months. She'd prayed with all her might that he'd been captured during the raid, but there had been no way to know. No one else knew what he looked like.

But Jimmy had apparently escaped capture, and now he'd shot Eliza. *It's my fault!* she thought in a sickening panic. *Somehow he did this because of me!* Everything seemed to rest on her shoulders - the chain of events leading to this moment. *How did he even find her? How did he know?* Rosa knew *The King's Messenger* article had been quite the topic of conversation, but she'd bet two nickels that Jimmy didn't even know how to read. And even if he did, why would he read a Methodist newspaper? It was a mystery, although irrelevant, since he'd come to be here all the same.

Self-reproach attacked her stomach like a poison, and she ran to the railing and retched over the side. She would never have come here if she'd suspected something this horrible would happen. But hindsight was one thing, and seeing the future another. She was no magician. Rosa's *brain* knew she'd done nothing wrong in coming here, but her *heart* told a different story.

Mamie knelt at Eliza's side, feeling totally impotent. What could she do to save her? Nothing. So she just held her hand, as one holds onto a lifeline, and hoped that Eliza could feel her, and know she was there. Eliza was breathing - taking small jagged breaths, but breaths none-the-same. Her eyes were open, but didn't seem to see. She seemed to stare up at nothing, or maybe at something only she could see. She blinked, but never shifted her gaze. Aside from the small raspy breaths, quiet as whispers, Eliza made no sound.

As she sat and held her hand, Mamie looked at the rose blooming on the entryway rug, where none had been before. Its petals grew silently, in a shade of deep cranberry red. Mamie knew what it was, but preferred to believe it wasn't Eliza's life slowly leaking from her torn body.

This woman had saved her from herself, and she didn't want to lose her. Mamie hoped that holding her hand would keep her soul in the real world, and not let it slip away into the shadows. So she sat, holding on for dear life, and prayed that her friend would make it through her struggle.

The men with the ambulance wagon finally arrived; ten minutes of forever. Dallas as yet didn't have a fleet of motor-powered ambulances, only one, and so far, it had been reserved for the north-end of the city. The upscale end. Ms. Dixie hurriedly explained that she thought the bullet had gone straight through Eliza's abdomen. She'd been applying enough pressure at the top so the bottom was also pressed tightly to the floor, hopefully slowing the blood escaping from the back. Dixie insisted on going with them; she would hold the compress to Eliza's wound as they traveled to the hospital. Although Parkland was close to five miles away, the attendants assured Ms. Dixie that Eliza must go there; it was the only hospital that could attend to wounds this severe. Five miles could well have been fifty. The horses' hooves seemed to beat the pavement in slow motion. There was nothing Dixie could do but hold the compress down with one hand and hold Eliza's hand with the other. Eliza's skin felt cold to the touch, although her brow was covered with perspiration. Her breath still came in short, rasping sounds, and her eyes still looked above, but what she could actually see, if anything, Dixie didn't know. Dixie prayed with all her might that Eliza would recover one more time. *Just one more time, please!* Her tears fell silently on the blanket covering Eliza, for she couldn't spare any hands to wipe them away.

Eliza wasn't sure what was real and what was in her imagination. One minute she was arguing with the bedraggled man on the porch, telling him to leave, and the next minute he'd pointed a gun at her. A noise exploded in her ears as a flash of light simultaneously exploded in front of her. She was fairly certain this had really happened, but after that, she didn't know. It might just be a dream. She thought her eyes were still open, but the only thing she could see was a bright white light. Her body felt as if it were floating high in the clouds, an odd sensation. There was no pain, so she assumed she wasn't hurt, or at least not badly. But what she was, she just couldn't figure out. Eliza wasn't sure what she was hearing, either. First there was total silence. Then only muffled sounds. She thought her body was moving, but not of its own volition. Something else was moving it. But what, she didn't know.

Best just to lie still and wait to find out.

Otto Heinrich was writing a report at his desk at the station when a street officer poked his head through the door.

"Hey, Detective," he said, "just got a report from Oak Cliff of a shooting at The Virginia Johnson Home. Weren't you just there a coupla months ago?" he asked.

The Johnson Home?!

"What? A shooting? What in the hell happened?" he demanded, bewildered that anything could happen at a place so innocuous.

"Seems a bum who'd worked at that crib you raided wanted to see one of the girls there, and tried to shoot his way in."

"Oh shit!" Otto cried in frantic desperation. "Was anyone hurt?!" Fear made its way from his stomach to his heart in one tenuous beat. *Please help Eliza be OK. Please!* he silently begged to a God he wasn't sure he still believed in.

"Yeah, one of the women, but don't have a name," answered the beat cop, as Otto grabbed his coat and hat and made his way to the door.

"What about the shooter? Did we get him?" Otto asked.

"*We* didn't get him, but apparently he was beat to a pulp on the front porch. Not sure by who."

"Thanks," Otto answered over his shoulder as he ran for the stairs. He had to find out what happened, and who was shot. He tried to remain stoic, befitting a man of his occupation, but tears of fear escaped his eyes nonetheless.

Chapter 52

Eliza

November 16, 1907

She thought the motion finally stopped. Eliza still hadn't been able to figure out what was happening to her, or why her body felt so odd. Or didn't feel. She continued her dream-like floating. She still saw nothing, save for the bright light, but she seemed to hear more and more as time crawled slowly forward. Eliza's head felt so heavy that for a time she'd decided to just lie and rest, giving her body up to the curious hovering sensation.

But now, she began to think again, trying to focus her scattered thoughts. What had happened to her? The memory of it slowly came back, in still, silent pictures. But images that adhered to each other, like individual raindrops combining to form a thin trickle of water. Slowly, slowly.

The dirty man on the porch, asking to see Rosa.

Eliza telling him no.

The man trying to push his way in, and Eliza blocking him.

The man pulling a gun from his pocket, and pointing it at her.

The horribly loud noise and blindingly white light.

The sensation of being catapulted backwards.

The sound of glass breaking.

Had he shot her? If so, why didn't she feel any pain?

Floating, floating, floating. That's all she felt.

Dixie sat by Eliza's side. The doctors had patched her wound as best they could. Although the bullet had passed right through her, it had shattered her spine in the process. Most likely, she was not able to move her body at all. She'd lost so much blood that Eliza's skin was pale as a magnolia flower, and cool to the touch. Eliza just lied there, with eyes open, staring at the ceiling, not moving. Dixie squeezed Eliza's hand, but got nothing in return.

As Dixie looked at Eliza, she noticed that the necklace and gold locket which normally encircled her friend's neck wasn't there. Had it fallen off in the havoc of the shooting? She glanced around the room and floor, but saw it nowhere. It pained her that Eliza was without her special touchstone when she needed its comfort and protection most. Hopefully it would turn up soon, and she made a mental note to ask the girls at The Home if they'd found it.

How could such a horrible act have happened to such a good person? Always concerned about others instead of herself? But wasn't that the usual way of life? Punishment for the good while those with evil hearts walked the earth unscathed.

It had taken Mamie, Rosa and Funk almost two hours and three different trolley cars to get there.

And then the indignity. The degradation of the courageous man who'd stopped Eliza's attacker. When the three entered the room, the nurse attending Eliza turned around, and was taken aback by what she saw, emitting a small gasp of utter surprise. A Colored man in a White hospital! In a White woman's room, no less! For a few seconds, the nurse was speechless, but then found her voice soon enough.

"You very well know Colored aren't allowed in this hospital!" the nurse barked at Funk, outrage seething from her entire being. "You'll have to leave immediately!" she ordered, assuming a protective stance to guard her patient, as if Funk had a virus that could be spread with only his presence. The unmistakable air of superiority filled her every word.

Dixie couldn't believe what she was hearing. "He just saved lives by restraining the man who shot this woman! What difference does it make that he's Colored? Doesn't he deserve more respect than that?" snapped Dixie, a dark red hue overtaking her cheeks with the impudence of it all. But even as she said it, she knew how it sounded.

The nurse just glared at her with the arrogance of one in control. "Respect is *one* thing," she answered, "but violation of the *rules* is *quite another*. He'll have to leave! Now!" she added.

"It's fine, Dixie," said Funk quietly, with his hat in his hands. "I know the rules better than most," he answered in a tone not of defeat, but of the practiced patience of waiting for justice that was so slow in coming. "I'll be outside. Please come let me know if anything changes," he said quietly, then turned and walked out the door.

Dixie glared at the nurse, throwing sharp stilettos with those green eyes. But there was nothing else to be done. Dixie had just suffered a lesson on the injustice of racism, something she admittedly hadn't thought much about before she'd met Funk and Rosa.

The nurse just sniffed and smiled at her, nose and chin still high in the air, then left the room.

Dixie felt the stark truth of the difference in their races. The challenge was huge, but she truly believed not insurmountable. She would have to bear the indignity of it, just as John. But that was fine; she would gladly share his trials. She knew there would be many more. *My, how fate tends to lend a hand with one's lessons,* she thought.

Total silence had turned into faint sounds, which had then slowly materialized into faint voices. People speaking. At first, she'd not been able to tell who they were, but Eliza's hearing was slowly, slowly returning. She now knew that Ms. Dixie, Mamie, and Rosa were in the room. She could hear them talking among themselves. At first, she couldn't make out all their words, or follow exactly what was being said, but now their voices were clearer.

Someone else walked into the room, it seemed. Mart. It was Mart! He was crying. Now he was close to her, but she couldn't feel anything. Couldn't feel him touching her, if in fact he even was.

Eliza still hadn't been able to feel anyone's touch. But it was comforting to know they were all there.

Mart shyly came into the room, not knowing what to expect, his eyes glistening.

"One of the girls sent word that Ms. Eliza was hurt. Shot! I came as quick as I could," he said.

As the women turned around, Mart saw Eliza lying in the bed, eyes open. He ran to her and crumpled at her bedside, taking her hand. "Ms. Eliza, please be all right. Ms. Eliza. Please!" he cried, not caring that the women saw him cry, not caring that his tears fell onto the sheet that covered her.

Mart's desperation was heartbreaking, and Mamie couldn't help but go to him and try to give him comfort. His head and back were wet with the perspiration of his travel there, but she didn't mind. Didn't mind at all.

"I don't know much else to do other than pray," said Mamie, "and we have been all afternoon." What more was there for her to say?

"Ms. Dixie, what did the doc say?" he asked, fearful of the answer.

Dixie just looked at him with sorrow; not just for him, but for all of them. The doctor had told her in private that it would be more than just a small miracle if she survived, and if she did live, she would be an invalid, most likely not able to move most of her body. "He said they're doing everything they can, and that we should try to keep ourselves in good spirits for her," she answered. She couldn't bear to repeat the doctor's words, as if saying them would somehow seal Eliza's fate.

Mart said a prayer for his earth-angel as he held her hand, then gave it a small kiss and placed it gently back on the mattress. He stood up and moved to the other side of the room to wait, just as the door from the hallway burst open, startling everyone.

Heinrich raced to Oak Cliff, to The Johnson Home. He had no other information about what had happened or who'd been shot. He had no choice but to start there. When he ran up the walk, three girls he didn't recognize were scouring the front porch with rags, and as he got closer, he could see that it was blood they were trying to scrub away. He also saw there was no longer glass in the panels of the front door. "I'm Otto Heinrich with Dallas Police. What in God's name happened?" he asked in panic.

The girls were confused, since the police had already come and gone, taking Jimmy's limp body with them. He was taken to Parkland Hospital as well, but the police thought him unworthy of an ambulance wagon. A regular wagon would do just fine for him. Otto noticed their confusion, and took out his badge. "I'm a detective," he told them.

"That horrible man was from the tenement Rosa worked in," one of the girls began. "He came here looking for Rosa, but

Ms. Eliza and Ms. Dixie wouldn't let him in. When they stood in his way, he pulled a gun from his pocket," the girl explained, her words becoming quieter, and choked with emotion.

Please don't let it be Eliza. Please!

"He shot Eliza when she was only a foot in front of him," the girl told him, beginning to cry.

As he heard her name, a deep pain pierced him like a lance. He wanted to scream out, to shout, to curse God for letting this happen. But he was a detective, and detectives were bound by certain rules. Hiding one's emotions was one of them.

Otto was scared to ask, but knew he must. "Is she still alive?" he asked timidly, in a whisper of his normal voice.

The girl looked at him as she wiped the tears from her cheeks with the hem of her skirt. "She was when they took her, sir. I don't know about now," she answered truthfully. "They took her to Parkland."

Otto looked at the girl, and the bloody porch, and the door without any glass, and knew it was bad. He had to get to her, and prayed to God she was still alive. He had to see her at least one more time. "Thank you," was all he could manage to say to the girls, as he turned and trotted down the stairs. It was all he could do not to run screaming to his car.

Otto just then noticed the carpet, rolled up and lying on the sidewalk, the red blossom now adorning its underside, almost glowing in the afternoon light.

Otto hadn't even bothered to pull his police car into the lot, but parked it at the curb, and ran through the front entrance of Parkland Hospital. The woman at the information desk told him where she was, and he raced there, the fear of being too late attacking his insides as if the clock on a bomb were just ticking away the few precious minutes left before the devastating explosion. He saw the room number and burst through the door, surprising everyone inside. A teenage boy was just leaving her bedside.

Eliza lay in the bed, her skin almost as white as the sheet which covered her. Her hair fell back from her face, vividly displaying the scar she'd so desperately tried to hide. He gently drew his finger over the wreckage of her cheek.

I failed her then too, thought Otto. It wasn't that he'd never admitted the fact - he'd always acknowledged he hadn't given her the justice she deserved. It was just that he tried to put it out of his mind. There'd been nothing else to do for it. His superiors told him to leave it alone. And he did.

His superiors. His job. Again.

How much had *he given up for his prized position at the police department? It was clear: his happiness. And Eliza's. His job owed him.*

Otto's gaze was drawn to the middle of her bed-sheet, a small crimson petal lying on a blanket of snow. Blood slowly leaking from her wound. He picked up her hand and held it in his own.

"What in the hell happened, Dixie?" he asked over his shoulder.

Chapter 53

Admissions

November 16, 1907

She heard him! It was Otto!

Eliza heard Otto's voice. He was close to her, at her bedside. Her hearing was much better now. And the fog seemed to be lifting from her brain somewhat. Maybe they'd given her painkiller, and it was beginning to wear off. She still had that strange floating sensation, as if her body were detached from her mind. But she felt more alert now, more aware than she did before. She still couldn't see, and when she tried to speak, or move her lips, nothing happened. Nothing! She didn't think she could move anything - at least, nothing happened when she tried. She didn't feel a thing. And it was curious that no one had touched her. At least, she didn't think so. Could her body just not feel at all?

Eliza wanted to call out, to scream that she'd survived. That she thought she was fine - she felt no pain. But it was as if everyone were somehow once removed, like they were in one room and she in another. Maybe she was a spirit, just listening to them? But no, she hadn't heard them say anything about her dying.

Eliza's heart jumped at the sound of Otto's voice. She was smiling on the inside, although she didn't know what the outside was doing. Nothing, she supposed. Then she heard Otto's voice ask about what had happened. She listened with all the intensity she could muster, hearing Dixie's voice describe the altercation and attack. She'd been shot by that horrible man! Her spine had been shattered, and her body was paralyzed. Paralyzed! That was why she felt nothing, and couldn't move. That was why she felt no pain.

Eliza tried again to call out to them, without success. Her mouth wasn't obeying her brain's commands, and no sound came from her vocal cords. Panic filled her as she heard Dixie explain what the doctors had said. She felt almost like she'd been buried alive, but above ground.

I just want to go home! I just want to go home! Help me! Someone please help me!

Otto listened to Dixie in horror as she described the attack. Rosa said the person she knew as Jimmy had been the mistress's right-hand-man at the tenement. Otto assumed he'd gone to The Home to exact vengeance on Rosa, the cause of his unemployment. Eliza had protected the girl and kept her from harm's way, but she'd paid the price. Dread and sorrow filled him as Dixie relayed what the doctor had said about Eliza's injuries. She was a fighter, he knew, but he didn't know how she could recover from this.

"Dixie, would you mind if I had a few moments alone with Eliza?" he asked quietly. This might be the last time he saw her, and *this* time he wasn't going to waste the chance to tell her how he felt.

"Of course," she answered, ushering Rosa, Mamie and Mart from the room.

Otto took Eliza's hand in his, and held it gently, stroking her fingers, the hands that had done so much for so many. He didn't know if she could feel his touch; didn't know if she could even hear him. But he had to tell her, regardless. He felt as if a dagger were stabbing him just under the breastbone, digging out the flesh where his heart should have been. Otto stroked the back of her chilled hand.

"Oh, Eliza," he said quietly. "I have to tell you the truth about how I feel. I've been taken with you since I first met you, during the investigation after your first attack." He remembered his interviews with her, the way she persevered in trying to help him find her attacker. The bandages on her face couldn't hide her determination, or her loveliness.

He'd tried his best to bring her attacker to justice, but then he'd just given up when his superiors told him to end the investigation. Otto could never rid himself of the guilt from his subservience; down deep he knew it wasn't the right thing to do. The image of her disappointment when he'd told her that the investigation would be closed continued to torture him. She'd never said a word about it to him; had only thanked him for his efforts and hard work. But he was certain she wondered how any self-respecting man could just stop trying to do the right thing, just because another told him it wasn't worth the time or money. *She* was worth the time, and he knew it.

Otto had always felt the spark between them. Always. As he imagined Eliza had as well. But he'd chosen to let that tiny flame flicker in a cold wind and die, the threatening fire ensuring a stunted career. He'd chosen safety. Yes, he'd been promoted several times since then. He'd made detective, just like he'd always planned, always dreamed.

But he'd also dreamed of Eliza.

When his wife, Lanette, put her arms around him, they were Eliza's arms. When he touched her under the sheets at night, it was Eliza's skin his fingers felt. Otto had tried to convince himself he was being juvenile, letting what surely amounted to a teenage crush get the better of him. He was an adult and needed to make adult decisions. He had responsibilities. He had a daughter. He had an impressive position with the police department.

But he didn't have Eliza, and that void continuously lured him into dissatisfaction. His life on the outside was admirable; his wife was perfect. But on the inside, he yearned for the passion of loving an imperfect woman with a scar running down the left side of her face.

"Eliza," he began, not sure of exactly what to say or how to say it, but knowing that he had to tell her - he might never get the chance again. "I don't know if you can hear me. I hope to God you can. I just want to let you know...no, I *need* to let you know that I love you. I know I was a coward, and I chose my job. I know I didn't have the courage to make a life with you, to just deal with whatever happened after. I *know* that, and I'm sorry. Yes, I'm married. But every time I look at Lanette, I wish to God that she were you."

Otto stroked her hand as his voice became hoarse with the emotion of a lost life that could have been. "I'm not proud of my choices, and ironically I almost hate my fucking job now. I know I'm not as strong a person as you. You've never tried to hide your past, and you've only tried to make yourself better, and everyone around you better. I admire you so much for what you've done with your life; what you've done for those girls. Please don't leave us," he pleaded, squeezing her hand with both of his. Wanting her eyes to open, her lips to smile at him. Wanting to hear the sound of her sweet Texas drawl.

But Eliza made no move, no flicker of eyelids, no hint of smile. And then, as if in answer to his pleadings, he noticed a small tear escaping from her left eye, pooling in the damaged flesh before rolling down her cheek.

"You *do* hear me, don't you?" Otto asked, as he gently swiped his finger across the wet trickle on her cheek, then brought it to his lips and kissed it. His own tears made their way down his face, and landed on the white sheet covering Eliza. The red splotch had slowly turned from a small flower petal to a large, blooming rose. He brought Eliza's hand to his lips, and kissed it gently. "I love you Eliza," he whispered, as he carefully laid her hand on the mattress and rose from her side.

Eliza heard Otto ask everyone to leave the room. She wasn't sure if he were touching her, but she hoped and prayed that he was. He said he didn't know if she could hear him.

She wanted to scream. Yes! Yes, I can! She tried again to speak, but nothing. She prayed sound would come from her throat, but none did. It was as if she were trapped inside a box that was sealed tightly, preventing any sound or movement from touching the rest of the world.

He loved her! She'd been wanting to hear those words for the last four years. And now that she had, she couldn't even say it back, couldn't even touch him or look into his chocolatey eyes. Life was cruel.

And he'd said the words that made her laugh inside. He wished he were as strong as she! She thought that was most hilarious; she'd never considered herself strong, but weak. But then again, he didn't know about her teenage infatuation with the boys, or her opium addiction. Or her lost baby, the child she'd chosen to rid her body of before it ever had a chance to grow. Strong! Her laugh turned into a wrenching heart.

Otto said he admired her, for what she'd done with the girls. Yes, The Johnson Home was her saving grace. It had saved her from herself, and made her a better person for helping other girls escape the same. She could admit to herself that she'd been important to the girls. She'd gotten Rosa and Mamie to move there, to begin their lives again. And she'd at least been successful in getting the police to close one of the tenements. It wasn't enough, by far, but it was a start.

And she'd saved Rosa from that horrible man.

In the end, she'd been successful in the last years. Was it enough to erase her failures? She didn't know. But she felt a calming peacefulness as she thought of the good they'd accomplished. Yes, she had been part of that. Maybe she wasn't the wayward degenerate her mother had always proclaimed her *to be. But a mother's words echo in their children's ears for many long years; they were only just now beginning to fade.*

"I love you, Eliza," Otto said, almost in a whisper. Close to her ear. Had he kissed her? Had he stroked her hair?

"I love you, too, Otto," Eliza whispered inside her brain, wanting to hold his body but forced to only hold his words for the time being. She was so very happy and so sad at the same time, as if both emotions had tired of the battle for control, finally giving up and becoming friends. Although she couldn't feel it, a tear silently escaped her eye, and slid down her cheek.

Then something strange and wonderful happened. Eliza was filled with an overwhelming sense of joy, a total and unrestrained happiness she'd never felt before. Peacefulness. A soft and calming light filled the room, coming not from the windows or the lamp, but somehow glowing from within. She looked down upon herself. Her face was beautiful: her scar not visible to her; her humiliation gone. The blacks and grays of a life filled with remorse and shame had been replaced with bright colors; pinks and golds shimmering in the bright light that surrounded her. She saw everything - her bed, Otto walking out the door, her friends in the hallway, the top of the hospital, the trees, the clouds.

From somewhere, she heard a baby cry. But that sound was now hopeful, making her smile, no longer echoing her regret and failure. She was speeding toward sunshine, no longer weighted by body or worries. She seemed to move faster and faster, the floating sensation replaced with purposeful movement. Her soul had an agenda of its own; she was needed somewhere else.

Eliza was the woman of a thousand lives.

Chapter 54

Conclusions

1907

Eliza was buried in a small Oak Cliff graveyard not far from The Johnson Home. There were so many people at the church it was hard for some to find a seat. Those who loved her were many - from The Home, Mart, John Funk, Mr. Gramercy, Mr. Linder, Otto, and others that some didn't even recognize. A surprise for all of them was to see her mother at the funeral. She was dry-eyed and stoic, exactly like the picture Eliza's few words about her had painted. Dixie thought it a dreadful waste and shame that she attended to her daughter in death, but not in life. Many people had eulogized Eliza that day, people that she'd touched with her kindness and compassion. Hopefully, Eliza's mother would realize, albeit much too late, what a wonderful and loving person she had been. One to be admired; not a wayward girl.

Eliza's friends looked over her grave as the minister read his parting words, and blessed her with the Twenty-Third Psalm. Dixie and John Funk stood beside the shoveled earth and held hands, having decided not to care what the rest of the world thought. Otto had looked at them with a longing he knew would never be fulfilled. The one he really wanted was being put to rest. Such a sad thing that he'd not listened to his heart when it could have made a difference.

Mamie, Rosa, Mart and Christian flanked the other side of the grave, all crying with the pain of saying goodbye. Mamie's hand was tenderly intertwined with Mart's. After Eliza's death, Mart was filled with a new-found courage. He saw the danger in waiting to express his feelings, in hesitating to tell Mamie that he loved her. When he did, her lips curved into the sweetest smile he'd ever seen, and she reached for his hand, and held it like she'd never let it go. Why shouldn't she? Sometimes life was just too short to waste a precious second. You never knew, it might be too late if you did.

With help from Mamie and Dixie, Rosa was slowly able to let go of her guilt over Eliza's death. Although she'd been the reason for Jimmy's visit, it was he who'd pulled the trigger. Rosa had been an unfortunate victim since the day she seated herself in Mr. Smith's wagon on the farm. She was no more responsible for Eliza's death than the girl who'd opened the door at Jimmy's knock. Eliza died because of a crazy man's anger, not because of Rosa.

Ms. Dixie wrote a compelling article for *The King's Messenger*, which chronicled Eliza's life and struggles, and her conquest over the obstacles she'd faced. She told the world of Eliza's concern for those who couldn't take care of themselves, for those who needed a little help along the way. She wrote of how Eliza had protected Rosa, even after she'd seen the gun; how she'd given her life to save another. Almost immediately after the article was published, an odd thing began to happen: The Johnson Home received so many donations they almost couldn't store them all. And money poured in, even from as far away as Oklahoma. As a result, The Home was enlarged to care for even more girls, and their educational program expanded. Dixie smiled when she thought of how Eliza managed to keep on giving and providing, even after death. She missed her girl terribly, and knew she'd never stop missing her.

The relationship between Dixie and John Funk had raised a multitude of eyebrows when it became known. They were in fact chastised by most of Dallas' upscale, but many others applauded their courage and resolve. They would follow their hearts, regardless.

Parkland Hospital. A woman had died in the room he was cleaning. The orderly stripped the sheets and blanket from the bed, careful not to touch the blood that had stained them.

The man was a tired sort, working fourteen hours a day to feed his family, barely getting enough sleep to keep his head clear, one day just rolling into the next. He picked up his broom and absentmindedly swept up the floor, thinking. Wondering how he'd scrape together enough money to pay for the turkey his wife wanted to cook for Thanksgiving. There was always something extra that someone needed, and it was up to him to figure out how to pay for it.

The man passed the broom under the bed, then under the small bedside table. Sweep, sweep, sweep. As if he were trying to sweep away the monotony of his life.

Then he saw it, glimmering on the floor amid the small pile of dirt his broom had gathered. A necklace. He bent down and picked it up. A shiny golden locket on a gold chain. The initials *EGD* engraved on its face. He smiled at its loveliness and sparkle. The man guessed that it must have belonged to the woman who'd died there, or maybe someone visiting.

The man held it in his hand, considering it. He should turn it in, so the hospital could try to find its owner. That was the rule, and the moral thing to do. But the thought occurred to him that this one necklace might pay not only for Thanksgiving dinner, but Christmas dinner and most likely some presents for his kids as well.

The orderly struggled with his conscience for less than a minute, until the decision was made. He put the necklace in his shirt pocket and resumed sweeping, smiling at his good fortune.

Chapter 55

Elaine Grace Dearborn

November 19, 2011

My last trip into the past is one I'm almost not able to get over.

After my visit to Jane, I've been rewriting my novel in first person, from Eliza Darling's point of view. As I rewrite word after word, it seems as though my personality is absorbing more and more of Eliza's. Although before I felt as though I knew Eliza inside and out, it now seems almost as if we two are inseparable, like we are one and the same. It feels as if I'm writing *my* life story instead of hers.

My last experience from 1907 left me a broken mess. I can't seem to stop shaking, or chase the horrible visions from my brain. Eliza came to the door of The Johnson Home to find a vile and vengeful man asking for Rosa. Even after he pointed the gun at her, she stood her ground. When the shot was fired, she flew backwards, through the doorway, landing on the rug and on the broken glass. I experienced her feeling of nothingness as she lay blinded, and bleeding.

As Eliza's friends buried her, I experienced a panic like no other, like I was being buried alive. I cried out but no one could hear me; my screams not even passing through my lips. I saw faces looking down at me, but then just as quickly I was looking down at them.

I soared with Eliza's spirit through the heavens after her death. I heard a baby's cry and felt hope, not guilt. I felt the total freedom of her soul, unconfined by the mortal world.

At first, I was left with a spirit-crushing loneliness, and felt like I was spiraling downward into black despair.

But now I have an irrepressible urge to be reckless and dangerous. I don't understand why - Eliza had traded that lifestyle for one of a respectable teacher. Why do I now feel drawn to the seedier side of life? One in which prostitutes work the streets day and night, where unemployed men loiter in front of convenience stores, holding their brown bags of malt liquor as if they are lifelines. I sit in my car, across the street from the Sunny Days Motor Court, a motel that might have been successful in the Fifties, boasting of its *Refrigerated Air*. But now it's been rolled over by the years of progress, left in the dust of a sad and deteriorating history. The women of this place, both young and old, lean against the building in their skimpy clothing, even though the air is chilly, smoking cigarettes, eying each car that drives into the parking lot, hoping that it brings the customer who will provide their next meal.

I feel as if I'm searching for something, or someone. I seem to crave risk and peril. But why here? What do I mean to do? Join the ladies of the night as they troll for customers? I start my car and drive away, no more at peace with myself than I was before I arrived.

These strange emotions have taken their toll; my middle-class life has shattered. I can't sleep, for the visions recur each night. I can't eat; uneasiness and panic make me want to vomit any minute. I cry for any reason, and for no reason. Just cry. Irrationally hoping that tears shed will lighten the burden of Eliza's ordeal, but they don't. They just seem to make it worse. I'm floating in a sea of devastation without a life preserver.

Drew is quite worried about me. If he weren't positively sure it couldn't happen, he'd swear I was pregnant. I've told him it's *the change*, which he accepts readily enough. As far as men seem to be concerned, a woman's instability is usually caused by her time of the month, pregnancy, or menopause, and just the mention of these subjects is usually all they need to know. Men really aren't fond of hearing all the details.

Again I call Jane, my hand shaking as I hold the phone up to my ear.

"It'll be OK, Elaine," she says, but I can hear the worry in her voice. I think she's trying to convince herself, as well as me. "I've made an appointment with a psychic healer. I think she'll be able to help you," Jane informs me. "She's the one I told you about the other day in my office."

"What in the hell is a psychic healer?" I ask her. I've never even heard the term before.

"It's a person who has psychic or paranormal abilities. They can heal by manipulating a person's energy, or channeling the spirit world to assist in curing them," Jane answers.

I've always been skeptical of people claiming to talk to spirits, never mind healing a person with energy. *What a load of crap!* I would have said, laughing at the total gullibility of people.

But that was then, and this is now.

Now I'm a disaster. Broken. In need of fixing. I've officially reached the final level of desperation, and on that floor any once-crazy idea is now a welcome friend. I've been reduced to a trembling, sniveling lunatic who's fallen into a well and can't seem to find a way out. Maybe this psychic healer will be the one to throw me the rope. I sure as hell don't know what else to do, and Jane is a well-educated person with a doctorate, for God's sake. Given what's happened to me during the last six months, my perspective about such things has changed. Why *can't* there be people who have the gift of healing with their hands? I think it's time to expand my faith yet again and open my mind to the possibilities that the paranormal is real, not just the subject of hokey reality shows where you never actually see the ghost.

"OK," I answer, nodding my head. I'm going to trust Jane on this one. I resume my crying as I hang up the phone, not able to shake the terrible feelings of hopelessness and loss.

"Hi. I'm Angelique Devereaux," she says, holding out her hand. "Nice to meet you." The psychic healer is a very tall, angular black woman with high cheekbones and stunning turquoise eyes. Blue gem-stones against a background of light mocha. Quite dazzling. Her hair is braided into a thousand tiny ropes, and pulled up into a pony tail. Not quite the five-foot-tall blond poof-haired Long Island Medium I was somehow expecting. *Too much T.V.,* I tell myself.

"I'm Elaine Dearborn. Nice to meet you too," I answer, shaking her hand. I jump as a small electric shock passes between us, as if I've just dragged my feet across a shag carpet. "Oh, I'm sorry. Static electricity I guess," I say. But she doesn't say anything in return. Just looks at me with a depth that's unnerving.

"Please sit down," she invites, "and I'll explain what I do." She has a New Orleans accent, and I automatically wonder if she was displaced by Hurricane Katrina. My mind also careens to the memory of a shaman from the Louisiana Bayou I saw on The Discovery Channel one night.

"Have you ever been to a psychic healer before, Elaine?" she asks me.

"No. I must admit, I didn't even know about psychic healing before Jane told me. I've got to tell you - I've never believed much in psychic phenomena - ghosts, talking to spirits, that sort of thing. But things have happened to me recently that are making me reconsider. I'm keeping my mind open," I tell her, as Jane just looks on.

"That's fine," Angelique answers. "I've heard that many times before. As you said, the key is to stay open-minded." I'm almost mesmerized by the shimmer of her bright blue eyes, tiny sparkles of sun on a Caribbean sea, almost winking at me. "I want to explain about what I do, and what will happen during the session. Every living thing is made up of energy. Your life force. Your *aura*. The energy should be evenly distributed throughout your body, shifting somewhat according to what parts of your body you're using more than others. Such as when you're fighting a cold, or grieving for someone who's passed. But sometimes life forces or events can cause your energy to shift unevenly, becoming imbalanced, or even blocked, so that parts of your body don't receive the energy they need."

Angelique looks for signs that she's lost me, but I'm still listening, trying to process what she's telling me. "My job is to identify and correct aural imbalances and blockages, and to rid you of them, replacing negative energy with positive, removing any heaviness that is draining you. I connect with your aura through my hands.

"You'll lie down on the massage table, fully dressed, and I'll first identify where your energy is balanced, and where it's imbalanced. I have a special amulet, my pendulum, that I'll dangle over different parts of your body. If your energy in that part is balanced, my pendulum spins in a clockwise circle. If it's imbalanced or blocked, it moves back and forth. I'll then lightly touch your body with my hands, moving them around. This is how I connect with your aura." She pauses briefly. "I also use the psychic realm."

Angelique can see my expression shift from a tenuous trust to one of uncertainty. I know I'm trying to stay receptive, but I just can't help it. "You mean like talking to spirits?" I ask, not able to prevent the incredulous look that I know has just covered my face.

"Well, yes. *Communicating* with the spirit world. Actually, I mostly just listen, and feel. And there are also the angels," she tells me.

"The angels," I repeat slowly. *Holy shit.* I know I'm desperate and need help, and I said I'd be open-minded, but I just don't know if I can buy into this. It sounds like some back-water hocus-pocus. I look at Jane who just gives me a quizzical expression that says *Why not?* as she slightly lifts her shoulders and cocks her head to the side.

Why not?

I remind myself of what got me to this point in the first place. Visiting the past through my computer. I know that sounds crazy as hell, but I also know it's real. I never in a million years would have anticipated what's happened to me during the last six months. I guess all things are possible. *Yes, why in the hell not?*

"All I ask is that you trust me for the hour we're together. I will do nothing inappropriate, but my methods are most likely not what you're used to," Angelique adds. "But just trust."

Trust. I usually have a hard time with that one. But what choice do I really have?

Jane and I had already agreed we weren't going to provide any specific information to her. Jane knows I've been skeptical of all things *psychic*, and with submitting myself to a healer, so we agreed to stay silent about my experiences. If Angelique is real, she should discover them herself.

It's curious, though, that Angelique doesn't even ask.

I lie down on the table, every nerve taut with anxiety, over-wound guitar strings ready to snap any minute. "Close your eyes," Angelique instructs. "Just try to relax."

Easier said than done, but of course I'm sure she knows this.

I lie still and glimpse Angelique's pendulum above my head as I close my eyes. A few seconds pass, and then an involuntary gasp escapes Jane's lips. My eyes instinctively pop open, and the amulet is moving wildly back and forth above my face, swinging so hard it's close to wrapping itself around Angelique's hand.

"Your third-eye Chakra. That of psychic vision and intuition. It's almost totally blocked. I've never experienced a blockage this severe before," Angelique responds to my look of surprised worry. "Just try to relax, and again close your eyes," she instructs, as she places her hands on my forehead, trying to calm me. "Let me do my work."

The only sound in the room is the quiet, tinkling music of chimes. Curious. They remind me of the sound I hear before I'm taken to the past. I try to focus on the beautiful melody as Angelique makes her way down my body with her amulet.

The healer then gently places her hands back on the top of my head, moving her fingers over my brow and temple, the touch of a butterfly alighting here and there on my skin. I will my muscles to loosen; I unclench my jaw.

Angelique lays her hands on my face, and my closed eyes see colors, and light, dancing together in front of me, playing chase in the field of my imagination.

I feel her hands gently brush over my neck, and shoulders, and chest. Moving down my body which prickles with a subtle electrical charge, as if I've just covered myself with a blanket fresh out of the dryer but had forgotten the dryer fabric-softener sheet.

Then something very odd happens. When the healer moves her hands over my left wrist, over my charm bracelet, there is a surge of electricity that makes me cry out, not in pain but in sheer surprise.

"Your energy seems to be pooling here," she explains. "Curious," is all she says, holding my wrist and bracelet. My wrist becomes so very warm, almost hot. "Just keep your eyes closed," she again instructs.

The colors continue to swirl beneath my eyelids, but now they're whirling, gyrating, spinning. Spiraling into a shape somehow. Light and colors blend, undulating in my mind until I see her. A woman. *Eliza!* I'm shocked that she's here. I am not *traveling* or dreaming - I'm wide awake. I make a sound of surprise, which the healer doesn't even question.

Angelique continues her way down my body, then back up. Once again, as her hands move over my bracelet, my wrist becomes hot. And not just my wrist, but the bracelet as well. Then her hands are over my face again, and she rests them lightly on my forehead and cheeks, covering my eyes. My skin is electrified by her touch, the energy alive and hot on my flesh as she holds her hands there, putting slight pressure on my temples.

"Eliza," she says, and I am stunned. An involuntary *Wow* escapes Jane's lips. I open my eyes and see Angelique's face hovering over mine. Her eyes close, and the pressure of her fingers is stronger on my forehead. "She's from the past. I can feel her, and see her. She's not a harmful presence, but she's more or less taken over your energy, almost intertwined with it. She doesn't know how to release herself from you," she says quietly, now rubbing my temples gently. I feel the heat from her hands, a touch charged with the power of the mind. I see Eliza, and *feel* her.

Angelique moves her hands in fast, plucking motions in the space above my head, her eyes closed and head swaying back and forth, almost as if she's in a trance. The plucking motions move downward, above my chest, above my stomach, until she arrives at my left wrist. She places her hands on top of my charm bracelet, and my wrist is again on fire. "You've seen the past," says Angelique. Not a question, but a statement. "Your amulet. Its energy is quite high. Between it and Eliza, your aura has become blocked; your energy is entwined with the past."

I hear the chiming pings of the music, and think of the tinkling of the charms on my bracelet, sitting before my laptop, right before I'm pulled back into another time.

"Eliza is speaking," Angelique tells me, and I lay as still as I can, with eyes closed.

And then she gasps - a quick intake of breath. My eyes again fly open, and I see Angelique's expression. Brows furrowed, eyes closed, fear covering her face like a dark shroud. She's shaking her head back and forth quickly, side to side, as if not wanting to hear the internal whispers, telling her more than she bargained to know.

I'm afraid. I'm supposed to be calm and relaxed, but I'm not. I close my eyes again, this time not in tranquility but in fear.

Angelique continues manipulating my energy, trying to bring balance back to my life.

I again see colors swirling under my eyelids, some beautiful and bright, but some dark and foreboding. The bright pinks and yellows are fringed with blacks and grays. Brief tingles of electricity ripple under my skin as Angelique again works her way over my body, laying her hands on me, plucking the air above me, trying to draw out the negative.

After what seems like a slow-motion picture, the tension and sadness and panic gradually start melting away, like the sun finally showing itself on a dreary winter's day.

I feel *me* slowly coming back.

"I believe a soul continues throughout the ages, inhabiting different human forms along the way," Angelique explains, as we sit with her after the session. Balancing my energy had taken twice as long as she'd expected.

"But why did Eliza choose me?" I ask her, still not understanding what has happened to me.

Angelique looks at me with the eyes of an ancient, knowing more than mere humans are supposed to know. "Eliza didn't *choose* you," she answers quietly. "She *is* you."

Her words reverberate in my ears, but I can't comprehend what she's saying to me. "What do you mean?" I ask in total confusion.

"Her soul is *your* soul, Elaine. She is one of your prior lives. You *were* Eliza," she answers.

I sit with a stunned expression on my face, and look at Jane, who is apparently just as shocked as I. "You mean, like reincarnation?"

"*Rebirth* is the term I like to use. You are one of the lucky people who get to experience who you were *before*, in the past. All of our souls have lived before, and continue to live. They are infinite. But because the body is finite, a soul must move to another human form when the body dies. Even though our souls begin complete, they continue to expand, and the only way to do this is to live again, as someone else. You're just one of the lucky ones who can connect with your prior lives," Angelique explains, smiling at me as if she's just told me I'd won the lottery. And maybe she thinks I have.

But I don't feel lucky. I feel more like I've been cursed. "I don't understand how all of this works," I tell her.

"Well, I can only give you my understanding of it," she says. "Most people aren't open to the idea of prior lives, and even the ones who are don't usually have a portal to visit who they were before. But you do," she says, as she touches my bracelet. "I think your bracelet is the amulet that somehow opens the portal to your previous lives."

"Prior *lives*?" I ask. "As in more than one?"

"Yes. Eliza is just one of the lives your soul has lived. There are many others."

Oh my God! This is going to happen again? I begin to panic.

"Are you telling me that I'm going to experience other lives as well?" I ask her, almost in tears at the thought of having to go through this again.

"I don't know if you'll travel back to them. But they were there, and they lived." Angelique looks at me in contemplation. "And I have to tell you that not all of them were positive. I felt darkness pass through your aura, more than once. Cold gray shadows," she says, looking at me with concern.

"What can I do about the dark presence? I'm afraid. I was shaken after my visits to Eliza. *Her* spirit wasn't dark, was it?" I ask.

"No, her spirit was filled with positive energy. It wasn't Eliza I felt. It was someone else, but I couldn't tell exactly who. Just be careful; negative energy can invade a person's spirit unforgivably. I don't know if you'll encounter this life, or even if this energy will touch you. Just be careful," she instructs, as if I have control over any of this.

I've barely been able to deal with Eliza's *positive* energy. How in the hell am I going to deal with *negative*?

I just sit in my chair and consider Angelique's prophesy, not knowing what to say. So I say nothing, holding Jane's hand, searching for some sort of strength that might prepare me for what may come.

"You are what the ancients used to call *One of a Thousand Lives.*"

Angelique says this and my jaw almost falls to the floor, the hairs on my arms standing straight up, a shiver running just under my skin. I remember that phrase from Eliza's diary. It's what the fortune-teller said to her at Lake Cliff Park.

"Eliza was told the same thing. In 1907. I read it in her diary," I tell her. I am even more afraid. Scared that I won't be able to handle what might be in my future. *The past.* "Is there any advice you can give me to help me keep my energy balanced, so I won't feel as if I'm losing my mind?" I ask.

Angelique considers me in silence, and then asks, "By chance, have you brought anything back with you from your past? A trinket, or keepsake?"

The thimble.

"Yes, a silver thimble. I think it was Eliza's," I tell her. "Why?"

"I had a client once who visited her past," she tells me. "Like you. After our session, she decided to wear her keepsake on a necklace, never taking it off. From then on, her past life didn't hinder her present. It was as if acknowledging her past life, and giving reverence to it, enabled her to keep her energy positive. She could move on." Angelique considers me a moment. "And with Eliza's necklace, the two will hopefully keep your energy balanced," she says.

"Eliza's necklace?" I ask in confusion. "What necklace?"

"The one you're wearing around your neck. The gold locket bearing the initials EGD. Eliza Genevieve Darling. It was her necklace," she explains.

My fingers immediately move to the locket, my touchstone. "This was Eliza's?" I ask incredulously. *What?*

"I'm certain of it," Angelique answers.

I can't believe the necklace Drew gave to me was Eliza's. I had assumed he'd had my initials carved into its face, but apparently they'd been hers. Either the science of coincidence, or destiny, has certainly had its way with me. Again I caress the small golden piece tenderly, brushing my fingers over the engraving of her initials. *Our* initials.

I wonder how and when it left her, and how the antique store acquired it. I'm sure there are many stories surrounding its hundred-year journey between then and now. But I don't think I'll ever know them.

I think about Angelique's words. *Move on*. What does that really mean? Will my soul move from one past life to the next? Will I be reliving history again and again? I decide to heed her advice - I will have the thimble made into a charm, and wear it around my neck.

"The thimble will remind you of where you've been and where you want to go," Angelique said.

I know I've heard those words before, but instead of frightening, somehow they're comforting.

"And I'm certain of something else," says Angelique. "Your children will ground you."

I instinctively know this; I *feel* it, throughout my entire being. Eliza gave up her child, and grieved over her decision her entire life, as short-lived as it was. She only found peace in the end. I know I gave my first child up as well, and have made mistakes throughout the years, but the fact still remains that I've successfully raised two wonderful boys. Two loving, caring human beings. I did my job - the most important job in the world - and regardless of what happens with my *travels*, or my writing, or anything else in my life, that success can never be taken away from me. My children are my foundation. I still grieve for the one I lost, but I smile at knowing the two I still have will always be the result of my existence.

"Holy shit," Jane says, shaking her head as we sit in the car after our visit with the healer. Jane is great at making funny understatements, at tempering tension and worry with humor.

"My words exactly," I reply. "I'm pretty much freaked-out." I just don't know what to feel. I think I need time to absorb the truth about myself, my *ability* to connect with my past. I was not prepared for what Angelique told me.

"Well, I smell a reality show gearing up," Jane quips with a smirk, and even in my apprehensive state, I can't help but laugh. Her quick wit and sense of humor are always ready to ease my tension. That's one of the things I truly love about her.

"Maybe I can give Ms. Long Island a run for her money!" I say playfully, the comic relief very welcome, but too short-lived.

Then I think about what I've just said, and what it means. I have special *abilities*. Hell, I didn't even believe in reincarnation before today. It's frightening, but then again exciting at the same time. *Who in the hell does this?*

"You know," Jane says in a contemplative tone, "you have first-hand knowledge of what happened in history. After all, you apparently lived it. You can bring history alive for people," she suggests. And then her lips spread across her face in a wide smile. "And what better marketing tool is there for your books? You could name them *My Life Before*, or something. Who in the hell wouldn't read a book written by a woman who visits her former lives?"

I laugh at my first impression of what Jane has just said, the absurdity of it, until it dawns on me that she has a valid point.

Every writer needs an angle, and it appears I've just discovered mine. I decide then and there to not only deal with my powers, but put them to good use, fear or no.

I am One of a Thousand Lives.

And so my writing career begins.

About the Author

K. L. Romo loves to make friction and sparks; now working on a bonfire. Come make some smores! She lives with her family in Duncanville, Texas.

You can visit her at www.klromo.com, and she'd love it if you signed up for her email newsletter on my website.

You may contact K. L. Romo: by email at klromo@klromo.com, or by Twitter at @KLRomo.

If you enjoyed the book, please consider posting a review to Amazon, Barnes & Noble, Goodreads, your blog, or any other place you like to talk about books. A review by you would be much appreciated!